LOVE'S GOLDEN SPELL

Borgo Press Books by WILLIAM MALTESE

LOVE'S GOLDEN SPELL

A ROMANCE

WILLIAM MALTESE

THE BORGO PRESS

MMXIII

LOVE'S GOLDEN SPELL

SECOND BORGO PRESS EDITION

Published by Wildside Press LLC

www.wildsidebooks.com

DEDICATION

For all of those individuals, present, past, and
future, who have devoted their lives, time,
money, and effort to the preservation of
endangered species everywhere.

CONTENTS

CHAPTER ONE

JANET HAD BEEN PREPARED to hate this handsome man whose touch sent uncontrollable sensations racing along her spine, whose low and melodious voice brought back memories of her childhood before it went sour.

"Welcome to Lionspride," Christopher Van Hoon said, and smiled. He didn't recognize her. She didn't expect he would. They weren't children now, and her name was Westover, not Kelley.

His teeth were brilliantly white in contrast to a tan burnished deep bronze by the South African sun. His golden eyes were black flecked. He didn't look like his father, Vincent. He never had. He took after his mother's side of the family. Janet didn't remember Gretchen Van Hoon, but she remembered Vincent. There was no forgetting or forgiving him.

"May I offer you and your crew something cool to drink before we get started?" Christopher asked, holding her hand, still smiling. Janet recalled a biblical quote about how the sins of the fathers were visited upon their children. "I've taken the liberty of having wine punch brought out on the terrace," he added, releasing her fingers. "Emphasize the punch. De-emphasize the wine—realizing, of course, that this is a working visit, isn't it? I mean, neither of us would want to end up tipsy in front of the cameras, would we?"

She should refuse. She had a job to do, and she wanted it over. She wasn't taking this as easily as she had planned. Seeing this place and Christopher brought back too many memories—

painful and otherwise. However, there was the crew to consider. The air-conditioning in the van wasn't working, and Tim and Roger could use a cool drink before setting up the equipment. So could Jill, the makeup artist.

"A drink of punch would be lovely," Janet said. She felt guilty. There was no reason to feel that way. Even though Vincent Van Hoon was dead, he had left an unpaid debt.

"This way, please," Christopher said. He motioned them along a walkway that circled toward the back of the main house.

Janet tried not to concentrate on Christopher. She wasn't successful, even with the wealth of distraction offered by the mansion, its gardens and the view from the terrace. All around were sights and smells that helped her to renew her acquaintance with exotic Africa: flaming aloes, unbelievably large proteas, flowering mimosa. In the distance, the well-remembered swimming pool and bathhouse were separated from the South African veldt by a line of dense acacia and blue-gum trees.

Lions had growled among those trees. Elephants had filled the air with their trumpeting. Quaggas had made shrill and barking neighs. A girl had felt the thrill of first love.

There were no longer lions and elephants this close to the Van Hoon estate. They were locked in parks farther inland. As for the quaggas and the girl—

"Miss Westover?" Christopher queried, interrupting her reverie, offering her a crystal glass filled with ice and an attractive amber liquid. She took the glass with thanks, careful not to touch his fingers with her own. She tasted the punch. It was tart but thirst quenching. She turned to the scenery, resentful that his presence wouldn't let her concentrate. She was resentful, too, that he didn't recognize her, although his recognizing her could ruin everything. She would know him anywhere.

"Is this your first trip to Africa, Miss Westover?" Christopher asked.

She would spoil everything if she made him suspicious, but she couldn't lie. "No," she said. "I was here as a little girl with my father." She didn't mention her father's name, and Christopher didn't press for it.

"Do you find the country much changed?" he asked. She was nervous. The seasoned hostess of *Animal Kingdoms in the Wild* was used to asking the questions, not answering them.

"All things change, don't they?" she replied. Often, as in the case of Africa, they change for the worse. There were those, Christopher included, who would consider her notions at odds with their definition of progress, but she couldn't help that.

"How so?" Christopher asked curiously.

Her velvety black eyes weren't looking at him but into her glass.

"We should start taping," she said, determined not to be sidetracked into giving herself away. "We're imposing on your hospitality as it is."

"Believe me, it's my pleasure," he said with a charm and grace his father had never possessed. She would have taken pleasure in fooling Vincent Van Hoon, but Christopher belonged to the good times.

"We'll be out of your hair as quickly as possible," she promised.

His blond hair was like sunlight. Touching it would submerge caressing fingers in molten gold.

"I've had far less charming things in my hair, I assure you," he replied gallantly.

He smelled of lime-scented after-shave. His dimples were deeper than she remembered.

On some mysterious cue, a black man appeared to collect the empty glasses, carrying them away on a silver tray. "What you've come for is this way," Christopher said, guiding her toward the open French doors, disappointing her when he didn't take her arm. The others followed in their wake.

The trophy room was immense. It was larger than Janet's childhood memories of it and filled with wall-to-wall animal heads and skins. The latter were also scattered on the hardwood floor and used as upholstery for the overstuffed furniture. The room smelled sensuously decadent, of time-worn leather. Over the mantel of a large walk-in fireplace was a sunburst of guns. Those weapons had killed the animals on display.

Janet shuddered. She always had when entering this room. Christopher, standing close by, sensed her reaction. His questioning gold eyes turned on her. She enjoyed a second shiver that had nothing to do with the first.

"Someone must be walking on my grave," she said, wishing for a better cliché.

She was rescued by Jill Marlow, who was anxious to start whatever makeup Christopher needed for the cameras.

Janet's husband had told her there were so few blond heroes in the early days of the movies because they didn't film well. Heavy makeup had solved the bleached-out problem for women but had never worked as well for light-complexioned men.

Christopher, though, didn't have to worry. Modern technology had improved camera, tape, and processing. The Robert Redfords of the world no longer took back seats to their dark-complexioned competition. In. fact, Christopher would come off too well on camera.

He was so tanned anyway, and too handsome, too clean-cut, too... well... appealing. He was the stereotypical Dutchman, and his robust attractiveness would work against what Janet had in mind. She needed an unattractive slob of a man with a two-day growth of beard, sweaty clothes, dirty fingernails and no finesse. She needed someone as thoroughly obnoxious as Vincent Van Hoon had been.

Not only was Christopher all wrong, but so was the setting. It was too genteel. The animal trophies were too sterile. A television audience, jaded by blood-and-guts violence, needed to see a downed beast in the wild bellowing out its death throes before the viewer would get her point.

"I think Mr. Van Hoon looks fine," Janet said to Jill, who was running a makeup brush over Christopher's tanned cheeks and strong neck, paying too much attention to the smooth run of muscled chest revealed by his open shirt collar.

"Yes, he does look fine, doesn't he?" Jill answered with schoolgirl gushiness that Janet found irritating.

The cameras were ready, and Janet turned toward an antler-bracketed mirror that commandeered a place on one trophy-littered wall. Reflected were her wide-set black eyes, pert nose and Cupid's-bow mouth, all framed by a mane of thick black hair. If there were traces of a thirteen-year-old girl in her face, there were none in her full-blown breasts, narrow waist and long legs. It was best leaving the memory of her childhood in the same grave as her father. Nothing good would come of resurrecting it. Oh, but if only she could turn back the clock.

The taping didn't begin well. She couldn't relax, and it showed. There was no hiding from the camera. She got curious looks from Tim, Roger, and Jill. Christopher looked at her in a funny way, too.

She shouldn't have come. Why had she? Her reasons for being in Africa needn't have brought her to Johannesburg, to this house, to this man, to these memories.

"And this?" she asked Christopher, commanding her mind not to wander. She pointed to a skin stretched on the wall. It was a reddish brown pelt with irregular, dark-brown striping.

"A quagga," Christopher informed her.

"And that one?" she asked. She pointed toward the mounted head of an antelope with long stout horns that swept back from its forehead in a saber-like curve.

"*Blaubok*—a bluebuck," Christopher said, providing the translation. At the same time, a glimmer of suspicion registered in his gold eyes.

She was going about it all wrong. She was obvious in her singling out the extinct animals. She should ask about the wilde-beest or the North American elk, those takes edited out later.

"You know, Janet," he said on cue, "they're extinct now—the quagga and the bluebuck, but it wasn't all that long ago that they roamed this very spot on which we're standing. There were thousands of quagga as late as the late the nineteenth century. My great-grandfather hunted them, but I can't. No one can. We can't even see them, except as bits and pieces scattered around museums and trophy rooms."

Yes, the quaggas were gone, and so were the bluebucks—as were the young girl and the young man who had stood on this very spot so many years ago.

"My response to the loss of those animals is a feeling of deep regret," Christopher continued. Janet listened for sincerity. She wanted to believe him, but he was saying it because she had tipped her hand. "Not only do I regret their demise," Christopher said, "but I regret that more effort by my family wasn't channeled into saving them."

He was saying the right words. There had been a time when she had known whether he was telling the truth or lying. Now she didn't know—not for sure.

"However, I've been doing my own small part by restricting my hunting to camera safaris," he said. "Possibly that's too little too late, but it's taken this long for the Van Hoons to shake off outdated family tradition."

The camera safari was a good touch. She would check on it. If it were true, she would give him good marks for trying. She couldn't go easy, though, on a family whose quest for corporate profits had wrecked the chances of more than one poor beast for survival—as well as killing her father.

"Thank you, Christopher Van Hoon," she said.

Within seconds, Tim and Roger were packing up the lights and equipment. Janet turned to Christopher and smiled nervously.

"Would it be possible to speak with you privately for a few minutes, Janet?" Christopher asked. During the taping he had called her by her first name, too. She liked the sound of it on his lips. It had been a long time.

"Privately?" she asked. He would confront her with his suspicions, no doubt.

"It'll only take a moment," he assured her persuasively.

"I really...," she began, wanting but not wanting to be alone with him.

"Please," he said. He put his hand on her elbow and delivered the shock of his touch. The sensation was more disturbing than his previous handshake.

The ever-present servant opened the door to the next room for them. Janet took a deep breath. She couldn't lie to Christopher if he pressed her for the truth, not even if it came out who she was and why she was there.

"I thought you might have supper with me," he said. It was the last thing she had expected. It was out of context. "I thought I'd be more persuasive in here, out of the hubbub," he explained as they entered the room.

"Supper?" Janet echoed, confused.

"I thought we should have more time together—to talk," he said. He leaned against the back of a wing chair and folded his arms. His muscled chest thrust forward, molded by the cloth of his shirt. "We do have things to discuss, don't we, Janet?" he said.

There was a way he might have spoken her name to tell her their talk would be of old times, of shared and happy memories, but he didn't speak it that way.

He was a man who had discovered a plot and was out to deal with the enemy. So, all his fine talk about camera safaris was pure garbage. He was his father's son after all.

"Thank you for asking, but I have a lot to do at the hotel this evening," Janet apologized. Her desire to accept was a painful violation of her promise to her father. It was a violation of her husband's memory. "We're flying to Salisbury the day after tomorrow and then on to Great Zimbabwe. There don't seem to be enough hours in the day," she explained.

"I think you'll find the time in this instance, though, won't you, Janet?" he said, sounding very confident—too confident.

"I don't mean to be rude, but it's quite impossible," she said. His father had killed hers. She wasn't here to dance to his tune.

"Very well," he said. His expression had changed little from when they had first entered the room. "More's the pity that your trip is wasted."

"I'd hardly call it wasted," she said with a nervous laugh. She caught a glimpse of the boy in the man. It wasn't difficult. He was eighteen when she last saw him. His body had worn the stamp of what it would become, unlike Janet who, at thirteen, was due for major physical changes. "I think a replay of the tapes will show we've accomplished a lot in a short time," she reminded him.

"I'm afraid I can't let the tapes leave the house," he said. His smile widened. "Not without your promise to stay for supper," he qualified.

"I'm afraid I don't understand," she said. It wasn't his threat to hold the tapes that she didn't understand. It was what her staying for supper had to do with it.

"It's simple," he said. "I've always been extremely attracted to clever women. What you almost accomplished this afternoon was a very good show. Admittedly, it was flawed, but that you got this far reveals an admirable piece of planning."

"I don't know what you're talking about!" Janet said, her resolve weakening. She could have turned and walked out of the room, but she remained rooted to the spot.

"Although I came out fairly well in the interview," Christopher explained, "I'm aware how clever editing of those tapes can make my father the greatest detriment to wildlife since the invention of the firearm."

"But why would I?"

"Come now, Janet," he interrupted her, a steely edge to his voice. "If I momentarily failed to recognize your true intent, please don't make the mistake of continuing to underestimate my intelligence. Considering everything, I'm asking a fair price for letting your friends walk out of here with their tapes intact. Don't you agree?"

She couldn't have heard correctly. "If you think I have ulterior motives, why let the tapes leave here at all?" she asked suspiciously.

"I thought I made that perfectly clear," he said, so close she was heady from the lime-based fragrance of his after-shave.

"You interest me more than the tapes—certainly more then whatever damage you hope to accomplish by having them."

His interest suggested more than supper. "I have no intention of going to bed with you to buy what is rightfully mine," she said, surprising herself with the vehemence of her outburst. Christopher laughed. She would have preferred disappointment to amusement.

"Please, Janet, do wait until I ask," he chided and laughed again. There was less humor in the sound than Janet expected. "I mentioned supper, didn't I?" he reminded her. "Although I might be persuaded to throw in a visit to the Ivory Room. Wouldn't that make a marvelous supplement to your interview: a firsthand account of the fabled Van Hoon ivory?"

She hadn't seen the Ivory Room. Her father had, and it should have served as a warning. Vincent Van Hoon, a man with that much evidence of mass slaughter in his basement, plus ties to the mining community, wouldn't have been interested in feasibility studies for a wildlife preserve—no matter how much he had pretended to be so.

There was a sharp knock. The door opened slightly, and Roger stuck his head in. "Sorry to interrupt, but we've packed everything," he said. "We're ready whenever Janet is."

"Janet has accepted my invitation to stay a little longer," Christopher said. "I'll have my chauffeur drive her back to the hotel later this evening."

"Right!" Roger said, not waiting for Janet to verify Christopher's statement.

"You had no right!" she said, anger coloring her cheeks. She wasn't pleased with Roger's hasty retreat, either.

"You are going to stay, aren't you?" Christopher asked, although it wasn't really a question.

She wanted those tapes. They were part of her only feasible plan for getting back at the Van Hoons. If Christopher was unimpressed by the damage the tapes could do, that didn't squelch Janet's overpowering need to use them. Her condemnation of the hunter-clan, money-mad Van Hoons might yet have repercussions Christopher couldn't imagine. She hoped so.

"Yes, I'll stay," she said.

"Good," he replied and kissed her.

She didn't believe it. Not with Jill, Tim, and Roger in the next room. It wasn't a peck on the lips, either. Nor was it a kiss she could enjoy, despite her curiosity about how kissing the man would differ from kissing the boy. It was aggressive, crushing her lips between her teeth and his. And his arms wrapped around her with a strength that made it impossible for her to move.

"There!" he said; his smile was the epitome of satisfaction. "Tell the world the Van Hoons attack women as well as wild animals."

She couldn't find her voice to scream. So when he released her, she slapped his face. The sound of flesh colliding against flesh was like a rifle shot. How apropos.

"How dare you!" she said, her breathing erratic. His continuing smile infuriated her.

"I'll be sportsman enough to accept a one-on-one exchange, but don't try to take advantage," he warned her.

"You bastard!" she accused, her voice dripping venom. She went quickly to the door, willing her weak legs to support her. She expected to find Tim, Roger, and Jill in the next room, but they weren't there. Nor was the camera equipment. She hurried through the French doors and around the house, praying she would be in time. She prayed in vain. The van was gone. She was alone with Christopher Van Hoon, except for the people who worked for him.

She could count on no one but herself. There was something disturbing about her predicament.

Christopher stepped out on the front porch like an Olympian god about to bestow his favors on an unwilling maiden.

"I insist you have someone drive me back to my hotel immediately!" she said.

"You'll be driven to your hotel—later," Christopher said, his smile mocking her demands." Right now, Ashanti will show you where you can freshen up. We do, by the way, dress for dinner."

The servant who had collected the punch glasses appeared on cue.

"Dress for dinner?" Janet echoed incredulously. She expected him to tell her he had raided her hotel room for the only dress she'd brought for formal occasions. She wasn't expecting opportunities for dressing up in the bush, where she was heading the day after tomorrow.

"I'm sure you'll find something in the room to fit you," Christopher said instead. "I'm partial to the black silk myself."

"Then you wear it!" She refused to humor him. "I'm returning to my hotel!"

"Suit yourself," Christopher said with a shrug. "I just hope you're up to the walk." He turned and disappeared into the house.

Janet looked at the driveway, knowing how far it was to the main highway, let alone to Johannesburg.

"Miss Westover?" It was Ashanti, waiting patiently for her to obey Christopher's wishes.

She didn't answer. She started walking away from Lionspride and the madman who owned it.

CHAPTER TWO

"YOU'RE LUCKY you're dark complexioned," Christopher said. He was sitting behind a large oak desk. "That bit of redness will fade, and you'll look even more beautiful in your new tan."

"Call off your goons, damn it!" Janet said. If she had originally looked upon the two men as her salvation, her opinion had changed when they'd driven her back to Lionspride.

"Bill and Karl, this is Janet," Christopher said, pyramiding his fingers beneath his chin. He looked disgustingly cool and calm, but then he hadn't been trudging in the South African sun. Janet, on the other hand, looked a sight, and she didn't need a mirror to tell her that.

"Ma'am," Bill and Karl said in unison. They'd been supremely polite until she'd tried to force her way out of the moving car. Even then, they had done nothing but keep her from jumping out and hurting, maybe even killing, herself. She should thank them instead of calling them names—except they had brought her back to Christopher. She was no better off than she had been a couple of hours earlier, although she was considerably more tired. And no matter what Christopher said, she felt the tightness of sunburn across her forehead.

"That's all for now, men," Christopher said. "I'll have Ashanti show Janet upstairs—that is, if she's finally decided to cooperate." Ashanti appeared: a man-robot getting messages via telepathy.

Bill and Karl left, Janet staying where she was. Christopher ignored her, attending to his paperwork. He looked up several minutes later, pretending surprise to find her still there. He made a great show of checking his wristwatch. "I really wouldn't recommend any walks after dark," he said.

"I refuse to believe this is happening!" Janet said, leaving the room. He would have left her standing there until doomsday.

"Miss Westover?" It was Ashanti, trying to perform the task Christopher had assigned him.

The view through the drapery-banked windows confirmed it was getting dark. Even with no wild animals around, Janet wouldn't tempt fate after nightfall. "Okay, Ashanti," she said, resigned—temporarily—to defeat, "where's this room?"

'This way, please," Ashanti said, leading the way to the sweeping stairway that reminded Janet of a set from *Gone with the Wind.*

Once in the room, she locked the door and looked for a telephone. There was none. The room wasn't one Janet remembered. She had never been in all of the rooms of Lionspride. Christopher used to joke that he hadn't, either.

The bathroom was well stocked, complete with expensive perfumes. Everything was obviously designed for the use of not one but a procession of women, of whom Janet was merely the latest.

Christopher had never married. The press kept Janet informed, because no matter what Christopher Van Hoon did, he made the papers. He was interesting copy, tremendously good looking and tremendously rich. That he hadn't married gave Janet satisfaction long after her marriage to Bob.

The bathroom mirror confirmed that she looked like hell. Her sunburn, though, wasn't as bad as she'd thought.

She started running the water in a bathtub as big as a swimming pool, liberally adding bath salts from two of six available jars of the stuff. The result was so inviting, she got into the tub before it was filled. She used her sore feet to turn off the faucets, then leaned back, closed her eyes and relaxed her weary bones.

Qwenella Fairchild might have enjoyed the luxury of this

sunken tub, Janet mused. Christopher had dated her in the States. That, too, had made the gossip columns. Qwenella was an ex-*Playboy* Bunny and centerfold. Compared to her, Janet looked like a man. Then, there had been the high-fashion model who had gone from the cover of *Vogue* to a big movie contract. Compared to her, Janet looked like a *Playboy* bunny. Then, Lady Bellona Morrel, who was related by blood to the Princess of Wales.

"Who knows, I may marry you when you grow up," he had told Janet sixteen years before. The sun was hot that day, a huge ball of molten gold behind blue-gum trees. Christopher's hair was long over his ears and collar. He looked like a young lion. "If you ever do grow up," he had added with a laugh, and kissed her.

She roused herself from a drifting lethargy, concentrating on her lips, sensitive from his most recent, stolen, kiss. What a world of difference between their first kiss and this last one. What a world of difference between the loving youth and the hateful man.

She hadn't stopped thinking of Christopher when she married Bob. Some of those thoughts she hadn't minded—those concerned her plans to get back at the Van Hoon family. Others, though, were betrayals of her father and of her wedding vows. That Vincent Van Hoon was dead and buried, her husband murdered by guerrillas in Central America, didn't make such thoughts less disturbing. She was never physically unfaithful to her husband during the years of their marriage; but, every woman indulged in fantasies. It didn't mean she didn't love Bob. It didn't mean she loved Christopher, either.

She came out of the bath like Venus from the sea, reaching for one of the Turkish towels monogrammed with the Van Hoon crest: a full-mane lion against a sun disk. She dried herself quickly, dispelling her disturbing thoughts. She needed her wits, and her memories were betraying her. She had been crazy, basing so many daydreams on an incident that had happened sixteen years ago.

She found a black silk dress on the bed. She hadn't put it there, and the door was locked. This didn't mean anything. It was Christopher's house, and he had the keys. He must have been there while she was in the bath, the bathroom door ajar. He must have watched ever so silently, and—

She was letting her imagination run away with her because of one unpleasant kiss meant to scare her. He had laid out the dress to scare her, too. He was getting back at her for her plan to blacken the Van Hoon name. Scaring, though, was as far as it went. Christopher, with all the willing women he could have, wasn't going to force himself on her. Janet wasn't a little Miss Nobody. She was a well-known personality in the States and in five foreign countries that syndicated *Animal Kingdoms in the Wild*. She could cause one helluva big stink that not even Van Hoon money could gloss over.

He was playing a game. She could play games, too. She walked over to the bed and lifted the dress for closer inspection. It was a Valentino: simple, expensive and with a revealing neckline. She checked the closets and dresser drawers for accessories.

He knew her correct size at a glance, because the dress fit like a glove. If the bodice was tight, the effect was sexy. It was so sexy, she wouldn't have worn the dress in public, but only the servants and Christopher would see her here.

She unlocked the door and stepped into the hallway, surprised when she wasn't confronted by guards. She could enter one of the other bedrooms to find a phone, but her rescue party would be spotted before it reached the house. Besides, she wasn't as frightened as she had been.

She paused at the top of the stairs, her fingers poised delicately on the highly polished banister. Her gaze followed the long downward curve of the railing, her mind flashing to long-ago rides with her and Christopher astraddle the thing. At eighteen, he had argued that he was too old for such antics, yet Janet hadn't had that much trouble changing his mind.

Janet was older now and wasn't dressed for a ride, but the

temptation was too great. She assumed an experimental side-saddle position, more weight on her feet than on her derriere. By the time she made her slow slide to the bottom, the silk dress was hiked well above her knees. She felt ridiculous when she slipped off, feeling more so when she realized Christopher was watching. It wasn't possible to guess how long he had been there.

He was dressed in a white dinner jacket with black tie, the jacket and white shirt contrasting attractively with the darkness of his tan. His cufflinks were small asterisks of gold.

"I used to be quite a tomboy," she said, recovering enough poise to speak. "Sometimes, I'm afraid, there's a reversion to childhood."

"Yes? Well, you could have easily fallen and broke your pretty neck," he said unsympathetically. He was the one who once had fallen from this particular banister, but reminding him would reveal too much. With a small cut on his forehead, he'd remained undaunted, immediately going back for another ride. Maybe the small crescent-shaped scar was still there, waiting for her to brush back the attractive tumble of his blond hair to find it.

"Where's supper? I'm starving!" she said, taking the last three steps to the marble floor. Her tone of voice said she was now in control.

"I'll do my very best to satiate your every appetite," he said suggestively. He was insinuating more than food, but she let his double entendre pass without comment.

"So, let's eat!" she said, sweeping grandly past him and leading the way to the formal dining room. A long teak table, set for two in the intimacy of one corner, was illuminated by three beautiful chandeliers. "I presume the head of the table is your spot?" she said. She would have said more to emphasize her new mood, but he was giving her a strange look.

"It has taken you an astoundingly short time to find your way around my house," he said.

Janet had made a very dangerous mistake by leading her host

to a room she had supposedly never seen. But she was far better at subterfuge than she expected when she said, "It's a knack I've always had," tossing off his observation as less than it was. "Most women have it. It comes with the territory." She walked to the table, not surprised when Ashanti was there to pull out her chair. Christopher hesitated, finally joining her.

They were served hotchpotch of curly kale, a hearty Dutch stew of cabbage, potatoes, sausage, salt, butter, pepper and chicken stock. The stew was anything but pedestrian, served as it was from a large Delft soup tureen into matching soup bowls and accompanied by a 1947 South African Cabernet Sauvignon from the Groot Constantia vineyards outside Cape Town. The wineglasses were Baccarat.

"You say you're going to Great Zimbabwe?" Christopher asked when they paused in their small talk about the food. Janet had told him her travel plans earlier, using them as her excuse for avoiding this very meal.

"I guess it's Great Zimbabwe, *Zimbabwe*, isn't it?" she said, and recalled her earlier confusion at the apparent redundancy. Great Zimbabwe was once only a group of impressive archaeological ruins on a high plateau in Rhodesia, she knew. When Rhodesia became officially independent from Britain in 1980, Zimbabwe also became the name of the new country, and Great Zimbabwe now also referred to the game reserve surrounding those ruins.

"The camera crew and I are going to spend some time with a government group," Janet continued. She didn't mention elephants. Christopher's promise to show her the Ivory Room was more of a bonus for her than he imagined. "We'll stop off in Salisbury first."

His right hand realigned the lush blond hair that tumbled almost to his golden eyes. She longed for the fluid movement of those silky strands through her fingertips.

"I was at the Great Zimbabwe ruins not long ago," Christopher said, putting Janet on her guard. He eyed her over the elaborate place settings, his eyes luminous and hypnotic. "There was a government team there, then," he added. "An encampment of soldiers, too, for that matter."

"Soldiers?" Janet asked nervously. Soldiers hinted of more unexpected dangers.

"There's a heavy poaching problem in the area," Christopher said. "The troops have been sent in to stop it." He, no more than Janet, mentioned elephants, but he surely knew which animals concerned the Great Zimbabwe research group. He knew how interested Janet was to see his Ivory Room.

He was taking her attempt at revenge too lightly—not that he seemed to recognize it as revenge. Her motivations probably didn't matter to him—he was that confident she wasn't a threat. He had not only let her crew leave with the tapes but had hinted at giving her more ammunition by showing her what was in the basement.

She was at a decided disadvantage. Her memories were interfering, while he thought her nothing more than a busybody television hostess. She would tell him who she was. If nothing else, that would assure him of her determination.

But she caught herself in time. She couldn't let more tender emotions take control. Her best chance for success was in getting the tapes to the States, editing them to emphasize the now extinct animals tacked so proudly on the Van Hoon walls. There would be footage shot at Great Zimbabwe about elephant herds endangered not only by encroaching civilization but by people like the Van Hoons who had encouraged the poaching epidemic in their eagerness to stockpile ivory.

She couldn't spoil her plans because she wanted Christopher to laugh as he once laughed, or because she wanted the sparkle back in his eyes instead of the glaring suspicion and distrust she saw there. She was a fool if she let those wants make her act rashly. There was no bringing back the past. Too much water had passed under the bridge. Christopher had probably not forgotten or forgiven the daughter of a man his father hired, used, and fired. And that was her fault. She had left him, had refused to answer his letters, not vice versa.

She had been only thirteen, after all, and needed desperately to blame someone. She had blamed him—herself, too. She and Christopher had chalked up too much happiness, and her father was the forfeit. Years later, of course, she realized the extent to which big business and politics were linked—business and politics concerning gold and Vincent Van Hoon's desire to control it—neither of which had anything to do with two adolescents enjoying each other's company. By then, though, it was too late to go back. It was too late to go back now.

"*Koeksisters*," Christopher said, startling her out of her reverie. Most of the dishes were cleared. She looked at him, embarrassed and confused.

"Are you all right?" he asked, sounding and looking genuinely concerned. Perhaps he was afraid she was suffering a delayed reaction from heatstroke.

"I'm fine," she said. It was a lie. She wasn't fine. She was hoarding memories as if they were priceless treasures. But revealing them to Christopher risked exposing them as nothing more than cheap imitations. "You were saying something about your sisters." He didn't have sisters. She knew that. She knew all about him. He neither knew nor cared about her.

"*Koeksisters*," he repeated, watching her more closely. "It translates 'cake sisters,'" he said, no doubt encouraged by the focusing of her eyes. "Braided dough, deep fried, and then chilled in syrup of water, sugar, cream of tartar, ginger, cinnamon and glycerine."

"Oh?" She laughed, picking up her fork and stabbing the pastry with apparent relish. "Delicious!"

They were served a chilled South African Riesling from a vineyard outside of Stellenbosch.

"South African wines were at their best in the nineteenth century," Christopher said. "They enjoyed a vogue in England and France that no other non-European wines have matched, not even your superb American vintages. However, something happened to that quality that has wine experts guessing—rather like Falernian, the most celebrated of ancient Roman wines.

Praised by Pliny and Horace as being 'immortal,' Falernian was uncorked to rave reviews for centuries. Today, those same hillsides are yielding wine that, while good, is by no means extraordinary and definitely not immortal." He pushed back his chair, and Ashanti appeared to assist Janet with hers. "But I promised you more than supper and wine trivia didn't I?" Christopher said. He started to take her arm, disappointing her, perversely, when he didn't follow through.

They walked through several rooms, each emphasizing the house's largeness. The Van Hoons had come a long way since Petre Van Hoon arrived from the Netherlands with his few personal possessions. The founder of the Van Hoon dynasty had lived in a mud shelter like the local natives. This house, with its silk-covered walls, gilded cornices, antique furniture and crystal chandeliers completely overshadowed those humbler beginnings, the opulence further widening the gap between Janet and Christopher. These Chinese porcelains, Japanese bronzes, Persian rugs, and Louis Quinze pieces could attract the wealthiest and most beautiful of women.

The Ivory Room was in the basement, reached by a curving flight of stairs behind a Gobelin tapestry. The narrowness of the stairs brought Janet and Christopher into constant contact, but neither made the move to descend single file. Janet reached the bottom feeling breathless, and not just because of the exercise.

"It's only a bit farther," he said. His smile flashed white in the dim lighting. It was a perfect spot for him to take advantage, but he didn't. Janet was disappointed, since she had decided how to handle it: not with fighting but with a bored acceptance—up to a point.

They stopped in front of a massive door that was too large to open into the narrow corridor. Christopher unlocked it and put his shoulder to it. It moved sideways, showing blackness in the space beyond.

"Here, give me your hand," he instructed.

She hesitated, embarrassed for doing so. If he were going to attempt something, he wouldn't ask for her hand. He'd take it.

"It's dark in there," she said, stating the obvious.

"Which should make you feel particularly safe," he said. She didn't see how. He laughed. "I prefer my lovemaking with the lights on. I don't know about you, but I like to see what's going on." He reached for her hand. She didn't give it to him, but she didn't resist, either. There was a comforting familiarity to his fingers closing around hers. She trusted her intuition and followed him through the opening.

Déjà vu: the caves of the Molapong Valley where she, with far less hesitation, had entrusted herself to the safekeeping of a younger Christopher Van Hoon.

He slid the door closed behind them, excluding all light. Being so close to him made her heart flutter. She gasped when his supportive fingers slipped free, leaving her helplessly adrift. "Christopher?" she asked the darkness.

The lights came on. He was amusing himself at her expense. He could have reached the switch from the outside. At Molapong, he had worn the same expression after telling her they were lost and then, magically, leading her to safety.

"Are you having fun?" she asked sarcastically. Her question was superfluous. Of course he was having fun! They were in an empty room with cement ceiling, walls and floors. This was a joke!

"Now don't get your tail in a knot," he said, mirth bubbling over with each word. "Everything in this world has its price. My amusement is certainly cheap enough for what you're getting out of the bargain.

"Yes, I suppose so," Janet said, an expansive wave of her arm encompassing the room. "I certainly don't get to see the likes of this every day, do I?"

"Ye of so little faith!" he condemned, and laughed as he had laughed at Molapong. The strain in his face dissolved, unmasking a Christopher years younger. His eyes twinkled. His dimples sank deeper as his smile widened. She wanted to touch his cheeks with her fingertips and explore those indentations.

She was distracted by the grating of metal against metal. One whole wall was moving. Janet watched, fascinated. She had been on the verge of saying something stupid. Had he waited one minute longer before pressing the button, he would have heard her confessing everything.

She was walking a fine line: on one side her loyalty to her dead father and to her dead husband; on the other her desire to salvage something for herself before it became too late. The thing she kept forgetting was that Christopher didn't offer salvation. He hadn't understood the girl turning away from him. He wouldn't understand the woman coming back.

She focused on the macabre reality of the room beyond the wall. On all sides, stacked in niches and on special supports designed to store them, one on top of the other, were thousands of elephant tusks. She was staggered by the sheer number. She had no idea what the collection was worth. Never in her wildest imagination had she thought to see this much ivory in one place.

She turned accusingly on Christopher, aware deep down that the tragedy behind this grisly collection was only one of her excuses for coming to Africa.

"How many elephants did you kill to give the Van Hoon empire this?" she asked, her voice trembling. He had hunted with Vincent before he met her. He had proudly shown her a gazelle killed on an afternoon hunt with his father. She had taken one look at the lifeless delicate animal, and been sick to her stomach. He'd promised he wouldn't kill another. His father, furious at such a silly promise, had boxed his ears, calling him a sissy.

The boy who made that promise wasn't the man whose handsome face was now showing none of the amusement of a few moments before. "I do all my hunting with a camera, remember?" he said, his voice so frosty it froze her to the quick.

"I want out of here," she said. A constriction in her heart made further speech impossible.

She didn't wait for his permission to leave. She managed to maneuver the sliding door, and then took the hallway to the stairs. If she tripped silent alarms on the way out, she didn't care.

She headed for the library, expecting Ashanti to appear out of the woodwork to intercept her. She didn't see anyone. She did see the Baccarat decanter of cognac standing on one of the elegant library tables.

She was cold, very cold. The burn of the brandy going down helped. She poured herself another swallow, sitting down in the nearest chair. She was trembling. She shut her eyes, trying to get control of herself. When she opened her eyes, Christopher was in the doorway watching her.

"What are you staring at?" she demanded, her nerves on edge.

She expected an immediate sarcastic reply, but he didn't answer for several long moments: When he did, his voice was strangely distant, even apologetic.

"I'm sorry," he said, "but you reminded me of someone."

She felt the shivers dancing along her spine. "Of whom?" she asked in a whisper so low she wasn't sure she said anything. Her breathing stopped. It was erratic when it returned.

"I don't really know of whom," he admitted.

She wanted to cry out that she reminded him of a thirteen-year-old girl he once knew, but a large lump in her throat wouldn't let the words slip past. There was little point in bolstering a memory so weak it was beyond recall.

She was on the verge of tears, and she wouldn't be able to explain them. She was saved by Ashanti. "Mr. Geiger is here to see you, Mr. Van Hoon," Ashanti announced.

"Excuse me, Janet," Christopher said, and left the room. By the time he returned with the man, Janet had regained her composure. "Janet Westover, Donald Geiger," Christopher said.

Donald nodded in her direction. He was in his forties, his short stocky body poured into soiled pants and shirt. His black hair was graying, his lips narrow, his suspicious brown eyes shifting from Janet to Christopher and back again. He was nervous.

Christopher locked the door. Janet came to her feet, not

appreciating the smile Christopher gave her.

"Don't mind Janet's apparent paranoia," Christopher said. He was talking to Donald but looking at her. "She sees me locking the door and lets her imagination run rampant."

Donald was embarrassed. "Maybe I should come back later," he said, proving he was as ill at ease as he looked.

"Nonsense!" Christopher said. "Janet is anxious to be entertained, and she hasn't been pleased with the job I'm doing. Maybe she'll be more receptive to what you have to offer."

"Maybe I should go?" Janet suggested.

Christopher wasn't accepting that alternative, either. "Don't be silly, Janet," he said. "Who knows, you might find this the most interesting part of your stay at Lionspride."

"Really, I—" Donald began but was interrupted.

"For the moment, we'll just pretend Janet isn't here." Christopher said.

He was baiting her. He was enjoying her discomfort in front of Donald. He was encouraged by the flashes of anger in her eyes. She had gone through so much that day it was difficult not to strike out at his sarcasm, but she controlled herself.

"Donald?' Christopher said, evidently pleased that Janet couldn't or wouldn't speak. He went to his desk and slid his paperwork to one side. From one of the side drawers, he took a square of black velvet and spread it over the cleared surface. "Let's see what we have, shall we?"

Donald was as glad as Janet that Christopher's attention had shifted. He reached into his pants pocket and pulled out a small sack closed off at one end with a drawstring. His large fingers expertly loosened the string. He tipped the bag and spilled out a stone onto the black velvet. The stone was a rough octahedron, and it was the color of Christopher's eyes, complete with dark specks that marred an otherwise translucent surface.

"Yes, that is nice, isn't it?" Christopher said. If his attention was diverted from Janet, it wasn't for long. "Do come on over, Janet!" he insisted. "You're not going to see this every day. And it's one aspect of the Van Hoon enterprise that has nothing whatsoever to do with blood sport. Or is it only the killing aspects of the family that interest you?"

She came to the desk and stood by it, drawn to the gold of Christopher's eyes rather than to the gold of the bauble on his desk top.

Christopher took a jeweler's loupe from a drawer. He picked up the rock and began a thorough examination of it. For a moment, he was totally occupied, and Janet willed herself not to wish that he would find her half as exciting as he found that piece of colored stone.

"Exceptional!" he said, putting the loupe to one side and rolling the glassy octahedron between his large and powerful fingers. How exciting those fingers would feel lovingly touching her skin, His attention shifted from the stone to Donald, Janet seemingly out of the picture. "What do you think?" he asked. "Thirty-two carats if we shoot for flawless?"

"Rubel said thirty-four," Donald answered. "He recommends we do it with a heart cut."

"Here, Janet," Christopher said, tossing her the stone. She caught it purely out of reflex. "What do you say?"

"What is it? Topaz?" she asked. When she and Bob were looking for her engagement ring, she had seen a yellow topaz. It wasn't as big as this stone, though.

Donald gave an audible intake of breath that dismissed Janet once and for all. Christopher's golden eyes sparkled more than the uncut gem.

"It's a diamond, Janet," Christopher said, shaking his head and clicking his tongue in mock disappointment. "I thought every woman knew a diamond when she saw one. Aren't they supposed to be a girl's best friend?"

"It's honey colored," she said, putting the stone back on the velvet. Donald's reaction, more than Christopher's statement, told her it was indeed a diamond. She was nervous with a stone that would cut to thirty-four carats, much heavier (more valuable) than Elizabeth Taylor's much ballyhooed ring. She rubbed hands together, renewing the warmth Christopher had passed to her through the cool crystal.

"It's a fancy," Christopher said. "Impurities make it that color."

"They make it a damned sight more expensive, too" Donald interjected, dispelling the notion that impurities equated with inferior quality, in this instance.

"Right," Christopher agreed. "We are always exceedingly pleased when one of these babies turns up."

He picked up the telephone on the desk, his gaze on Janet. There was humor in his eyes. Again, he had made her appear foolish. "Bartlet, will you send Samuels around front with the car, please?" he said into the mouthpiece before replacing the receiver. He walked over to the door and unlocked it. "I'm afraid Donald and I have things to discuss that you'd find horribly boring, Janet," he said. "I hope you'll accept my apologies for cutting our evening short." He smiled that same maddening smile. "I'll make it up to you later, I promise."

"That won't be necessary, I assure you," Janet said, more affected by her dismissal than she would admit.

"Feel free to take the dress with you as a consolation prize," he called after her, making her skin turn hot with embarrassment. She knew what Donald Geiger was thinking. "You certainly look better in it than the other women did," Christopher added. His amused laughter was still ringing in her ears when she reached the top of the stairs. She was tempted, but she didn't slam the door of the bedroom. She refused to give him the satisfaction.

She had no intention of keeping the dress. The tapes were all she wanted from him. By tomorrow, they would be safely on a plane for Seattle. Whatever glimmer of hope she had had of dissociating him from his despicable father was shattered.

The zipper stuck in her hurried attempts to shed the offensive silk, and she began to panic during the following moments of struggle. She couldn't go back to the library for help, but the alternative was to tear the dress. She couldn't ruin something so lovely that, by her standards, was so extravagantly expensive, even if Christopher cared less.

"Thank God!" she said, heaving an audible sigh of relief when the zipper came loose.

She changed, knowing Christopher would be curious about the delay. He would think she had misgivings about leaving Lionspride. The sooner she set him straight on that score, the better.

Ashanti was waiting patiently at the front door. There was no sign of Christopher. Janet was the last thing on his mind at the moment. A large golden diamond was more interesting than a busybody come to do him mischief. At least that's the way Janet saw it.

CHAPTER THREE

THE ROLLS ROYCE SILVER SPIRIT was long, roomy and had all the creature comforts, including a television set and a bar. However, Janet couldn't get comfortable. She was leaving Lionspride. Again. Nothing horrible had developed from Christopher's stolen kiss and his insults. They merely confirmed what she had known all along: the past was over and done, never to be lived again.

She was disappointed and knew why. She touched her fingertips to her lips. The feel of Christopher's stolen kiss lingered somehow. She was disgusted by the pleasure evoked by the memory of his mouth on hers.

That kiss set her up. It took her by surprise, as though hinting of worse things to come. The resulting horrors, though, were figments of Janet's overactive imagination. Christopher had enjoyed a delicious meal. He'd played games in the darkness of the basement. He'd terrorized her with a few suggestive words and looks. Then, satisfied that he'd paid her back for her plotting against him, he'd sent her on her way. He was a king tired of his court jester, offering her a used dress in reward for stale amusements.

She put herself in his position. He graciously consented to let her into his home. He personally greeted her, trying to make her feel comfortable. He offered her punch after her long drive from the city. He cooperated in every way, only to have it dawn on him that she was there to do a hatchet job on his family.

Well, Janet didn't feel guilty. Fair play was a luxury owed

those who played by the rules, and the Van Hoons never did that. Their fortune originated with Petre Van Hoon's swindling of a poor native who didn't know a diamond from a pretty stone.

Janet laughed—not in amusement, either. It was ironic to have witnessed Christopher drooling over a diamond just as Petre Van Hoon must have done. Christopher was no ragged vagabond with only the belongings on his back, but the same greedy gleam was in his eye. She had seen it there when he was packing her off moments after that precious stone had entered his life.

She leaned into the luxurious leather of the seat. Ahead, the largest man-made structures in the world were piled high across the horizon. Some of the rock crystal in those enormous heaps of mine tailings were dragged from over two miles beneath the city. The foundation of Johannesburg was honeycombed with kilometers of tunnels stretching in all directions. As much traffic went on below the surface as on the streets above. All for the sake of gold.

Christopher's hair was gold. Christopher's eyes were gold.

She wouldn't think of Christopher's hair, or his eyes. She wouldn't think of him, period. He had lost something in his transition from boy to man, just as Janet had lost something in her painful journey from girl to woman.

The car stopped. She didn't wait for the chauffeur to get out and open the door for her. She opened it herself. She wasn't a pampered woman who couldn't take care of herself without a paid retainer's assistance. Those women were of Christopher's world. She was of quite another. Those women draped themselves in animal skins that brought the leopard, cheetah, lynx and tiger to the brink of extinction. Janet wanted to save those animals. Not just the ones killed to satisfy some society matron's twisted notion of fashion. Not just those massacred to bolster some hunter's macho image. Rhinoceros were slaughtered for their horns, believed to restore sexual prowess to impotent Asian men. Elephants were killed for their tusks, made legal tender by uncaring speculators.

Christopher had a room full of elephant ivory. With each elephant killed, the source of that ivory was depleted by one. Christopher became richer. When all the elephants were dead, like the quagga and bluebuck were dead, Christopher would be a very rich man.

Damn it, he was rich enough already! He shouldn't think of how to add more money to the family coffers. He should take steps to insure that his children would see live elephants instead of just pictures of them.

But Christopher was childless. He wasn't married. Janet felt funny inside as she swept through the doors of the Carleton Hotel. The hotel was part of a vast complex of boutiques, movie theaters and restaurants, none of which claimed her attention. She wasn't all that interested in the spectacular view of city lights from her hotel window, either.

The bed had been turned down by the night maid. Janet searched a suitcase for her cotton pajamas. Her negligee was in the closet, but she didn't want it. It was too provocative against her skin. She shouldn't have brought it. It was extra baggage. Pajamas were more practical where she was going.

The negligee was black silk. Christopher had dressed her in black silk, like a doll, tossing her aside as soon as a honey-colored diamond came along.

The phone rang. Her sweet visions were of his calling to apologize—better yet, telling her that he realized who she was, that he was angry for not realizing it right away, that he wanted to see her again. She was a fool for letting them get off to such a ridiculously bad start. There were memories to talk about after sixteen years.

It was Jill. She wanted to make sure Janet was back safely. She wanted to satisfy her curiosity. Tim and Roger had rushed her away from Lionspride grinning from ear to ear like two Cheshire cats. "Janet really landed herself a big one this time!" Roger had said as they drove off.

Janet was in no mood to talk about Christopher. She wanted to forget him. All the interesting tidbits Jill wanted to hear hadn't happened. "Did you get the tapes ready for shipping?" Janet asked, using business to counter Jill's snooping. There was silence at the other end. "Well?"

"You've the tapes," Jill said. "Don't you?"

"How could I have them?" Janet asked. Frustrated. Something was wrong. She didn't need this. "I stayed at Lionspride, didn't I? You called to see whether I was back. Right? Right!"

"But he said...," Jill replied, leaving the sentence hanging.

"Who said what?" Janet asked, her heart sinking.

"The man who stopped us at the gate," Jill continued tentatively. "He told us you wanted the tapes to play for Mr. Van Hoon at the house. He ran them back to you. Didn't he?"

"Don't worry about it," Janet said, keeping her cool. There was no need to take out on Jill what wasn't her fault. It was logical for her to have accepted the information as given. Everybody had video equipment nowadays. Christopher could afford the very best. "I'll talk to you in the morning, okay? I'm a little tired right now."

"But what about the tapes?"

"I'll talk to you tomorrow!" Janet insisted with finality. She hung up the phone, her hand gripping the receiver so tightly her fingers were bleached white across her knuckles. "That rat!" she forced out between clenched teeth. He was a liar like his father! If Donald Geiger hadn't distracted him with that diamond, he would still be lying, insisting he wanted fair payment for tapes that he had no intention of letting her have.

She released her grip on the phone, her fingers hurting as she uncurled them. She paced, but it didn't help. She lay down on the bed. She would sleep and worry about this in the morning. She didn't need the tapes. She could say the Van Hoon wildlife collection contained extinct species, and Christopher couldn't deny it. There were people who had seen the trophy room, and they could substantiate her story if Christopher called her a liar. Of course, a picture was worth a thousand words. Television audiences were visually oriented.

He was less flippant about the threat she offered than he

appeared. The Van Hoon name was vulnerable to attack after all.

She squeezed her eyes shut, trying to clear her mind. She was enveloped in the smell of exotic perfume. She had splashed the fragrance on extravagantly at Lionspride after finding a sixteen-ounce bottle in the bathroom. She had used too much; she smelled cheap. She felt cheap. Christopher Van Hoon's toy, his plaything—tossed aside when he tired of her.

She wished he could be guiltless. It was his father— and the Van Hoon tradition most of all—that she hated. If she was obvious in pinpointing the extinct animals before the cameras, it was because she wanted Christopher to convince her she was wrong to condemn him. At eighteen, he had promised he would never kill another animal. Or was his promise never to kill another gazelle? It didn't matter. It was a lie. He had said she could have the film if she stayed for supper. A lie. She had endured the brunt of his amusement for nothing. He had been laughing at her.

She got up, stripping off her pajamas, and went into the bathroom to take a shower. She scrubbed her body until her skin was raw, exchanging the exotic muskiness for the antiseptic blandness of soap. She would wash away all memory of him.

Her pajamas reeked of the perfume. She threw them in a corner and climbed into bed naked. She wanted to sleep, but the caress of the sheets against her nakedness was sensuously distracting. When she did sleep, she dreamed of Christopher.

He was young. He was standing in the shade of a blue-gum tree. He didn't need the sun in the sky, because he carried sunlight in his hair, in the glow of his eyes, in the tan of his skin. Janet was in the dream with him. She was happy. God, it was so good to be happy! Ahead of her stretched unlived years of pain in which her father and husband died and left her. She would pick up the pieces each time she had this dream, remembering how it was to live in innocence, to laugh and touch in innocence, to kiss in innocence. Was it wrong to want it back?

She was filled with loss and futility when she awakened. She was Janet Westover, not Janet Kelley. She was twenty-nine, not thirteen. She was a widow, not a virgin. She wasn't innocent, and there was no bringing back the past.

A knock on her door brought her back to reality. A second knock made her moan and wish whoever it was would go away. She was tired. It had taken her an eternity to get to sleep, and now this. She opened her eyes, surprised to see that the sun was shining through the window.

"Give me a minute!' she said, throwing back the blankets. "I said, just...a...minute," she erupted irritably as a third knock sounded. Her robe was in the closet, hanging next to her black silk negligee. She put on the robe, securing the belt at her waist. She opened the door.

He was standing there with his blond hair and golden eyes, deeply dimpled cheeks, and wide smile. "Hi!" he said. She was dreaming. His left hand was behind his back, his right hand extending a bouquet of golden roses. She could smell the heady fragrance of the flowers.

"There's only one thing I want from you!" she said, wishing he wasn't so handsome, wishing his eyes weren't sparkling with good-natured humor.

"And surprise, I brought that, too," he said, producing the tape spools from behind his back. "I did promise them to you, didn't I? In exchange for supper, wasn't it?"

"I suppose you spent last night erasing them," she accused, taking them anyway.

"Janet, Janet," he said, his low voice as teasing as it was chiding. "May I come in?"

"I'm not dressed," she said, watching his wide smile spread.

"I know," he retorted.

"No, you may not come in," she replied. He was too handsome, too charming, too capable of being nice one minute and hurtful the next.

"Then will you come out?" he ventured playfully. "I'm taking a look around one of the Van Hoon gold mines this morning, and I thought you might like to ride along."

His hair was gold, his eyes were gold, his skin was gold. She was dreaming. "What makes you think I want to see a gold mine?" she asked when he didn't dissolve into thin air.

"What woman in her right mind wouldn't want to see one?" he countered.

"So what makes you think I want to see a gold mine with you?" she amended. What was he trying to pull? She preferred him less friendly, less pleasantly playful, less the Christopher she remembered. She was vulnerable, and he was clever enough to see that.

"What woman in her right mind wouldn't want to see one *with me*?" he said. "So what do you say? You're not crazy, are you?"

"I'd be crazy if I did go with you," she said, determined not to be persuaded. He was up to no good.

"You make it damned hard for a man to apologize, Janet," he said, shaking his head.

Surely, he understood why this was so impossible. "That's what you're doing, is it?" she asked. "Apologizing?"

"I behaved abominably last night," he said. "I was hoping the flowers and tapes would say that for me, but I'm willing to eat more humble pie."

"Why?" she asked suspiciously. "That's what I want to know."

"Why?" he echoed. "Because I finally remembered who you remind me of." She didn't ask. She couldn't. He answered anyway. "A girl I once knew," he said. His bright smile dimmed. "A funny thing: her name was Janet, too." Janet was charged with emotions. There were memories of her alive within him. "But enough of *that* Janet!" he said, erasing the warm sensuousness of her discovery. "She was a child. You're a woman. She was unable to reason as an adult. Your job demands adult objectivity. You wouldn't peddle distortion just because it raises your television ratings, would you?"

Christopher's images of Janet Kelley were anything but pleasant, tainted by all that came after. Even if she had been a child at the time, he hadn't forgiven her for thinking and reasoning as a child.

"You're telling me your family hasn't exploited the land and the wildlife?" Janet demanded, drawing her robe more tightly around her. There was something about this man that physically affected her, something far more noticeable now that she was a woman.

"It's the nature of things to change," he said "You told me that at the house. Nothing is static. Not Africa. Not its wildlife. Not its people. Many have prospered from Van Hoon mines. I guarantee fair wages and decent working conditions. And why condemn me for animals slaughtered in my grandfather's and father's times? Their generations lived the grand illusion of unending natural resources."

"That doesn't excuse their excesses!" she said, vehemently. His rationalizations of innocence wouldn't defuse her outrage.

"I shouldn't be expected to make excuses for people over whom I had no control," Christopher said. Janet wasn't responsible for circumstances over which she had no control, either. Her father had forced her to leave Africa, Lionspride, and Christopher. A thirteen-year-old girl doesn't disobey a father loved for a lifetime. It was only now, sixteen years later, that she could say she had loved Christopher, maybe as much as she had loved her father. "I'm asking you to take the time to get to know me a little better," Christopher said. "Is that too much to ask a woman who can bad-mouth me to a few million people at one shot?"

"And by getting to know you, I'll come to love you, I suppose?" Janet asked with sarcasm in her voice. She hurried on. Joking about her feelings for Christopher made her uneasy. "In one afternoon, you'll convince me that a line of despots ended when your father died, you springing on the scene as pure as newly fallen snow."

"I'm Christopher Van Hoon, remember—not a saint," he said, a wry smile playing at the corners of his sensuous mouth. "I'm not faultless. It would be wrong, though, to paint my picture blacker than it is. If a man isn't patted on the back a few times in his life, encouraged for his attempts to make amends—no matter how feeble those attempts might appear—he'll think further effort hardly worth the effort."

"I can't believe you're concerned about what I might or might not say about the Van Hoon family on television," Janet said. He had shown his contempt for her and her position by engineering that embarrassing scene at Lionspride.

"I'm not concerned," he admitted, and Janet flushed with anger. Suspecting her ineffectiveness was one thing. Having it confirmed was another. "Actually you're a surrogate," he said.

"For whom? For what?"

"For that other Janet who never gave me the chance to defend myself," he said, filling her with the guilt she had tried to deny.

"You seem extremely confident of your powers of persuasion" Janet said, stung by the accusation in his voice. He was condemning a virtual child for not allowing herself to be persuaded by letters still unopened and ribbon-tied. A young girl's grief allowed no separation of grain from chaff, of son from father. By the time she could forgive the boy for being a Van Hoon, he was a boy no longer. He was head of Van Hoon Afrikaner Minerals. He was the only Van Hoon she had left to hate; a hate she had struggled to overcome, to no avail.

Besides, the real villain was Van Hoon Afrikaner Minerals, a corporate profiteer. The hiring of her father all those years ago and the commissioning of his feasibility study for the Lackland Animal Preserve had been a cover for company machinations. Because of the attention drawn to the study, gold exploration could be conducted without arousing the suspicion of the competition or her father. When gold was found, Jack Kelley and the Lackland Animal Preserve project were dumped by the wayside, having served their purposes.

Her father hadn't survived that betrayal. He had been deeply committed to the preservation of African wildlife. His study had shown a locale excellently suited to that purpose. Sixteen years after he had submitted his paperwork to that effect, there were no animals in the area he had mapped out for Lackland.

There were three deep holes in the ground, their openings surrounded by smoke-belching buildings that converted tons of crushed rock into ounces of shiny gold. Trains chugged where antelope once roamed. Winders, trucks, conveyer belts, drills and explosives bled sounds to a veldt that once knew only the sounds of animals, the wind, the rain.

The impetus behind that perverted metamorphosis of the African landscape hadn't died with Vincent Van Hoon, any more than it had died with Petre Van Hoon. Van Hoon Afrikaner Minerals remained a nefarious entity, guiding human actions from behind the scenes. Christopher Van Hoon, as sole heir to his father and grandfather, *was* Van Hoon Afrikaner Minerals. He was the personification of that evil, and Janet could fight it only through him. If she was his surrogate, he was hers.

"I'll give you fifteen minutes to decide whether you're here to do a hatchet job or to do things fairly," he said, tossing the unclaimed bouquet onto a nearby chair. The discarded roses bruised their golden petals on the chafing upholstery. "I'll wait in the lobby."

The door closed behind him. She glanced at the travel clock on the bedside table. She needed to know how long she had. She picked up the roses, cradling their long stems in her arms, smelling their sweet fragrance. Bob had never bought her flowers. Bob was practical. Why spend money on something so transitory? Better a toaster or a tape deck. Now Bob was dead, his life as transitory as cut roses.

Time was passing, seconds turning into minutes. She needed more time.

There was no vase for the flowers. If she left them, they would wilt before the maid found them. The roses seemed important. Concern for them kept her from thinking about Christopher waiting in the lobby.

She went into the bathroom and filled the sink, propping the ends of the stems in the water. Too many things died in Africa. Flowers. Animals. Dreams. Expectations. Love.

"Damn!" she said, bracing herself against the edge of the

sink. She was as conscious of the ticking in the other room as tourists were of Big Ben's chimes at noontime.

Less than fifteen minutes—that was what sixteen years of memories came down to. She could let the clock tick away the final ending, or she could hope for a miracle in a world devoid of miracles. She could hope to reclaim the unclaimable, even if Christopher offered no real solution. He wasn't waiting to tell her everything was all right, the sixteen years forgotten. He was playing games—not because he saw her as a threat but because she was a woman. Success with any woman offered him consolation for an ego bruised sixteen years before when Janet had been unable to succumb.

She wanted to be fair. She wanted more. Too late. Sixteen years too late. Fifteen minutes too late.

Her robe was off before she reached the closet. She didn't look at the clock, fearing what it showed.

She dressed quickly, choosing a brown pullover. She had no trouble with the button and zipper on the matching slacks. The strap on her left shoe was less obliging. She softly cursed it into submission.

She grabbed her purse, finding her comb in it by the time she reached the hallway. She shared the elevator with two men who eyed her appreciatively as she put her hair into some semblance of order. There was no time for makeup.

She asked one of the men for the time; she'd left her wristwatch in her room. The man's watch was an expensive Piaget. No chance of the wrong time. A Piaget only lost one second every two years, according to the ads.

She was beyond the fifteen-minute deadline. She had made the right decision too late. There would have been plenty of time if only she had started dressing the minute he left. Sixteen years and fifteen minutes to end like this, before any new beginnings.

He was waiting, his muscular body leaning against a pillar facing the elevator. He smiled, walking toward her. "I knew you'd come," he said confidently. Her anger flushed her cheeks. She shouldn't have come running. She should have denied him his obvious satisfaction. "Not because I'm personally so irresistible," he added quickly, intuitively sensing her second thoughts. "I merely knew you had a sense of fair play."

"I thought you'd be gone," she commented with feigned coolness.

"I've never known a woman who could get ready for anything in fifteen minutes," he said. "You must have set some kind of record as it was."

"My being here doesn't mean I'm making any promises," Janet said. Too many promises were regretted later.

"I'll get the Van Hoons," she'd promised her father. He hadn't heard. He was dead. It was a promise nevertheless. Now she was consorting with the enemy.

"My car is outside," he said, his fingers on her elbow. Fire ran the length of her arm. He did that with his slightest touch.

Because it was early, the hotel lobby was almost deserted. Shops, theaters and restaurants that would soon pull a crowd into the Carleton Complex were closed and awaiting proprietors. Beyond the revolving door, the city stirred. There was a vital pulse to Johannesburg that existed night and day. That activity had begun on a deserted piece of wasteland less than one hundred years before, conjured by the discovery of gold, still the main reason for Johannesburg's existence.

Gold raised a city where there should never have been one. Perched on one of the highest ridges of the South African plateau, seventeen hundred meters above sea level, it had no water that wasn't pumped in from the Vaal over sixty kilometers away. Its petrol and diesel came all the way from Durban, 720 kilometers to the southeast, where tankers from the Persian Gulf fed an insatiable pipeline.

Johannesburg had a population of nearly a million and a half people. It was nearly twice the size of Durban and Cape Town, South Africa's other big cities, and three times the size of Pretoria, the republic's administrative capital.

Christopher was driving a Mercedes sports car. He opened the door on the passenger side for Janet and went around to the other side to slide in beside her.

"Relax," he said, smiling. His teeth were white, his hair as golden as the metal dug beneath the city. "I'm really not a dentist out to yank your molars. I'm here to show you a good time."

There was no denying that Janet was tense. She was debating whether she had been right in coming. There was something about being with Christopher now that muted the unhappiness of the past sixteen years. With his handsome face and muscular body so near, Janet could forget her father and her husband. She knew it was unhealthy to escape reality by recalling the past. She was with Christopher Van Hoon not because they were children, enjoying each other's company, but because they were adults engaged in adult games.

She settled back in her seat, caressed by the luxurious softness of expensive leather. The leather smells became more erotic when mingled with the scent of Christopher's distinctive after-shave. The car was moving toward the maze of great mounds, evidence of three thousand million tons of rock pulverized in the search for gold. But these mine tailings were less the unsightly boils on the landscape they had once been. Years of experimentation and large outlays of cash had resulted in the discovery of ways of getting hybrid vegetation to root in the unsavory mixture of silica and cyanide. The dumps looked more and more like low-lying foothills: the Johannesburg Downs. A standard joke on the stock exchange was that the mining companies took all the ups, leaving the city the Downs. The still un-vegetated segments caught the early-morning sunshine, telegraphing flashes of gold.

The same sunlight caught in Christopher's hair, held captive in silky strands glowing with luminescence. Janet wanted to comb her fingers through that mating of hair and celestial fire. Electricity built inside her without the touching.

"The Cassandras have been prophesying an end to the gold for years," Christopher said, steering the car along a highway that sliced one man-made dune into mirrored halves. "As far back as 1911, the mines were supposedly about to give up their last. New discoveries, however, combined with advanced technology and periodic increases in the selling price of gold, now project the life of the mines into the year 2030.”

“There used to be wildlife wandering here in vast herds,” Janet said. “Where do you suppose they are now?”

“Mining companies in Johannesburg employ over four hundred and fifty thousand men,” Christopher answered; his reply automatic. He was programmed for his response. “Without the profits from the mines, this country would be very poor indeed, attempting to eke an existence from the export of agricultural products at the mercy of periodic droughts and severe crop failures.”

“Yes, well, I imagine there is a rationalization for everything, isn’t there?” Janet said, refusing to be impressed. She knew the arguments for industrial development versus maintenance of an ecological status quo. Christopher wasn’t the only one who considered corporate profits more desirable than environmental preservation. Unfortunately, there were too many like him. If they weren’t the majority, they were still in positions of power that gave them the edge.

“I suppose it all depends on one’s priorities,” Christopher said smugly. “Some people seem more concerned about the welfare of four-legged animals than the welfare of their own two-legged species.”

“Some people find the four-legged varieties far less able to take care of themselves,” Janet said. “I don’t see animals lobbying for their grazing land while greedy businessmen divvy up the pot.”

There was an uneasy silence. Her every moment with Christopher was a battle. Perversely, she had hoped for something more.

“Look,” he said finally, his thoughts parallel to hers, “surely we’re not going to be the only two people on this lovely day who refuse to enjoy ourselves, are we? Couldn’t we try for a truce? It’s unlikely we’re going to resolve, in one day of bickering, any profit-versus-ecology questions that have been around longer than either of us."

"Then what's the purpose of this little outing?" Janet asked.

"I want you to know there are members of the opposition who are charming human beings and not the ogres you, and many of your cohorts, seem to think," he said, flashing a wide smile that invited seduction.

"Is that what you think you are?" Janet asked, wanting to believe but refusing to do so. "A charming human being?"

"Oh yes," Christopher said, ignoring her sarcasm. "As you shall soon see if you give me half the chance."

"A preacher pontificating his own virtues must surely do so to a congregation of one!" Janet said, wishing Christopher's charm was more the natural variety of his youth than the calculated efforts of a shrewd businessman out to win converts.

"Touché!" Christopher said with a laugh so infectious Janet couldn't help smiling. She shouldn't have smiled; it gave him the proverbial inch that would encourage him to go for the mile. "There," he said; "isn't that better?"

It was better. It was some of what she wanted; it was what she feared, too.

"I didn't mean to sound pompous," she said. He was right. There would be no miraculous conversions in their short time together. She knew that when she came down the elevator to meet him in the lobby. That was never her real purpose. She wanted a piece of her past. She was willing to settle for one day of renewal, here and now. Offered the chance of that day, she would be a fool to refuse it.

"We won't mention it again," he said, sounding too triumphant.

She didn't like losing ground. "Tell me about this girl who I remind you of," she said.

"I thought we were going to have fun?" he demanded, his golden eyes shooting condemning daggers.

"How can you have fun when I remind you of someone you'd rather forget?" Janet replied, hurt by his change of mood, even though she had anticipated it. She feared giving in to inner needs that could weaken her resolve.

"There are good memories as well as the bad," he said. She shouldn't have pried for that admission. Despite her heartache, it was easier thinking he remembered only the bad. "Nothing is ever truly black or white," he said, turning his face toward her, unreadable. "Don't ever let anyone tell you that it is. Relationships are painted in grays."

"I'm sorry," she said, meaning it. "For some reason, I feel compelled to be on the offensive."

"We do seem to be having our problems, don't we?" he said, the humor back in his voice. She was glad for the return of lightness; it was contagious. "So, I will apologize, too," he said, "and bring us back to square one. After all, why shouldn't you be curious? Who knows, it may do me a world of good to talk about it."

Janet didn't want him to talk about it. She didn't want to open that can of worms, appalled that she had been the one to provide the instrument. He would paint her the villain of the piece. It would be easy to do. She had never answered his letters, never even read them, fearful that they held the magic to seduce her from her father. Janet couldn't join in her father's betrayal, and only Christopher had had the power to make her do so. She had hated her father for taking her from Africa and from Lionspride—from Christopher. The hate had been there, as well as the love, when his heart attack killed him. And she felt guilty, prepared to compensate for her feelings of disloyalty.

"I knew her when we were children," Christopher said, making Janet uneasy. How could she stop him? His memories weren't hers, and time distorted things. The reality of her dreams might be inaccurate. "She hated to see animals killed," he said. "She liked sliding down the banister at Lionspride. You see the similarities?"

"I like her already," Janet said, nervously glancing from the car window. Mine tailings stretched to either side of the highway. She and Christopher were driving the Golden Arc of the great South African gold fields. Millions of years ago, heat, cold and storms scoured debris from gold-bearing mountains into a great inland sea that was now the Transvaal Highveldt and the Orange Free State.

"She was very likable..." Christopher said.

"But?" Janet prodded. Pure curiosity made her want to hear the rest.

"But she was a child," he said. Maybe he understood after all. "I wasn't more than a child myself."

"First love?" she suggested. She was torturing herself, making things worse. She was hoping he would recognize her as that thirteen-year-old girl.

"Actually, I fared far better in my teens than most," he said, steering toward an end to that line of conversation. He was laughing it off. It wasn't special; it was only a phase of adolescence that everyone went through. Children grew up. Things that seemed world shattering were recognized later as mere childish exaggerations.

CHAPTER FOUR

IT WAS A JOKE: a very funny one about a black cat, an Englishman in a bowler hat, and an American tourist in Cairo. Janet would try to recall it later, but the punch line would always elude her. All she'd remember was how she was laughing when Christopher pulled the car to a stop on the small rise. He pointed through the windshield and down into a shallow valley, and the laughter died in her throat.

The mine was called the Van Hoon Deep Levels. Of course it would be the one Christopher would select. It was the company showpiece—the biggest, the deepest. It was the most profitable gold mine ever discovered. It produced more gold in one year than all the mines in the United States could produce during that same year. "Something on the order of eleven-million rand a month," Christopher boasted, his voice filled with an owner's pride.

Janet looked through a lattice of high-power electric lines held aloft by giant four-legged supports. There were massive piles of mine tailings, three perfectly pointed like candy kisses done up in gold foil, the fourth a massive volcano whose top seemed blown away. The summit of the latter was misted in water from sprinkler systems designed to keep down the dust from the additional waste rock continually being dumped to build the pile higher.

There was a cluster of buildings. Christopher isolated the structures, one by one, as if they were priceless jewels in a necklace. "The maintenance shop, the riggers' shop, the smelter, the uranium and sulfuric acid plants. Uranium, and sulfuric acid are by-products of the operation."

"No animals," Janet said. She hadn't meant to say it aloud. It just slipped out. "There should be animals." That barren landscape was denuded of wildlife by man's burrowing in the ground like a mole.

"Damn it, if you're so hot for animals, why don't you go to Kruger!" he suggested, angry at her return to a topic they had agreed to avoid. Kruger National Park was a game reserve of two million hectares in the northeastern corner of the Transvaal. Its wildlife population was enough to attract half a million visitors a year.

"I'm sorry," she said, but their former levity was shattered. Christopher brought her here—of all places. She couldn't keep the disappointment out of her voice. The Van Hoon Deep Levels was the major of three mines rising from her father's useless dreams for the Lackland Animal Preserve. This shallow valley had been set aside as part of that proposed sanctuary. Now there were no animals. The lake, which might have sustained wildlife through the longest droughts, was stagnant behind the ugly mine tailings.

The movement of cars, trucks, and people—all ant-like in the distance—wasn't the vital sign of something vibrantly alive. It was a sign of death. Because of this abomination, thousands of animals lost a home. In the year 2030, with modern technology leeching the last of the gold from the rock below, nothing would live on the resulting desolation.

Christopher pulled the car back on the highway. He exuded coldness. The illusion of truce was ruined. He was showing her the pride of the Van Hoon corporate complex, and she was committing the ultimate sacrilege of criticizing the necessary displacement of a few antelope, zebras and ostriches.

She wanted to return to Johannesburg. There was no hope for her and Christopher—that was clear now. They were too far apart. Sixteen years might as well have been sixteen hundred. She had once persuaded him never to kill another gazelle, but she had surrendered all other influence over him by leaving him to his father. The Christopher she loved wasn't here. What was beside her was a duplicate of Vincent Van Hoon. If more attractive and more charming, that was a veneer. The core of his being was no longer malleable.

Vincent hadn't liked her. The idea of his son promising her not to kill another gazelle had made him livid. He had got rid of her and her father none too soon. The death of Jack Kelley must have pleased him. The less anti-capitalistic idealists, the better!

They took the road that led down toward the works. The Van Hoon name was proudly displayed on a high archway, whose gates opened for the car.

Guards ushered them through the checkpoints. They knew Christopher. He authorized their paychecks. He kept this place running. He turned a vast deposit of compact, gray-green pebbly stone into gold. He was an alchemist extraordinaire.

Without a word, he steered the car into a parking spot and stopped it. "Come on," he said, breaking the silence. He didn't open her door. He didn't turn to see if she was following. He disappeared inside the nearest building.

She would sit there until he was ready to return to the city. She had seen all she wanted to see. Only an insensitive, avaricious man would view such an unsightly conglomeration of metal buildings, rumbling trucks, and floating dust and find satisfaction in the man-made desolation. What few trees, flowers and shrubs were planted by someone, to give the illusion of natural beauty among the expanding lunar landscape, were ghostly efforts thickly shrouded in dust. She hated this place and all it stood for. She wanted out.

She got out of the car. She would insist he take her back to her hotel. It wouldn't be the first time. She had made the same request at Lionspride. It got results when Christopher was ready—not before. It would be no different this time.

He was coming to get her. She could tell by the determined expression on his face when she opened the door of the building and saw him facing her. "Good!" he said. "I would have hated a scene."

"I want to go back to Johannesburg," she said, echoing her request at Lionspride. He might yet have an unwanted scene on his hands. Everyone was an employee of his here, as at Lionspride, and these men were as likely to gossip as household servants.

"No, you don't," he contradicted. "And shall I tell you why?" If only he didn't look like the Christopher she remembered. If only he were fat or bald. If only he were taller, skinnier, dissipated by vice. It was painful recognizing the boy within the man when that boy seemed only an illusion. "Because this visit is giving you more ammunition for your smear campaign against my family," he said.

"I want to go back to Johannesburg!" she insisted. She wanted to step back in time—if not sixteen years, then to the truce of a few minutes before. It was marvelous when she had pretended they hadn't a care in the world, hearing his jokes, laughing with him—his eyes sparkling and his dimples deepening. Both of them had seemed like children again, their world less complicated than the world of adults. Wishful thinking!

The present was real.

"Do you know what this mine sits on?" Christopher asked. He made no move to walk her to the car. "It sits on land once destined for an animal preserve. Think of that. Here was to be a sanctuary for all those little furry, cuddly beasts you so love; the Van Hoons marched in and claimed the land in the name of corporate profits. Won't that make good editorial material for your television program, thrown in to emphasize the trophies on the walls and the ivory in the basement?"

"Why are you doing this?" she asked, hurt by the challenging mockery of his voice. "What's the point? You think so little of the threat I offer that you feel safe in what you're doing—but why bother? The great Christopher Van Hoon spending so much time and effort on a minor irritant doesn't jell."

"I go after what I want," Christopher said. "You don't bait a lioness with a piece of sugar. You give her the prey she wants."

He smiled at her confusion. It wasn't a pleasant smile, either. It was a Vincent Van Hoon smile. "Where would you have been if I hadn't offered you a look at the Ivory Room?" he asked. "Huh? I'll tell you where. In a van, with your camera crew, heading back to Johannesburg. Where would you be if I hadn't revealed to you what this might have been? You would be hurrying back to the city. I tell you what I tell you, I offer what I offer, because it keeps you where I want you."

"What do you mean, 'where you want' me?" she asked, finally getting the question out. Some equipment started in an adjacent building, and she shouted over the noise.

"Is it necessary for me to spell it out in graphic four-letter words?" he asked. There was something about his voice that made it easier for him to be heard above the racket.

"You want another Janet," she argued, her throat dry. "Not me."

"I assure you, my needs aren't those of one child for another," he contradicted. The noise stopped, his words hanging in the uneasy silence.

"Take me back to my hotel. Please," she said, saddened more than ever. He was hinting at a liaison, at a way to bridge the ideal past with the real present. She couldn't risk the passage. Fantasies were perfection; reality flawed. Succumbing to temptation only cheapened the preciousness of moments gilded by time. There were too few remembered good times to surrender them for something that couldn't possibly be comparable.

"Tell me you really want to go back to Johannesburg, and I'll take you," he said confidently.

"I want to go back," she said. She didn't recognize her own voice.

"Now, tell me with your eyes," he insisted, stepping in closer. "Tell me with your eyes that you don't feel something between us that goes beyond our differences about wildlife preservation and corporate profits—something that goes beyond any possible differences that could ever arise."

"You're mistaken," she said, hardly managing the words.

Because he wasn't mistaken. There was something between them: a segment of shared childhood. That's what it was. He misinterpreted in ignorance, believing it was something as mundane as lust. That was the way he thought. He was more animal than any beast that had once roamed this valley.

"Deny it all you please," he said. He didn't touch her. She wanted him to touch her. His touch would be the magic to convince, and she wanted to be convinced despite the danger. "Deny it to yourself," he said. "Deny it to me. Deny it to the world. You'll be lying!"

He still didn't touch her. He left her the will to protest. She didn't thank him for that. "If I stay, it won't be because of anything felt for you in the disgusting way you're suggesting," she said. "It will be because I'm willing to accept any scrap of incriminating evidence you're prepared to throw my way in your smug belief that your position is invulnerable."

"Then, let's get on with the feeding, shall we, my beautiful lioness?" he said, stepping back. He extended his hand, but she didn't dare take it.

"Afraid?" he asked, his smile cynical and mocking.

"No," she said, "I'm not afraid." It was a lie.

"Then, you're very lucky," he said, pulling his hand back without insisting. "Because I'm afraid, Janet Westover—and not of your design to crush the Van Hoon Empire in a deluge of public recrimination, either." He didn't explain. Janet didn't press for him to do so. It was enough that he was afraid and she was responsible. It gave her power—but an uncomfortable power that sent shivers cascading her spine.

He didn't look afraid. He looked anything but. He wanted her to assume an advantage that wasn't there. He wanted her to think he was vulnerable. Vulnerable men were more lovable, he must know. He must have used that ruse on many women before her.

He was right about one thing. She was interested in the scraps he tossed her—not only because they were ammunition but because they were reason enough to follow him deeper into the building. The machine, wherever it was, started again. The sound of Janet's footsteps was absorbed by the greater rumbling. He led her into a large locker room. The place smelled disturbingly of sweat, of dripping shower faucets that washed male bodies free of a grime that was later filtered from the drains for precious gold. He gave her a pair of rubber boots, a rubber coat, a miner's hat. He strapped a power pack on her back, paying scant attention to her protests that she could manage on her own. A cable connected a light to the power pack. He showed her how to turn on the light by twisting a knob on its back.

"If you look good in this getup—which you do—you'll look good in anything," he muttered. She didn't look good. She looked ridiculous. She wasn't spared seeing herself, either. A full-length mirror on one wall reflected her figure in all-too-vivid detail.

Christopher belonged. Like a chameleon, he traded the guise of businessman for that of miner. The change was more complete than Janet had imagined possible, but he was nonetheless handsome. If anything, the costume emphasized his good looks. He would look good in any clothes... or without any.

In their youth, they had swum in the pools above Lisbon Falls: he, already boasting the physical trappings of manhood; she, grown-up enough to be thrilled by the sight. He had since disrobed more completely for other women, of course, all shyness shed with his boyhood.

They exited into sunlight. The yellow rubber of their coats was more lemony in the brightness. There were several cages giving access to the mine. They were raised and lowered on a counterbalance, one cage always traveling in the opposite direction to the other. The electric pulley, around which the control cable wound, was a massive affair. Whatever else might be turned over to computers in a mine, the winder was always operated by a man. A miner, below ground, wanted the security of knowing there was a thinking, caring human being on the other end of his lifeline.

Three bells were echoed by three more. The gate of one

cage opened with a clatter. A casual wave of Christopher's arm motioned her forward. She wasn't looking at his arm. She was looking at the expression on his handsome face.

She didn't accept the invitation. She turned from the cage and all it symbolized and went back to the locker room. She couldn't trust herself alone in an elevator with Christopher, nor could she allow herself to be isolated with him below ground.

She took off the power pack and the miner's helmet.

"Janet?" He had followed her. She answered by taking off the rubber coat. She sat down to remove the boots.

"I'm afraid the thought of going down makes me claustrophobic," she said. "You go down if you must. I'll wait here."

"And miss the surprises I've planned?" he asked, smiling his little-boy grin. Janet wasn't up to his surprises.

"Yes, and miss the surprises you've planned," she said wearily, trying not to be sarcastic.

She stood, and he automatically reached for her. His rubber boots squeaked. His large hands wrapped around her wrists. "What if I told you there is a VIP room down below?" he cajoled, "with rugs on the floor, tapestries on the walls, tables, chairs, a basket of pâté de fois gras, chicken in aspic, asparagus and caviar waiting to be eaten—and a bottle of vintage champagne chilling in a silver ice bucket."

"I'll bet there's a bed, too, right?" Janet said intuitively. Now, there was no hiding her sarcasm. He took women there, surprising them with a cubicle of civilization in primitive uncivilized surroundings. "Really, I'm tired," she said. "I want to go back to my hotel."

He seemed genuinely disappointed. "What about your souvenirs?" he asked; his voice and eyes pleaded for her to be amenable. His eyes were such a beautiful gold. His hands were hot brands around her wrists. Her souvenirs from this place were of the mind: visions of what might have been compared to what was. "Your souvenirs are down below," he said, contradicting her thoughts. If she could resist the temptation to be alone with him, she certainly wasn't going to be enticed by trinkets that would end up displayed on knickknack shelves back home. "Gold," he said, surprising her. "Krugerrands. Five of them."

"Krugerrands?" she said, her interest piqued. Each Krugerrand coin contained a troy ounce of gold. At the going rate of gold, the famous South African coins were hardly distributed as gratis souvenirs.

"What better way to remember a gold mine than with gold?" he coaxed. He gave her a gentle tug, starting her on her way.

She knew, though, what he was suggesting. Humiliation burned through her body. "You're trying to buy me!" she accused, her voice calm. She wasn't calm.

"My God, Janet, how could you suggest that?" he said, all wide-eyed innocence. Despite his act, he looked like a young boy caught and embarrassed by being caught.

"There isn't enough gold in this mine, nor enough in what's already come out of it, to pay me to do what you want— above ground, on ground, or underground," she said, fighting for control. She felt dirty. Once again he had made her feel cheap. He didn't respect her as a professional in her field—or as a woman. That hurt. It made no difference that he offered a payment for sexual services that was generous—but then he was a generous man.

"You could donate the money to a worthy charity," he said with a smile, as though a woman in her right mind couldn't resist going to bed with Christopher Van Hoon and getting paid in the bargain. "Maybe to some foundation out to save your furry friends," he suggested, mocking her compassion.

He was despicable! She jerked both her arms, loosening his grip but not dislodging it. "Let me go," she hissed, "or I'll scream so loudly that this damned gold mine of yours will cave in beneath our feet!"

"Maybe the lady doth protest too much?" he suggested. He didn't believe she was saying no. He was used to getting his way. This time he had another think coming.

"This lady hasn't even begun to protest, which you'll find out if you try anything funny," she promised through teeth clenched so tightly her jaw ached "Now, turn me loose!" She gave another tug, no more successful than the first.

"Don't be a tease, Janet," he said, releasing her wrists. His arms went securely around her before she could prevent them.

"You're mad!" she said. Her face was close to his. She marveled, even in that moment, at his unflawed handsomeness.

"Mad because I want you?" he asked incredulously. "I'd be madder if I didn't want you."

She had dreamed of his saying that. She had come awake feeling guilty with Bob beside her, or with Bob off reporting some jungle war. Christopher wanting her—in every sense—had been her ultimate fantasy, her dream of him the wonder she had tried to preserve. But Christopher seemed about to destroy it. In dreams, he spoke to her in love. In reality, he spoke to her in lust. There was a world of difference. She wasn't even sure it was genuine lust. Maybe he was out to master a woman who had come into his home under false pretenses to trick him. In that case, she could have weighed three hundred pounds, had missing front teeth, been bald, and it wouldn't have mattered. If he wouldn't win her with distorted logic, he could master her in the bedroom. It was caveman mentality.

"I wouldn't go to bed with you if you were the last man on earth!" she cried. Her statement was trite, but it fit the occasion. It was never said in her dreams. In her fantasies, she never protested but waited breathlessly for his every whispered invitation. Such anticipation had been centered on a boy who no longer existed.

"You're lying, Janet!" he accused. His audacity! "You broadcast your desires, and I pick up every last signal!"

His grip tightened, pulling her closer. There seemed nothing between them. His chest and stomach muscles were chiseled contours pressing into her flesh. She felt more, and she no longer questioned his desire. She did question the reason behind it.

He wouldn't let her go.

This wasn't the way she had always imagined it, yet the physical image of the real man wasn't so different from her fantasy. The reality was more in focus: eyes more golden, dimples deeper, jaw squarer, hair blonder, body harder, kisses —

She turned her face to avoid his kiss. His lips followed the movement and claimed her mouth anyway. She mumbled a protest. Her words were lost as he muffled her complaint with his tongue. He teased her lips with his mouth, and though it seemed as if his lips would at any moment relinquish hers, for endless minutes, they did not.

Her struggles ground her against him, making him more excited. She began to be affected by his unyielding hardness, too. "Scoundrel!" she gasped, finally given air to breathe.

Yet her mouth enjoyed the taste of him. Her ears eagerly accepted his low whispers, while he breathed warm caresses against her cheek. "You're so beautiful," he said. "So very beautiful."

He was a master of seduction. He had practiced on Qwenella Fairchild, on that Vogue model, on Lady Bellona Morrel, on countless women in and out of the bedrooms of Lionspride, in and out of the VIP room in the mine. He had cut his teeth on jaded women, and Janet was a defenseless innocent by comparison. It made no difference that she had once been married. Bob had come to her with less expertise than Christopher mustered with one kiss. Bob had loved his work more than he'd loved his wife. It seemed to her that he only made love to her because that was one need his job couldn't satisfy.

"Please, let me go!" she begged. She was rationalizing what was happening by blaming Bob and his inadequacies. She had known his inadequacies before she married him. She had known he was dedicated to his job, that he would be out of the country for long periods, that he walked a constant tightrope between life and death in his coverage of countries at war. It was because she knew and understood that he proposed to her in the first place. She had married him though he was less than perfect, as all men were less than perfect.

"I never plan to let you go!" Christopher said. His lips settled for the sweeping curve of her neck when she denied him a return to her lips. His mouth was hot, burning her flesh, his licking tongue fanning the fire.

He backed her against one of the lockers. She heard metal sing as it gave beneath the pressure of their combined weight. She freed an arm. He tried to reclaim it, but she wouldn't let him. She anchored her fingers in the sensuous silkiness of his hair and took hold.

"Let me go!" she insisted. She no longer said please. This wasn't a moment for politeness. He was decimating her fantasies, and she refused to let him continue. If he was an uncaring brute, she didn't want ultimate proof. She wanted to retain at least a piece of her illusion.

She tugged on his hair, jerking his head back, not to hurt him, merely to make him stop. The curve of his throat as he followed the motion of her hand was a sensuous arc. Powerful muscles and tendons stretched into high relief with the esthetic beauty of an anatomical drawing. He shook his tousled hair from the grip of her trembling fingers, and she let the golden strands slip away. Then, he merely returned his lips to hers.

His kiss sucked her strength away. In any case, there was no denying the power of his body, while Janet's reserves were nearly exhausted. Her struggles were hopeless. She conserved what little strength she had left by no longer resisting. His hold immediately relaxed, but not so she could pull free. His lips became more insistent, but gentle as they caressed with a pressure that kept her lips parted for the maddening dart of his tongue.

There was the clatter of metal against metal, echoed by the same noise elsewhere in the room. She recognized the sound. So did Christopher. Locker doors were being opened. Men were arriving to change and go down into the mine. They also changed and showered when they came to the surface. Some were there now; more would come. It was almost time for the noon shift.

Christopher broke the kiss, listening.

"I'll scream," she told him. She should scream. She didn't— she hadn't, and that bothered her. Had she thought no one would hear over the noise of the machinery? Hardly, since she clearly heard the opening of lockers. "There may not be anyone working for Van Hoon Minerals who will risk interfering when his boss is involved," she continued, "but I'll guarantee a performance that'll be the talk around here for weeks to come." He released her. She missed his strong encircling arms. She missed the burning heat of his kisses. "If you'll excuse me, then," she said. Her studied calm belied the rapid thumping of her heart. "I'll see about getting other transportation to my hotel. I've seen more than enough of this place and you, thank you."

She expected him to protest, but there was only the answering clatter of more opening lockers. Someone laughed. She had laughed at Christopher's joke about a black cat, an Englishman in a bowler hat, and an American tourist in Cairo. That seemed years ago. A few seconds of laughter was all she had salvaged from the whole morning.

There was a phone in the office. No one was surprised to see her. No one questioned her right to be there. Word had already filtered down of Christopher's bringing her through the gates. They only wondered why he was letting her get away so quickly. A basket of food was down in the VIP room. Champagne was chilling.

"Something came up, and Mr. Van Hoon has decided to stay on," she told the man who pointed out the phone. She needn't have lied to protect Christopher's good name. It was ironic how she came to blacken the Van Hoon reputation and ended up protecting it.

"Your boss attacked me!" That's what she should say. She felt guilty for having been on the verge of premature surrender, lulled into submission by the warmth of Christopher's muscled arms and the sensuous movements of his hips against her.

There had never been that ecstasy of danger and desire with Bob. Bob had held her, had kissed her. His love for her was never as intense as it was for his job, but Christopher didn't love her at all. She responded to Christopher's lust in a way no decent woman should. His power over her was as complete as he suspected. To let him know that, though, was to put a dangerous weapon in his hands. Janet wasn't about to arm the enemy. Thank God, she had seen the last of him. Tomorrow she would leave this country, these memories, this place—him. She shouldn't have come.

The area outside, once deserted, was now filled with people arriving for the shift change. Christopher knew they were coming. He knew the work schedule. He knew the only thing possible, in the short time available to him and Janet in that locker room was a few stolen kisses. A man didn't make love to a woman with a crowd of witnesses due on the scene. Not even Christopher Van Hoon dared that. He had once again subjected her to a sense of danger when there was no danger.

Except there was danger! Janet knew it whether Christopher did or not. She had unwittingly flowed with that erotic moment. Thank God there had been no more time! Had there been, she would have regretted it later. She wasn't the kind of woman capable of deriving any long-lasting satisfaction from sex with a man who didn't love her.

She had demanded love from Bob and got it—at least as much as he was capable of giving. She had given him love in return. Their kind of love had nothing to do with the perversion of Christopher's well-choreographed kisses.

She was intelligent, practical, and rational. She enjoyed her control of her life. She didn't appreciate the chinks Christopher exposed in her armor. It had been a long and tough struggle to reach her present independence. She wasn't turning over one small segment of hard-won victory to a man who saw her as one plaything in a long procession of playthings. For too many years she had been dependent on men who pulled out and left her at confusing loose ends. First her father, then Bob. She was no longer leaning on any man. She refused to lean on one as mercurial as Christopher.

And if her nights were painfully lonely, filled only with ethereal fantasy, that was the price she paid. Her dream lover didn't use and abuse her, tossing her aside when he was done. He was a figment of imagination, but he was a more substantial friend, confidant, and lover than his flesh-and-blood counterpart could ever be.

The taxi arrived. By then Christopher's car was gone, Christopher with it. She was far better off with him out of her life. He didn't deserve the few hours she had given him. She had solved no problems by coming—she had made new ones.

Christopher was a product of his environment. She no longer blamed him for what he was. She couldn't expect more from a man raised in the shadow of a father who set so bad an example. Still, it pained her to see what the boy had become. He had once had such potential for becoming a truly caring human being. It saddened her to think she had somehow failed him.

And Janet Kelley Westover wished Christopher Van Hoon was created in her image of how she thought he should be!

She was daydreaming again. Daydreams were healthy only when kept in perspective. The chances were good that Christopher would have turned out no differently had Janet never left Lionspride. There were constants in every family, passed from father to son. Vincent Van Hoon inherited his greed for profit from his father. Such motivation controlled the Van Hoons. Christopher was too successful for it not to be part of him, too. Company profits soared under his expert guidance, the result of profits from gold and other South African minerals.

South Africa's control of the free world's chromium and platinum was almost total. Bob had told her that. Bob had told her about man's insatiable search for power, and he had died covering such struggle. As long as Christopher controlled vital natural resources, he held the trump cards. It was ludicrous for Janet to try winning a hand. Money wouldn't cease pouring into Van Hoon coffers just because the hostess of *Animal Kingdoms in the Wild* got up on her soapbox and bemoaned the extinction of the quagga and the bluebuck, the threatened extinction of the elephant.

The Van Hoons weren't totally to blame, she admitted. She was mistaken if she tried making them the sole culprits. Oh, Vincent Van Hoon contributed to her father's early death. That provided sufficient fodder to feed her bitterness. But her father's death and what led up to it were part of a far bigger picture in which countless Vincents, countless Van Hoon Afrikaner Minerals played a role.

She and Christopher never had a chance.

The cab stopped at her hotel. She paid the driver, and the doorman opened the taxi door. Her legs hardly supported her weight. She hoped a hot bath would help, and maybe some food. She hadn't eaten all day.

Christopher had offered pâté de fois gras, chicken in aspic, asparagus, caviar, champagne. He wanted her body in return. She wasn't that desperately hungry!

She went through the revolving door and headed across the lobby to the elevators. There was no need to detour at the front desk. Her room key was in her purse.

He had chosen a chair purposely situated behind a pillar, clandestinely waiting to intercept her. "Are you going to walk by without at least saying hello?" he asked. The familiar sound of his voice stopped her, but she quickly started walking again. "Janet! Please wait!" He was up and after her.

Whatever his invisible hold on her, it was unholy—a connecting web of memories, past and present, good and bad. Did he know that? How could he? Maybe he sensed it as a hunter senses a weakness in its prey. "I'm tired," she said, but she stopped anyway. She faced him, prepared for his look of repentance. He was a consummate actor. He should be on the stage. He was wasting his talents on her—or was he?

"Sit down for a moment... please," he said. He dropped to a small couch, patting the empty space beside him.

"'Will you walk into my parlor?' said the spider to the fly," she quoted. She took a chair across from him. It was either sit or fall. She was emotionally drained. He knew that; he was used to taking advantage. "We have nothing to say," she said wearily.

"We said it all. We said more than enough."

"I'm afraid you've been left with less than a good impression of me," he said. What unmitigated nerve it took for him to be there at all!

"That, I'm afraid, is a gross understatement," she said, gazing over his head. Looking directly at him was painful. His eyes were too seductive. He was too disarming. Only minutes before he had been stealing kisses.

"I won't blame myself," he said. Naturally. What Van Hoon would? It was always someone else's fault. If he thought he was dropping all the blame at her feet, he was overestimating his powers of persuasion. She was partially responsible—for reasons he would never know. But she refused to let him squeeze out blameless. "The culprit was time," he argued, naming his scapegoat.

How right he was! Time was the culprit. Sixteen years of time, although Christopher hardly knew that. Unless...

She examined his face for some sign that he knew her real identity.

"You gave me only two days," he said. She missed his meaning. She was too caught up in her own thoughts. But her confusion was short-lived. He was mentioning mere days, not years.

"What *are* you babbling about?" she asked angrily. "Gave you only two days for what?"

"I was desperate and running out of time," he said, so appealing in his role of penitent. "Offering you money was a spur-of-the-moment mistake, a last-ditch effort to save a sinking ship. It was unforgivable, I know."

"I don't accept your apology!" she said, standing up. The sooner he was out of her sight the better. She reasoned more clearly when he wasn't around. He confused her too easily. "Some things are not forgiven at the mumbling of a few 'I'm sorry,'" she insisted. "And if that sounds unsportsmanlike to you, then I'm sorry."

"Come on, Janet. You can see I like you," he said.

He was a chameleon; potential seducer, diamond merchant, gold baron, boy, man....

"'Like' has never been enough in my book for what you're suggesting," she said. He could have said he loved her, a lie or not. She was glad he had been honest enough not to. It was a cheap shot to mouth dishonest sentiments to a vulnerable woman.

"I don't believe in love at first sight," he said, standing up. His nearness disturbed her, as always. "I don't believe in love in two days, either."

What about love born of one summer, sixteen years before? Did he believe in that, or would he think her a foolish woman, indulging in memories of childhood puppy love? She didn't ask. She wouldn't be mocked. "I doubt you believe in love—period!" she accused. "Or, maybe you can love gold, or diamonds, or chromium, or platinum, or a piece of land like Lionspride. But love a person? That's far beyond you. My life is too short to waste time on an emotional cripple. I have more important things to do—like catch a plane in the morning. And I'm not packed."

"I do believe in immediate physical attraction," he said, and she walked away. His hand roughly clamped her arm to stop her. She was furious at his inability to accept that not all women were captivated by the Van Hoon charm—furious because she was one who was, in spite of herself.

"We aren't at Lionspride now," she said coldly. She wasn't cold inside. She was boiling with the mysterious heat always flamed by his touch. "Nor are we at one of the Van Hoon mines. There will be someone in this lobby who doesn't know the Van Hoon influence or doesn't give a damn. So if you'll turn me loose, it will save us both a good deal of unwanted embarrassment." She gave her arm a tug, surprised and disappointed when he released it. They were attracting attention.

"Give me one more chance," he said. She was tempted. She'd been tempted before, and look what that got her. "We'll have supper," he said. "Here at the hotel—anywhere you want.

There'll be people around, so you won't have to worry."

"You must learn when it's time to give up," said, speaking her words to herself as well as to him. She had to think of herself—no one else was. There was nothing but heartache in seeing Christopher one more time. She wasn't careless enough to risk it.

"I won't accept that!" he said. She marveled at his monumental conceit.

"Even the Van Hoons can't win all the time," she said with little satisfaction. She was possibly cutting off her nose to spite her face. She wanted supper with him. She wanted to give him another chance. However, some people never changed, whatever the high hopes for them. Christopher was one of those people. He would benefit from learning there were no rewards for violating basic rules of civilized behavior. The feelings of others merited as much consideration as did his own. "I'm sorry," she said, meaning it. "Really, I am."

"I'll be here at eight o'clock," he said, refusing to give way, eating his portion of humble pie. And Janet, acting so superior, knew she wasn't guiltless. She had responded to him, however belatedly. "I'll wait for you until nine," he added. He smiled... so guileless when he smiled. It was hard to remember he was the enemy, a dangerous enemy. How close she had come to surrendering to the persuasiveness of his seduction. "An hour is forty-five minutes more than I gave you last time."

She didn't crack a smile, proud of her self-control as she gathered her defenses around her. "Save yourself the wait, Mr. Van Hoon," she said, "by not bothering to show up at all."

She didn't remember her walk to the elevator. It was a few moments stolen from time. The ride up to her room was vague. She looked into mirrors of the elevator and hallway and couldn't place the face staring back at her.

In her room, there were golden roses, rescued from the bathroom sink by the maid and arranged in a crystal vase. The vase sat in the center of the vanity table. Janet saw the flowers, smelled their fragrance, saw her reflection in another mirror and thought of Christopher. She looked tired. The man who had given her those flowers was fresh and alive. A skillful hunter, he thrived on the chase, whereas Janet felt run to ground by their encounter.

A bath didn't help; the water was too hot. She stayed in too long, hardly pulling herself out of the tub finally. Her resolve twirled down the drain with the water.

She was a fool not to give Christopher another chance. She had come all this way and then had failed to go the final mile. There was a barrier of sixteen years between them, but she wasn't taking every advantage to break through. She wasn't as strong as she had thought. But then, Christopher was more dangerous than she'd imagined. She faced losing what little she had salvaged from her childhood. There were no guarantees of reward for further sacrifice—quite the contrary.

The meal she ordered from room service helped, even though the chicken sandwich was dry enough to choke her. Washing it down with a glass of milk, she glanced at the clock—again. She was counting the hours, the minutes, and the seconds until eight o'clock: five hours, ten minutes, forty-five, four, three... seconds. She was an unwilling subject pulled from an audience and given a post-hypnotic suggestion: *at eight o'clock, you will be dressed for supper and will go downstairs, where you will enthusiastically greet Christopher....*

She was not going downstairs to meet him. She was not subjecting herself to the temptations of uncaring lust. It was difficult, since her childhood love for him wasn't dead, not yet. It made her believe in the miracle of his loving her again—if he had ever loved her.

"Do you really love me?" That's what she had asked him sixteen years before in the grove of blue-gum trees.

"I love you, and someday I'll marry you," he had replied with the simple determination of youth. Her lips had burned from his kiss. Oh, the sheer beauty and wonder of that moment! The glory of the sun, piercing high branches to reach them among the cool shadows! It had been like worshipping in a cathedral, wherein sunlight was made more golden by its passage through stained-glass windows. Christopher's golden hair had shifted in the caressing breeze. She had been jealous of the liberties so freely taken by that wind. Christopher was hers alone. She had loved him as only a romantic girl could. She had taken his answer as a promise. Sixteen years later, she still savored the illusion that that promise might be fulfilled.

She got dressed, picked up the tape spools and walked down the hall to the room Tim and Roger shared. Roger came to the door. He was direct from sunning on his balcony. His skimpy bathing suit was orange, visible through the open front of a short robe. His chest was visible, too. It was hairy. Christopher's chest wasn't. At least, it hadn't been when he was eighteen. What Janet had seen since, glimpses of tanned smoothness beyond Christopher's unfastened shirt buttons, gave no indication of change.

"Would you check these out, Roger?" she asked, extending the spools to him. Another woman would have been affected by Roger's remarkable physique. He had been a gymnast in college, not too long ago. His muscle tone was excellent, his chest and stomach well-defined. Janet hadn't seen Christopher in a swimsuit since their interlude at the pools above Lisbon Falls, but already she knew Roger didn't stand a chance in comparison. "I want to be sure the tapes weren't damaged on their run through Mr. Van Hoon's equipment," she said.

"Jill told us the clever bastard pulled a fast one," Roger said, stepping back to let her in.

"Let's just hope something can be salvaged," she said, not speaking only of the tapes. She nodded when Roger pantomimed the offer of a drink. He knew her preference, and mixed a rum and Coke. He and Tim had brought a good supply of liquor with them. The Coke and ice were compliments of room service. "There's the possibility he didn't erase anything," she said. The outside of her glass quickly beaded with condensed moisture. The sliding doors to the balcony were open. The temperature was in the eighties.

"You think so?" Roger asked, fixing himself a drink, clearly dubious.

"He doesn't believe we're much of a threat," Janet said, and laughed with little amusement. "I daresay, he's probably right." She took a large swallow of her drink, suddenly sorry she had asked for it. Visions of turning into a helpless alcoholic in frustrated old age flashed before her. But she was stronger than that. One drink didn't make her a boozer.

"I thought you two hit it off rather well," Roger said, eyeing her over the rim of his glass. He, Tim, and Jill had probably spent the morning comparing notes. Men were as gossipy as women; Janet had never believed otherwise. "We tried to call you earlier," he continued. It sounded like a subtle shift in conversation, but it wasn't. "You were already up and out. Making the most of your last day, were you?"

"Mr. Van Hoon—" she almost said "Christopher," but she caught herself in time. It was best to keep things formal "—was gracious enough to show me around one of his gold mines."

"One of them?" Roger asked, impressed. Even now, he didn't realize how much money and power were tied up in one man. He thought in terms of Rockefeller, Mellon, Getty. He would recognize the name Rothschild, but others were less easily placed in his mental financial hierarchy. Even avid readers of gossip columns, bombarded by Christopher's name, his picture and accounts of his social exploits, couldn't fully comprehend the much-used adjective "wealthy" as it applied to Christopher Van Hoon

"He has several mines," she said, taking another swallow of her drink. She walked to the open doors of the balcony, looking out over the city in which Christopher merely lived—sometimes. When you were as wealthy as he was, you bore no allegiance to any place or any person. His loyalty was to money, power and ways of increasing both. Cities were stopover spots. Women were decorations and momentary diversions. "Several gold mines, several diamond mines, several chromium mines, ad infinitum," she added bitterly.

"He would make a fine catch for some clever woman," Roger said, prying for a confidence.

"You like women, don't you, Roger?" Janet asked, putting her glass down. The glass wasn't empty, but she was through with it. She needed her wits, and alcohol wasn't going to help matters. "I mean, you *really* like them, yes?"

"Sure," he said suspiciously.

"Then don't do any woman the disservice of wishing a man like Christopher Van Hoon on her, will you?" she said. She smiled, wanting him to know she forgave him. It wasn't his fault he equated money with happiness. Many people did, but it was a mistake.

No insurance company would touch Bob, the odds accurately projecting him dead by thirty. But he had been frugal. There were few luxuries in the jungles, deserts and war-torn cities where he went with his beloved camera. He didn't drink. He didn't smoke. His job was his only vice and his chief pleasure. He had left Janet very well fixed... financially.

She went to her room. It smelled more of roses than when she'd left it. She sat on the edge of the bed and looked at the clock. Three-thirty. In four and a half hours Christopher would be in the lobby. Janet was determined not to be there with him.

* * * * * * * *

BY SEVEN, she was packed. Her lone cocktail dress had been the first thing in her suitcase. She had arranged it to maximize wrinkles. It was impossible to get to it now without disturbing everything. She was protecting herself, raising small obstacles to prevent any change of mind.

A few things remained unpacked: her toiletries for morning and the skirt, blouse and shoes she was planning to wear the next day. Someone who "dressed" for supper at home, like Christopher, would consider any of her presently readily available apparel as unsuitable for dining out.

Her black silk negligee was still unpacked, too, substituting for the pajamas still reeking of perfume. She should have sent them to the laundry. The scent, like the fragrance of the golden roses, conjured up unwanted memories and emotions. She was tempted to set the roses in the hallway. She couldn't do that, though; they were too beautiful. Besides, it was a long time since she had last received flowers from any man.

Three years ago, John Pettering, an old friend of her father, had sent flowers to celebrate the high ratings following the debut of *Animal Kingdoms in the Wild*. It had been John who had initially suggested that Kenneth Bainbridge talk to Janet about hosting the show. Kenneth, a Seattle producer, was looking for a program to syndicate in the family-hour time slot. He approached John with the idea of the animal format. Many people seemed to find the intricacies of nature quite fascinating, and John was a logical choice to head the project. He was director of the Seattle Zoo, a position Janet's father once held. John had trained under Jack Kelley in the old days.

John, though, was aware of his limitations as well as his strengths. He was confident and knowledgeable in his field, yes. Those qualifications held him in good stead in his chosen profession, but they wouldn't charm middle-America on a weekly basis. He didn't see himself as a television personality, and no amount of support from the most charming of four-legged critters was going to help him, either.

John suggested Janet for the job. She was at loose ends since Bob had died. She had literally cut her teeth at the Seattle Zoo, had spent some time in Africa, and her husband's profession as a cameraman had given her more than a nodding acquaintance with the media. Besides which, she was strikingly beautiful— an interesting counterpoint to the cuddly domestic animals, and a complement to the more exotic types. If she wasn't outgoing at the time, it was because she was unhappy.

Based more on John's recommendation than on Janet's resulting interview, Kenneth had given her a chance. If Janet was unsure at first whether it was the right step for her, she was soon glad she had made the commitment. It gave her something to do. The show required location shooting. Africa was a possibility. Christopher and childhood memories were in Africa.

A big mistake: the detour to Lionspride. She should have gone immediately to Great Zimbabwe. Her future was with four-legged animals, not with the two-legged kind Christopher had become.

She slipped off her robe. The clothes she had worn that day were in the suitcase. Her negligee was soft against her fingers. Christopher's hair was soft. She had buried her hands in the glistening strands while fighting him off in the locker room at the mine.

Christopher was out of her life. She was thinking about him too much.

The sensuous slide of the material over her naked body wasn't appreciated. It recalled to her the black dress at Lionspride, the one Christopher chose for her to wear at that painful charade.

She went to the vanity table to brush her hair. The smell of the roses was especially strong. She moved the flowers to get better access to the mirror.

The roses were lovely, a unique shade of antique gold. She touched one, tracing the intricate layering of petal over petal... so soft. Christopher's body was hard to the touch, golden with tan.

She refused to look at the clock behind her by the bed. She consciously avoided focusing on the clock hands reversed in the mirror. It made no difference what time it was. She was going to bed. There was an early plane to catch in the morning. She needed her rest, and a supper with Christopher would be anything but restful. She was only now recovering from the strain of being with him that morning.

She put her brush to one side and stood up. Her negligee molded her body with sensuous flowing drapery. The black emphasized the ebony of her hair and her deepening tan. Her adventure at Lionspride had left her pleasantly brown, as Christopher had predicted.

Janet had bought the negligee during one of Bob's lengthy

absences, to reaffirm her femininity. It was a magic talisman to keep her husband around longer next time. Bob, though, hadn't cared what she wore to bed, hadn't mentioned it when he finally saw her in it. He'd said he was going to Central America on assignment. So much for magic!

She didn't wear it for a long time after his death. Black might have been the traditional color of mourning, but silk somehow seemed inappropriate for widow's weeds. The feel of it against her skin wasn't conducive to grieving.

Men who imagined silk lingerie as a tool primarily to aid in their seduction were dead wrong, she mused. That was a lucky by-product, although a pleasant one. In truth, the feel of silk against a woman's body was a pleasurable aside from the reaction of any appreciative male. Wearing it made Janet feel more a woman.

In sleep, she found the silk a stimulus to make her dreams more vivid... dreams of happier days with Christopher.

She was tempted to strip off the offending nightdress and put it in the suitcase. She would sleep without it or pajamas, as she had the night before. But nakedness, for someone who grew to maturity wearing a nightie to bed, was disturbingly sensuous in its own right. She couldn't win either way.

It was seven-thirty.

Her suitcase was across the room on a luggage rack. It was locked, secured with an additional belt that was buckled. The key to the suitcase was on the dresser, easily reached. There was time to unpack her cocktail dress. There was time to steam out any wrinkles in moist heat from the bathroom shower. She could dress within minutes, despite the stumbling blocks she had cleverly laid in her way.

She went to the phone and dialed. She opened the room service menu. Supper in her room was one incentive to stay put. Appetizer: *Hoenderersmeer.* Soup: *Hoender en noedelroomsop.* Entrée: *Kopenhaagse schnitzel.* Did she want dessert? Yes: *Verskeie soorte roomys.* A drink? "Milk. No, wait!" she insisted. She scanned an accompanying wine list. *"Oude Libertas Dry*

Steen," she said, having picked a bottle at random. That was her meal. She didn't have the vaguest notion what it was. She went back over the menu, looking for an English translation. She was having tasty chicken livers, blended with brandy and cream into a smooth light pâté; cream of chicken and noodle soup; veal steak garnished with smoked salmon, Danish caviar and anchovies—she hated anchovies. As well as assorted ice creams; and a full-bodied, dry white wine with a fragrant bouquet.

Red wine went with red meat, white wine with white fish. Veal vaguely seemed an exception. Christopher would know. She laughed nervously. This was ridiculous! She wasn't even hungry.

What would the room steward think when she greeted him in a slinky negligee, like some character from a sleazy, X-rated movie? She put on her terry-cloth robe. She wasn't dressing for the short time it took someone to wheel in a serving cart. Waiters saw hotel guests in one state of undress or another during every workday. With her robe pulled tightly around her, Janet was the only one who knew what was underneath. Besides, dressing now, for the waiter, would make it too easy for her to be dressed for Christopher who waited for her downstairs.

When the knock came, long minutes later, it startled her. Reflexively, she checked the time. It was after eight. Christopher was taking matters into his own hands. Nonsense! It was the waiter. Christopher wouldn't show. The victory wasn't worth the effort of the chase.

She opened the door. The waiter smiled, said good evening and rolled in the cart. He didn't give her a second look. Real life wasn't the movies. She tipped him from the small pile of change on the dresser. He left.

The meal was enough to feed two people. Christopher would take one look and think she had arranged for them to have a quiet supper in her room. She would point out there was only one place setting. Better yet, she wouldn't let him in far enough to see the cart.

She was playing mind games. He wasn't in the lobby, or in

the elevator, or walking down the hall. He had crossed her off as a lost cause. He thought her a tease. He couldn't know it, but whatever she had done had been done to renew an old and precious acquaintance, not start a new relationship based on less than mutual respect.

She lifted a cover from one of the chafing dishes, revealing the beautifully prepared veal dish. She tried to recall the Afrikaner name from the menu, was distracted by a sound at the door.

Someone was there. She didn't need to see to know. The presence announced itself clearly in her stomach. Her heart beat faster. She glanced at the clock and then at her reflection in the mirror. She looked excited. She was.

A light knock. Deceptive. Christopher was the type to batter down the door. Another knock—harder. The waiter was back, delivering something he'd forgotten the first time. He knew she was in the room. She wasn't dressed to go out. She couldn't have finished eating already.

"Janet, are you in there?" It wasn't the waiter. It wasn't Christopher.

"Tim, I'm sorry. Do come in," she said, opening door. "Have you been there long?" She sounded guilty. She felt silly. "I was occupied in the other room." She let him in. She was as safe with him as she was with Roger. She preferred a sense of danger.

"Looks like there's little point in asking you to join your crew for supper," Tim said, eyeing the overflowing service cart. "Smells good, though. Maybe we should join you." He lifted a lid to reveal a drooping mountain of multicolored ice cream.

Tim was the youngest member of the film crew. He looked young, too; the type who would look twenty when he was forty. He was blond. Christopher was blond. His eyes were blue. Christopher's eyes were golden. He was a boy. Christopher was a man.

"I decided to pamper myself on my last night in Johannesburg," Janet said, listening for the sound of footsteps in the hall. She heard the elevator opening. No, she was mistaken. "I didn't feel like dressing up to go out."

"We'll miss your company," he said. He was charming. He had been charming from the start, and he could have turned out to be such an obnoxious person. He was the producer's nephew, after all, joining the show after he'd dropped out of his senior year at high school and had given his parents apoplexy. School was "a drag," to hear Tim tell it. He'd never given Janet any cause to bemoan his uncle's nepotism.

"You'll see more than enough of me before this trip is over," she joked. Christopher had said he would wait until nine. It wasn't nine yet. He wouldn't come up until he was sure she wasn't coming down.

"Maybe so," Tim said, giving her a smile. His cheeks dimpled. He looked nothing like Christopher although some of the same basic ingredients were there: "Probably not, though," he added gallantly, his smile growing wider. "Anyway, I'll leave you to resume your gourmet glut and beauty rest. Roger said to tell you the tapes turned out A-OK—nothing erased. He ran them this afternoon. Do you want them shipped this evening, or is tomorrow at the airport, on our way out, soon enough?"

"Tomorrow is fine," she said. There was no hurry. Christopher didn't want them. They didn't threaten him, his precious family name or his corporate profits. Such a confident egotistical bastard "And speaking of tomorrow, I'll expect to see three of you bright-eyed and bushy tailed," she said.

He left her with her meal. She picked at the veal, methodically shifting the decorative anchovies from one side of her plate to the other and then back again. The meat grew cold. The ice cream grew warm, melting into an attractive rainbow of chocolate, vanilla and strawberry.

It was after nine. Christopher wasn't knocking on her door. He wouldn't, either. She had been crazy to think he would. Look how many times she had shot him down. He was tired of trying, bored. Janet wasn't such a good catch that he would go out of his way any more than he already had.

She lay on the bed. The silk of her negligee settled provocatively around her. She shut her eyes. Had she played her cards right, she wouldn't be alone. Had she not insisted on love, Christopher would be here—except her need for Christopher was so tied up with feelings of love that she was cheating herself even to consider settling for less. Lust wasn't the stuff of which romantic dreams were made.

She was on the verge of tears. She had cried when she'd left Lionspride and Christopher the first time. She had come full circle.

She had cried when her father died. She hadn't cried when Bob died. She'd expected Bob's death and was prepared for it. She should have been prepared for this. She wasn't, because dreams died hard.

And that was why she was crying.

CHAPTER FIVE

"JANET?" SHE THOUGHT IT WAS CHRISTOPHER, because she was thinking of him. A mistake. He wasn't there in Salisbury with her. He was a plane ride and a country away. "I'm Craig," the man in the office doorway introduced himself, noticing her confusion. "Craig Sylo."

"Oh, of course, Craig," Janet said, standing. "Dr. Cunningham mentioned you were in the city."

He wasn't Christopher. Not in voice—more gravelly. Not in appearance—as opposite to a blond as most white men would likely ever get. He was handsome in his own right, though, rugged and dark complexioned, lacking Christopher's outward polish.

His hair was coal black, and his eyes were large and velvety black, like those of a deer. His eyelashes were sooty, his eyebrows thick, dark and lush. Good bone structure enhanced his square face. His powerful neck flowed into a vee of hairy chest visible at the open collar of his shirt, which was short sleeved and well-tailored, displaying his impressive arms and muscled torso to good advantage. He had narrow hips and a flat stomach. Beneath his shorts, his legs were solid, brown from many hours in the sun.

His short haircut was decidedly military, which was appropriate. Craig Sylo was the captain in charge of the military contingent assigned to the Great Zimbabwe Wildlife Reserve. His job was protecting—trying to protect was more accurate—the elephants scheduled for relocation to Wankie. Land reform had diminished the size of the Great Zimbabwe Reserve to the point where it could no longer support either elephants or big cats.

Craig took her hand politely. There was no electricity—not like when Christopher touched her. Of course, she hadn't expected any. Her chemistry with Christopher was unique, the result of misunderstanding, disappointment, and frustrated love.

"I'm told there's a transportation problem," Craig said. He held her hand longer than necessary, but she didn't mind. Here was a man to take her mind off Christopher. He was on her side, unlike Christopher, who was the enemy.

"A short delay," she said. "Our flight has been canceled because of engine trouble. Things are supposed to be straightened out by tomorrow."

"I'm here to offer on-the-spot aid," Craig said. "I'm heading back to the reserve this afternoon. My plane is small and pretty cramped with supplies, but I can squeeze in one passenger. Are you interested?"

"Am I?" she asked. Interested was an understatement. She couldn't believe her good luck.

"I'd take your whole crew if there was room. As it is, they'll find tomorrow's commercial flight more comfortable."

"I'd love to go in today," Janet said and shuffled data sheets on the table into an unruly stack. She knew the facts and figures on them too well. Going over them wasn't holding her interest. She had spent the morning mentally rehashing her catastrophic confrontations with Christopher. Getting her mind off him in this way would be a welcome relief.

"We're in no big hurry," Craig said, smiling at her eagerness. He checked his wristwatch. "How about we meet up, again, here, in an hour? After which, I'll take you to your hotel to pick up your things, and even buy you lunch before take-off."

"It's an offer I can't refuse," she said and meant.

"It's settled, then," he said, giving her a smart salute. "An hour it is."

The time didn't pass fast enough. As soon as Craig left the

room, Janet lapsed into thoughts of Christopher. How badly things had turned out between them. The tragedy had plagued her since she'd left Johannesburg. She needed immediate and deep involvement in the project at Great Zimbabwe, work that would snap her out of her depression. The cancellation of their scheduled flight that morning seemed like a horrible conspiracy. Craig Sylo's arrival and rescue were heaven-sent.

She dutifully re-filed the data sheets and said good-bye to Dr. Cunningham who, as an advisor to the Department of National Parks and Wildlife Management, had had a good deal to do with her invitation to come to the Great Zimbabwe Reserve. She had enjoyed the week she had just spent working with him here in Salisbury, and assumed that he had enjoyed it, too, though the elderly professor seemed happy to see Janet going off with the handsome Craig Sylo. No doubt he thought they made a suitable couple.

It was an hour later, to the minute, when Craig reappeared. "Ready?" he asked.

"More than ready," Janet agreed.

"You're checked in at the Monomatapa, right?" Craig said, stepping to one side as she entered the hallway ahead of him. His body was hard muscle; she brushed it as she passed. Still no electricity. She wished there was.

"Right," she affirmed. Monomatapa was also the name of a line of African kings to whom early explorers and adventurers paid tribute. In return, the foreigners had been awarded (awarded themselves) the right to export the country's gold. An estimated twenty-five million ounces of gold had been taken from ancient workings. The Christophers of the world existed even then, Janet thought sadly. They had laid the groundwork for mineral exploitation that had escalated alarmingly.

"I hear you're from a long line of animal lovers," Janet said, settling in the passenger seat of his Jeep, which was, as described by Craig, "Spartan but functional." It was a change from Christopher's plush Rolls and Mercedes sports cars. Janet was better suited to this less opulent life-style.

"Two years after my grandfather arrived from India, he had quite a menagerie—spent what little money he made on his animal collection, too. Some of his caring rubbed off on my father, then on to me. Like father, like son." Like Vincent, like Christopher.

"You don't look Indian," she said. His naturally dark complexion was emphasized by a mahogany tan, but his features were decidedly British.

"India was part of the British Empire in my grandfather's day, remember," he said. "Granddad originally came from a small town outside of Bournemouth, England. The military was his last chance to better the gloomy lot that fell to the youngest of twelve kids—little or sometimes nothing to eat, an old man who was a drunkard, a mother old before her time and on her last legs, suffering from tuberculosis. Not much left at the end of that tunnel. The military gave him a sense of adventure, so when he got his discharge, he came out here to make his fortune."

"Did he," Janet asked, figuring she knew the answer, "make his fortune?"

"He died poor but well respected," Craig said. He wasn't mercenary enough to make it big."

She couldn't help comparing the Sylos with the Van Hoons. Petre Van Hoon, too, had arrived in Africa with little to his name, but he had quickly learned the tricks of exploiting people and land for substantial profit. Craig's grandfather, more caring, naturally reaped less material reward. That, unfortunately, was the way the deck was stacked. It didn't make the Sylos any less men than the Van Hoons. Quite the opposite.

Craig Sylo's grandfather had been one of the men who was all for the founding of the Great Zimbabwe Reserve. Set up as a wildlife sanctuary of nineteen thousand square kilometers in 1900, the reserve didn't fare as well as the Sabi Reserve, established in South Africa two years earlier. When Sabi and the Shingwedzi Reserves merged to form Kruger in 1926, the Great Zimbabwe Reserve had already lost a third of its area to land reform. Further shrinkage occurred in 1932 and 1944. In 1951, there began a twenty-five year program to convert a substantial segment of the remaining Great Zimbabwe Reserve acreage to productive farm and ranch land. By 1976, the wilderness area that remained was deemed inadequate to support elephants or big cats. The cats were relocated first, since their smaller size made them more manageable.

The country's eruption into bloody revolution stopped the transfer of elephants before it started. As a result, the elephant population at Great Zimbabwe had, for years, been trapped in an area admittedly too small to sustain it. The wandering pachyderms were continually rebelling against their confinement, raising havoc with whatever man-made barriers were raised in an attempt to keep them from remembered trails and food sources. Farm crops were trampled and domestic livestock scattered through toppled fences.

Enticed by a sudden trickle of Great Zimbabwe ivory, channeled into the black market by disgruntled farmers and ranchers taking the matter of ruined crops and dispersed livestock into their own hands, poachers arrived en masse. Experts at exterminating wildlife for profit, they were quietly accepted by landowners as a means to an end. Speculators welcomed the prospect of swelling their existing ivory stockpiles. The Department of National Parks and Wildlife Management had its hands full.

Christopher, with his ivory cache, would be the first to point out that profit motivation was the government's reason for finally rushing to the aid of the Great Zimbabwe's long-neglected elephants. After years of scant attention to the acute poaching problem, some bureaucrat in finance had the sense to realize that tourists, with their needed tourist dollars, came to Africa to see animals. They didn't come to see fields of corn or herds of docile cattle. They had those at home.

Even then, the government response wouldn't have been as swift if the problem at the Great Zimbabwe Reserve had been an isolated one. After all, the cost of getting two hundred elephants relocated hundreds of kilometers away was a major expense in itself. The problem at Great Zimbabwe, however, was only the tip of the iceberg.

Game reserves like Wankie, which pulled in the bulk of the country's tourist dollars, were losing animals to poachers at a disturbing rate, too. There weren't enough park rangers to prevent it. Concentrating heavily threatened animal groups in one or two of the most visited reserves meant that rangers from depleted parks, like Great Zimbabwe, could be reassigned to those areas needing their services the most.

Janet had never found out what had happened to the animals in the territory her father had marked off for the Lackland Animal Preserve. Dr. Cunningham had scratched his head over that one. Sixteen years was a long time. When the men and equipment moved in to sink the initial shaft for the Van Hoon Deep Levels Mine, the animals moved out—that much was clear.

The doctor did know about Van Hoon Afrikaner Minerals, though. The company had its greedy tentacles everywhere. Zimbabwe's asbestos, copper, iron, coal and chrome deposits made the country fair game. Unlike the large deposits of gold-bearing rock farther south, Zimbabwe's gold sources were depleted. Great Zimbabwe, the ancient city supported by the gold trade, had been abandoned. Its ruins were a national monument located within the reserve.

"So you're here to help in the transfer of elephants to Wankie," Craig said. She nodded her head. His job was protecting those elephants until they were moved, but he was having little success. "I hope the poachers leave you a few to transfer."

Christopher had mentioned the problem of poaching when Janet was at Lionspride, and Dr. Cunningham had verified the information. Craig wasn't in Salisbury just to pick up supplies. He had to explain to his superiors why the job was proving more than he could handle. "We're up against smart cookies this go-round," Craig explained. "They know where I'm sending my patrols before I do. It doesn't help that the locals are so glad to get rid of the elephants that they look the other way whenever one goes down. Poachers are clearing the land faster than we can. The government isn't known for its speed."

Christopher had tusks that came from dead elephants, Janet thought bitterly. He wouldn't miss the chance of adding to his bloody collection. If only he were more caring—about animals, about her.

The top of her hotel appeared over the low-lying city buildings, the high rise a monument to the growing importance of tourist dollars in the country's economy. A few years back, there were no such oases to give the modern traveler all the conveniences of home. Today, thousands of locals might be without plumbing, but Mr. John Q. Public from Chicago got a hot bath, his evening cocktail, plenty of food, and a good cigar.

"Shall I get a table by the pool?" Craig suggested when they pulled up in front of the Monomatapa. They left the Jeep with an attendant who seemed surprisingly little pleased with the prospect of parking it. "It's far too beautiful a day to be cooped up inside, wouldn't you agree?'

"I certainly would," Janet said, checking her watch. She spent a good deal of time checking her watch lately. "Give me fifteen minutes to stuff the rest of my things into a bag." What seemed like century ago, Christopher had given her fifteen minutes to meet him in the lobby of another hotel.

"I'll get the jump on things and order you a drink," he said. "What'll it be?" He belonged in a more rugged setting, whereas Christopher would have blended in perfectly here.

"A glass of white wine, please," Janet said. "The house wine will be fine." It was okay saying that to Craig. Christopher would wrinkle his nose in disapproval. In Christopher's world, the only wine worth drinking was vintage and came from a bottle uncorked at the table.

"White wine it is," Craig promised.

Janet took the elevator to her room. There was little to do when she got there. Expecting to be on a plane that morning, she had left out only the bare necessities the night before. It was reminiscent of the morning she had left Johannesburg, everything packed except her toiletries, robe, and negligee. The negligee continued to remind her of what might have been if she hadn't insisted on love in the bargain. So did her perfume-scented pajamas. At Great Zimbabwe, she would wash her pajamas first thing.

She tried to call Tim and Roger but got no answer. Jill wasn't in her room, either. Janet jotted down a short note on the hotel stationery and left it at the front desk. She needn't have bothered. Tim, Jill and Roger were at the pool.

"Our Great White Leader decided to roost for a while?" Tim asked. Tired of waiting for drinks, he had gone up to the service counter. Roger and Jill were waiting impatiently for him to return with liquid refreshments. They saw Janet and waved. "Want to pull up a chair and join the peons for rest and relaxation?" Tim asked.

"Why is it I find myself refusing you once again?" she said. But the last time she had been expecting Christopher. Now Craig was waiting at one of the nearby tables.

"I don't know," Tim said, grinning from ear to ear. "Why are you refusing? I suspect you're not up to the temptation of my fantastic body." She laughed. She had needed someone as easygoing as Tim when she was very much younger, but fate had chosen Christopher for her, instead.

"Come on," Janet said, heading for the couple by the pool. "I see two very thirsty people waiting none too patiently for their drinks. I might as well explain to all of you at once."

Jill nodded hello, her short-cropped blond hair glistening in the sun. "Hi, stranger!" Roger said. "You decide to quit cramming dull facts and join the fun? It's mighty cold where you and I come from. Enjoy this lovely sunshine while you can."

"No time," Janet said. "I just left you a note at the desk. I'm flying on ahead to Great Zimbabwe this afternoon." She wished she was at the reserve already. She wanted a full routine to keep her mind occupied. "Someone offered me a ride, and I accepted."

"A man?" Jill asked. She had the curiosity of a cat. It went with her green eyes and lissome figure.

"As a matter of fact, it is a man," Janet admitted. She should have known what Jill would make of that.

"Christopher Van Hoon?" Roger and Tim chimed simultaneously, forestalling Jill.

Janet laughed nervously. She was sorry to disappoint them. She was sorry to disappoint herself.

"I don't know what kind of fairy-tale romance you three are concocting for me," Janet said indulgently, "but there's absolutely nothing to it." It pained her to admit it. "Nor has there ever been." That was even more difficult. Saying it, though, helped the truth to sink in. Those wonderful times in childhood were imagined, conjured up from a world that never existed. She was finally exorcising those illusions. "You've had too much free time," she chided her crew. "That will change tomorrow."

Craig saw her and waved to let her know where he was in the crowd. Janet waved back. "Your pilot?" Jill asked. She and Tim were a couple, but still there was a tinge of envy in her tone. First Christopher Van Hoon, now this attractive man who had stumbled in from only God knew where, she was no doubt thinking.

"He's in charge of the military encampment at Great Zimbabwe," Janet said. She was a teenager again, explaining to her aunt why there was no need to worry about some boy. Then, as now, it was impossible to admit no one was interesting after Christopher. "He flew in for supplies and happens to have an extra seat. Dr. Cunningham told him I was anxious to get to Great Zimbabwe."

"Janet, you could fall into a manure pile and come up smelling like a rose, couldn't you?" Roger said.

"I won't bother asking what that enchanting vulgarity is supposed to mean," Janet said, but she knew what it meant, and so did Tim and Jill: she lost out on Christopher, but she immediately latched on to Craig.

"The gentleman is certainly attractive," Jill said, insisting on teaming Janet with the captain. Janet wished she were right.

There was nothing like one man to make a woman forget another. The trouble was that she hadn't met anyone in sixteen years to make her forget Christopher. "Not as attractive as Christopher," Jill added, "but he'll do. Right? Christopher is in Johannesburg, isn't he?"

"You're hopeless romantics!" Janet admonished them. Craig had waited for her long enough, and this conversation was getting ridiculous. "I'll expect you more clearheaded tomorrow. Right? Right!"

"You know we only wish you the best," Roger said.

"I know you do," Janet admitted. She was getting emotional. It was embarrassing, and she blamed Christopher. She had controlled her emotions better before her return to Lionspride. "But let's not have me involved prematurely, okay?" She was pleased there was no tremor in her voice. "I just met the man, didn't I?"

She joined Craig at his table. "Your crew?" he asked.

"You can see how disappointed they are that I'm leaving them to sun by the pool, instead of dragging them to Great Zimbabwe today, can't you?" she said. Her wine was cool and pleasant.

Craig ordered a "Salisburger". It arrived open faced with two large meat patties and all the trimmings. Janet ate a club sandwich. This meal was certainly different from the one at Lionspride! This one was more her style.

He had another beer and persuaded her to have a second glass of wine. Then, since Roger, Tim and Jill were still by the pool, she took Craig to meet them. They were dutifully restrained, except for Roger's mischievous wink as Janet and Craig were leaving. Janet shook her head in mock disgust, but she couldn't help laughing.

"You've thought of a joke you're dying to tell me," Craig said. He hadn't seen Roger's wink.

She needed a joke. There was the one about the black cat, the Englishman in a bowler hat, and an American tourist in Cairo, but she couldn't remember the punch line. She tended to forget the amusing things in her life, retaining the unhappiness. "I'm afraid they think we're a twosome," she said. It was an embarrassing admission, but she couldn't think of anything else to say.

"Maybe they're psychic," Craig suggested. His teeth were a brilliant white when he smiled. "Would that bother you?"

"Not if it doesn't bother you," she said. She didn't know what she thought of Craig as a romantic interest. It was too soon. She did know he made her feel good. With Christopher, she always felt like crying.

"That means you're not already promised to some lucky man in the States?" Craig asked, still smiling.

"Yes, that means I'm not promised," Janet answered.

"Good," he said. She didn't ask him why it was good; she knew. She hadn't discouraged him, either. That was unfair to him. Still, if there was a chance....

They reached the lobby, and Janet signaled the porter who had taken charge of her bag earlier. He brought her suitcase to the waiting Jeep. Craig helped her into the front seat with a touch that was comforting and self-assured. She could feel safe with this man, which was a relief. She never felt safe with Christopher.

The weather was beautiful but muggy. It was colder in her hometown. Seattle was having snow flurries, she'd heard, although the temperature seldom went below freezing.

"Dr. Cunningham said you stopped off in Johannesburg for a while," Craig began. He was making small talk. "I suppose you saw a gold mine and all that." She grimaced from the pain that comment caused her.

"It seemed the thing to do," she managed. "Who knows when I'll get back?" She had left Christopher twice. There wouldn't be a third time.

"There's more to see here," he boasted. "I know Great Zimbabwe is on your list, but you shouldn't miss Victoria Falls."

She had seen Victoria Falls at thirteen with Christopher. She didn't want to see them again. Luckily, there were no such memories of Great Zimbabwe held over from sixteen years before. There were only so many things they had been able to accomplish in that one short summer. "I'll be too busy to play typical tourist," she said, determined to steer the conversation elsewhere.

"We could go tomorrow morning," he suggested, catching her off guard. "You can't do much at the reserve without your film crew. We could see the falls and be back while your people are still settling in."

"Actually, I've seen Victoria Falls," Janet admitted. That was the best excuse for not going. It wasn't her real reason for putting the place out of bounds, but her relationship with Christopher was too private to expose to a stranger. "I was in Africa when I was quite young."

"Oh," Craig said. His evident disappointment made Janet reexamine her reasons for refusing. She was keeping Victoria Falls, and her memories of it isolated like some holy shrine. It was a place of good times, as Lionspride had been. So much of her make-believe world had been spoiled that she was reluctant to destroy more. She was a fool. Whatever memories made Victoria Falls sacred, they were no more substantial than those that had gone up in smoke after renewed contact with Christopher. It was best to wipe the slate clean. She couldn't straighten out her life if she didn't clip all the strings that bound her to childhood love.

"But the falls are worth a second visit," Janet said. "Why don't I think about it? Some things are better the second time around." Most things weren't! Her return to Lionspride proved that.

"Fantastic!" Craig said. He seemed to want to spend more time with her, and his enthusiasm was flattering.

At the airport, they bypassed the major terminal buildings. The small private planes were lined up in neat row along one edge of the tarmac.

Craig's plane was as crammed with supplies as he had said. Strapping herself in the copilot's seat, Jane wondered if they would get off the ground.

"All this stuff isn't as heavy as it looks," Craig encouraged her, guessing her thoughts. "I've had heavier cargo and there was still no problem."

"I wish us luck," she said. Going belly up in an overloaded airplane wasn't the way she envisioned leaving Africa.

"Trust me," he said, patting her knee in friendly reassurance. Had Christopher done it, she would have reacted differently. Christopher wouldn't be offering comfort. His intentions would be less chivalrous.

"So, I trust you," she said. She was committed to the trip.

The radio crackled instructions for takeoff, and the plane moved.

"There, that wasn't bad, was it?" Craig said a few minutes later. They were airborne. Janet was recovering from an imagined close call with the treetops at the end of the runway. She flew in small aircraft all the time, but she never felt as safe as in the larger jets. Unfortunately, few good camera shots of wildlife were available through the window of an aircraft at thirty thousand feet.

"Not too bad," she admitted. Craig was a good pilot, had flown for years apparently. Even if he hadn't, it was a little late to question his credentials.

The plane veered tightly toward the south. The resulting sensation reminded her of one of those twirling rides at an amusement park.

"Great Zimbabwe is that way!" Craig said, pointing straight ahead when the plane leveled. "We have an almost direct line of flight." Janet was glad.

"So how did you end up commanding the troops at the reserve?" she asked. The suburbs of Salisbury were beneath them. "Dr. Cunningham said your father was assigned there, too."

"Father was," Craig affirmed. On the radio they heard of an aircraft landing nearby. Craig watched it descending on their left. "But not now, and never in a military capacity. He spent twelve years on the reserve as assistant game warden. I was born on reserve land that has since become some farmer's corn-field." He sounded less than pleased.

"Are your parents still living, then?" Janet asked. Below her, the signs of civilization weren't disappearing as quickly as they would have done a few years back. The area was now more inhabited and cultivated, a patchwork quilt of farm and grazing land that stretched to the horizon.

"No, and it's just as well," Craig said. "They were extremely fond of the Great Zimbabwe Reserve. They would have been disheartened to see it come to this, even if they were around for the beginning of the land reform that's shrunk it to its present pitiful size. They were killed during the revolution."

She didn't miss the verb "killed," but she didn't press for details. When the new African country of Zimbabwe was arising from the collapse of Rhodesia in 1979, a lot of people, white and black, died—were killed—during the birth of that nation.

"They were returning to the reserve from Fort Victoria," he said without her asking. "It was dark. They were ambushed. I heard the gunfire from the house. It didn't last long."

"My husband was killed by guerrillas in Central America," she said. A bond shared. It was a better reply than stock phrases of sympathy. She knew what it was to lose someone under wartime conditions. It was a grief different from losing a loved one to natural or accidental causes. It was even different from how she had lost her father. What killed Jack Kelley was more subtle than a bullet, although no less lethal. "Bob was a cameraman."

"Killed in a mess he volunteered to cover for some news-paper, I should imagine," Craig said. "My parents were killed in their own backyard."

She had been stupid to reach for comparisons. Bob had engi-neered his own death. He had gone into those jungles with his eyes wide open. Craig's parents were cut down while driving home from a night on the town. It wasn't the same thing. "Yes. I suppose you're right," she conceded. "However, it didn't make his death any less final."

"Of course it didn't!" Craig said apologetically. How did we get on the depressing subject of death anyway? There's no point in dredging up the past." He wouldn't approve of her reasons for returning to Lionspride, then. He wouldn't approve of her years of living with bitterness. It was the present that counted. That's what he was saying. Why should anyone screw up her present by dwelling on things over which she had no control? "A lot of water has flowed under the bridge since that bloody hell left blacks and whites its victims," he said. "We're all sleeping more soundly now."

Not as soundly as they might. There were those who said Zimbabwe wasn't entering the twentieth-first century rapidly enough. There were whites and blacks who argued constantly that the other had too much power. Interparty politics still resulted in murders on night-darkened streets. It was all very complicated, and Janet didn't pretend to understand it. Her job in Africa was to save animals. As difficult as that was, it was invariably less complicated than saving people.

"So you're familiar with the Great Zimbabwe Reserve," Janet said. The plane dipped slightly and returned to a steady flight line. Her stomach adjusted less quickly. "And that's why you were assigned there to settle the poaching problem?"

"Right. And for reasons already discussed, my knowledge of the area hasn't been of much use," Craig said. The only animals below them were domestic. Wildlife didn't stick around when cattle, dogs and people moved in. They migrated with the same swiftness they had exhibited in fleeing from the Van Hoon Afrikaner Minerals site sixteen year before. They ran until there was no place to go. Then someone either came to their rescue, or they died. Such was the predicament of the elephants in what remained of the Great Zimbabwe Reserve.

Craig cared what happened to the elephants. Christopher would lift a hand only when the elephants were dead, their cold-blooded killers peddling the ill-gotten ivory. Then his hand would be lifted to pass out the cash and pull in more tusks for his macabre collection. How could she love such a man? She didn't! She loved the boy the man once was.

"You have no idea who's leaking information?" she asked. It was an unnecessary question. His look told her that he didn't know. If he did, the leak would be plugged. Right? He would have accolades instead of criticisms of incompetence. "I'm sorry," she apologized. "That was silly."

"At least you recognize it as such," Craig said grudgingly. "My superiors haven't your insight. Next they'll accuse me of consorting with the enemy."

"I do doubt that," Janet consoled him. His grandfather had been one of the original supporters of the Great Zimbabwe Reserve. His father had been an assistant game warden there for twelve years. Generations of the Sylo family had been devoted to saving animals. Had Christopher been on the scene, she would have pointed a suspicious finger in his direction. And yet, even if Christopher's purchase of ivory was contributing to the problem, he wouldn't involve himself in something illegal like poaching, she was sure. Even the seizure of the land once scheduled for the Lackland Animal Preserve had been above board. Her anger and hurt painted him blacker than he was. He had warned her about doing at.

"Hell, I'm beginning to wonder if I *am* somehow responsible," Craig said. "There's seemingly no other explanation for their knowing my every move except them somehow having hot-wired my brain."

"I don't see any protruding electrodes," Janet said, hoping to inject a lighter vein into the conversation. "So I think you can discard that possibility."

"They're too often in the right place at the right time to rely on *just* luck," he said, not taking her cue. "There's a spy in my camp, and I have every intention of flushing him out."

"He'll make a slip," Janet said encouragingly. "He can't be so damned clever forever."

"He doesn't have to be clever forever," Craig reminded her, "but only until the last elephant on the reserve is dead."

If Craig didn't find the leak, she realized, it could damage his military record. Things like this were important to a career man's chances for promotion.

Janet looked out the window. There were finally a few sections of untilled land below. So close to civilization, they offered sanctuary for squirrels, groundhogs and birds—nothing bigger.

"The problem at the Great Zimbabwe Reserve has always been its fertile land," Craig said, following her gaze. "You don't allocate such land to four-legged animals when people are starving. If you do, they don't hold it for long. A field of corn feeds more people far longer than does a dead gazelle. If there are people finally realizing how valuable animals are for the tourist trade, they were a long time in seeing that, probably because there was so much wildlife at one time that few people imagined there ever would be a shortage."

The reserve boundary, when it appeared, was a visible line where fences stopped and complete wilderness took over. Animals sought sanctuary in that wilderness, although there were no guarantees of safety even there. Why maintain small reserves when there was giant Wankie a few hundred miles to the northeast? Not to mention Matopos National Park or Victoria Falls National Park. So much of a poor nation's valuable land turned over to animals!

Janet didn't think it was too much. There were, however, too many people like Christopher. Christopher saw a herd of animals on land, and he didn't question that the land was more important. Even though the Great Zimbabwe Reserve had been whittled down for farms and not for mineral development as had happened on the Lackland Preserve, Christopher's indifference indicated where his sympathy lay. Show him how a herd of wildebeest could fatten his pockets, and he would save it fast enough.

His fine talk about putting down his gun for a camera was worthless. The proof came with the Great Zimbabwe Reserve shrinking to nothing while he was in his counting house, counting out his money, and his diamonds and his precious gold. He had the power and the influence to champion wildlife preservation successfully. If he only would!

"Lake Kyle." Craig announced. They were approaching the man-made body of water resulting from the back-up of the Mtilikwe River behind the sixty-meter-high Kyle Dam. The lake and the dam were part of a vast water-storage system designed for the same agricultural network that had doomed the Great Zimbabwe Reserve to its present depletion. "Ninety square kilometers of water," Craig informed her, and then pointed to the right. "Fort Victoria is that way." Fort Victoria was the first town established by pioneers after their struggle up from the low country. In the 1890s, during the rebellion of the warlike Matabele tribe, the town had been an important stronghold for the white settlers. There had been plenty of animals back then.

Janet surveyed the shoreline. Somewhere among those trees were the elephants she had come to save—how many she didn't know. Part of the project in which she was involved required a counting before transfer. Estimates were well over a hundred, but there were fewer elephants now than a week or two before. Poachers had seen to that.

"Giraffes at eight o'clock!" Craig said. He banked the plane to give her a better look. There were three, their tall necks extending fragile heads into the treetops. Mobile lips gently plucked the tender leaves. The gold-and-black high-rises paused, instinctively aware that they were being watched but unsure from which direction. The noise of the plane gave no clue until the aircraft passed between them and the sun. Startled by the eclipse, they set off in a surprisingly graceful gait.

Janet was moved by the tragic beauty of these confined animals who had once roamed far and wide. Christopher would condemn her feelings as mere sentimentalism.

Craig turned the plane back toward the south. The terrain was hillier than that around Salisbury. Large ridges of stone bulged to form rich, flat-bottomed valleys between them. Slopes and depressions were verdant with velvety foliage. Here and there, variegated gray-granite domes alleviated the monotony of green. Centuries of weathering had peeled Zimbabwe granite as if it were a multi-skinned orange. The resulting scree slid to the base of the outcrops. But there were fewer loose stones than there might have been. Most had been picked up centuries ago and used for building the city of Great Zimbabwe.

The ruins that remained of that city had been legally protected as early as 1893, when the British Africa Company began to fear the destructive nature of early settlers scrounging for the legendary wealth of the region. Made a part of the Great Zimbabwe Reserve in 1900, they were proclaimed a national monument in 1937.

Two thousand people had once lived in Great Zimbabwe. It was once, according to one school of thought, the capital of biblical Ophir, famous in King Solomon's time. Other historians believed it was the capital of Havilah, where the gold of Ophir originated in the second and first millenniums B.C.

A later theory, based on the radiocarbon dating technique, put the city's heyday in the thirteenth and fifteenth centuries A.D. The theory postulated that a small African village had grown into a mini-nation as a result of old trade, and then was abandoned when the violated environment was depleted not only of gold but of the resources necessary to sustain its inhabitants.

All that remained were scattered ruins through one valley and more ruins atop one hill. The former was dominated by the Great Enclosure, the latter by a warren of stone walls and rock passageways. It was the Great Enclosure that first captured Janet's attention as they flew over. It was an oval wall, 253 meters in circumference, as high as nine and a half meters in many places, and more than five and a half meter thick at its base—a stupendous achievement of dry-stone construction, encircling what was once supposedly a royal residence. The tall red milkwood trees, clustered mainly inside the eastern curve, hadn't rooted until after the place had been abandoned, several hundred years before. They now extended a canopy of leafy branches that concealed a solid stone tower. The tower had a base diameter of almost six meters, tapering in its eleven-meter height to a summit only two meters across.

"The military accommodations," Craig informed her as he buzzed over the tents pitched among the trees outside the Great Enclosure. "Yours are a little less rustic. We've booked you into the tourist hotel—over there." The Zimbabwe Ruins Hotel was a cluster of one-story buildings within a fifteen-minute walk of the Great Enclosure. Janet, who was expecting far less, was pleased by what she saw from the air. "Once more around the block," Craig said, "and then I'll set us down." Janet didn't see an airstrip. Craig pointed to a stretch of dirt road. "We'll land there!" he prophesied confidently.

"Which you've done plenty of times without accident," Janet said, not enthused. Landing too close to the trees could lose them a wing. The plane was overloaded with cargo and therefore wasn't as maneuverable, no matter what Craig said. She glanced toward the horizon, because she didn't want to increase her fears by a further examination of the pitiful runway.

"We'll be down before you know it," Craig assured her, preparing her and the plane for touchdown.

Janet, though, was suddenly no longer concerned about landing. She had spotted the lazy vortex silhouetted against the bright blue of the African sky. "Vultures!" she exclaimed.

"Damn!" Craig replied. His thoughts were the same as hers. He immediately aborted the landing and headed for the whirl-pool of birds.

"It could be an injured animal," Janet said without conviction.

"Quite a few scavengers for one wounded animal," Craig observed.

Janet prepared herself mentally for what was coming. She had seen death in the wild before. She had filmed in Mexico and South America before coming to Africa. Death was part of the natural order.

Not death like this, however!

"Oh, my God!" she cried, sick to her stomach. Nothing could

prepare her for the six slaughtered elephants around a blood-dyed waterhole, a seventh partially submerged in the water. The seven mounds pulsed, not because they were alive, but because they were covered by birds. As the plane swooped closer, some birds took wing. Others scattered along the ground, too glutted by the frenzy of feeding to get their bloated bodies in the air. "Poachers did this?" Janet asked, knowing the answer. Her first sighting of the Great Zimbabwe elephants was a grisly one.

"I'll wager not one of those elephants has its tusks any longer," Craig said, making another approach. More birds scattered. Those too heavy to fly were grotesquely comical as they flapped their wings and wobbled in futile attempts to get airborne. "There's no place to land here," Craig said. "I'll come in by Land Rover."

"I want to come with you," Janet said. It was a lie. She had seen enough. Still, it was important that she expose herself to the full horror of a closer inspection. If she hoped to portray graphically to her viewers the extent of the tragedy, she must immerse herself in it. Tomorrow she would bring the camera crew to this spot, too. Even a jaded viewing public couldn't remain unmoved by this. If they did, there was no hope for the animals.

"It was predictable," Craig said. She must have misheard him. If it was predictable, he would have taken steps to prevent it. Even if he had been in Salisbury at the time, there was open communication between him and the camp. "They knew, don't you see?" he continued. Janet didn't see anything but the sickening sight below her. "They knew exactly where to strike most effectively. My patrols were concentrating on the north and northeast sections. The poachers struck exactly where there was the least chance of detection."

"Haven't you enough men to do the job?" Janet asked. Her voice was strange. She was nauseated from the sight blessedly left behind her.

"We have enough to stop any group who doesn't have inside knowledge of our every movement," Craig said.

"Ask for more men, damn it!" She was getting hysterical. She fought to control. Nothing was accomplished by falling to pieces.

"We have all the men who can be spared," Craig said. "There are problems like this other than at Great Zimbabwe, you know—quite aside from the fact that most of the military can't be bothered. I don't know how much you know about the political situation in Zimbabwe, Janet, or if you know what's happening in the other emerging nations of Africa. It's volatile, to say the very least. We had a revolution a few years ago, and we're still picking up the pieces. For every two people who thank God for the end of the bloodshed, there's another who thinks the killing stopped too soon. No one is sending troops to Great Zimbabwe that are needed to guarantee footholds of power. The death of seven elephants—or seven hundred—isn't going to change that. Whatever our problem is here, it must be solved with the men we have. We're not getting more. We're not the highest priority."

The plane landed at Great Zimbabwe without incident. Janet's thoughts were still on those seven dead elephants. Their tusks might someday be padlocked in that room in Christopher's basement, she reflected angrily. He should see this! Not even he could be unmoved by the brutal carnage.

Craig turned her over to Sergeant Timbuti, a neatly uniformed black man who was waiting when the plane taxied to a stop. "The sergeant will take you to the hotel," Craig said. "You take a few minutes to get settled, and I'll make arrangements to pick you up in—" he checked his watch "—about fifteen minutes." Christopher had given her fifteen minutes to meet him in the hotel lobby in Johannesburg, and the echo was disturbing. "That is, unless you've decided you've seen enough," Craig ventured, giving her an out.

"I want to go," she replied quickly before she could have second thoughts.

Sergeant Timbuti said little, and Janet wasn't up to initiating conversation. They drove directly to the Zimbabwe Ruins

Hotel. There was no formal registration. The whole complex had been commandeered, staff and all, by those involved in Project Pachyderm. Dr. Nhari, the man she was to contact on the site, was out in the field and wouldn't be back until late evening. There were no tourists, because the area was off limits to unauthorized personnel.

The accommodations were deluxe compared to what Janet had expected. In her room, there was a double bed, a sofa, three chairs, a coffee table, a desk and various end tables, even air conditioning and a telephone. There was even a bathroom with a shower-tub combination that would have sent her into fits of ecstasy if she hadn't been so numb from the sight at the water-hole.

Splashing water on her face, she looked in the mirror over the sink. Despite the coolness of the water, her skin remained hot. Her pupils were dilated. "If you can't stand the heat, you shouldn't be in the kitchen," she said, drying her face with a towel.

She went into the bedroom. Craig had said fifteen minutes, but he might be longer. Whoever he had left in charge would be briefing him now on what had happened while he was in Salisbury.

When she dialed the phone for an outside line, a male voice answered. There was a corporal on the switchboard. She asked him for the Monomatapa Hotel in Salisbury. The line crackled and someone answered, seemingly from a great distance away. It was a bad connection. She asked for Roger's room three times before she was understood. She heard muted ringing but no answer. Someone knocked on her door. "Come on in, Craig!" she said, hanging up the telephone. "I'm ready."

The door opened. "I'm not Craig, but I'll come in anyway," Christopher said, his too-bright smile illuminating his too-handsome face.

"You!" Janet accused, not knowing what she was feeling. Her mind was cluttered with conflicting emotions. She was glad to see him; she was furious that he'd refused them a clean break.

She resented his intrusion on a spot untainted by childhood memories of him; she yearned for his arms around her, his lips against hers. Her mind simultaneously flashed visions of seven dead elephants around a bloody pool and bloody ivory stacked to the ceiling in a basement room at Lionspride. "What are you doing here?" she demanded.

"That must be obvious, Janet," he said, arching his left eyebrow, as though her surprise was unwarranted. "I came running, as you knew I would." She didn't know any such thing. She had presumed he was out of her life forever. She had hoped he was anyway.

"I thought I'd seen the last of you," she said.

"Then you underestimated my determination," Christopher returned, shutting the door and leaning against it. "You certainly underestimated your charms."

"Get out!" she commanded. She couldn't think. Too many things were coming at her—first the miseries of meeting and leaving Christopher in Johannesburg, then the dead elephants with their throbbing shrouds of feasting vultures. Now this. Why couldn't he leave her alone? She wanted to forget him, but that was impossible with him standing there. If there were still enough good times to outbalance the bad, there soon wouldn't be. "Will you get out? Please."

"Come on. Janet, don't be so inhospitable," he pleaded play-fully. "I just got here, didn't I?"

He started across the room toward her.

CHAPTER SIX

IT WAS THE LAST THING she wanted; it was what she wanted most in the world. He took her in his strong arms. She didn't stop him. He smoothed her hair, brushing away a few unruly strands that clung to her right cheekbone. His fingertips were excitingly sensuous as they touched. "Tell me you're glad to see me," he said, both his hands sliding up the back of her neck and cupping her head, tilting her face upward. She looked into his startlingly golden eyes, drawn to them like a moth to a flame. He was so handsome, but so callous. Yet she was glad to see him. Dear heaven, she was glad!

"Only someone with your ego could think I'd be happy to see you after Johannesburg," she said noncommittally. His power over her was great enough without giving him more. She knew the triumph he wanted. She wouldn't give it to him. Not in Johannesburg—not now, not ever.

"Then tell me you're not glad to see me," he challenged. His right thumb gently traced the line of her jaw. She trembled.

"I'm not glad to see you," she said. She should struggle. She should pound on his muscled chest with her fists—scream, shout. She didn't.

"You're not much of a liar," he said, his smile dimpling both cheeks. She wanted to kiss those dimples, feel the sweetness of them beneath her lips.

He was back in her life—if he had ever left it. She was thrilled and disturbed. She was at Great Zimbabwe to forget him. She arrived with no childhood memories of this place.

She had a job to keep her mind occupied. Craig Sylo might fill her emptiness, at least partially. Christopher would spoil it all. She couldn't reason properly with him around. He distorted her common sense.

He kissed her.

Her arms went stiff at her sides. She waited impatiently for the kiss to end. When it did, it was replaced by another, this one more determined to melt her facade. That's all it was, too—a facade. If she was cool on the outside, her blood boiled in its race through her veins.

Christopher's kisses were lethal, even that first one, sixteen years before. If this kiss was different from the first one, it was no less deadly. It thrilled her as no other man's kisses could. If that was unfair to Bob's memory, it couldn't be helped. If that was embarrassing for her, the kiss a result of his lust and not of his love, that couldn't be helped, either.

Lust was what he felt, lust and a need to conquer a woman who offered him the challenge of resistance, a woman who had come to Africa to blacken the Van Hoon name. On the other hand, Janet felt love for whatever trace of the boy remained in the man. Understanding his hold on her didn't make it easier to bear.

His large hands slid down her back, cupping her hips. He pulled her lower body in closer. The pressure of his lips opened her mouth wider. His tongue tantalized the breach, tasting sweet honey beyond. His hot breath fueled the flames inside her.

It was hard to remain passive. She wanted to wrap her arms around his neck and pull his head, his kisses closer. She wanted the muscled hardness of his chest pressing unyieldingly against the softness of her breasts. She wanted him to stop. That was the conflict raging inside her.

He lifted her in strong arms. She automatically locked her hands around his powerful neck, simultaneously shaking off his demanding lips. "Put me down!" she insisted.

"I have every intention of putting you down," he said. He carried her to the bed and dropped her on it.

"I don't want this." she said. "Can't you tell?

"I want it, though," he countered. He began unbuttoning his shirt. "Can't *you* tell?" His motivations were inadequate. They didn't balance Janet's needs. Whatever satisfaction awaited from a few minutes in bed, it wasn't enough for Janet. Not with Christopher. Not with any man.

Yet here was the means to shatter the remaining fantasy, to put everything into perspective, to wipe the slate clean. By surrendering, she could force herself to face reality. The loving boy was gone. All that remained was a brutish lout driven by passion and resentment. He would use her body and arise proudly triumphant. She would triumph, too. She would no longer think of him as the hero of her childish fantasies. She would know better. He was the villain. If he mocked her when he was finished, and he would, that would hammer the valuable lesson home. If he left her afterward, and he would, she would pick up the pieces. She had picked up pieces before and survived—when her father died, when Bob died, when she left Lionspride and Christopher the first time. It was worth a few minutes of physical discomfort to prevent more years of mental torment. It was time to cast off childhood dreams and get on with living in the real world.

"It makes no difference to you what I want, does it?" she said. His shirt was open, giving her a glimpse of his muscled chest and scalloped abdomen. That hint of bare flesh excited her more than she would have thought possible.

"I'm not convinced you don't want it," he said. He sat on the edge of the bed. His weight dipped the mattress, shifting her closer. He leaned over, one hand on each side of her body. The front of his shirt opened wider. She saw the full excellence of his bare chest and stomach. His skin was golden velvet stretched over hard hot steel.

"But if I'm convinced of what I want?" Janet asked. Even though she had made her decision, something made her want to delay. Traces of his lime-based after-shave mingled with the natural aroma of his body. The combination was potently sexual.

"You don't know what you want, Janet," he said with conviction. He began unbuttoning her blouse. "Do you?"

Yes, she knew. She wanted an end to her heartache, an end to the illusion that life could be better. She wanted an exorcism of childhood dreams that had damned her marriage to Bob even before it was consummated. Had Bob lived, they would have separated. Dreams had been calling her back to Africa even then. She was tired of bedding a figment of her imagination. Bedding the real thing would confirm how distorted her dreams had become.

She shut her eyes. She couldn't help her sadness.

He peeled back her cotton shirt to reveal creamy breasts. She wasn't wearing a brassiere; it was too hot. Yet it was hotter with her nakedness exposed to his smoldering eyes. "Beautiful!" he sighed appreciatively, and bowed his head. His tongue was a brand against her flesh, a running fire that seared one nipple.

"Please, don't!" she begged, forgetting she was committed. He paid no attention. The hardening of her nipple was all the invitation he needed to continue.

She ran her hands up his back, wishing his shirt were torn away. She wanted his hard muscle against her palms. She buried her fingers in his silky hair. She didn't take hold. She didn't pull him away. He licked her nipples to painful hardness. He flattened the nakedness of her breasts beneath the weight of his bare chest. He burrowed his face against the side of her neck. His exploratory kisses were maddening.

She was afraid. This wasn't the horror on which she had counted. This was the stuff of which dreams were made. She couldn't surrender herself to enjoyment without love. His seducing her to unexpected pleasure was a triumph she wouldn't allow him.

He was going to reject her when he was through. He was going to throw her aside like all the other women who surrendered to him. She would be left with the pain of knowing the pleasure of a dream that existed in reality. What's more, the dream existed without love, hers to experience only in the arms of a man who, once he'd gotten what he wanted, would want nothing more to do with her.

That was exchanging a dream for a nightmare! She wasn't taking the risk. She gripped his shoulders, her fingers grasping his golden flesh. "The door, Christopher," she said. "It's unlocked." He kissed her neck, and then attempted to cover her mouth with his.

She refused to be silenced. "I'm expecting someone," she insisted.

"Forget the door," he said. "Forget whoever you're expecting." His hands slid down her body, spreading fire wherever they went. If she didn't get him away soon, there would be no turning back for either of them.

"Craig knows I'm in here, Christopher," she said. Her voice was breathless. She didn't have the strength to force him physically, so she used words. "He'll worry if I don't answer. He'll try the door. He'll come in." She was close to panic. Her words tumbled out, hardly decipherable. "It's Craig Sylo, Christopher. Captain Sylo," she emphasized, enunciating distinctly. Christopher's right hand crept up beneath her skirt, caressing with startling expertise. She must stop him. "Please, Christopher—the door. At least lock the door!"

"I'm not afraid of Captain Sylo," he said, kissing her cheeks, her forehead, her chin. He tried for her mouth again, but she jerked her head from side to side to prevent him.

"Will you think of someone besides yourself for a change!" she cried, mustering as much disgust as she could. "What will Craig think, walking in to see us like this?" Janet would be mortified.

"He'll be jealous," Christopher said. "I would be, too, if I found you in bed with another man."

That was a laugh! She didn't say so. He was smooth talking her into submission, hinting at a shred of emotional involvement. It was bull! He wasn't thinking about anyone but himself when he got to his feet. He didn't want Craig walking in and interrupting a good thing.

"Thank you," she said, missing the press of his weight against her.

"Don't go away, will you?" he said. His blond hair was tousled. The pupils of his golden eyes were large. No one was more handsome. Her heart beat faster. A heat burned inside her that Christopher was able and willing to quench. She had been four years without a man, but it was a mistake letting things go this far. She had rationalized herself into an unforgivable spot. She would be more careful next time. *Don't let there be a next time*, her mind screamed.

"I'll be right back," he said. He went to the door and locked it. Janet locked another door, after completing a record sprint to the bathroom. "Janet?" He was confused. She was supposed to lie there, waiting for him to take up where he had left off. He was wrong!

"I want you out of my room and out of my life!" she called out, bracing her body against the door. She wasn't safe. The door was a flimsy barrier in the face of the strength in Christopher's muscled body. She had felt the strength of his body against her own.

"I don't understand, Janet," he said. He was feigning ignorance. The man was unbelievable!

"I can't make it plainer," she said. "Get out and leave me alone. Craig will be here any minute," she added in warning.

"You and Craig Sylo have something going?" he asked. Typical. His mind was one-track. His interest was purely sexual, and he believed that to be true of any man. Where was Craig? He should be there. The fifteen minutes had passed. Maybe he'd gone to the waterhole without her. "Janet?" Christopher insisted.

An inch of weak wood kept her from him. She was tempted to open the door and surrender again to the crush of his body. "It's none of your business what I feel for Craig!" she said. Let him think there was another man in her life. She needed all the insulation she could get—real or otherwise. "It *is* your business that you're an unfeeling monster!"

"Janet," he said and was so close to the door that the wood creaked with the pressure of his body against it, "it's time we talked seriously."

"You were talking a few minutes ago," she reminded him, "and I didn't like what you said." All their talking would be done through closed doors from now on. She wouldn't be taken in by craftiness, with no avenue of escape.

"I came to Great Zimbabwe to say something important," he claimed. That was a laugh! She knew what was on his mind. It was the same thing that had been there since that day at Lionspride. How close she had come to giving him his victory. How close she still was to ultimate surrender. She was angry and disappointed in herself. "After you left Johannesburg, I got some things in perspective," he said. He didn't give up. The man's conceit was monumental! "I made certain decisions." He had certainly done that. He had decided to come to Great Zimbabwe and take up where he'd left off. "It's important that you hear and understand them."

"I can hear them from where I am," she said; she wasn't leaving that bathroom.

"Janet," he pleaded. He was so damned persuasive. Such a sexy voice—all golden peaches and heavy cream.

"Whatever talking you want to do, you should have done a long time ago," she said. "We've gone beyond the talking stage. I can't trust you. That's what it boils down to. That's why I'm not opening the door until you're gone." She didn't trust herself, either. She was vulnerable and had been all along. He would mutter some lie about how it wasn't lust that brought him back to her, and she would convert to putty in his hands at just that suggestion of love.

"Look, I'm sorry," he said. "Really, I am." She needed Craig right now, not unfelt apologies. "I've been thinking of you all the way from Johannesburg," he said, "and suddenly there you were. I wanted to say, 'Janet, let's sit down and talk,' but you looked too damned beautiful to resist. I couldn't help myself. You weren't beating me off, either," he reminded after a pause.

He wanted to shift the blame onto her. It wasn't the first time he had insinuated she was a tease.

"Get out, Christopher!"

"You can't stay locked in there for the duration," he said. She was lucky he wasn't breaking down the door, no doubt. That would have been more in keeping with his caveman style.

"I have no intention of staying locked up in here much longer," she informed him. "I have every intention of coming out when you leave, and/or when Craig arrives. He'll be here any minute."

"I'm not leaving Great Zimbabwe until we have our talk, Janet," he said grimly. "I haven't run all of this way like a love-sick calf to leave things unsaid."

"Don't you dare mention love!" It was what she had expected from him. He was pulling out all the stops, sinking to new depths. At least in Johannesburg he had been honest enough to admit he wasn't capable of love. But no. All he had admitted was that he didn't fall in love at first sight, or in two days' time. The third day was some kind of charm, was it? "The only one you love is Christopher Van Hoon," she said angrily. It was sad but true. "I will not be fooled by anything you have to say!"

He was laughing at her. She had given way in his arms once too often to be believable. She cursed her weakness. She cursed childhood memories that contributed to that weakness. She cursed the fantasies of Christopher that had made her life bearable for so many years and now made it a living hell.

"If you're so sure of yourself, why are you afraid to hear me out?" he asked. He was good with words. He was good at playing with emotions. She was dealing with a pro—out of her league. Damn it, she should be capable of holding her own.

"I'm not afraid to *hear* you," she said. She was furious. "I'm afraid *of* you. You're ten times stronger than I am, you know."

"Come on, Janet," he said. "Don't be so dramatic. All I'm asking is that you listen to me."

"You expect me to believe that?" she demanded sarcastically. He didn't answer. Of course he didn't. Christopher was irresistible. He was the Greek god every woman dreamed would descend from Mount Olympus to take her in his arms and into bed. He was good-looking, physically superb, powerful, and wealthy—each factor alone a potent aphrodisiac. Together, they were an elixir no woman could resist. Until now. "I'm saying no, damn it!" she said. "No, no, no! Accept it! I have more important things to do with my life than fight off a lecherous egotistical child."

"We'll talk when you're less hysterical." His patronizing attitude made her livid. "It won't be a conversation through a closed door, either," he promised. His footsteps faded as he made his way to the outside door that opened and closed.

"I promise you it won't be in any bed!" she screamed. She was shaking. She needed to get control of herself. She shouldn't let him affect her this way. She shouldn't have gone to Lionspride. What a mistake that had been!

She looked in the mirror over the sink. She didn't like what she saw. Her hair was mussed, her lipstick smeared. Her blouse was open, her breasts tingling from the horror she had endured in the other room. She resented how much she had reveled in it.

Re-buttoning her blouse, she tucked it into her skirt. A tissue removed her smeared lipstick. She combed her hair. She looked too good after such a trauma.

There was a distant knock. Thank God. Craig! At the bathroom door, she paused without opening it. Christopher hadn't left. He was waiting beyond the barrier. It wasn't Craig knocking. It was Christopher, trying to trick her.

"Janet?" Muffled through two doors and the length of the room, the voice sounded as though it could be anyone's. The outside door opened. "Janet?" It was Craig.

She came out, checking to make sure Christopher was gone. She smiled a warm welcome. Christopher wouldn't try anything stupid with Craig there. Craig was a match for him.

"Sorry I'm late," he apologized. She was sorry, too. "I thought you may have given up on me and gone for some fresh air and sunshine. Ready?"

She was as ready as she would ever be, and delighted to feel safe. She hooked her arm through his gratefully as they walked toward the parking area, the afternoon sunshine bright and hot. Its heat might explain the flush that gave Janet's skin its special glow, but she knew better. Her blood was rushing furiously through her as a result of her latest encounter with Christopher.

"They found five more dead elephants yesterday," Craig said. "Dr. Nhari and his team stumbled across them."

"It's all so horrible!" Janet exclaimed. Concentrating on the plight of the Great Zimbabwe elephants could take her mind off Christopher, she thought. But she was wrong.

Christopher was waiting in the Land Rover. Janet stopped dead in her tracks when she saw him. "Hello, Janet!" he called, waving.

"You know each other?" Craig asked curiously. The answer was obvious. What else did her expression tell him?

"Unfortunately yes," Janet said. She tried not to sound bitter. Craig would ask too many questions.

"He wanted to come along. If you'd rather he didn't...."

"Oh, I don't mind," she said. Christopher should see those dead elephants. It would shake him out of his lethargy as far as wildlife preservation was concerned. "I was surprised to see him, that's all." She tightened her hold on Craig's arm. Christopher had better watch his step. She wasn't undefended any longer, and he had more than tried her patience for one day. "I interviewed him in Johannesburg. His family has a huge ivory collection."

"Yes, I've heard," Craig said. He spoke with the right degree of disgust. His family was concerned with saving animals, not killing them and tacking their heads on trophy boards.

"Janet, what a surprise!" Christopher greeted her. No one would have known they had parted only minutes before under less than congenial circumstances. "A pleasant one, however," he added quickly. He could save his gentlemanly claptrap. He was no gentleman, and she knew it.

"The surprise is mine," she assured him. "You didn't mention you were coming to Great Zimbabwe."

"Didn't I?" He was all innocence.

"Definitely you did not!" she said icily.

"Odd. It was a well-thought-out decision," he said, a wide grin making his handsome face even more appealing. "We'll talk about it later."

Fat chance of that!

"Is it all right if I sit in front with you, Craig?" she asked sweetly. "I'm sure Mr. Van Hoon wouldn't mind getting in back."

"The front seat it is!" Craig obliged. Christopher got in the back without protest.

Two more Land Rovers arrived, filled with armed soldiers. In the lead, Craig took a dirt road for a couple of miles before veering into the bush. Janet moved closer to him. She was isolating herself from Christopher as best she could. Forgetting he was there was impossible.

They disturbed a herd of zebras that spurted into a wild gallop before deciding the Land Rovers were no direct threats. There were wildebeests among the herd. The two species were often found together. Wildebeests ate the leafy parts of young grass that were more difficult to digest than the young shoots preferred by zebras. The wildebeest was a survivor. It managed to proliferate against all odds. Possibly it was left alone because it was so ugly, and ugliness was never in demand. Its tail and hindquarters were horse-like, its shoulders those of an American bison, its head an ungainly appendage that was long, flat, bearded and horned. When it ran, it was far from graceful, its bucking gait awkward beside the smoother movements of the zebra.

The caravan flushed out two ostriches, which ran beside the Land Rovers for a mile before peeling off. The male bird was over nine feet tall and must have weighed close to three hundred pounds.

"They were clocking over thirty," Craig informed her as the flightless birds disappeared among the distant trees. The Land Rovers weren't always that fast over the rough terrain. Janet's spine ached from continual jarring.

She searched the sky for circling birds but didn't see any. Distances were deceptive in Africa where ground travel seldom went in a straight line. The route snaked around clumps of underbrush and trees, detoured around dry gullies and rugged outcrops. Craig knew where he was going. Janet was lost in the maze, but it couldn't be much farther. The sun was dropping toward the horizon, and they probably wouldn't stay out after nightfall.

Janet was daydreaming about the luxury of the shower-tub combination waiting for her in her hotel room when the Land Rover came to an abrupt stop. Janet was strapped in with a seatbelt and shoulder harness, but Craig's arm automatically extended in front of her as a further safety precaution.

"Melissa and Suzy," Craig said. His index finger was at his pursed lips, signaling for silence. Janet didn't understand at first. But when she spotted the rhinos, she wondered how she had missed them. The one was as big as a Sherman tank. It wasn't just the size of Melissa that made her unique, although two tons of animal, standing six feet at the shoulders, was impressive enough. It was the size of her horns. There were two, one behind the other on her snout. The first was three feet high, the other almost as large. "Take a good look," Craig said, "You don't see horns like that very often, certainly not around here. Melissa might as well carry a sign saying, 'Shoot me!'"

In the Far East, it was believed powdered rhino horn restored sexual potency, Janet knew. That superstition had played a big part in bringing Asian rhinos to the brink of extinction. African rhinos were seriously threatened; their horns used more and more to fill the Asian demand. "We try to keep a close watch on her, especially now that she has Suzy," Craig said, "but a twenty-four-hour guard in the wild is impossible. And with rhino horns bringing in twice their weight in gold on the black market...." He shrugged in helplessness.

Suzy's horns weren't nearly as impressive as those of her mother. They were small nubs that hardly seemed attractions for poachers—except that anyone who shot Melissa might decide the smaller horns of her daughter were frosting on the cake. Janet shuddered in disgust. Once there had been thousands of rhinos in the area, some with horns that dwarfed those of Melissa. A pair of rhinos in Masai Amboseli, a famous reserve in Kenya, were of record length. Tourists had flocked to see them. Both animals were killed by poachers, their popularity more an invitation to slaughter than an assurance of protection.

When her father had been the director of the Seattle Zoo, one of the black rhinos had died during difficult labor. A team, of which a far younger Janet was a part, worked around the clock to save the calf. Despite their efforts, the animal died. That childhood sadness made Janet particularly sensitive to Craig's pessimism for the survival of this calf. Living under normal conditions was hard enough for these animals without their worrying about two-legged killers sneaking up on them in the bush.

"Funny what people pay good money for," Craig said, shaking his head in disbelief. The horns were similar to animal hooves and human fingernails in texture. Nothing scientific verified the substance as being the least aphrodisiacal, but superstition died hard... like memories. All the rhinos would be dead before the last man stopped believing his virility could be restored by swallowing what was knocked off the snout of a dead animal and ground to fine powder.

Melissa and Suzy were white rhinos, although both white and black rhinos were actually the same dirty gray. The whites were merely bigger with wide mouths. Blacks had lips that were narrow and pointed. Both had bad vision and were known to charge trees, termite mounds and an occasional Land Rover. Meeting the charge of a two-ton animal could do a good deal of damage to a vehicle. To avoid frightening mother and daughter, Craig put the Land Rover in low gear. Melissa and Suzy watched nervously, seeing a disturbing blur as the caravan moved slowly by them.

"Mr. Van Hoon has several rhino trophies with horns bigger

than Melissa's," Janet said when they were out of attack range. "Don't you, Mr. Van Hoon?" She cast an accusing glance in his direction.

His gaze greeted hers without flinching. "Yes," he admitted without pause. "Killed, I might add, when the species was more abundant than it is today. Or doesn't such a small fact matter? I've never heard of a Van Hoon shooting one animal after it was added to the endangered species list. Maybe you know something I don't? Maybe I kill them while sleepwalking. Do I, Janet?"

She didn't answer. She couldn't think of a reply. He was right. She was blaming him for animals killed in his father's and grandfather's time, a time when most animals were so abundant that few hunters thought there could ever be an end to them. She had no proof Christopher had gone off on any recent big-game hunts—with or without a gun. He was too busy with Van Hoon Afrikaner Minerals to be bothered—one way or another.

Craig gave her a sympathetic smile. It embarrassed Janet that he knew Christopher could get the best of her. She must reason things out more carefully before saying them. She needed to get her facts down pat. Around Christopher, it was her unreliable emotions that controlled whatever she said or did.

She concentrated on getting comfortable but was unsuccessful. Besides the bumpiness of the ride, thoughts of Melissa's and Suzy's dismal future disturbed her, not to mention the grisly sight awaiting them by the waterhole. Christopher's disrupting presence in the back seat didn't help matters.

"We're close, aren't we?" she said. She didn't see the circling birds but knew it couldn't be long before they reached the ugly scene. For a moment she was sorry, very sorry, she had decided to return. Yet it was her job to understand exactly what was happening to the animals she was so determined to save. She pulled herself together. She was a professional, and it wouldn't look good to act like anything less.

"The waterhole is through there," Craig said, pointing straight ahead. The Land Rovers entered a cluster of flat-topped acacias.

With umbrella branches, the trees rose to forty feet on all sides, displaying thorns often three inches long.

As if on cue, the birds became visible through a break in the leafy canopy of branches. Silently the aerial deathwatch progressed. Large-winged vultures hovered on warm air currents until satiated diners below made room for them.

"You okay?" Craig asked Janet.

"I'm fine," she said. She appreciated his concern. She resented her obvious squeamishness.

The Land Rovers broke into the clearing that separated the cluster of surrounding trees from the water. Their emergence was a catalyst. Startled vultures rose like swarms of giant flies. Some took full flight. Others resettled immediately, reluctant to leave what wasn't finished. The nakedness of their heads and necks, easily exposed to the cleansing rays of the hot sun, was nature's hygienic protection from the bacteria rampant within carrion. They were grotesque as they eyed the approaching vehicles. Their flapping wings stirred the smell of death, making that sickening perfume more distinctive.

Hyenas with sloping backs and bare faces, also feeding off the carnage, were spooked. But they retreated only as far as the tree line. Like the birds, they were reluctant to leave their meal. Their stares were malevolent. Two of them harmonized exceedingly dismal and melancholy notes of protest. Their crackling affected "laughs" were indescribably wild, sending shivers up Janet's spine. Her skin went rough with goose bumps. Even the usually nocturnal jackals were out, made skittish by the interruption; small coyote-like carnivores, they stood about a foot and a half at their shoulders and weighed about twenty pounds each. Their attractive gold color was incongruous in a setting worthy of a painting by Hieronymus Bosch.

Craig drove the Land Rover upwind and parked it. "This won't take long," he said encouragingly. Soldiers spilled out of the other Land Rovers. They knew what to do; they had been this route before.

"Here, this might help if the wind turns," Christopher said.

Janet was startled to realize he was still in the Land Rover with her. She took his offered handkerchief. It was blessedly scented with the same lime-based fragrance she associated with him, and she put the handkerchief over her nose. She didn't wait for a further assault of the far less pleasant aroma riding the warm air.

More birds scattered. The interruption of their feeding wasn't as temporary as they had hoped. A soldier shot off a quick round of ammunition that sent even the most reluctant bird skyward. Jackals and hyenas disappeared among the trees.

"Well, I must admit this is grisly," Christopher observed behind her. Janet was too busy combating nausea to bask in the victory of hearing his admission.

After what seemed an eternity, Craig returned. "They used machine guns," he said "They waited in hiding and picked them off en masse when the herd came in for water. They had a truck ready to transport the ivory."

"Surprisingly close to your main camp, isn't it?" Christopher asked. Janet wasn't feeling well enough to say anything.

"No one said they weren't brazen bastards," Craig observed. "They timed it to perfection, knowing my teams were on the other side of the reserve at the time."

"How did they know?'" Christopher asked.

"You tell me, and we'll both know!" Craig snapped. Janet expected Christopher to make some sarcastic remark about Craig's competence, or lack thereof. She was surprised, pleased and relieved: when he didn't.

The ride back took forever. As the sun dipped heavily on the horizon, the lengthening shadows gave the landscape a gloomy turn that did nothing to lift Janet's sagging spirits.

The caravan reached the mouth of the Great Zimbabwe Valley at the moment when the setting sun performed one of those miracles only possible in Africa. Within a split second, the gloominess was eradicated in a burst of glorious sunshine that set ground and trees aglow with tawny fire. Everything was magically dipped in gold—each leaf, branch, shrub, puff of dust, and blade of grass. The distant Great Enclosure was a glowing diadem: the crowning treasure. The sky was awash with variegated shades of peach, the sun melting behind gilt-edged clouds.

The beauty of the scene contrasted with Janet's memory of the waterhole. She felt confused by a country so cruel one minute and so breathtakingly wondrous the next. She was tempted to turn to Christopher and see what the dying rays did to the blondness of his hair and the golden hue of his eyes but resisted. She resented this finish to the day—it was too splendid. She would have preferred no muting of the horrible scene that had preceded it.

The Land Rovers moved through the valley, reaching the dirt road that paralleled the military encampment. The two escort vehicles peeled off. Craig drove Janet and Christopher to the hotel. It was dark when they arrived, the parking lot milky in the weakness of a few phosphorescent bulbs.

"How can you let those poor animals be butchered?" Janet asked, turning on Christopher with a fury she didn't know had built to fever pitch.

"How can I?" Christopher asked, confused. "I hardly see how I have anything to do with it, Janet. From, what I under-stand, the killing took place before I got here."

"You've power. You've friends in high places. You've clout," Janet insisted. She sounded like an ad proclaiming reasons for taking on a credit card.

"Maybe we should talk about my power, friends and clout," Christopher said seriously. "We have to talk about many things. Why not those, too? Shall we begin our discussions over supper?" Supper? Janet was aghast. The thought of food after what she had seen that afternoon was enough to bring back waves of nausea. "I understand the food isn't gourmet here" he continued, "but I'm sure that can be overlooked in the presence of pleasant company."

"How can you think of food?" she condemned, unable to believe his callousness. "Didn't you see what I saw? Didn't you feel what I felt?"

"Listen, Janet," Christopher said patiently. "Our starving isn't going to resurrect seven dead elephants. You want to talk about how to save the ones that are left, that's fine. I'll be happy to hear your ideas on how I can be of help. But it's not going to do you, or the elephants, or me, one bit of good to make yourself ill. What you saw this afternoon is tragic, yes. But it's also a fact of life around here. You'll be lucky if you don't see far worse before you leave. So try to get hold of yourself."

"Well, I'm not hungry!" she said with finality. It angered her that what he said was true. The elephants were dead. They were evidence of a problem that had existed long before she arrived at Great Zimbabwe. Her irrational emotions were at work again, but she couldn't help it.

"Very well," Christopher said, seemingly disappointed. "We can do our talking over breakfast. I presume you'll be eating by then?"

"Breakfast is out of the question!" she said, furious that she wasn't as calm and cool as he was. "Craig and I are flying to Victoria Falls in the morning." It just came out. She was grabbing for excuses, and there it was. She was afraid something might have changed since Craig had issued the invitation. The poaching situation had obviously escalated in his absence. Maybe he couldn't spare the time to show her the sights. Maybe—

"That's right. I did promise her Victoria Falls," Craig said, coming to her rescue. "We'll leave before dawn and eat a little something after we get there."

Janet was afraid Christopher would ask to tag alone. The idea of facing Victoria Falls with him wasn't something she relished. Their last time there conjured up too many precious memories, now, that she didn't want shattered any faster or more completely than she could manage on her own. There was no doubt in her mind that the memories must be destroyed. But as with much-loved pets, there was a right way and a wrong way of putting them to rest. Christopher at Lionspride had raised havoc with

Janet's attempts to erase the past. Christopher at Victoria Falls would make things equally impossible.

He didn't ask to join them. What he said, though, was no less disturbing. "How does it feel, Captain Sylo, to know Janet is using you to make me jealous?"

"Is that what she's doing?" Craig asked. He was unfazed; he was amused.

"Aren't you, Janet?" Christopher persisted.

"You're crazy!" she said, hating the way he put her on the defensive.

"Maybe that's true, but it doesn't answer my question, does it?" Christopher pointed out, his voice triumphant.

"No, I'm not trying to make you jealous!" she said with all the insistence she could muster.

"And that little lie fools no one!" Christopher said. "Not me, not Captain Sylo, certainly not you. Drop by for our talk when you're through playing games."

She watched him go. As always, she was saddened by the way they never managed even a slight rapport. There was a time—fading fast and far distant—when they had never quarreled, had never said one harsh word to each other.

"Sounds as if there was more between you two in Johannesburg than one interview," Craig said. She had forgotten he was there.

"Less than he's willing to admit," she said bitterly. Perhaps more than she was willing to admit?

"He's a fine catch," Craig said, echoing Roger's sentiments in Johannesburg. Christopher was monopolizing everyone's thoughts. There were other things that were more important— like those poor dead elephants.

"What if it turns out to be true that I am using you without knowing it?" Janet asked quietly. Craig was an innocent third party. It disturbed her to think she might inadvertently be entangling him in her and Christopher's emotional web. She didn't really see much of a possibility of having an intimate relationship with the captain. On the other hand, she dated lots of men who could be regarded simply as friends. It was ridiculous to reject Craig as a possible friend because of half-baked innuendos thrown out by a pouting Christopher.

"I'm a big boy," Craig said. "I can handle my own with Mr. Van Hoon."

"I wouldn't want to be unfair in any way, Craig," she said, turning to him in the darkness. He was such a considerate man. Why couldn't she love *him*?

"I promise I won't be hurt," he assured her, "no matter what you decide in the end. How's that for a guarantee?"

"You're very nice," she said. "Really, you are."

She let him kiss her, hoping for fireworks that didn't materialize. After sixteen years, Christopher retained a hold over her that still made her unfit for any other man.

CHAPTER SEVEN

VICTORIA FALLS never seemed to change. Any differences were the kind that required thousands of years to be noticeable to the naked eye. The government worked to maintain the natural unexploited look that was almost un-American in its absence of concession stands and falls-view tourist hotels. The hotels, three of them, were built a good distance from where the Zambezi River widened to seventeen hundred meters and plunged into a vertical chasm the width of the river. All that was visible of the falls from the veranda of the Victoria Falls Hotel, from which Janet and Craig started out after a late breakfast, were clouds of spray often reaching five hundred meters in height. The African name for the spectacle was *Mosi oa tunya*—the smoke of many thunders.

It was a good kilometer walk to the gorge, almost another two kilometers along the edge opposite the tumbling water. The un-commercialized beauty gave the illusion that civilization was miles away. On November 16, 1855, David Livingstone was the first white man to see the view. "Scenes so lovely must have been gazed upon by angels in their flight," he wrote in uncharacteristically flowery prose and christened the spot after Queen Victoria.

Rumbling thunder on their left, rain forest on their right, dense growth periodically opened into pristine clearings in which antelope grazed. Wild monkeys played in a nearby tree. Antelopes and monkeys had been there sixteen years before, but the present-day wildlife appeared somehow less vibrant to

Janet's eye.

Raincoats they had rented at the hotel protected them against sudden updrafts of steamy spray. The yellow slickers were reminiscent of the rubber coats Janet and Christopher had donned at the Van Hoon Deep Levels Mine. Less careful on their previous visit to the falls, Janet and Christopher had braved shifting mists without protection, getting exhilaratingly soaked. Christopher had hugged her on the edge of the precipice, while rainbows arched almost full circles. Craig obliged her with a protective hug as the two peered cautiously over the steep edge. None of it was the same.

She wasn't glad she had come. Thinking about the good times was too painful. Rather than blotting out those memories she reinforced them. Helpless comparisons emphasized all that was gone. She was just another tourist; before she had been more. At eighteen, Christopher had added an elusive magic.

"Does it bring back old memories?" Craig asked. It was undiplomatic question, but he couldn't know that.

"It's beautiful," Janet said noncommittally. They reached the end of the pathway and stood on another brink of the gorge. Around them, mist shot upward. Moisture tingled their skin with refreshing dampness. So many small birds darted on the updrafts that it was a miracle there were no collisions.

"Rainbow!" Craig said. The sun penetrated a drifting curtain of moisture, imposing a multicolored arc on the ethereal canvas.

There had been another morning on the edge of this precipice, another rainbow, another man who had taken her in his arms. There had been another kiss that was the chief reason Janet allowed this one. She was comparing again, when comparisons were unfair to Craig. His kisses wouldn't stand up to those received when she was thirteen and dewy-eyed with illusions of first love.

Craig wanted another kiss, but she shook her head sadly. He didn't press for an advantage. He was a gentleman—something Christopher had forgotten how to be somewhere along the line. Christopher would have persisted. He would have taken full advantage of their precarious perch, locking her in his arms, his mouth greedily drinking from the spray-splattered wetness of her lips.

She shook off those day dreams. Christopher wasn't here. She didn't want him here, but she missed him anyway.

"Still worried about using me?" Craig asked. There was a miraculous shift in the wind that bared a segment of pathway. The ground was damp, leaves glossy with moisture, but the sun was warm.

"Sometimes I get confused," Janet admitted, "about my feelings for Christopher." She hadn't intended to speak of him, especially to this near stranger, but Craig seemed sympathetic.

He answered her in a quiet reassuring voice. "He seems less confused about his feelings toward you," he said, pushing back a water-laden branch that bled liquid down his arm.

"Oh, he knows what he wants from me all right," Janet said, her voice dripping sarcasm. "However, you'll excuse me if I find it not in the least romantic."

"I see," Craig said. She wondered if he did.

"It seems to me," Janet said carefully, "that people these days jump into physical intimacy without considering any other kind—I mean without taking emotions into account. Not that I'm emotionally involved with Christopher," she hastened to add. "It's just that his standards of behavior are very different from my own. Do you see what I mean?"

"Sure, I understand," Craig answered. "Christopher's problem is that he comes from another world. The rich have their own morals. Most of us poor slobs are unhappy because we can't pay our bills, or build houses, or buy cars. Love makes our disappointments bearable. The rich don't have those everyday disappointments. Love is, therefore, less necessary as a panacea."

"To Christopher, money is paramount," Janet said sadly. "But money isn't everything, as the old cliché says."

"So why does everything else come in a distant second?" Craig asked, surprising her with his sentiment.

"You don't believe that!" Janet chided. A wispy veil of moisture shrouded them for seconds before releasing them to more sunshine.

"Sometimes I do," Craig admitted. "I find myself wishing I were in Christopher Van Hoon's shoes for a day to see what it's like to get the money, the power, the women." Was he thinking of her in particular, Janet wondered?

"Don't you dare wish such a thing on yourself!" she insisted. "You stay the way you are. There are too many emotional weaklings in the world—there's no call to wish you were one. Money makes a man believe everything is for sale. That simply isn't true."

The wet fog moved in. Cool drops of water seeped beneath the collar of Janet's slicker and trickled between her breasts. On the trail just ahead, a man sought momentary protection beneath the shelter of a tree. A persistent ray of sunlight illuminated his wet hair, converting blond to radiant gold. Janet thought it was Christopher. She expected him at every turn. He followed her to Great Zimbabwe. Why not to Victoria Falls? Her legs were weak. Her mind flashed memories: two kids drenched to the skin and futilely trying to escape the deluge beneath branches too wet to shelter them.

"It's not Christopher," Craig said, giving her hand a squeeze. It wasn't. It was a young man. Eighteen? There should have been a thirteen-year-old girl with him.

"A little wet!" the young man said. Janet was embarrassed—because she had been staring, because Craig had read her thoughts.

"More than a little wet," Janet amended, her laugh unreal to her ears.

"It's worth it, though, isn't it?" he said. He wasn't wearing a slicker. The muscles of his chest showed beneath his plastered shirt. Sixteen years before, Christopher's shirt had been the same way, and his pants. Now there was sexiness to the memory, even though Janet hadn't used that word in those days.

"Yes, it is worth it," Janet agreed. She looked away, fearing the boy might misconstrue the message in her eyes. The message wasn't for him. It was for someone who was a boy no longer. She gave Craig's arm a tug, and they moved on. "How did you know I thought he was Christopher?" she asked.

"He fooled me for a minute, too," Craig admitted. "I guess I've been expecting Christopher all along. He had a determined look last night. He's not the kind of man who gives up what he wants. Any idiot can see he wants you."

"He wants another acquisition," she said bitterly. It wasn't an easy admission. It was painful, humiliating. "I'm one more tomato in the supermarket." Craig laughed at the simile, and his laughter made Janet feel better. "Why are we spoiling the morning by talking about Christopher Van Hoon?" she asked incredulously, determined to shift the conversation. "I can't believe, with all this natural wonder around us, we're wasting our time on him."

"It sometimes helps to talk things out," Craig said.

"I'd rather not if you don't mind," She couldn't share her memories with anyone. Not yet.

"Then maybe you should at least talk to Christopher," Craig said. His suggestion surprised her. She was a little let down that he would surrender her to Christopher so easily. Craig read her disappointment. "Actually, that wasn't Craig Sylo, adviser to the lovelorn, you just heard," he commented. "It was a concerned naturalist who sees the possibility of Christopher's becoming a major force in animal preservation. That same naturalist sees a lady who might convert him." Janet wasn't sure she found that flattering, either. "I'm not for a minute suggesting you compromise yourself or your morals by encouraging Christopher in order to bribe him to join our cause," Craig said hurriedly. He was ahead of her every step of the way. "It's just that, whether or not you care to admit it, I sense electricity between you two that hints at something more lasting than an overnight roll in the hay. Why not use it for a good purpose?"

"You're imagining things!" Janet snapped.

"You know better than I do," Craig granted. After a pause, he qualified that with a, "Maybe."

"What's that supposed to mean?" Janet asked, piqued by the turn of the conversation.

"As a third party, I'm possibly more objective," Craig clarified.

"And possibly you're not!" Janet said with a finality she hoped ended the subject of Christopher Van Hoon once and for all. It didn't.

"He offered to talk about saving the animals," Craig reminded her. "That's a concession I doubt he's made to anyone before. Talking doesn't mean you have to go to bed with him, does it?" They walked in silence, taking the cutoff that led back to the hotel.

Christopher had offered, and Janet had let the offer slide by. If she were as concerned about animal preservation as she pretended, she would have swallowed her pride and jumped at the opening he'd given her.

"I can't blame you if you're skittish," Craig said, "especially if, as I suspect, you've been burned by Christopher before. He's a formidable opponent, no matter what the game. But you're not playing alone this time, Janet. I'm here—to talk if you want to talk, to run to if our friend finds it too difficult to take no for an answer."

She knew it was a reason to continue a relationship with Christopher, even if it wasn't the reason or the type of relationship she wanted. She didn't plan to go to bed with him, even if he offered the salvation of every last animal in Africa. But she could make him see his duty to keep alive a part of Africa—that was important. "I'm not promising anything," she said. They were some distance from the falls now, and she unsnapped her slicker. Craig helped her off with it.

She didn't see Christopher until he spoke. He was off the trail in the shade. Even in shadow, however, his hair glowed golden, his skin glowed bronze. "Fancy meeting you here," he said, stepping into the sunlight. Apollo in the sacred grove, Janet thought whimsically. He conspired with nature to make the day brighter, the greens greener, the browns browner.

After the false alarm on the trail, Janet wasn't expecting him. "Yes, I imagine you're very surprised," she said, glad her voice functioned on command. For a brief moment it had caught in her throat. "Especially since you knew we were here."

"You've caught me in that truth," he admitted with mock chagrin, "so there's no use continuing any attempt at ruse. Yes, I knew you were here. It was a case of the mountain not coming to Muhammad, so...." He shrugged his broad shoulders, letting Janet fill in the rest of the time-worn expression.

"I haven't the time nor the inclination to play your games this morning," she said, proud of her control. She derived strength from Craig beside her. "I'm here to see Victoria Falls with Captain Sylo. So if you'll excuse us...." She hooked her arm through Craig's. It wasn't only a signal for Christopher to leave. It was a bid for needed support.

"Haven't you already seen Victoria Falls with Captain Sylo?" Christopher asked. "Unless things have changed, the falls are that way, aren't they?" He nodded in the direction from which Janet and Craig had come.

"I'm sure you know what I mean," Janet said, not amused. "There's more to Victoria Falls than the falls."

"In truth, I felt it best to see you while Captain Sylo was standing guard," Christopher said. "Knowing you're afraid to talk with me alone—"

"I'm not afraid!" she interrupted him. It was a lie. What's more, she was wasting her breath trying to convince anyone otherwise.

"I figured you would he more comfortable with him in attendance," he completed his sentence.

"I don't need a bodyguard or a chaperon!" Janet snapped. He smiled. He had anticipated her response. She played mouse to his cat every time they met, and she hated the role.

"Then maybe he'll excuse us for a couple of minutes?" Christopher suggested. He hadn't missed the opening. "I promise not to keep you long."

She glanced nervously at Craig for help. "I could take the

slickers back to the hotel and wait for you there?" he proposed. He was no help at all! He was the sheep dog turning over his charge to the wolf from the woods. Janet's panic showed through. "Or maybe you'd rather put off discussions with Mr. Van Hoon until later," Craig offered quickly. "Maybe even indefinitely." It was the out she wanted. His initial response, she suspected, had come from their mutual concern for wildlife. Janet was their hope of persuading Christopher to join their side.

"I suppose I can spare Mr. Van Hoon a few minutes," she said reluctantly. Her heart beat faster. The sun was overly warm against her face "If you're sure you don't mind, Craig."

"You're sure *you* don't mind?" Craig double-checked. He was chivalrous to the last, thinking of her sensibilities. He wouldn't condemn her if she decided not to take the risk.

"This won't take long," Janet said, committing herself. She wanted Christopher converted to the cause. If she could bring him around—without compromising herself—she owed it to the dwindling animals of Africa to give it her best shot. However, she admitted to herself that her excitement had nothing to do with the possible salvation of any four-legged beast.

Slickers in hand, Craig diplomatically headed up the path toward the hotel. "I don't particularly care for that man," Christopher said when Craig rounded a bend in the trail and disappeared. Janet was furious at his unwarranted attack. The nerve!

"I don't find your dislike surprising," she said sardonically. "He's all that you're not—gentle, kind, courteous, caring."

"You think so?" Christopher asked. He was doubtful. Of course he was. Craig was strong, good-looking, and he stood between Christopher and what he wanted. "I'm a good judge of character," Christopher said. "I'm wrong sometimes, but seldom. I'd watch myself with Captain Craig Sylo if I were you."

"I can take care of myself, thank you!" Janet said, her voice trembling with anger. "If you're here to bad-mouth Craig behind his back, we can call our conversation quits as of this moment."

"I didn't come to bad-mouth Craig," Christopher said, taking her arm. He nudged her toward the falls.

"I can walk perfectly well on my own!" she said, jerking her arm away. "Or hadn't you noticed?" Her arm tingled where his fingers had been.

Christopher seemed to be somehow in mysterious communion with Mother Nature. The mist cleared before him, baring segments of path whipped by soaking spray seconds before. The falls emerged, unveiled and beautiful, sunlight enmeshing in the webs of fog to add the right touch of rainbow enchantment.

They passed Devil's Cataract and moved on to the ninety-three-meter-high Main Falls. Their view of the gorge was breathtaking. Across the way was Livingstone Island, where its namesake had canoed to peer over the lip of the chasm. When Janet and Craig had passed the spot, the rumble of the water had been a deafening thunder. Now the roar was muted, blown away with the spray.

"I haven't been here for sixteen years," Christopher said. Janet's heart rose to her throat and stayed there.

"That's a long time," she managed finally, hoping the thunder of the cascading water was loud enough to conceal the break in her voice.

Luckily, Christopher didn't notice. He was lost in his thoughts. "Every place a person visits becomes a backdrop for memories," he continued. "Memories good, bad, indifferent."

"And Victoria Falls?" Janet asked, wishing she were less curious. "What kind of memories does it hold?" What if he said bad ones?

"Good ones," Christopher said. "So good that I was reluctant to return today for fear that meeting you here might taint them."

Janet was simultaneously thrilled and heartbroken—thrilled that his memories were good, heartbroken that he thought her capable of damaging what her presence had conjured up sixteen years before. Good memories weren't easily destroyed. They held on tenaciously—sometimes for longer than a person wanted. Her good memories were still strong, further intensified by Christopher's nearness. Sixteen years seemed like yesterday.

"I came to Great Zimbabwe and to Victoria Falls to find you, because I felt something for you from beginning," he said. He folded his arms across his chest.

"What you feel is a desire for revenge," Janet said. She was familiar with the emotion. She had lived with it for years, although there was something about the present scene, about Christopher, that diminished that drive in her.

"Not just revenge," he contradicted, "although I wasn't too pleased to realize what you and your camera crew were up to."

"What do you mean, 'not just revenge'?"

"I'm not sure I know what I mean," Christopher admitted with a nervous laugh. "For a time, I wasn't sure I wanted to know, either."

"Something changed your mind?" Janet asked, her heart pounding, her throat dry despite the surrounding water.

"You were the catalyst who brought back memories of a time in my life I'd almost forgotten. Maybe it was your crusade against killing animals, or the way you looked so ridiculously sexy sliding down the banister at Lionspride. Maybe it was your name."

"Were you here with that other Janet, Christopher?" she asked, willing to face the danger inherent in what he might answer.

"Some memories aren't shared!" he said tersely. For him, she was a burglar caught in the act. He didn't know his memories were already hers. "Hell, why not share them?" he amended, which cut Janet to the quick. He was right in what he said about memories. He should no more expose precious times to her, thinking her a complete stranger, than Janet was willing to reveal them to Craig. She prayed for the mist, the gusting wind, the noise to shut out his words. "I've always felt guilty," Christopher said, plowing ahead. Janet couldn't stop him without running away or revealing her secret.

She did neither. She needed to hear him out. She wanted her ghosts put to rest, and maybe this was a solution. She doubted it, but nothing else had worked. "She was only thirteen,"

Christopher continued. "It made little difference that I was only five years older. She was vulnerable with childish thoughts. I was already a man."

He felt guilty? Oh, the silly fool! He was tormented because he thought he had taken advantage of a young girl. What he had done was to give her the happiest moments of her life.

"Oh, don't get me wrong!" he said quickly. He didn't know she was fully aware of how wonderfully harmless it had all been. "It wasn't anything deliberately sexual. No matter the playboy I became—" he gave a sad smile "—I assure you, I wasn't one at the time."

A faint gust of wind blew up from the gorge, baptizing them in a short-lived sprinkle of mist. There wasn't enough dampness to keep his hair down. Silky strands lifted to accept more haloing sunlight.

"I thought she would be around forever," he said. "This goes to prove I was as much a child as she was. I thought there would be plenty of time to sort out confusing emotions. As it turned out, there was only one summer—one very short wonderful summer. You'd think memories would pale after sixteen years, wouldn't you? You'd think remembering wouldn't be so easily triggered by meeting someone called Janet, long after the fact," he said. He faced her with an unexpectedly tender expression on his face. "I hated you for making me remember," he said simply. "I hated you, because I'm old enough to know there's no bringing back the past, and the memories made me want a return of that one summer of my childhood, although that other Janet wouldn't thank me for the replay."

He was wrong—even if she had come to Africa to erase the memories. "Somewhere there's a young woman, once thirteen, who's thanking you for that one cherished summer," she said.

He shook his head. He didn't believe her. Why should he? She had never left a clue, had cut him off without a word, without reading his letters. She had feared he was writing about how foolish he was to love her. She had mistaken him for a man who would recover more easily than she would. She had mistaken him for a man who was as glib about kisses and whispers of love as those men in Janet's life who came after. But at eighteen he had still been a boy in many ways. Would Christopher lie about love at eighteen when he refused to lie at thirty-four?

"I don't believe in love at first sight," he had told her. "I don't believe in love in two days' time, either."

"I loved her," he said, another gust of windy spray tousling his gilt-edged hair. "A few kisses, a few good times, a tragic end, and I loved her. I haven't loved anyone since. Maybe I did use the motive of revenge to rationalize my attempts to seduce you, but really I was hoping you could do more than trigger memories. You have the same name, the same coloring, the same need to condemn the slaughter of wildlife as she did. You slide down banisters as she did. If there's no reliving the past, there is the present, isn't there?"

"Yes," she admitted. He was right. She had come to the same conclusion. What was done was done. Fools spent lifetimes looking back, hoping for a return of the past. She'd been a fool.

Keep the good memories, she saw that now. Savor them. But they were so precious only because they were one of a kind, not to be lived again.

"I want to explore the present, Janet," he said. "I want to sort out whatever it is that draws me to you. I want to know if it's only memories of another Janet, or if I'm rediscovering feelings buried so long I can't remember them. I want a little of your time, not to maul you at every opportunity but to get to know you better. You needn't feel anything in return. You can go your way when your project at Great Zimbabwe is finished. I'll be satisfied with the inner knowledge that something vital inside of me didn't die when I was eighteen. That's not too much to ask if I behave like a gentleman, is it?"

She closed the space between them. She looked into the deep gold of his eyes and slid her hands around his hard waist. "No, it isn't," she said, her lips inviting his to kiss them.

"You won't regret your generosity, Janet," he said, touching her mouth in a tender exploration that recalled the joys of kissing when the experience was new and full of wonder. It was an exquisite resurrection of pleasure that left her hungry for more—much more—of the same. "You see, you needn't think I'll try to devour you like a beast at one sitting," he said.

He bent his head to offer a gentle kiss. Her mouth eagerly responded, her body molding itself closer to his. Her hands caressed the contours of his hard and muscled back.

The wind changed, hurling a curtain of spray over them. They didn't move, oblivious to everything but the ecstasy of the moment.

When they came apart, it was with mutual wonder at the miracle of pleasure enhanced by invisible bonds between them. For a moment, she had reclaimed her past, relived a moment of first love on the edge of the gorge.

She was happy.

He took her hand, laughing as he rushed with her to the shelter of sunshine beyond the enveloping mist. She ran with him, fleeing the premonition that such uninhibited innocence and childlike joy couldn't last.

* * * * * * *

"YOU DIDN'T TOSS him over the falls, did you?" Craig asked, greeting her return to the lobby of the Victoria Falls Hotel.

"No," Janet said, laughing. It had turned into a wonderful few moments! Her clothes, drenched during those final seconds on the lip of the gorge, had pretty much dried during her walk back. "Surprisingly, Mr. Van Hoon was downright civil."

"Is that the comment of someone trying to hide the blame for his disappearance?" Craig asked, making an exaggerated search of the area for Christopher.

"He's alive and well," Janet assured him in continuing good humor. She would have been on her way to the airport with Christopher if she hadn't been obligated to Craig. She wasn't the kind of woman who came to a party with one man and left with another, even if her escort probably didn't care. More to the point, she wanted a little time away from Christopher to analyze this new turn of events. It was so fantastically wonderful, and she couldn't believe it was true. Christopher was drawn to her without realizing he had known her before. There was a chance for them in the present, as there had been in the past. That was as frightening as it was exciting. Disaster was on the horizon. The gods wouldn't let her remain this blissfully happy for long. She knew from experience.

"So, how did it go?" Craig asked, walking back with her to the main door. Her meeting with Christopher put them behind schedule; it was time to leave. She had come to cancel memories, and she had ended up gathering a whole new beautiful bouquet of them.

It had gone better than she had hoped—even the part that interested Craig. "He said he'd have his people look into it," she said, running her hand through her damp hair to further dry it in the brilliant sunshine that greeted them. "They'll come up with the best way for him to help. He made no promises to follow through on any of their suggestions, mind you, and I didn't feel it wise to press him at this stage of the game. But he seemed receptive."

"I'm glad for the wildlife he'll be helping," Craig said, signaling for a cab.

"So am I," Janet said. Craig didn't know how glad.

The airstrip was a short drive from the hotel. Christopher had taken off in his private plane by the time they got there. Within minutes, they were in the air and circling the falls for a final goodbye. The deep scar on the earth boiled its puffs of ominous white-to-gray spray.

Craig flew upriver to where a group of hippos wallowed in deep clear water, visible like submarines. He veered southeast for Great Zimbabwe.

They didn't talk much, Craig occasionally pointing out buffalo, kudu, and waterbuck on the landscape below. It was after they had left Victoria Falls miles behind, farmland heralding their approach to Great Zimbabwe, that Craig inadvertently dropped his little bomb. Janet didn't miss the irony, either. After all, Craig was chiefly responsible for Christopher and her making a new beginning at the falls.

"Damn!" Craig said, priming the explosion. He shook his head, and for a moment Janet thought something was wrong with the plane. "Sorry," he said, seeing her worried expression. "I didn't mean to disturb your snooze."

"Actually, I was just resting my eyes," Janet confessed. She had feigned sleep, because she preferred savoring her recent memories of Christopher in silence. It didn't look or sound as if there was any problem with the aircraft.

"I'll check with Christopher's people when I get back to Great Zimbabwe, but it would have been better for me to talk with Christopher in private," Craig said.

"Talking to him about what?" Janet asked. Craig wouldn't likely have brought the subject up if it was a purely personal matter.

"'I need to know where his people are off to tomorrow," Craig said. Alarm bells went off in Janet's head. Somehow this sounded like a warning—and she didn't want to know what she was being warned of. "They're supposed to file daily reports," Craig continued, "but they've been straying from their official projections as of late. I'm technically responsible for everyone's safety, including theirs. It's difficult when I don't know where they are. Poachers aren't above killing men as well as beasts."

"Christopher's *people*?" Janet asked. The term he'd used came off as a strange one. There were Craig's people, and there were government people at Great Zimbabwe. Even her people were probably there by now. But Christopher's people?

"His work team," Craig said. "I'm sorry. I thought he would have told you. I thought that's what you meant when you said his people would be looking into 'it.'" Noticing Janet's blank expression, he elucidated, "From V.H.A.M." He pronounced V.H.A.M. to rhyme with WHAM, leaving Janet confused—until the implication became clear.

"Van Hoon Afrikaner Minerals has a work team at Great Zimbabwe?" she asked, a chill creeping over her. There had been a team with her father's party, too, although that was more undercover than this one apparently was. There was a V.H.A.M. team at Great Zimbabwe, and that's why Christopher was there. Oh, what a fool she was! He hadn't chased her. As usual, his actions had been profit-motivated. He was doing business, taking advantage of the coincidence that had her there, too. He had sensed how close she had been to surrendering to him in Johannesburg, and he had decided to use a more subtle approach. It had fooled her. How he must have enjoyed the success of his little speech about childhood memories, so expertly delivered on the brink of the gorge. No woman, not even Janet, could resist an admission of vulnerability by he-man Christopher Van Hoon against such a stirring backdrop.

"What exactly is this team from V.H.A.M. doing?" Janet asked. The question was superfluous, she realized. They were out for something in the ground that could be removed and sold for a profit. They were after the same thing that they had wanted—and had found—on the property that had been slated for the Lackland Animal Preserve.

"Gold," Craig said. The chilling of Janet's blood was complete. "The area around Great Zimbabwe is riddled with old workings," he continued. "The economy of Great Zimbabwe was once based on the gold trade, remember."

"And the city was left to ruin when the gold sources dried up," Janet recalled. She had done her homework.

"They couldn't get it all out with their primitive techniques," Craig said. "Taking into account modern methods and higher gold prices, V.H.A.M. is checking out the possibilities."

"What happens to what's left of the Great Zimbabwe Reserve if and when V.H.A.M. finds gold there?" Janet asked.

"The same thing that happens whenever the prerogatives of men take precedence over the prerogatives of animals," Craig said. "It will go industrial, too. But I thought Van Hoon was reconsidering, Janet. Wasn't that the point of your discussion at the falls?"

"It's obvious he was just soft-soaping me," Janet replied grimly. The nightmare was starting over. Last time, it had been the Lackland Preserve. Her father had died of a heart attack after that failure. Well, Janet's heart was sound, no matter how much Christopher's betrayal pained her at the moment. She wasn't going to take this sitting down, although she was probably as powerless in the face of the Van Hoon resolve as her father had been.

"It's not just Christopher and V.H.A.M., Janet," Craig reminded her. "If it were that simple, we'd have a fighting chance. All third-world countries are striving to advantage the twentieth-first century but are finding the entrance fee damned expensive. Gold is better currency than wildlife—an unfortunate fact of life. Our best weapons are cooperation and compromise. Surrender a piece of land here—better protect a piece elsewhere."

"And when gold, or something else, is discovered in those places elsewhere?" Janet asked cynically. "I'll tell you what happens. Goodbye to that land and those animals, too—that's what!"

"There is land that is unsuitable for mining, farming or settling," Craig remarked.

"And not fit for animals, either, I'll bet you!" Janet said, angry that Craig was giving her these arguments. They were more what she expected from Christopher.

"There has to be cooperation and compromise, Janet," Craig repeated. "That's the only way, believe me. That's why it's important to persuade men like Christopher to join us. They have the clout to deal successfully with their own kind. Without them, the animals don't have a chance."

"Animals bring in tourist dollars," Janet argued.

"Granted," Craig conceded, calm and objective, "and how much do you suppose Wankie and Kruger bring in a day, combined? On the other hand, how much is brought in daily by one of the Van Hoon gold mines?"

"Something in the order of eleven-million rand a month," Christopher had boasted at the Van Hoon Deep Levels Mine. She could imagine what that must round off to per day.

"How can you be so complacent?" Janet demanded, striking out at Craig because Christopher wasn't handy.

"Because I saw the writing on the wall a long time ago," Craig said. "I saw my father's anguish as he watched an area of nineteen thousand square kilometers dwindle to what little there is of the Great Zimbabwe Reserve today. He wasn't for compromise, either, and what did it get him? If one way doesn't work, we have to be flexible enough to try another. It's not doing the animals any good when marvelously intentioned people fight like hell for a losing cause. As for V.H.A.M., I'd rather they found gold here than at Wankie or Kruger."

Well, Janet had seen the proposed acreage for Lackland go for mining, had seen how that decision affected her father. That didn't lull her into complacency—quite the contrary. She was more determined than ever to fight.

"We've lost too many battles by beating our heads against brick walls, Janet," Craig said.

"I hate Christopher Van Hoon!" Janet said. "I hate what he and others like him are doing—not only in Africa but elsewhere."

"Don't lose this chance to win him over, Janet," Craig pleaded.

She wasn't moved. This wasn't just about saving animals. Christopher had lied to her. He had used her, had tricked her into believing the present had possibilities to rival the past. She couldn't forgive that. "He's beyond helping us!" Janet said with finality. "He's beyond helping himself!" Vincent would be proud of the creature he had created.

"I'm sorry to hear that you feel that way," Craig said. Maybe he now regretted letting out the information about the V.H.A.M. team, but Janet would have found out, even if left on her own. Her relationship with Christopher had been a bonus for Craig to explore. Nothing ventured, nothing gained.

Janet was not surprised at Craig's sudden diplomatic silence. She shut her eyes, trying to tell herself Christopher's lies didn't hurt.

"Our stomping grounds," Craig said, announcing the appearance of Lake Kyle on the horizon. This time they put the lake on their left behind them. Vultures still flew in lazy circles in the distance.

The plane touched down on the dirt road. It wasn't as scary as the first time. A person's system adjusted to certain things quickly, and to other things not at all, Janet reflected.

Christopher had landed at Fort Victoria, probably gloating over how he had pulled the wool over her eyes. Or maybe he had beaten them to Great Zimbabwe and was waiting.

It was the members of her camera crew who were waiting. "We're ready for work whenever you get back from sight-seeing," said the note slipped under her door. "I'm in Room 24. Where are you?" It was signed, "Roger."

There was no time like the present to begin some hard work. She needed the distraction it offered. She was in bad shape after her betrayal by Christopher at Victoria Falls. She went to Room 24 and knocked.

"Can it be our boss?" Roger asked in mock wonder "Come on in, stranger" He stepped back to let her enter. Tim and Jill were inside, sitting on the bed.

"I could swear you said you were anxious to get to Great Zimbabwe," Tim said, his voice bubbling over with amusement. "Was it really Victoria Falls you said you were anxious to see?"

"Did you take a commercial flight?" Jill asked gleefully. "Or did you utilize the volunteered services of our favorite pilot, Captain Sylo?"

"Vacation is over, people!" Janet said, not bothering with answers. They had obviously asked around when they arrived. They knew who she had flown off with before dawn. "As soon as you get your things, we've shooting to do in the field."

Dr. Nhari had arranged for a guide and Land Rover the night before. He had stopped by Janet's room after learning she wasn't feeling up to supper. When he knocked, Janet had thought he was Christopher, and she almost hadn't let him in.

She left Roger, Tim, and Jill to get organized on short notice, then went to the hotel office to ask for Arusha, the guide Dr. Nhari had promised. Arusha arrived in the Land Rover a few minutes after the corporal on the switchboard put through Janet's call. Arusha was a middle-aged black man with pleasantly nondescript features and short-cropped hair. He spoke fairly fluent English with a clipped British accent.

Their gear loaded, they headed out, stopping at the military encampment to report their intended movements to Craig. Craig instructed them to turn around at the first sign of anything suspicious. While he doubted the poachers would strike so close so soon after their brazen slaughter of the seven elephants, it was hard to second-guess them. They were dangerous if surprised in the middle of an operation. More than one inadvertent witness was dead to prove it. Craig added bitterly that the poachers probably knew where the camera crew was headed anyway and would steer clear.

The captain does look mighty good, doesn't he?" Jill said as soon as Craig was out of hearing.

Janet didn't bother to reply.

* * * * * * *

VIEWED A THIRD TIME by Janet, the scene at the waterhole lost some of its shock value. There were fewer birds, and the elephant carcasses were quickly deteriorating.

Jill, though, seeing it for the first time, got sick, hardly clearing the Land Rover in time. Janet ended up applying her own last-minute makeup.

"Shoot it all," Janet instructed, not mentioning the fact that she hadn't been nearly as calm the last time. "Some of it might come across strong, but we can edit later." She took up a position in front of one mountain of birds. The vultures were as jaded to her presence as she was to theirs. They hardly stirred.

"These are seven of the ever dwindling population of elephants in Zimbabwe," she said as the cameras rolled. "Not a very pretty picture but one becoming more common every day. The current round of killing has increased with the skyrocketing value of ivory over the past five years. The elephant—largest of the land mammals—might not survive. Out of the millions that once roamed this continent, there are less than one and a half million left—a number that present-day poachers are depleting by fifty thousand to one hundred thousand each year. A single pair of tusks can bring in thousands of dollars. Natives, earning less than a thousand dollars a year, are easily persuaded to supplement low incomes by killing elephants for ivory. But poachers aren't just individuals. More and more, they're highly organized groups, killing with poisons, snares, guns—even rockets. These seven elephants were mowed down by machine-guns." On cue, Arusha fired his rifle and theatrically sent the vultures skyward.

The wind changed, subjecting everyone to the stench that had escaped them until then. Jill was sick again, and Janet almost joined her. Masquerading behind facades of male bravura, even Roger and Tim looked green. No one complained when Janet wrapped the session.

She wasn't entirely through shooting, though. There was something she wanted before getting caught up in the everyday activities of the government work team. "Arusha, can you locate Melissa and Suzy for us?" she asked. She had watched for the two rhinos on the trip in and had seen no sign of them. She feared they had met the same fate as the seven elephants, although there were no new vulture swirls blackening the sky.

"Maybe," Arusha said. "I can try." He expertly maneuvered the Land Rover through the gauntlet of acacias and left the dead elephants and the bloody water behind.

"Who are Melissa and Suzy?" Roger asked. Jill wasn't asking any questions. Janet felt guilty about not warning the other woman about what to expect. She had been too engrossed in eradicating thoughts of Christopher to pay attention to Jill's sensibilities—which was a good sign that priorities were screwed. The members of her crew were her friends. She should be thinking of their welfare, not of Christopher, who was the enemy.

"Jill, are you okay?" Janet asked before answering Roger.

"Okay? No! Better? A little," Jill said, leaning her head against Tim's supportive shoulder. Janet turned to Roger.

"They're rhinos," she said. "Two of them. One has the longest horns I've seen outside of the Van Hoon trophy room. Craig says it's only a matter of time before the poachers get them."

"Planning before-and-after shots, are you?" Roger asked with all the acumen of a cameraman analyzing the possibilities of a story. The comment was cold-blooded, but Roger was being more objective and professional than Janet at the moment. Janet was disturbed by the thought that he might be right. Maybe she was setting the animals up for before-and-after shots. It would be dramatic to show rhinos peacefully grazing one minute and gruesomely dead and dehorned by poachers the next. Janet's blood chilled. She didn't want Melissa and Suzy dead. She was overjoyed when Arusha spotted the two animals among the trees. She had been heartbroken as a child when the rhino calf had died at the Seattle Zoo. She would be heartbroken if this calf died tragically in the wild. Since there were fewer rhinos now than when Janet had fought vainly as a girl to save the one born in captivity, Suzy's death would be even more poignant.

Roger and Tim were delighted at the opportunity to turn their cameras on Melissa and her calf. Jill, who didn't need to prepare either rhino with makeup, watched nervously as Roger and Tim carried portable cameras within a few feet of mother and child.

"You sure they're tame?" Roger joked, preparing to move closer.

"Don't believe it!" Janet warned. "You try anything funny, and I'll get you if the rhinos don't." Roger, who had enough experience with wildlife to have a great deal of respect for it, wasn't about to try anything funny. If Melissa and Suzy were docile at the moment that could change at any time. Rhinos weren't known for their cheery dispositions, and a mother with a calf to protect wouldn't stand for much nonsense.

Janet wished Melissa was less obliging, despite the fantastic shots Roger and Tim were getting. The cameramen might be poachers carrying guns, for all the rhinos knew. It wasn't good for them to become accustomed to men. That's what had happened to the two big-horned rhinos in Amboseli. So many tourists had flocked to see them at close range that the rhinos weren't in the least concerned when a few more men moved in to blow them away. "I think that's plenty of footage, you guys!" Janet called as soon as Roger and Tim were out of immediate danger. The idea that because of this kind of exposure, Melissa and Suzy might allow poachers to sneak up more easily didn't leave a pleasant taste in Janet's mouth.

They headed back to camp, stopping at Craig's tent to let him know they'd returned. Craig reported on Christopher without Janet's asking. "He went out with one of his team," Craig said. "There's a site close by that warranted a check."

"What he does is no concern of mine!" Janet said with finality.

"Want me to offer moral support at supper?" Craig volunteered, changing the subject without really changing it.

"That scene at the waterhole still kills my appetite," Janet said. "I'll skip supper tonight, thank you."

"You skipped supper last night," he reminded her. You didn't eat a big breakfast this morning. We missed out on lunch. I wouldn't skip too many meals if I were you." He knew as well as she did that she wasn't missing this meal because she was a little queasy. She needed to get her thoughts together. She didn't want to give vent to impulsive anger in front of Christopher, which she was going to do if she didn't retreat from things for a while to calm herself down a bit.

"I'll be back to normal tomorrow," Janet promised. It was a promise she doubted she could keep. After Victoria Falls, she would never be back to normal.

"Well, if you change your mind, have the front desk ring my tent. I'll willingly play escort."

"Thanks, Craig—really," Janet said, once again wishing she

could respond to him the way she would have liked.

"And you're off tomorrow morning with Dr. Nhari, right?"

"He's filed his report, has he?" Janet asked.

"He's always good about it," Craig admitted. "That is more than I can say for the men working for someone else we know."

"What are the chances that the informer sees those reports, too?" Janet asked. It was a logical question, although she was sure Craig must have thought of it before she'd brought it to his attention. She was right.

"The reports are never out of my sight," he assured her. "They go in a safe to which only I have the combination."

"Maybe the poachers *have* just been lucky up until now," Janet said, suggesting that alternative. She couldn't fault Craig for lack of caution.

"No one can be *that* lucky," he said. "And I promise you, I intend to find out how they manage it, if it's the last thing I do." He slapped the door of the Land Rover emphatically in emphasis. It was also Arusha's signal to move on. Janet silently wished Craig luck. She didn't want to cover another slaughter, no matter how well the footage emphasized how animals were being butchered to the brink of extinction.

"Who's out with one of his team checking on a nearby site?" Jill asked. Either she was on her way to recovering from the scene at the waterhole, or her curiosity conquered all. Janet suspected the latter.

"Christopher Van Hoon is here," Janet said. "There was no need to make a secret of something she couldn't keep under wraps for long.

"You don't say?" Jill and Roger chimed in unison. Tim smiled at their impromptu response.

"A team from Van Hoon Afrikaner Minerals is checking out the possibility of redeveloping mine sites left from the gold drain of a few centuries ago," Janet explained. Her friends would accept Christopher's lies about coming all this distance to see her if she told them. Damn, she wished she could!

"He's here for gold, is he?" Roger said, flashing a don't-feed-me-that smile.

"Yes, gold!" Janet emphasized: "Mr. Van Hoon's main interest in life is profits, whether any of you choose to believe that or not."

"I do see your predicament," Jill said, ignoring everything Janet had said. "Craig and Christopher are a bit too much of a good thing to deal with at one time, aren't they?"

"I'm so pleased your recent bout of sickness hasn't damaged your sense of the absurd," Janet said with no trace of amusement. Arusha stopped the Land Rover in the hotel parking lot.

"What time are we out tomorrow, Janet?" Roger asked, deciding it was best to change the subject.

Janet told him, thankful the teasing had stopped. It was painful knowing that everything that they playfully hinted at was what she wanted to be true. They couldn't know that, but it still hurt. "Arusha will see that the Land Rover is out front before breakfast, so you can load before or after you eat. Any questions?" Thankfully there weren't any. "If you think of anything later, I'll be in my room, although I do plan to make an early night of it. I've a splitting headache."

"Is that what we tell Christopher if he asks?" Jill asked with a wide smile. She was clearly feeling much better. "That you have a headache? Not very original, Janet!" She giggled, and Janet was hard put to control her temper.

"Yes, that's what you tell him," Janet said, knowing Christopher would ask. She had agreed earlier to eat supper with him. He would wonder why she had changed her mind. It might even be better if she left a written message for him. She didn't want him on her doorstep for explanations that evening. She couldn't handle any confrontations with him until she had had time to get her thoughts and emotions in order.

She wrote him a note in her room, saying the day had taken more out of her than she had bargained for. That was an understatement! She said she had taken her crew to the waterhole, and that hadn't left her feeling well, either. She had decided on bed instead of eating. She hoped he understood.

The officer on duty at the front desk assured her that Mr. Van Hoon would get the message.

She returned to her room and put on her pajamas. Washing them free of perfume was the first thing she had done after unpacking the night before. She had thrown the black silk negligee in the wastepaper basket. If the maid had rescued it, she was welcome to it.

At first, Janet couldn't sleep, anticipating Christopher's knock. When she finally dozed, it was to enter a restless dream world in which she desperately searched endless rooms and hallways, looking for something very valuable that she'd lost.

CHAPTER EIGHT

JANET'S HEART STOPPED. When it started again, its wild thumping battered painfully against her rib cage.

Christopher stood in the door of the restaurant, the gaze of his black-flecked golden eyes sweeping the room. Displaying a wide smile, he spotted Janet and headed toward her.

Her hopes of reprieve vanished. For a short while, she had thought she would get to finish her breakfast and leave with the government team before Christopher's arrival. She should have known better. The fates never gave her any breaks, and they weren't starting now.

"Hi!" he said cheerily, joining her in the corner booth she had chosen for its inconspicuousness. "Feeling better?"

She had slept horribly, her attempts at rest disturbed by haunting nightmares. She was torn apart by what had brought him to Great Zimbabwe, and she hadn't recovered from the shock of losing all hope for happy tomorrows. "I was just leaving," she said. That wasn't what she had planned to say. She had planned painful accusations. Suddenly, though, she didn't have the willpower to go through with them. She needed more time. She should have skipped breakfast, but she was hungry from missing lunch and supper the day before.

"Oh, stay for a couple of minutes more," he cajoled, reaching for the menu. "It looks as if your teammates are taking care of everything outside. Why be the big cheese if you can't delegate authority on occasion?"

"Really, I have to go," she said, starting to stand up. It wasn't any physical move on his part that caused her to sink back into her seat, other than his pained expression. He put the menu aside, no longer interested in it.

"There's something wrong, isn't there?" he said. How very perceptive!

"I don't want to go into it right now," she said. He wouldn't let it go at that.

"No, I see you don't," he observed dryly. "But I do. I thought we were off to a fresh start. Why the change? Did your friend, Captain Sylo, do some bad-mouthing on your flight back yesterday? Was that the reason you skipped supper last night and are running scared this morning?"

"Don't blame Craig for any of this!" she said angrily. "He tried his best to make me see your good points."

Christopher settled back in his seat and folded his strong arms across his chest. Not many hours ago, she had been in those strong arms, had felt their sensuous embrace as he kissed her breath away. How cruel life was. "Why do I find the thought of Captain Sylo championing my romantic interests so unbelievable?" he asked sarcastically.

"Why shouldn't he?" Janet wanted to know. "He wants you on the side of wildlife as much as I do. He thinks I can persuade you."

"Do you find it flattering that he's willing to foist you off on another man for the sake of a few animals?" Christopher baited her. "I wouldn't give you up for that cause or for any other. I'm suspicious of any man who claims he could."

Janet was torn between feeling flattered by his compliment and feeling disgusted by his disdain for the cause to which she and Craig hoped to convert him. "I didn't need Craig to tell me what really brought you to Great Zimbabwe," she said, fighting for self-control. She didn't want to become hysterical. She wanted to put her case to him, and she wanted him to come up with excuses to make her doubts disappear once and for all. Unfortunately, not even the Great Van Hoon was that extraordinary a magician! "You're part of a Van Hoon Afrikaner Minerals work team." She was challenging him to deny it.

"That didn't bother you yesterday," he said. He wasn't denying anything. He was condemning her violation of their verbal truce.

"I didn't know it yesterday!"

"Captain Sylo told you on the plane ride home, did he?" Christopher asked, a mocking grin twisting his usually handsome features.

"There's no point in trying to discuss this!" she said, standing up.

"Sit down!" he commanded, the power behind his words in no way diminished by the low timbre of his voice. She hesitated. She didn't like him ordering her around. She had a will of her own. She wasn't a puppet on strings, getting up and sitting down whenever he wanted. "Please, sit down," he amended softly.

She sat. Her legs wouldn't support her anyway. "When Craig mentioned the V.H.A.M. team, he thought I knew," she said with a defeated sigh. "So don't blame him."

"You did know," he insisted. He lifted his right hand to stop her interruption. "I told you over supper at Lionspride."

"You did not!" she protested. He was always trying to put the blame on her.

The waiter appeared, and Christopher impatiently waved him off. "Why else would I have been here a couple of months ago?" Christopher challenged. His eyes sparked golden fire.

"How should I know?" Janet replied, frustrated. "You said nothing about a V.H.A.M. team." This was true. But he had insinuated as much over supper at Lionspride when mentioning his visit to the ruins, Janet now recalled. Great Zimbabwe had been cordoned off for months because of the poaching and the proposed elephant transfer. Christopher's connections might have gotten him special permission to play tourist, but it was more likely his presence was authorized because of other reasons—such as researching the possibilities of converting old gold mines into new for government—and Van Hoon—profits. Janet hadn't put two and two together fast enough, which left her arguments less forceful than they might have been.

"Yesterday I thought you intelligent enough to see how I used the presence of my team here as a convenient excuse to join you," Christopher said. "It was the excuse my ego demanded if you didn't believe the truth and left me feeling like a fool for running after you. I could tell myself I really came to look in on business. But damn it, I didn't come for business! And you have no right to make a turnabout at this late date and make me lie to myself or to you that I did."

"I don't believe you. And now I'm sorry I was too busy wanting to believe you to think clearly," she said bitterly. She hated the ease with which he always came out on top. "I would like more than anything to pretend it doesn't make any difference that your men are out digging for evidence that will convert this land into one massive landscape of mine tailings. But I'm here to save wildlife, and you're here to destroy it. I can't stand the idea of this becoming another Lackland."

"What about Lackland?" Christopher asked, his eyes darkening with suspicion.

Had he finally guessed who she was? She should have told him, not betrayed her secret like this. But she still felt he wouldn't forgive her for a thirteen-year-old girl's apparent rejection of his well intentioned love. "You told me at the Van Hoon Deep Levels that the mine was built on the frustrated plans of that animal preserve, remember?" she said, desperate to cover her trail. "You boasted about it in fact."

"And that's what you think is happening here?" Christopher asked. "That's the fear that made you go from hot to cold overnight?"

"I can't help my convictions," Janet said. It wasn't an apology, either. "I've had them a good deal longer than I've known you." She had nursed the dying rhino at the Seattle Zoo before she came to Africa for that long-ago fateful summer. "And I can't imagine even you respecting me for dumping them on such short notice just because you want me to."

"Damn it!" he said. He gripped the edge of the table and

pushed himself deeper into his seat, scrutinizing her carefully. He was going to get up. He was going to leave. It was the final goodbye of all their goodbyes. "Why did this have to happen?" he asked, shaking his head in disbelief. "Can you give me the answer to that? I would appreciate hearing it." He released the table, leaning across it. "It is happening, though, isn't it— another conflict of interest, shall we say? I'm stuck with that, aren't I? So if I make an ass of myself, at least I can rationalize that an occasional failure builds character, can't I? You might remember that axiom, too, Janet. It's not healthy to insist upon winning all the time. In fact, life is full of compromises." Janet wondered how many times Christopher had been defeated or forced into giving way an inch. "Are you following this, Janet?" he asked.

She knew what he was saying. She wanted to believe that he cared enough about her to be upset at the thought of their being at cross-purposes. But wanting to believe and believing weren't the same thing. "No?" he challenged her. "Then at least follow this much. Our efforts indicate there's no profit to be made from reopening these old mines. I'm not saying we won't come up with something yet. I'm telling you what we've got so far. So for the present you're battling a boogeyman that isn't there. That's a waste of effort, don't you think?" He reached for her hands, resting nervously on the tabletop, and squeezed them. She didn't pull away. She wanted the reassurance he was giving. "Janet. Janet, Janet," he chanted. The way her name sounded on his lips sent shivers of pleasure along her spine. "Why make life more complicated than it is? If my team turns up a bonanza of gold in the next couple of days, can't we deal with that when it happens? There are too many constructive things we could be doing in the meantime—getting to know each other better, for one. Don't you want that? I thought you did yesterday. Was I wrong?"

"Hey, you two!" Janet and Christopher were so engrossed that Roger had reached the table without their noticing. Janet was startled, and quickly attempted to pull her hands free of Christopher's strong fingers. Christopher refused to let go, however. A glass of water almost tipped over during the momentary tug of-war. "We're moving out," Roger announced, flashing an I-hate-to-bother-you-two-love-birds smile.

"Fine," Christopher said, unfazed by Janet's embarrassment. "We'll be along in a minute. Oh, yes, Janet will be riding with me for the first few miles. Right, Janet?" As usual, he caught her off guard. She had expected to use the next couple of hours to carefully analyze all he had said to assure herself that it made as much sense as she thought it did. "I have an old mine site to check out in the direction your group is headed," Christopher explained. "I've arranged to tag along part of the way—something about safety in numbers."

"Oh," Janet said, wishing she had something else to say. She was on an emotional roller coaster. She went from the depths of despair one moment to the heights of ecstasy the next. She was definitely on an upswing now.

Roger didn't stick around for Janet's confirmation, already out the door to tell Tim and Jill the latest development. He had done the same thing at Lionspride when Christopher had told him Janet was staying for supper. This time, however, Janet didn't mind as much. She would find time to herself later. She would methodically go over all of this. She was enjoying this latest turn of events while she could. Heaven only knew what waited around the next perilous corner.

"Ready?" Christopher asked, coming to his feet without releasing her hands.

"Yes." she said, standing. She wasn't angry with him any longer. She was angry with herself for not getting things out in the open the night before. She could have saved herself a night of tossing, turning, and worry.

They followed Roger outside to the official caravan. As head of the government research team, Dr. Jom Nhari was in the first Land Rover with three associates. Dr. Nhari was one of the Shona tribe, whose forefathers were thought to have built the city of Great Zimbabwe. His ancestors had walked the land when there had been nothing but themselves, the wildlife and the uncivilized landscape. Dr. Nhari had two degrees from Oxford and could hold his own in any intellectual circle. However, he hadn't lost sight of his roots. He had been one of the first exiles to return to Zimbabwe after the revolution, bypassing far more prestigious jobs to join the Department of National Parks and Wildlife Management. Even then he had balked at any cushy desk job, preferring to spend his time in the field. He, unlike Christopher, saw the importance of insuring that wildlife remained part of the African heritage.

In the second Land Rover were two more of Dr. Nhari's assistants and the tagging equipment. Arusha was driving. Roger, Tim and Jill, all grinning from ear to ear, were in the third vehicle, Roger behind the wheel.

As soon as Janet and Christopher appeared, the cars started up. Christopher's Land Rover brought up the rear as the expedition took to the dirt road. At the military encampment, two armed soldiers joined the party. Craig didn't make an appearance. He knew where everyone was going. Christopher and Dr. Nhari had dutifully filed reports the night before.

The ruins of the Great Enclosure were a ring of blackness in the morning twilight, exuding a special aura of enchantment. The ruins on the Acropolis were undefined among the shadows still shrouding the hilltop. A two-man helicopter lifted from a spot among the nearby trees, its lights preceding the caravan into the gradually diminishing darkness.

Fifteen to twenty elephants had been spotted the previous afternoon, and it was those animals that concerned the team today. A radio transmitter would be attached to one of the elephants, making the whole herd easier to locate in the future. This method of marking, already used on several elephant groups, monitored herd movements. Knowing where the elephants were at any given time allowed the research team to return later for more detailed counting and the final transporting to Wankie.

Any interruptions of a signal, or its too-long transmission

from the same place, warned of a possibly dead elephant. Daily checks from the air were run on all "bugged" herds in hopes of keeping poachers in check, but the method wasn't foolproof. Time and expense prohibited the team from affixing transmitting devices to every elephant, and poachers had no trouble spotting those animals wearing them. By leaving a marked animal alone, but killing its unmarked companions, poachers could remain undetected on government monitoring devices.

The dawn broke in the east, splashing pale yellows across the horizon. The tip of the sun appeared through a break in the distant trees. "Beautiful!" Christopher said. He wasn't looking at the sunrise but at Janet.

"Flattery will get you nowhere," she said, nonetheless pleased by his compliment. The only thing making the morning less than perfect was the presence of his high-powered rifle.

"I'm not the only one in the group with a weapon," Christopher reminded her. Just by looking at her, he seemed to be able to tell what she was thinking. "It doesn't mean I'm hell-bent on killing every helpless animal I see. It means I have protection against the men who might not like me nosing around."

"I know that," Janet said. Christopher had more than enough money. She didn't envision him stalking animals on the game reserve when there were spots in Africa where he could legally hunt most animals, elephants included, by paying across the table.

The next couple of hours were wonderful. The presence of the gun continued to disturb her, so Janet blanked out the thought of it. Her immediate concern was saving elephants, and his rifle wouldn't be used for killing any of them—not here anyway.

She and Christopher didn't keep up a running conversation, which was more relaxing than making the attempt. Only people uncomfortable with each other tried to fill every silence. If Janet wasn't completely at ease, she wasn't in her usual state of panic, either. It helped that Christopher was being less aggressive these days. At the falls, it had been Janet who had initiated the kiss on the edge of the gorge. It had been Janet who had ended it. If she could continue at her own speed, there was a chance they might discover the joys of a meaningful relationship. Not that Janet was holding her breath. She had been dealt too many blows in the past to hold out much hope for Christopher's becoming a major part of her future. But she was learning to seize the pleasures of the moment. Riding with Christopher, his hair catching the morning light, was definitely a pleasure. He looked more at home than at Lionspride, or decked out in gear for a descent into the mine.

The morning became more wondrous once they had sighted Melissa and Suzy in a distant patch of underbrush. Each day that those rhinos survived in the wild was an occasion for celebration.

They spotted giraffes, buffalo, and zebras. Some species were holding on, no matter how fragile the thread.

"Without something to do, I would spend my days mooning around, waiting for you to return from your daily jaunts to save the animals in the bush," Christopher said with a smile. "I'd be miserably bored."

That was his rationalization for his daily treks in search of gold, but Janet wanted none of it. "I'm sure we could find you something more worthwhile with the research team," she said. "Working with animals would give you a better understanding of what some very concerned people are trying to achieve."

"Touché!" he said, his golden eyes flashing sunlight, his grin warm with amusement. She wanted him to volunteer his services. She wasn't above that daydream. She knew, though, that reality was a different ballgame. She was content—for the moment—to leave things as they were. If Christopher gave her half a chance, she would win him over to her side. There was more chance of that now than there had been only twenty-four hours earlier. That was enough triumph to savor at the moment. Any journey was made one small step at a time.

The Land Rovers stopped. Dr. Nhari got out and came back to them. He had shining black eyes set in a charcoal-colored face. "The helicopter pilot has spotted the herd among the trees up ahead," he said. Janet saw no sign of elephants, but she heard the distant drone of helicopter rotors. "He's singling out an elephant now for darting," Dr. Nhari continued. A special hypodermic would be shot from the helicopter once the animal was sufficiently isolated from the herd. The team would move in as soon as the drug took effect.

"Dr. Nhari," one of the doctor's associates called from the front vehicle, "it's about to clear the tree cover!"

"We'll be moving out shortly," Dr. Nhari informed them, heading back to take the binoculars held by his assistant.

"That's my signal to leave you, I guess," Janet said, sliding out of her seat. She didn't want to leave Christopher. She didn't want him to leave her. Their drive had been so enjoyable; she hated to see it end.

"Why not skip this tagging?" Christopher suggested. "Your crew can handle it on its own. They're professionals. They know what to do."

"And what would I do in the meantime? Help you look for gold?" she asked, shaking her head in amusement, not anger.

"I could take the day off, too," Christopher said. "My people are happiest when the boss sticks his nose elsewhere. You and I could spend the day together, just the two of us."

Janet was tempted. He didn't know how tempted.

"Elephant at the tree line!" someone shouted. Everyone scanned the edge of the clearing, except Christopher and Janet, who were looking at each other.

"Let's not move too fast," Janet said. She cherished their morning together, but she was afraid of any attempts to extend it. The fates were jealous of too much happiness.

"Elephant down, Janet!" Roger called. The front two Land Rovers immediately headed for the elephant collapsed a few meters into the clearing. If the crew was going to get the shots wanted, it had to move, too. Dr. Nhari couldn't wait. Once the animal was down, it had to be tagged as quickly as possible. Elephant herds were social groups and were known to rush to the defense of one downed member. That offered fewer complications to poachers with guns at the ready than it did to Dr. Nhari's team, which was out to save life. There was another possible complication. The drug used was a powerful relaxant; a downed elephant could suffocate under its own massive weight if it was too long without an antidote.

Janet was torn between joining the rush and telling her team to go on without her.

"Janet!" Roger persisted. He was all cameramen now, and he knew good shots were a matter of good timing. Time was running out.

"Maybe you're right about not moving too fast," Christopher said, reading the conflict on her face. "Things are going so well, I don't want to spoil them, either. Besides, you were right when you said I wouldn't respect you for dumping your convictions just because I asked."

"Janet!" Roger yelled. Dr. Nhari was almost at the elephant, and Roger was tempted to head after him without Janet along.

"You go with your team, Janet," Christopher said, smiling. "We'll talk later. If I've started falling in love with a lady do-gooder, I wouldn't want that lady changing horse midstream. I might not know how to handle it." He drove away.

She turned and ran to her crew. "About time, boss lady!" Roger said, peeling rubber as soon as Janet was on board.

Christopher was right. Part of her reason for coming to Africa was a need to save the animals. She wouldn't forgive herself or him if she threw it aside for purely selfish satisfaction.

He had said he was falling in love with her, and Janet was shaken by that revelation. Her legs had hardly gotten her to the Land Rover before the vehicle began racing with bone-jarring speed over the rough ground. Janet was filled with wonder at Christopher's admission, not knowing how to deal with it. It was too impossibly wonderful to be true. It was what she wanted more than anything. It was the fulfillment of her dream of sixteen long years. But dreams didn't really come true. This was no different. She needed time to think. Things were moving too fast, whether she wanted them to or not.

Janet couldn't tell Roger, Tim, or Jill that Christopher had admitted beginning to love her. She couldn't admit it to herself. It was a possibility savored in secret. If it were to be a dream, never fulfilled, the fewer people she told the better. Even if it was true, there was rough sailing ahead. Christopher didn't know she was a ghost from his past.

Roger concentrated on making up for lost time. His passengers held on for dear life as he brought the Land Rover to a screeching halt. He and Tim scrambled for their equipment. Jill set to work, making Janet look presentable for the cameras.

The next few minutes were a dream. Janet was a professional, operating on remote control. She performed everything with her mind elsewhere—on Christopher. She checked her face in the mirror Jill held for her. She knew what additional makeup she needed, and Jill applied those finishing touches. Janet stepped out of the Land Rover and went to work. All the time she marveled at the unbelievable wonder of Christopher saying he loved her. He hadn't said it before. He wouldn't say it unless he meant it, would he? He sounded so sincere. But because he sounded sincere didn't necessarily mean he was.

Dr. Nhari and his associates were skilled at performing within a minimum time limit. While the specially designed collar was attached to the downed animal's thick neck, the rest of the group took the elephant's physical measurements for future identification. Roger busied himself with close-ups. Janet commandeered Tim for her on-the-spot commentary. The two soldiers took up guard positions as a precaution against possible trouble from poachers out to take advantage of the vulnerable elephant.

"Are we done?" Dr. Nhari asked, verifying once more that the collar and its transmitter were securely in place. Janet told the shooting camera that the elephant would be revived by an injection of the antidote into one of the large veins latticing the pachyderm's ear. "Everybody back, then!" Dr. Nhari instructed, hypodermic in hand.

Tim joined Roger in recording the injection. Janet stepped

back to avoid the groggy elephant's complete return to consciousness.

What happened next wasn't clear in Janet's mind. Nor was it clear to anyone else.

The antidote apparently just worked faster than expected. The elephant began struggling to its feet before Dr. Nhari pulled the needle from the vein. The man scrambled nervously but dexterously to avoid the kicking legs and whip-like trunk. Well-trained assistants gave him a hand.

The two soldiers bolted in fear of the thrashing beast. Watching from the Land Rover, Jill remained riveted to her seat. Tim panicked for one short second until he realized Roger, the more experienced of the two, was coolly recording the whole thing. Tim turned his camera back on the elephant's unsteady return to its feet. Fascinated, Janet watched. She wasn't feeling particularly threatened. Dr. Nhari's laughter—albeit nervous—assured them the danger was over.

It wasn't!

There was an explosion among the nearby trees. Two tall acacias tumbled in a mushroom of fire and smoke. When her ears quit ringing, Janet found she was still standing on vibrating ground.

The revived elephant trumpeted its fright, stumbled on legs too wobbly to support it and dropped heavily to its front knees.

"Stampede!" somebody yelled. Not Janet. She was speechless as fast-moving elephants materialized from among the trees.

It was a dream—that was her first impression. It was inconceivable that she was in Zimbabwe, about to become a victim of stampeding elephants. When the truth hit her, she was left with no choice but to get out of the way. Easier thought than done. The elephants were in a wide and cluttered line that made it useless for her to go left or right. She couldn't reach the Land Rovers, because the collared elephant, visibly panicking, was blocking that route. The poor beast's eyes were wide, its ears flared, its trunk thrashing wildly. Anyway there was little chance of Janet reaching the Land Rovers before the elephants reached her. She had but one alternative. She turned and started running.

There was a distant outcropping of rocks that offered sanctuary. It seemed too far distant, but that didn't stop her from trying.

She heard the elephants behind her. Their trumpeting got louder and louder. The ground shook more noticeably beneath her—a veritable earthquake caused by elephants run amok. It was difficult to keep her footing. She moved in staggering slow motion across a plain seemingly of Jell-O.

An elephant thundered by on her right. The dust stirred up in its wake clogged her aching lungs, making it even harder to breathe. The tremendous size of the animal was unreal! How could something so big move so fast? She was slower—much slower. Her brain admitted escape was impossible. The outcrop of rocks was closer, but not close enough. An elephant rushed by on her left. The wind of its passing buffeted her with dust. It was only a matter of seconds before one of them would take her down with ease, perhaps not even noticing that small obstacle in its path.

She was going to die. Her mind was amazingly clear. She saw the irony of being killed by the animals she had come to save. She saw the irony of dying when Christopher's words of love made her less willing to die now than at any time during the past sixteen years. Her thoughts of Christopher, her realization of lost possibilities for happiness, kept her on her feet long after she was exhausted.

Thoughts of her love conjured him up before her. She was in no condition to believe he was actually among those rocks. It was disappointing that her last vision of him was with a rifle in his hands.

She didn't hear the shot; she heard the horrible scream of the elephant behind her. There was the hardness of vibrating earth coming up unexpectedly to meet her. The collapse of the elephant caused further reverberations that made Janet's ungainly sprawl more painful.

She had died and gone to hell; there was no question about it. The smoke of eternal fires surrounded her, filling her lungs with burning dryness. Her eyes stung even though she kept them tightly shut. Her mouth was stuffed with nettles. Her head ached from the banshee cries of lost souls committed, like she, to everlasting damnation. It was her punishment for hoping for happiness in Christopher's arms. She wasn't surprised at her fate. It was always this way. There were no happy-ever-after endings.

The screaming faded. The rumbling decreased. There were other sounds: distant trumpets, her breathing, running feet. She wasn't running. She was down and out for the count of ten. How cruel life was. It dangled possibilities of happiness before her eyes and then snatched them away.

Christopher, Oh, Christopher. Life is so unfair!

"Janet? Janet!" His voice. She opened her eyes. Hell was a blur. She shut her eyes. "Janet? Janet!" The illusion was too much to bear. She started crying. Bitter sobs racked her body, tearing her insides. Something wrapped around her tightly. She was lifted. There was a comforting hardness hugging her. "Tell me you're all right!" he commanded. "Tell me!"

How could she be all right? She had lost him. She had lost the one thing she wanted most in the world. Or had she? Maybe she wasn't dead. Maybe she had survived, Christopher to the rescue.

"Christopher?" she asked. She opened eyes glued with tears and dust. "Oh, Christopher, is it really you?" She locked her arms around his neck. He was there, an illusion that might slip away if she didn't hold on to him with all her might.

"It's all right, Janet," he soothed, rocking her in strong arms. She was like a frightened child. She buried her face against his chest, resting her cheek against the vee of smooth skin revealed by his open shirt. The smell and the feel of him excited and comforted her at the same time.

"I thought I was dead," she cried, shuddering at how close she had come. A miracle had saved her—but at what cost?

"It was close," Christopher admitted. "It was too close for comfort, but you're safe now. That's all that counts."

Was it, though? She shut her eyes: an ostrich, sticking her head in the sand. She wasn't making the truth go away by refusing to face it. An act of violence had saved her.

She pulled her face away from the comfort of his neck. Still holding on to him, she twisted to see dust everywhere. The sun was liquid gold within the haze. She saw a dream-like, landscape.

The elephant was dead, its bloody eye socket already attracting flies. Vultures, likewise, had caught the scent of death and coasted nearer on the wind. How lucky the birds were to have so many men anxious to set food before them.

Just as there had been irony in the possibility of her death, there was irony in her salvation. Because of her an elephant had died. The man she loved had pulled the trigger.

The implications were too much to face at the moment. Her mind relieved her of the burden. She fainted.

* * * * * * *

THE NEXT THING she knew, she was in her bed at the hotel. For a wishful moment she thought it was all a bad dream— except there was someone standing by the window.

"Christopher?"

"Shall I get him?" It was Roger. He sat on the edge of the bed, his handsome face etched with concern. "He was here until a few minutes ago. I told him to get some rest. He's been awake since it happened."

"How long have I been out?" Janet asked. It didn't seem long.

"Last night. All today." He put a cool hand on her forehead. "The doctor gave you a shot. He was concerned about the terrible fright you had. We've all been worried."

Suddenly the memory of what had happened came back full force, and a shudder passed through her. She shook it off. "Tim and Jill are all right, aren't they?" she asked. She didn't know what she would do or say if they weren't.

"They're fine," Roger assured her. "Jill is naturally shaken. She stayed in the Land Rover, rooted to the spot throughout. It turned out to be a good place. Out of all the vehicles, only one got damaged. Tim's a little frayed around the edges. He insists he's more upset about losing his camera than about almost getting squashed by the same elephant that smashed it." Janet smiled at Tim's masculine posturing in the aftermath of disaster.

"Did any of the others get hurt?" Janet asked. There was a dead elephant. Christopher had killed it to save her.

"One of the soldiers was badly injured. They rushed him to the hospital in Fort Victoria. We're still waiting to hear, but it doesn't look good. Aside from him, everyone came through with minor cuts and bruises. We're extremely lucky," Roger said, "considering what could have happened."

"What was it all about?" Janet asked, remembering the explosion, the mushroom of smoke and fire, the two toppling acacias, the line of elephants emerging from the trees.

"Captain Sylo says it was the work of poachers," Roger said. "They booby-trapped the place, knowing the elephants were there and we were coming to tag one."

"They wanted to kill us?" Janet asked, shivering at how close they had come to succeeding.

"It looks that way," Roger admitted. "Captain Sylo figures they wanted to kill us, scare us, or both. They hate us roaming around. Although they somehow have no trouble finding where we are and when, it's easier for them when we're not here at all. Captain Sylo, by the way, is anxious to see you. But right now I suppose you'd prefer seeing the man who saved your pretty neck, yes?"

Somehow she felt she couldn't bear to face Christopher just then. The thought of the elephant that had died, instead of her, preyed on her mind. "Didn't you say Christopher was tired?" Janet said. "Maybe we'd better let him rest."

"He won't be pleased when he finds out," Roger said. "I only got him to leave by promising I'd wake him at the first sign of your revival."

"I'll take the responsibility," Janet said. It sounded as if she was thinking of Christopher's needs. It wasn't that at all. She needed time to think.

"Damn, Janet, it was exciting to see!" Roger said, his eyes lighting up at the memory. "I got it all down, too, and it's going to make fantastic footage to show your kids and grandchildren someday. Your television audience is going to love it, too." She found it a bit cold-blooded that he had been able to shoot her race with death so calmly, but let him continue. "I couldn't believe what was happening," he explained. "I went running after you, camera in hand, hardly realizing I was getting it all."

"You're a good cameraman," Janet complimented him. Her husband had been, too. Bob would have kept his camera rolling. He was doing just that in Central America when he went down. What his camera recorded during those last moments had made poignant footage on network news across the country.

"Christopher downed it with one shot!" Roger said. She knew what he was saying. Roger might have died in the stampede. And Tim. And Jill. And Dr. Nhari. And Janet. Even Christopher. They didn't. An elephant did. Except for one soldier, everyone managed to get out of the way. One of the animals was dead, because Janet wasn't as quick as most of the others. One bullet was all it had taken—far more efficient than poachers who peppered their victims with machine-gun fire. "His aim must be as steady as a rock," Roger said appreciatively. "The elephant went down within feet of you," Roger said. "The rest of the herd split around it, missing you and Christopher. Damned unbeliev-able!"

There was no denying it. It was recorded for posterity. Anyone could sit in front of a television screen and watch it happen again—her frantic run, the elephants behind her, Christopher among the rocks, aiming his rifle, the elephant's death, its fall, the wedge it made to divert the stampeding herd around her.

If she had stood right where she was when the explosion went off and the elephants emerged from the trees, would they have missed her? Jill was saved by not moving. Granted, Jill was in a Land Rover, but that wasn't adequate protection from a herd of stampeding elephants. If Janet hadn't panicked, that elephant might be alive.

She tried to recapture the moment of the explosion. It was blurry. Strange, because everything had seemed clear at the time. She remembered analyzing possible escape routes and rejecting them one by one. She couldn't go forward, left or right. She turned and ran. She didn't consider the possibility of staying put.

"You should see the tusks on that baby," Roger said. That didn't make her feel better. "The poachers would give their eyeteeth to add those to their stockpile."

"I'm grateful to Christopher," she said. She was, too. At the same time, each elephant's death narrowed the chances of the species surviving to see the turn of another century. "I'm tired, Roger," she said. After a night and a day of sleep, she shouldn't be tired, but she was. "I'll rest now, if that's all right."

"You get all the rest you need, boss lady," Roger said, smoothing her hair back from her forehead. His hand was cool. "We've everything under control."

Far better control than Janet was managing. Her team was well oiled. Roger, Tim and Jill were pros. Roger had kept his camera rolling through it all. He had footage to prove Christopher had saved the hostess of *Animal Kingdoms in the Wild*. Janet hadn't come all this way to make Christopher a hero—quite the contrary. But Christopher was being congratulated on all sides for a killing well done. Even Roger was full of praise.

Everything was topsy-turvy. Everything was wrong. She needed to think. Not now though; now she was tired. She would think tomorrow. There were answers, and she would find them.

She shut her eyes. Roger didn't leave the room but took a chair by the bed. Janet was worried. She was in Africa to exorcise memories, but she wasn't succeeding. She was here to help save elephants, and one was dead because of her. She had come to deny her love for Christopher but seeing him had only confirmed that her love was stronger than ever.

She dreamed she was in the middle of a clearing. She watched a brilliant explosion set fire to some nearby trees. The air was hot with the flash of the flames. She knew what to expect. She had been there before.

She contemplated escape routes. There was no going to the left or right. There was no running forward to meet the charge, although someone had once told her that was one sure way of stopping any attacking animal. An old-wives' tale. She had two alternatives: stay where she was or turn and run. She would stay where she was. Jill had stayed put and survived.

Elephants charged from the trees, and suddenly Janet was turning and running. The elephants charged closer and closer. One in particular was on her trail. It was determined to run her down. It had a mad and evil glint in its bloody red eyes. It was bigger than the others, its tusks huge and bleached with age.

There was an outcrop of rocks up ahead. There was no chance of her reaching it. It didn't matter. Christopher was there with his gun. He would save her.

Only he wasn't there, and the elephant behind her came faster and faster, closer and closer. "Christopher!" She opened her eyes to the darkness of the room.

"I'm here, darling," he said. Roger had kept his promise to wake him despite Janet's urgings to the contrary.

"You saved me," she said, lost between dreaming and consciousness.

"It's the least I could do for the woman I love," he said, kissing her warm cheek.

"I love you," she said. A dream?

"I suspected that," he said, smiling.

"No, you didn't suspect a thing," she contradicted him. She was Janet Kelley. She was thirteen and in love. He knew nothing, nothing at all.

"I certainly was hoping," he amended. She slept peacefully through the rest of that night and into the next day.

CHAPTER NINE

HE WAS ASLEEP in the chair. He looked younger in sleep, as though he were eighteen again. But Janet wasn't thirteen. She looked and felt older.

He stirred without waking. How handsome he was, his eyelashes thick against his tanned cheeks, his blond hair attractively tousled. His sensuous lips were parted and invited a kiss. His shirt was unbuttoned part way, revealing his muscled chest. His legs were spread wide for balance, their splay decidedly sexy. Janet blushed like a schoolgirl.

He raised his right hand to his square jaw line and casually massaged a colorless stubble of beard. His eyes fluttered and opened, his dilated pupils taking a few seconds to focus.

"Good morning," she said, and he stretched sensuously. He was an exotic jungle cat reveling in the first warming rays of dawn. Several cramped bones cracked audibly as he worked them into proper alignment.

"How are you feeling?" he asked. His voice was husky from sleep—or lack of it. "You're looking none the worse for wear."

"That's more than I can, say for you," she observed with a smile. It was a lie. He looked as good as ever, but she knew he couldn't have had a good sleep where he was. "Why don't you find yourself a bed?"

"Is that my long-awaited invitation to join you?" he asked with a wide grin. She was tempted.

"I was thinking of the bed in your room," she said.

"Oh," he pouted, his disappointment only partially faked.

He placed his palms over his handsome face and rubbed his sleep-filled eyes. He had been in that chair since shortly after midnight.

"I appreciate the vigil," she said, "but you and I have things to talk about, and we can't do that until you're rested. I wouldn't want to take advantage."

"One of those kinds of talk, huh?" he said, but he wasn't arguing.

"In the meantime, the patient can take care of herself," Janet assured him.

"Your teammates are out in the field," he informed her. "Five more dead elephants were found yesterday."

"Oh, no!" Her mind flashed a vision of the elephant she and he were responsible for killing.

"Sylo thought it best that your group get what shots they could," Christopher said. "He's hinting at tightening up security until the poaching problem is cleared up once and for all. That could mean an attempt to withdraw all civilians. You'll admit the problem is getting out of hand."

The thought of Craig issuing orders to vacate the area made Janet panicky. Granted, she wouldn't stay much longer anyway. As soon as the first of the elephants was transferred to Wankie, she would wrap up shooting. She had never intended staying through the whole process. It would be weeks before the last elephant was delivered to its new home. But she didn't want to be kicked out early. Not now. Not after waiting all these years to find this chance with Christopher.

He said he loved her. The sheer wonder of it! He had saved her life. In the light of day she saw the difference between killing for ivory or for sport and killing to save a life. She wanted to sort out other conflicting emotions as easily.

"I think I'll take a hot bath," she said. That would help. Being so long in bed had made her sluggish.

"I could use a bath, too. You wouldn't be up to sharing one, I suppose?" Christopher said, only half-teasingly.

"I won't say I'm not tempted," she said, giving him that much.

The idea of taking a bath with him was exceedingly sexy. Her husband hadn't been much for variety. Bob's imagination had shown in his work, not in his lovemaking.

"However, now isn't the time or the place, right?" Christopher filled in for her. He stood up and stretched, elongating exquisitely developed muscles as he reached for the ceiling. Her pleasure in watching was almost painful. He came to the bed, a strange glint in his golden eyes. Janet shivered in agitation. She was in no condition to fight him off. She didn't want to fight him.

Her fear was short-lived. "You do remember you saying that you loved me last night, don't you?" he asked. "Or are you going to hide behind the excuse of delirium and say you don't remember a thing?"

"I remember what I said," Janet admitted. There was no forgetting. "Do you remember what you said?"

"You're hinting that I said I loved you, too?" he asked. Her pain at even his joking denial was sharp. "Well, I did say it. There's no denying it," he said, filling her with joy. "And I don't make the statement as lightly as some of the other men you might have known in your life."

"I know. You don't fall in love at first sight," she said, quoting his words. "You don't fall in love at second sight, either."

"I was unabashedly lying when I uttered that bull!" Christopher said. "I was running scared because of the hold you had on me from the start." He sat on the edge of the bed, exciting in his nearness. "I did love you at first sight. I felt I knew you from before. You know—in another time, another place, another existence. I'm sure someone with a belief in Oriental religions and reincarnation would nave better words to describe it."

She knew why he felt that way. She would explain. But no. She was held in check by her fear of his reaction. He had once loved a thirteen-year-old girl who had betrayed him.

Christopher brushed the back of his fingers gently along her cheek. She thrilled at his touch. "I wouldn't want to lose you," he said, tracing her lips with his right index finger and increasing her pleasurable chills.

He had lost her sixteen years earlier—without a word, without a letter—because the Lackland Animal Preserve had gone up in a puff of her father's frustrated hopes and dreams. Very little had changed over the past sixteen years. The problem was now the Great Zimbabwe Reserve. A barrier still existed, not dissolved by the passing years. Christopher would see his love threatened now by the same things that had wrenched it from him when he was eighteen.

There was a trace of her fears written on her face. "You're sure you're okay?" he persisted, apparently reluctant to leave.

She couldn't be okay! Her love hung in precarious balance. The slightest mistake could shatter its delicate foundations. There would be no other chances. It was now or never for the two of them. "Yes, I'm fine," she insisted. A commitment could be made by wrapping her arms around his neck and pulling him down with her. How tempting to run her hands through his tousled blond hair and feel the warmth of his body. She wanted him. She wanted the ecstatic joy of his lovemaking. He held the power to touch spots of wonder inside her that Bob had never explored. He was hers for the asking, made more irresistible by his admission that he loved her.

She would never go to bed with a man who didn't love her. She would never go to bed with a man she didn't love. Those were her guidelines—only she discovered there was more. There was the matter of degree. Janet loved him with all her heart. He loved Janet Westover. Did he still love Janet Kelley? The two women were the same—two halves of a whole. His loving one and hating the other wasn't enough, even if it was possibly all that was available.

"How about lunch together?" he suggested.

Janet checked the travel clock by her bed. It was almost ten. "How about supper instead?" she offered. She needed time. "Once you hit a comfortable bed, you're not going to feel like getting up too soon anyway."

"There's something about most of our previous supper

engagements that leaves a bit to be desired," Christopher reminded her. "You never showed up for most of them."

"Let's make it supper anyway," she insisted. "I have to break my present record of no-shows sometime, don't I?"

"Okay," he said, grinning. "Columbus took a chance and died in prison." He kissed her. It was too brief. She wanted more, but she resisted the temptation to carry the contact further. She must be very careful from here on in. Things must be thoroughly thought through.

He paused a moment longer on the edge of the bed, his temptation to lift her into his arms and shower her with kisses quite evident from his expression. And she was glad he wasn't rushing her. She needed to be coaxed gently, suspecting now that his initial clumsiness with her had been born of his own fears. "I do love you, you know," he said.

He didn't love all of her. He loved only a part of her, Janet was sure. He didn't know that—not yet. Maybe he never would. She must decide if she would tell him or not. She knew a piece of his love was better than nothing. She was reluctant to gamble what she had in a last-ditch effort to have all or nothing. "I love you, too," she said. She would love him forever and ever. She had been bolstered by dreams of returning to Africa, Lionspride, and Christopher. She had dared hope for the miracle to make all the pain of the past perish before the wonder of resurrected love. But there was no coming back a next time. There was no third chance to set things right. This was it.

"I'm satisfied with that," he said, getting to his feet. "For the moment," he added, and Janet couldn't help feeling flattered and excited by his obvious desire for her. "I'll be looking forward to supper. Say seven o'clock?"

"I'll be ready," Janet promised. There was no more running. No matter what the consequences, things must be settled between them at Great Zimbabwe. She prayed to make the right decision. She was risking so much.

He bent to kiss her forehead, and then went to the door.

"Christopher!" she called. She wanted him to stay. She

wanted him with her on the bed, naked next to her. She wanted the ecstasy of his hard body making love to her yielding softness. "Is it true about Columbus?" she asked instead.

"What about him?" he asked curiously.

"That he died in prison."

"No," he said, laughing. "Which is encouraging, isn't it?"

There was a noticeable vacuum when he left. For sixteen years there had been emptiness in a part of her heart. She didn't have the strength to endure its permanent return. That's why she so feared Christopher finding out that she was Janet Kelley. He would find out, too—if not now, later; if not from her, from someone else. The subject would come up. Someone would drop the fact in passing. Janet would inadvertently mention something from those long-ago years. Bliss would be shattered in an instant. Would the few moments she had stolen by deception have been worth it?

She threw back her bed covers and got up; her legs weak. She was in her pajamas. She didn't remember putting them on. She blushed with thoughts of it having been Christopher who'd undressed her, but Jill probably had done the honors.

She began to run the water in the bathtub. There was a bathtub at Lionspride far more luxurious than this one. She had bathed there once. Afterward, she had put on a chic silk dress and slid down a banister. He had seen her, had been reminded of a girl he had known and loved a long time before. She offered the same first name, the same complexion, and the same ideals. He wouldn't thank her for offering the same hurt. She didn't want to hurt him again, and she didn't want him to hurt her.

The hot water soothed her bruises, which had turned the same color as the rainbows at Victoria Falls. It was mental relaxation she wanted. She folded a towel to pillow her head. She shut her eyes. Everything would come together. It had to.

Minutes drifted by, robbing the water of heat. But Janet stayed there, finally able to analyze her long nurtured bitterness. It had never been anything but her excuse for keeping Christopher's memory alive. It had given her a reason to come back to Africa, to Lionspride, to him. It was a tool, no longer as important once it was used. She had sworn revenge on her Father's deathbed, but Jack Kelley had never asked her for the oath. He wouldn't have thanked her for it had he been alive to hear it. He fought his own battles, winning or losing them on his own merits. He wouldn't approve of her wasting her life on his account. He would have wanted her to be happy.

"What did Christopher write?" her father had asked one day, long ago. She had received another letter from Lionspride, he knew. He knew about all the letters. He sorted them from his mail and gave them to her. He never steamed them open, never held them up to the light. He never insisted she let him read them. He honored her privacy. It pained him to see what his feelings about Vincent had done to her. "Why don't you at least read his letters, Janet?" he'd asked. They were tied with pink ribbon in a box beneath her bed. "Why don't you answer them? What was between you and him has nothing to do with what happened between me and his father." But it did. It put her in a position of choosing. A thirteen-year-old girl had no real choice but her father.

A thirteen-year-old girl hadn't been able to get her emotions sorted out. A twenty-nine-year-old woman was having the same problem—only now there could be no further procrastination. Her whole life depended upon these next few hours. She was faced with a choice between either heart-rending despair or momentary passion with a man who loved only a part of her. She could delude herself into believing one moment of mutually shared enjoyment wouldn't cheat them both.

She stepped from the tepid water and dried herself, dressed in a pale green blouse and gray slacks, then left her room.

The restaurant was deserted. The research team would be in the field, her camera crew with them. Most of the soldiers ate in their own mess. Christopher was in his room sleeping. Janet welcomed the peace and quiet; she didn't feel like talking.

"Yes, please?" It was the waiter.

"Is the restaurant open?" she asked. Nodding, he led her

into the dining room, showed her to a booth, and handed her a menu. It was the same booth in which Christopher had joined her for breakfast the morning of the stampede. Everything had been made so right between them then. The drive had been marvelous, sixteen years gradually melting away. Illusion. Those sixteen years had burned indelible imprints on both their psyches, and Janet had to decide if anything was salvageable. If so, she had to decide if the remains were enough.

She was eating a chicken sandwich when the Land Rovers pulled up in the hotel parking lot. She watched through the window as the research team and her camera crew piled out, Jill and Tim laughing at something Roger was saying. Janet wanted to live a normal life, as they did, not haunted by her past. The two crews made beelines for their rooms, anxious to wash and eat.

Janet wasn't ready to talk business, discuss the day's shooting or rehash her narrow escape. She left the restaurant, keeping to the edge of the road. She prayed no one would see her, and no one did.

She reached the guardhouse that overlooked the entrance to the ruins. There were no guards on duty. The barricade was tilted in an upright position. Since the area was virtually a military encampment, there was no traffic control at this point. Anyone who hadn't heard that the entire Great Zimbabwe Reserve and the ruins were sealed off was stopped long before reaching this spot in the road.

To her left, across a wide stretch of uncultivated field, was the Acropolis. Janet picked out the walls erected on natural bedrock. In the fourteenth century A.D., that fortress had been part of a flourishing community. The valley had teemed with activity and people—some ten-thousand residents. Six centuries later, the population had shrunk drastically.

An empire could rise, flourish and fall in a few hundred years. Change sometimes happened overnight. That's how long it had taken at Lionspride. She had gone to bed one night, only to be shaken awake by her father. The next morning they were gone.

There had been no time for goodbyes. Christopher had been sleeping. They were supposed to have gone horseback riding the next morning.

She spotted a Land Rover leaving the military camp, heading toward her. She stepped deeper into the shadows of the trees and remained there until the vehicle passed. The lone driver was no one she knew. She had expected Craig. She especially didn't want to talk to him. Her decisions were hers to make, and she didn't want to be influenced. She knew what Craig thought. He wanted her to take advantage of an opportunity to convert Christopher in order to benefit wildlife preservation. Well, things weren't that simple. There was more at stake than the influence Christopher could wield in saving animals. Craig didn't know that, and Janet wasn't prepared to fill him in.

She bypassed the tents of the encampment, heading away from the Acropolis, since she didn't have the energy to make the climb. She moved instead toward the Great Enclosure, along the pathway that meandered through some minor ruins, once part of a sprawling city complex.

Even during tourist season, there were few out at his time of the afternoon. It was summer. The equator was only a few hundred miles to the north. It was hot; the temperature was nearly ninety. Whenever possible, Janet stayed in the shade.

The Great Enclosure was impressive this close up. Before she had only seen it from the air. At ground level the walls dwarfed her.

She circled to the Northwest Entrances. The interior was open to the sky, resembling a courtyard. The grass was surprisingly green in the heat of midday. Tall milkwood trees beckoned with their enticing blots of shade.

She turned left, entering the welcome coolness of the Parallel Passage, a pathway between walls that were high enough to keep the sun out most of the day. Apparently the builders hadn't been satisfied with the first wall and had begun the second, leaving the walkway between. The passage extended around a good third of the circle, opening onto the courtyard of the

Conical Tower.

Janet chose a pile of rocks and sat down. The sun couldn't reach her. There was a breeze blowing somewhere in the overhanging branches, rustling the leaves. This setting was meant to be shared, but Janet was alone. She had always been alone, even when she was married. After Bob's death she had made few friends outside the television business. There had been men, mostly inconsequential. She didn't remember their faces or their names. She saw them for a movie or for dinner, and that was it. Few returned, none she cared to see again. Her aloneness was cultivated. Her good looks and position would have given her access to a lot of people and places, but she never bothered. She returned to the same dream world she had enjoyed prior to her marriage.

Always she had planned to come back to Africa. Always she had avoided whatever ties might divert her from that objective. Only once in her life had she faltered, convincing herself she was ridiculous to devote so much time to daydreams. That's when she had married Bob, and regretted it afterward. He was a deterrent, someone to keep her fantasies in check, and that was no basis for a lasting relationship. It put unfair pressure on him, continually forcing him to compete with fantasies Janet had had before and during their marriage. When he died, she had felt guilty that she'd given him so little. And, yet, she had given him all she could.

There came a time when she thought not even Christopher could live up to the ideal that she had embellished with years of fantasy. At that moment, she had felt safe in arranging her return to Africa—on the one hand, hoping to prove he wasn't the Adonis she made him out to be, and on the other, hoping to prove he was. Either way, she had wanted the certainty only a revisit could give her.

Well, she was in Africa now. She had returned to Lionspride, even to Victoria Falls. She had seen Christopher sixteen years after the fact, and the magic hadn't died. He loved her, and she loved him with a mature woman's love. It should be so simple.

Love should conquer all, but it didn't. There were sixteen years to consider. She hadn't read his letters. She hadn't answered them. She hadn't paved the way for fairy-tale endings.

Suddenly she was startled out of her reverie. Realizing she was no longer alone, she looked up quickly. Dr. Nhari was standing a few feet away with an embarrassed look on his face. "I'm afraid I disturbed you," he said apologetically. "I was about to sneak away."

"Don't go," she said. She didn't want to be alone, after all. She kept coming back to the impossibility of her relationship with Christopher. "I wasn't reflecting on anything too important," she said. What a—mammoth lie! "Mainly daydreaming. The spot is certainly conducive to it."

"How are you feeling, then?" he asked in his clipped English accent. He chose a place nearby and sat down. "That stampede was quite an experience for all of us."

"I'm feeling much better, thank you," Janet answered. At least physically that was true. "How did it go today in the field?"

"Quite well. We made it through the whole morning without one explosion, or stampede, or dead elephant. We tagged another elephant with a transmitter, and I'm inclined to believe its group is the last of the lot. We can begin serious transferring of elephants to Wankie within the week if Captain Sylo doesn't decide to interrupt our schedule."

"Christopher says Craig will possibly move us all out to enforce more stringent security here," Janet said. Her hope of getting Christopher off her mind wasn't succeeding. He was too much a part of everything—too much a part of Africa, too much a part of her past and her present. She wanted him to be part of her future.

"Captain Sylo thinks that by moving us out he'll be better protecting the elephant," Dr. Nhari said, shaking his head doubtfully. "The only thing that will save these elephants is getting them out of here and to Wankie. He can't do that. I can."

"He's thinking of our safety, too," Janet reminded the doctor. She felt obliged to defend Craig, ever though she no more approved of what he was considering than Dr. Nhari did. Janet's objections were less concerned with the speedy transfer of elephants than with the cutting short of her time with Christopher.

"Yes, I suppose he is," Dr. Nhari said with a loud sigh. "And when those elephants came charging, I was willing to see the man's point. However, today I've regained my courage. And you?"

"Me, too," she said, and smiled. She didn't want to leave Great Zimbabwe—not yet. If it meant facing another herd of stampeding elephants, then so be it!

"Good for you!" he said. He left the subject of elephants to turn to another obviously as close to his heart. "And what do you think of the ruins?" He waved his arms at not only the immediate relics but also at those scattered farther afield.

"Magnificent!" Janet admitted. "I've wanted to see them for years."

"We'll go to Great Zimbabwe," Christopher had told her. "Father's pilot can fly us there in no time." They never made it. Her father shook her awake one night, and the next day she was gone. Not enough time. There still wasn't.

"Yes, quite impressive," Dr. Nhari agreed. "So much so that it took three-hundred years for the authorities to admit the ruins were the remains of a city built by the Shona." He spoke with the bitterness of an African long denied his rightful heritage. "They attributed the city of Great Zimbabwe to Semetic builders from the Mediterranean, or to the Sabaeans, or to the Phoenicians— even to the Egyptians. When radiocarbon dating eliminated the Phoenicians, Sabaeo-Arabians, and pre-Muslim Arabs, there were still diehards who refused to give credit where credit was due." He looked embarrassed, a smile and uplifted palms asking her for forgiveness. "That does sound bitter, doesn't it?" he said. He laughed but soon regained his seriousness. "My Shona fore-fathers built Great Zimbabwe, and I'm extremely proud of that fact." He came to his feet. "Shall we walk, or would you rather I left you to yourself?"

"Let's walk," Janet said, standing up to join him. She would think out things about her and Christopher later. She had until supper, at the very least.

They skirted the Conical Tower and proceeded through a ruined doorway that gave access to an expanse of lawn. The Great Outer Wall circled inward to the left of them.

"I was born here," Dr. Nhari commented. "Oh, not here in the Great Enclosure, mind you, but nearby."

"I think Dr. Cunningham mentioned that in Salisbury," Janet said.

"Yes, I suspect he did," Dr. Nhari said, a gleam in his eye. "He told you to tread carefully and not suggest in front of me that the ruins were anything but a city of native origin. Yes?"

"Well, as it turns out, I happened to concur, even before Dr. Cunningham's forewarnings," Janet said, pleased to see his face light up with satisfaction.

"Dr. Cunningham is a fine man," Dr. Nhari remarked. "A great diplomat, which is what he must be to work within the bureaucracy. If he met someone at a cocktail party who insisted the city at Great Zimbabwe was built by Martians, he would smile politely and neither agree nor disagree. On the other hand, I would certainly take immediate exception, which is why Dr. Cunningham sits behind his impressive desk in Salisbury and I get to bore a beautiful young woman in the field."

"I'm hardly bored," Janet protested. She admired Dr. Nhari tremendously. Dr. Cunningham insisted the man could have a post behind a Salisbury desk whenever he expressed the slightest interest in one.

They exited from the West Entrance and walked as far as the Ridge Ruins before stopping. Dr. Nhari pointed over a low wall to where a large rock was balanced against another, reminiscent of the toppled prehistoric ruins scattered across Europe. "One by one, we went into the darkness beneath that overhanging rock," Dr. Nhari said, "and had our fortunes told by an old man who tossed worn stones and bones in the dust. How times have changed!" He pointed to trees in the distance. "My parents had a hut over there. It was part of a village. The village was considered an eyesore when the tourists started coming to Great Zimbabwe in earnest. So the village was moved—lock, stock and barrel. We no longer came to the rock to have our fortunes told. And that, my dear, is progress!"

He looked at her, his eyes sparkling amusement. "Ah, you say, sour grapes! But you're wrong. It's acceptable to reflect upon the past on occasion, even if it's neither desirable nor preferable to wallow in such memories. The present is never as perfect, but it's all we have. Yes?" She knew what he meant, but she had more trouble dissociating herself from her past.

They continued along a pathway leading to the hotel. Janet stopped, not yet ready to go back. "Don't walk in the sun too long at a stretch, will you?" Dr. Nhari warned. He was politely acknowledging his dismissal.

"I'll be careful," she assured him.

"And a word of advice," he said kindly. "Don't let the plight of these animals get the best of you. It's tragic, yes. We must do all we can, yes. But extinction isn't anything new. Where is the saber-toothed tiger? Where is the Tyrannosaurus-rex? Where is the dodo? A change in climate killed them. A meteorite killed them. Disease killed them. Stronger animals killed them. What is man but a stronger animal? Who's to say it isn't his right to kill all that is weaker?"

"Or to save them," Janet injected.

"Yes, or to save them," Dr. Nhari agreed. "Man does seem to have that choice, doesn't he? But in the end whatever he decides is all part of a greater plan. A plan over which man—and that includes you and me—has no control whatsoever."

As far as animals were concerned, Janet found some solace in what he said. But when she applied his precepts to her relationship with Christopher, his philosophy was little consolation. The idea that she might be part of some preordained plan, no matter what she did, left her cold—although she sometimes wondered if this wasn't the case, considering how things had worked out for her. She had known so little happiness until now.

It didn't seem likely that she could expect any future improvements from the same master plan.

She backtracked through the Ridge Ruins to the Great Enclosure. She didn't enter the walled circle but skirted the outside. Nine hundred thousand blocks made up the enclosure—the equivalent of two and a half million bricks, or forty-five normal-sized houses. The fact that no mortar had been used made the stacks of stone even more impressive.

She walked through a series of minor ruins: the Plateau Ruins, the Mauch Ruins, the Phillips Ruins, and the Mauhd Ruins. A labyrinth of low walls overgrown with vegetation, they were of more interest to archaeologists than tourists. The pathways were blocked with rubble and tall grass, the perfect hiding place for the snakes that Janet hated. But she didn't turn and run in fear. The last time she'd done that, an elephant had died. There were no elephants here. Too many people had traipsed through these ruins over the years. Elephants had retreated deeper into the reserve. Soon there would be no elephants in all of Great Zimbabwe. They would be transferred to Wankie, or they would be dead. If gold were found, there'd be no Great Zimbabwe Reserve at all.

The ruins this far off the beaten path had sameness. One rock was much like another, and Janet welcomed the redundancy. It allowed her to think of other things. Time was short; there were decisions to be made.

Despite the warren-like nature of the maze, there was little chance of getting lost. Going eastward meant keeping the distant dirt road on her left. She stopped to rest beneath a large milkwood tree in the East Ruins. She picked off the miniature seedpods clinging tenaciously to her clothing from her waist down. They had hitched a ride during her hurried walk through high grass and weeds. When her grooming was complete, she stayed where she was. It was comfortable in the shade, and the sunshine beyond was extremely hot in its bright and glaring beauty.

There was a good view of the Acropolis from where she sat.

She was determined one day to make it to the top. But not today.

Seated there in that spot where few tourists bothered to explore, she decided to go for broke and tell Christopher everything. She should have done so long ago. She had set herself up for more heartache by delaying this long. Had she spoken at the outset, his rejection would have come after she'd prepared sixteen years for it. Now things were more complicated. He admitted to loving her. She admitted to loving him. It would make his rejection all the more painful. If she let their relationship progress without saying anything, she risked a rejection at a future date when she would be even less able to handle it. Possibly she was already beyond handling it, but nothing would grow easier with more delay.

She couldn't settle for less than she needed from a man and a lover. She'd already made that mistake. She needed complete love. He must accept the thirteen-year-old girl inside her, understand and forgive her betrayal sixteen years earlier.

But Christopher was his father's son, and Vincent Van Hoon hadn't been a forgiving man.

Her resolve to confess, so strong beneath the milkwood tree, weakened with each step taken toward the hotel and Christopher. But perhaps the more time she gave him to love Janet Westover, the more likely he was to overlook the faults of Janet Kelley.

She checked her wristwatch. It was almost five o'clock. In two hours she would see him over supper. He would sit across the table from her, his golden hair catching candlelight and holding it, his golden eyes reflecting flickering flame, his dimples sinking in his tanned cheeks whenever he smiled. He would hold her hand. He would tell her he loved her. No matter how much that love lacked completeness, Janet couldn't risk losing it by admitting she was an unwanted ghost from his past.

She was afraid, very afraid. She shivered, even though she was now walking in the full blast of the afternoon sun.

"Janet!" It was Roger calling her from the dirt road. He had spotted her emergence into a small clearing. She didn't hear him. He called again, but she was still preoccupied. He hurried to intercept her, standing directly in her path. She looked through him, her thoughts elsewhere. "Janet? Are you okay?" he asked in a concerned tone.

Her eyes focused. She was surprised to see him. "Where did you come from?" she asked. He seemed to have materialized from thin air.

"The question is: where were you?" Roger countered. "You looked a million miles away."

"Did I?" Janet said noncommittally.

"I've spent hours looking for you," Roger chided. "I never would have found you if Dr. Nhari hadn't told me where he left you earlier."

"I had some thinking to do," Janet confessed.

Roger didn't pry. "Well, now you've packing to do," he said. "We're kicked out as of ten o'clock tomorrow morning. This latest incident was the proverbial straw that broke the camel's back."

"Which latest incident?" Janet asked. Time was rapidly running out for her.

"One of Christopher's people was badly wounded," Roger said. "The guy apparently stumbled onto a couple of poachers knocking the horns off a rhino they'd killed."

"Melissa? Suzy?" Janet asked, horror-struck.

"No, but those poachers weren't too happy to see him," Roger said. "They turned on him. It's a wonder he didn't die on the spot. I got some footage, in case you want something besides the stampede to emphasize how poachers are no more concerned about human than animal life. But it might be too gory." They were walking side by side. The hotel appeared through the trees. "That makes two, and Captain Sylo refuses to take the responsibility for one of us making it three," he said. He anticipated her question. "That soldier who got it in the stampede died early this afternoon."

"Oh, no!" Janet said, shaking her head. She had to talk to Christopher, even if she didn't know yet what she planned to say to him. She hoped she would when the time came.

"Christopher was anxious to tell you himself," Roger said. "He ran around like a chicken with its head cut off, looking for you a while ago. I told him I'd get word to you that supper was off for this evening. He seemed sincerely disappointed about breaking the date." Roger suppressed a smile. The moment didn't call for levity. "But he felt his place was at the hospital."

"Does he know about Craig's decision?" Janet asked. If Christopher was at the hospital, he had too much on his mind to hear her confessions.

"I'll say he knows," Roger verified. "Captain Sylo was seeing red when he told him. The wounded man was shot miles from where he was supposed to be. Captain Sylo kept waving papers in Christopher's face, saying the military wasn't responsible when people filled out reports that put them in a different place from where they actually were."

Janet could imagine Craig's frustration. He had expressed concern about that very problem when he and Janet were returning from Victoria Falls. He had regretted not talking to Christopher about it then. He couldn't position his men to protect someone when he didn't know where that someone was. It was natural that he would want the area cleared, considering these continual violations of procedure.

At least Christopher knew Craig's deadline. He would get to her before then. He loved her. It wouldn't end like this. They had arrangements to make; there were things unsaid that needed saying.

"Janet, are you sure you're all right?" Roger asked.

"I'm fine," she insisted, and gave him a reassuring smile. She wasn't fooling anybody—not Roger—certainly not herself.

CHAPTER TEN

ROGER, TIM, AND JILL insisted she join them for supper. They argued that her missing another meal was the last thing she needed.

The restaurant buzzed with the latest gossip, and it didn't take Roger long to find out what had happened. He was in good with most of the men on Dr. Nhari's research team, the doctor included. He table-hopped after he ordered his meal.

"Okay, fill us in," Jill said, chewing on a piece of tough steak. She hadn't waited for Roger's return before starting to eat and had avoided close-ups of the wounded man from the V.H.A.M. team for fear of ruining her appetite. She was learning how to survive in the field.

"Looks like Van Hoon threw a monkey wrench in Captain Sylo's attempts to vacate the area of all civilians," Roger informed. "Van Hoon went over Sylo's head with a few phone calls. Word came down that the captain was overruled. He's understandably miffed."

"We get to stay?" Janet asked, her heart leaping at the news of her reprieve. She should have known Christopher would find a way for them to stay together awhile longer.

"Not *we*," Roger said, digging into his steak and mashed potatoes. "Van Hoon and his team. If you can convince the government people in Salisbury that we're here to make them rich by finding gold, too, we might get to stay. Since that's unlikely, we're scheduled to leave tomorrow. So are Dr. Nhari and his people. Think we've got enough footage to put a show together?"

Janet didn't know or care about the footage. She didn't care about her show. Christopher was staying in Great Zimbabwe, and she was leaving. Christopher's primary concern was the possibility of finding gold. Company profits came first. He apparently thought he and Janet could pick up their relationship elsewhere, at any time. Maybe in Fort Victoria. He could stop by a seedy hotel room on weekends and tell her he loved her between references to the latest geological reports. She could go back to Johannesburg and wait for him at Lionspride, amusing herself with closets full of designer clothes and shelves stocked with expensive perfumes. Of chief importance was the Great Zimbabwe gold potential and the efforts of Christopher and his team to define it.

She needn't have been worried about the part she'd played in his past. He didn't really care. She was a diversion, cast aside whenever more important things came along. It had happened at Lionspride when the diamond showed up. It was happening here with the gold. If he came back and found her gone, he would accept it with a shrug. He had succeeded in keeping his men on the spot, and that was what was important. They could give him gold. He was lucky to get a kiss from Janet.

"Excuse me," she said, getting up from the table. None of them was surprised, but their sympathy for her was evident. Janet wished she had someone to talk over her problems with—maybe Roger. But no, she couldn't—not with him, not with anyone. What was wrong with her was too personal to be shared, even now.

She went to her room and packed, after which she sat in one of the armchairs and waited. An hour later, Roger, Tim and Jill stopped by to make sure she was okay. She said she was fine and sent them on their way. She went back to the chair.

She waited for Christopher, even though she knew she waited in vain. He was too tied up in outmaneuvering Craig to give her a thought. Nevertheless, she wanted him to care.

By five after two in the morning, the normal sounds of the

hotel had long since subsided around her. She heard the tapping on her door. The sound was almost imperceptible. So was the voice. "Janet?" It wasn't too much to hope it was he, even it 2:00 A.M. Her room lights signaled her invitation. She opened the door.

"Hi," Christopher said. "Sorry about the hour, but I couldn't get away sooner." Because she thought it was a dream, she fell into his open arms. Because she wanted it to be real, she lifted her eager lips to his. She experienced the wondrous taste and feel of him. "A greeting like that makes me want to turn around and come back in again," he said, ending the deep and lengthy kiss. His hair was golden. His eyes were molten, as hypnotizing as the glow of the porch lamp that mesmerized dancing night insects. "Think it's safe to let me in?" he asked. A wide smile dimpled his cheeks. "It might cause talk."

She stepped back, dazed and overjoyed by his return. "I'm sorry about the man from your team," she said.

She suddenly knew why Christopher was there. He wanted to convince her it was now or never for them. She must leave Great Zimbabwe, kicked out as a result of Craig's understandable paranoia. Christopher must stay on for business. They didn't have much time. He'd gone through too much trouble to let things stand without one final shot. He'd played the perfect gentleman since Victoria Falls, and he wanted his just desserts for his restraint.

"Hey, what's this?" he asked. It was obviously her suitcase, and he knew it. He looked at her, shaking his head. "You think I'm going to let you walk out of my life!" he said. It wasn't a question.

"Do we have a choice in the matter?" she replied. She wanted him to say yes. "Craig's instructions say ten o'clock tomorrow morning."

"I fixed that, or didn't you hear?" he said. Janet resisted her desire to return to his arms.

"You fixed it for you to stay," she said, and moved farther away from him. "Something was said about the government's greed for gold overriding Craig's concern for your safety. That has nothing to do with me."

"Oh, Janet, you little fool!" he said.

"Don't touch me, please!" she warned him. If he took her in his arms again, she was his—for a moment, for an evening, for as long as he wanted. She wanted her pride, and he could steal it with a kiss. He won, but she didn't want him to know about his victory. Yet she was disappointed when he didn't reach out and take her triumphantly in his arms, when he didn't kiss her, when he didn't take her in his arms.

He took hold of her suitcase instead. He would help her on her way. Good riddance to a tease! The suitcase keys were on the corner of the dresser; he saw them. "Christopher?" He opened her bag, carried it effortlessly to the bed. "Stop it!" she insisted as he upturned the contents on the spread. He dropped the empty bag on the floor.

"I've unpacked for you," he said, scooping her belongings up in two massive fistfuls and stuffing them into the dresser drawers. The scene was so ludicrous, she almost laughed. "There," he said. One drawer was so overflowing he couldn't shut it. He folded his arms across his chest, leaned against the open drawer and faced her. "You should have known better than to pack in the first place."

"Oh? How should I have known that?" Her heart beat faster. Her throat muscles constricted, making it difficult to speak.

"You knew I was staying. You didn't think I would let the woman I love leave, did you?" His left eyebrow arched. "Or did you?"

She could play his game, fall into his arms and thank him for not forgetting her. She could surrender her body to his. In the morning, when it turned out he was lying and she must leave anyway, she would have memories of one night together. But that wasn't enough.

"What do you want?" he asked. She hated the easy way he put the responsibility on her shoulders.

"You didn't make arrangements for me to stay," she accused

him hotly. "You know why? I'll tell you! I don't have the expertise to find gold. Gold is your chief interest. All the rest is a clever diversion to get me into bed. That's all it's ever been."

He was surprised. Apparently he didn't think women had much reasoning power. They merely fell all over him, believing every lie and cockamamie story he told them. She was the exception. It made no difference that she wanted to believe him, because she knew better.

"And that's what you think?" he asked, shaking his head. He almost managed to make her feel guilty for seeing through him. "Well, that's great. Great! I do all I can to get us more time together, and you think it's a plot to get you in the sack for one evening. Well, I won't deny I want you in bed, although God only knows why I'm stupid enough to keep trying for the impossible! But you're wrong to think I'd be satisfied with one night. As I've told you before, you underestimate yourself—which continues to be to my advantage. You'd have a field day if you knew what control you really have over me."

She wouldn't be fooled. She wasn't buying his role of gullible male. She'd bought it at Victoria Falls, and look what it had gotten her. "Why here at Great Zimbabwe?" she asked, pleased with herself. He looked confused, and she made her question clearer, "Why not invite me to Lionspride for a get-acquainted holiday? Or suggest I take a hotel in Johannesburg while we explore our relationship a little further? It's Great Zimbabwe because of the gold. You can't simultaneously find gold and seduce me elsewhere."

She sensed his anger. His muscles tensed beneath the hugging contours of his tight-fitting shirt. "I have more faith in our relationship than you apparently do," he said. He was twisting things. He always did. He was good at shifting the blame, but she was prepared this time. There was no way this was her fault.

"Gold!" she repeated. "It's what runs in your veins instead of blood. If you really cared, you'd leave with me instead of staying to find it."

"I seriously considered leaving with you tomorrow," he said.

He was up to something. She could feel it in her bones. He was determined to win her over. It was a game, always a game. The more she insisted, the more important it was for him to triumph. "How easy running would be," he said. "Too easy."

She didn't see it that way. What was he saying? He wanted to confuse her. "I see what I see!" she said with finality. She saw a man she loved and had loved for sixteen years. He was pretending to offer her so much while offering so little.

"You think our running would solve the problem?" he asked. "It wouldn't, Janet. Whether the elephants get to Wankie or are slaughtered on the spot, the Zimbabwe government will want mineral experts back here. You and I won't change that by leaving before the job is done. Nor does the Great Zimbabwe Reserve have a better chance of survival without Van Hoon Afrikaner Minerals poking around. My company isn't the only one with the expertise to analyze the area's gold potential. We happen to be the one contracted for the job. Pull V.H.A.M. out, and someone else takes our place and reaps the profits. That's the reality, but you and I surely can face it and survive." Oh, he was so clever! "Finding gold here can bring the bogeyman out of his closet and make us deal with him. I've been in business long enough to know a satisfactory compromise can be worked out between two people. You may not see one right now—I might not see one, but we're not solving anything by refusing to admit the problem exists or by refusing to look for a solution. No relationship is perfect, Janet. Never. In fact, perfection is horribly boring, don't you think?"

She wanted perfection. She had had it sixteen years before. Or had she? All the heartache, longing and sorrow that had come after that summer was what had made those weeks so special in the end. She resented Christopher for giving her that insight. It made no difference that she was in Africa to smash childhood illusions; she wasn't going to let them go. She had never intended to let them go. She wanted a return to those good times; that's what she was doing here. He was telling her there wasn't perfection in his arms, and there never had been. Not only that—she would find it boring if there were. "I think. I might like a perfect relationship—for once in my life," she said.

He shook his head. He knew better. He knew everything. He knew nothing! "It's the downs of a relationship that make the highs so ecstatic," he told her. "It's the give and take, the ability to make something work, no matter what the odds, that give the greatest satisfaction. Our love can work, Janet. We can make it work—together I'm willing to take the chance. You should be willing, too."

"I'm scared," she said. She was, in fact, panic-stricken. She wanted it to work too much, and that was the problem. When her marriage to Bob had been on the rocks, she had told herself it would have been different with Christopher. Whenever she found her life wanting, she had told herself the same thing. What if it wasn't?

"Of course you're scared," he said. He came to her. She wanted him to take her in his arms and hold her close, and he did. She wanted him to tell her everything was going to be all right, but he didn't. "I'm scared, too," he said. "More scared than you, because I haven't loved in sixteen years. At least you had your husband." Yes, she had loved Bob in her way. Not this way, though—neither this deeply nor this intensely. The fear of losing Bob had never filled her with the horror she felt at even the prospect of losing Christopher again. "But fear is part of it," Christopher assured her. "Conquering fear is another part—a wonderful part," he insisted.

He kissed her then. It was a kiss like none she'd had before, not even in his arms. It took hold, its magic once again transforming dreams into reality.

He loved her and he wasn't going to let her leave. He wanted them together, facing whatever the future held. He was confident things would work out, and she couldn't be a coward. She was a fool to complicate their lives with problems that hadn't materialized and possibly never would. So far there wasn't enough gold at Great Zimbabwe to warrant the expense of getting it out. There was a good chance there never would be. She hoped so, but Christopher was right. Maybe if they worked together they could find a solution to whatever emotional conflict a major gold discovery at Great Zimbabwe would bring.

With hungry lips, he demanded the willing response she gave him. Their mouths opened slightly with the pressure. He took her breath away, and his own breath was ragged with emotion.

She slid her arms around him, savoring the hardness of his muscle beneath his contoured shirt.

"I love you," he said. There was never any doubt in Janet's mind that she loved him. She had loved him for sixteen long years.

He kissed her chin, and she seductively arched her neck to give him access to her breasts. He took her cue, simultaneously finding the buttons of her blouse with his skillful fingers and unfastening the material with gentle insistence. Green silk parted with a whisper like a lover's sigh. His hot kisses branded the creaminess of her breasts.

"Oh, Christopher," she moaned. Her voice was a low purr from sensuously parted lips. Bowing her head, she saw his mouth closing over the bud of one nipple. The nipple plumped in the fire with which his hungry mouth consumed it. He teased it further, nibbling it gently with his teeth. He caressed her other breast with his lips, his hands warm as toast as they cupped her.

He sank slowly to his knees, his hands skimming her hips as he pulled her closer, his tongue wet and alive against her navel. He moaned softly at the taste of her. He followed the waistband of her slacks from back to front with his fingers, expertly unfastening the side buttons. She buried her fingers in the soft silkiness of his hair as her slacks slid down her shapely legs and made a gray puddle around her feet. Hooking his thumbs in the elastic that hugged her waist, he peeled the pink silk downward, his hands searing her hips and thighs.

Convulsively she took hold of his hair as the caress of cool air against her newly naked skin was replaced by the heat of his maddening kisses. Her pleasure was unendurable, and she pulled his face upward, bringing him back to his feet. He was eager to reclaim her delicious lips, drinking in the sweetness of her breath, his hands guiding her blouse down over her shoulders. She dropped her arms to her sides, letting the clinging material come free and float dreamily to the floor behind her.

She stood in exquisite nakedness, more aware of her body than ever before. A vague guilt and painful shyness, never shaken throughout her marriage to Bob, were miraculously shed with her clothes, purged by Christopher's searing kisses and his touch. She was a pagan Venus born from a sea of pink and gray and green swirls.

He lifted her in his arms, leaving her clothes and shoes behind her. She held on tightly, burrowing her cheek against the straining cords of his neck. The frantic beat of his pulse vibrated against her lips, matching the racing of her heart. She nuzzled the sweet saltiness of his golden flesh.

In fact, she'd been wrong to think that the reality matched the fantasy. Nothing in her dream world rivaled the pleasure of Christopher's touch. Nothing in sixteen years of anticipation had prepared her for this moment or for the wonders she knew would follow.

He laid her gently on the bed, sitting beside her. His hands ran the length of her trembling body, exploring intimate places no other man but Bob had known before. "You're as beautiful as I imagined you would be," he said, his eyes never tiring of her sensuous curves. He cupped her breasts, his thumbs gently massaging her sensitized nipples.

He loved her, and she loved him. He preferred her body to precious gold. There were ways to work out any problem. If that wasn't perfection, it was as close as she was likely to come in the real world.

He eased away from her, standing by the side of the bed. He slowly unbuttoned his shirt, enjoying her enjoyment as he revealed the magnificence of his muscled torso. The smoothness of his golden flesh was stretched over a scalloped pattern of bone and muscle. What she remembered from their swims in the pools above Lisbon Falls, the memories upon which she had built her fantasies, was nothing compared to the wonders worked by Mother Nature on the real flesh and bone. He was her ideal man. He always had been and he always would be. She would find greater happiness in his arms than in the arms of any other man. She knew that with a certainty that scared her.

A sudden chill overcame her, a fear that she would not be able to fulfill his fantasies. Although Christopher talked about perfection as an illusion, it didn't mean he didn't picture an ideal woman. What expectations did he have—and how completely could she meet them?

He said he loved her, and she believed him. He said he wanted her, and she believed that, too. She had told Bob she loved him and meant it at the time, knowing he was less than the ultimate. Was that why Christopher said he loved her now, because he had given up looking for anything better?

He hadn't really loved since he was eighteen, and at eighteen, he had loved an innocent thirteen-year-old girl who had hurt him badly. Deep inside, she feared that Christopher loved only that part of her, the Janet Kelley of his past. Yet Janet couldn't respond to him from the depths of her being while suspecting that he would come to hate her if he ever found out who she was. And if she couldn't respond from that depth, she couldn't measure up to his ideal. She was destined to come out second best, as Bob had come out second best. She was cheating herself and she was cheating Christopher. Sometimes it had to be all or nothing, as pleasurable as mere fragments might be.

He unbuckled his belt, releasing its small metal catch. Within a matter of seconds his trousers would drop, and Christopher would be more powerfully attractive in complete nakedness than he was now. There would be no turning back then. Janet was only human, and she knew her weaknesses. But she also knew that their relationship could be better than second best—if she took a chance.

"Christopher, my maiden name was Kelley," she said, the words strangled in her throat, so that she didn't think he heard her. His belt was open, his pants unzipped. Golden hair curled on his lower stomach, disappearing beneath the snug fit of his blue jockey shorts. Having second thoughts about her confession, she now hoped he hadn't heard. She wanted him as naked as she was. She wanted him on the bed with her, making love.

"Kelley?" he asked, shaking his head to clear it. Where had his mind been before Janet wrenched it back to this less pleasurable reality?

"Janet Kelley," she said. She took the plunge, for better or worse. There was no turning back. "My father was Jack Kelley."

"No," he said simply. He didn't believe her. He thought she was joking. But it would have been a joke in poor taste, and he had obviously come to the same conclusion as comprehension dawned. "You?"

"I'm sorry," she said. She turned her head, unable to look at him. It was too impossibly painful to sort out the emotions that flashed across his handsome face. It was too painful to realize, she had come so close to the fulfillment of her fantasy, spoiling the moment because greediness made her hope for more.

He should love her despite her revelation. Their good memories should override the bad. He should realize the rare opportunity they had to rise above their parents' conflicting past. He had promised they could challenge all obstacles and beat them. He had lied—to both of them.

The door opened and closed softly behind him. She began to cry, her body aching from needs aroused within her, then left unsatisfied.

"Oh, Christopher, I do love you!" she said, sobbing. She sat up on the edge of the bed. Inner heat, a raging fire that had warmed her only moments before, had been doused by his rejection. She was icy cold.

She got up and pulled back the blankets, hoping to find warmth beneath them. Her legs hardly supported her. She saw Christopher's shirt, left where he had dropped it on the floor. He had been in too much of a hurry to bother taking it with him.

How exquisite his body was when it was free of that shirt. How near she had come to seeing the rest of his powerful physique, never to see it now. She picked up his shirt, rubbing it against her cheek, soaking its softness with the wetness of her tears.

The shirt smelled of tangy lime. It was a fragrance she would forever associate with her shattered dreams for happiness.

CHAPTER ELEVEN

SHE WAS A MAGNET, drawing them all to her that morning, except the one person she wanted. Even Craig was there, confused by her suitcase. "I thought Van Hoon arranged for you to stay?" he said. It was the cue for Roger, Tim and Jill to give her curious stares.

"When was this?" Roger asked.

"I found out last night," Janet said. Fat chance anyone would leave it at that!

"Van Hoon was insistent," Craig added.

"Well, I'm not staying," she said. "I told him so, too. I couldn't do much here without a camera crew."

"Ah!" Roger exclaimed. Christopher's arrangements hadn't included Roger, Tim or Jill.

"I'm not on vacation," she reminded them all. "I'm covering a story—on elephants, not on the search for Great Zimbabwe gold. While the discovery of gold would have an impact on whatever future there is for the reserve, I already have enough footage to emphasize that point. Now shall we go for breakfast?"

They wanted to hear more. Her crew no doubt remembered Janet's private supper with Christopher at Lionspride, her private trip with him to the Van Hoon Deep Levels Mine, and his unexpected arrival at Great Zimbabwe. And Janet knew Craig was probably recalling Christopher's appearance at Victoria Falls.

She had said all she planned to say. What had happened the night before was too painful to relive in conversation. Such wounds were a long time in healing—if they ever healed.

She wasn't hungry. Her trip to Africa had been wonderful for her waistline. She would write a book: *The South African Diet Book* by Janet Westover AKA Janet Kelley. Americans were forever trying to slim down. They were always ready for the latest diet fad.

Roger carried her gripsack to the Land Rover. From there, they all went to the restaurant. Janet ordered tea and toast. Everyone else was hungry and tackled large servings of eggs, ham and potatoes.

"I hope none of you take your expulsion personally," Craig said over a forkful of food. "You see my position—a stampede, a shooting, one man dead and another one dying. I'm no longer in any position to guarantee your safety. Van Hoon is staying, knowing I'm refusing all responsibility for him and his team."

"We have plenty of footage for a good show," Roger said. "I'd be less willing to go if we didn't." Tim and Jill nodded agreement.

Christopher wasn't in the room. Janet glanced toward the door, hoping he would appear. She was still praying for happy endings and should know better. *Janet, you silly fool!*

"Well," Roger said, pushing away his empty plate, "it's about that time, so I'll get the rest of my stuff loaded."

"Same here," Tim said. Both men got to their feet. "Jill?" Tim asked.

Craig would be less diplomatic about his curiosity once he got Janet alone, she feared, and Jill seemed reluctant to leave at this crucial moment. "I'll finish my coffee," she said. In the silence that followed, she got the hint. She excused herself, too.

"I guess I'd better do a once-over of my room in case I missed something," Janet said,, hoping to head off the cross-examination. She should have left with the others. There was anonymity in numbers.

"Why don't you stay until I finish my coffee?" Craig suggested. "I haven't seen much of you the past couple of days."

Janet nervously checked her wristwatch. "It's getting close to ten," she reminded him. "I'm famous for leaving things in hotel rooms."

"We've plenty of time," he assured her. "The plane is here to fly certain people out, and it won't go without everyone. In the meantime, let's talk about you and Christopher."

"I don't want to talk about me and Christopher," Janet said. She couldn't be plainer than that. It wasn't that she didn't want to talk about them. She couldn't talk about them. Let Craig play policeman. His interrogation would get nothing from her that she hadn't already volunteered.

"I was delighted when Van Hoon insisted you stay," Craig said, surprising her. "Do you know why?"

"You're going to tell me anyway, aren't you?" she said. She tried for sarcasm, but her curiosity came through. She did want to know.

The V.H.A.M. team has been lax from the beginning on its itinerary reports to me," Craig said. "I mentioned that to you on our flight back from Fort Victoria, remember?" Janet nodded. "This thing with Spencer has them momentarily realizing the error of their ways," Craig continued. Paul Spencer, the wounded member of the V.H.A.M. team, was in critical condition. He wasn't expected to pull through. "It's surprising, though, how quickly we forget. Christopher and his men will be back to their irresponsible habits in no time. I was hoping you'd serve as their insurance policy."

Me?" Janet wasn't following.

"A smile from a beautiful woman, accompanied by her, 'So where are we off to today?' would produce more accurate information than anything quickly jotted down on paper for me the night before," Craig said. He smiled. He really was handsome, and Janet regretted never having fully explored their possibilities. If only Christopher had stayed in Johannesburg! "You would have been able to double-check on their movements," Craig continued. "Van Hoon thinks he can handle himself in any situation, but Paul Spencer thought the same. I'm hoping to keep Van Hoon and his men alive in spite of themselves."

It gave her an excuse for staying—to help guard Christopher's life. Craig's reasoning seemed valid to her. Christopher's interest in Janet had been more than evident. Her interest in Christopher was as easily assumed. So she couldn't be angry at Craig for again wanting to use her. When he had pleaded for her help at Victoria Falls, it had been because of his concern for the animals. This time he had human life in mind—Christopher's life. "Unfortunately, whatever was between Christopher and me ended last night," she said. Who said talking helped?

"Irreconcilable differences?" Craig asked.

"I'm afraid so," she said, but didn't leave it at that. "We knew each other before—years ago, as children. There were bitter feelings then, and the years have changed nothing. For a while I hoped, but..." She shrugged helplessly. It was out of her hands. She wanted more from Christopher than he was prepared to offer. His fine talk of love as the universal cure-all was really meaningless.

"You're sure?" Craig persisted. "You're sure it wasn't just a simple lovers' quarrel?" Clearly, his job was complicated by the uncooperative V.H.A.M. team. He had enough problems with poachers, elephants and his superiors. The latter had not only countermanded his eviction of the team but had threatened to pull him out before he accomplished all that he'd set out to do. Janet regretted that she couldn't help him now.

"I'm positive," she said. She couldn't do any good by staying. Christopher wouldn't confide anything to her, no matter how much she smiled and wished him a pleasant day. He would avoid her like the plague. She wasn't about to submit to daily rejection.

"I'm sorry," Craig said, putting down his cup and getting to his feet. He read the impossibility in her eyes. "Well, he and his men have been warned. If they refuse to keep me informed of their movements, it's out of my hands."

"I'm sorry, too," she said, the words catching in throat. He didn't know how sorry, and neither did Christopher.

They walked into sunshine too bright for Janet's depressed

state. A dreary, cold, rainy day would have been more appropriate.

"Will you ride with me to the airport?" he asked when they reached the parking lot. Dr. Nhari and his men were busy loading their gear. Roger was storing the last of the camera equipment in one Land Rover. Tim and Jill were relaxing in the nearby shade. Janet was in no mood for further attempts by anyone to change her mind, and Craig seemed to guess her thoughts. "We won't talk about Christopher or poachers," he promised.

"Then I'd love to ride with you," she said. "Just let me check my room."

There was nothing of hers left there. She had spent the morning going through it time and time again. She had packed meticulously, folding the clothes Christopher had unceremoniously stuffed in the dresser drawers. He had looked so silly emptying her bag on the bed. He had looked so silly ramming fistfuls of clothes into the drawers. So silly and, oh, so lovable!

How high Janet's hopes had soared when he'd said he wasn't letting her go. She had believed him. How naive she was after all these years! Christopher was letting her go, and he was glad to be rid of her.

She splashed cold water on her face and checked for signs of her pain reflected in the mirror. That's what she had really come to her room to do. She wanted to put on a good face for the world.

She didn't look much the worse for wear, considering what had happened since her arrival in Africa. She was thinner, more tanned, a little haggard around the edges, but she wasn't the mess on the outside that she was on the inside. Her body was a marvelous performer. Her experience as a television personality helped her to mask her emotions further.

"Oh, Christopher, damn your lies!" she said, placing her hand on the mirror to blot out her pain-darkened eyes and give herself needed support. She was going to be sick. "Pull yourself together, Janet!" she commanded. This wasn't the only setback in her life. It wasn't even unexpected. She pushed away from the sink and forced herself to smile. "Your smile has to be more sincere," she criticized herself. She was actress and director. Her smile widened. "Better, better," she commented. "Not perfect, not good enough for an Emmy, but it's passable."

She didn't look at the bed on the way out, just as she had avoided looking at it on the way in. She might have experienced infinite bliss among those sheets and covers, Instead she had ended up shivering away the previous night like a feverish child, holding Christopher's shirt as if it were a security blanket or a favorite teddy bear. The shirt was now in the wastebasket by the desk. It had suffered the same ignominious fate as her silk negligee. She didn't look at the shirt, disturbed by the temptation to take it with her as a macabre souvenir. Her break must be a clean one.

She smelled the fragrance of lime as she opened the door and stepped outside. Her pulse quickened expectantly, but it wasn't Christopher. There was an orchard of lime trees behind the hotel. The fragrance stayed with her as she headed down the pathway toward the people waiting for her. Christopher wasn't waiting. He had left early to scour the hillsides for gold.

So much had happened for nothing to have happened at all.

"I'm riding with Craig to Fort Victoria," she said when she reached her group.

"We know!" they chimed in unison. "He told us." Janet laughed. She couldn't help herself.

"Now that's the Janet we remember!" Roger said approvingly—which wasn't true, she knew. Her laughter had an unfamiliar brittleness.

"I'm trying my best to get back into the groove," Janet said. Leaving Africa and Christopher would help. "You've all been marvelous, by the way."

"That's what friends are for," Roger replied. He would have said more, but Jill interrupted.

"Here comes guess who!" she announced. Janet turned, expecting Christopher. How foolish to hope at the last minute! It was Craig. Since everything was packed, he wanted them to be on their way.

"Ready?" he asked. Janet didn't know. She was tempted to stay, even knowing it was hopeless.

"Yes," she lied. She walked with him to the lead Land Rover and climbed in. There was no staying. She had given it her last shot and had come up with nothing. It was time to move forward, get on with her life and jettison the excess. To Christopher, she was excess already jettisoned.

Craig kept his word. They didn't talk about Christopher or the poachers. Avoiding those subjects, they had little else to say. It was just as well, because Janet didn't feel like talking.

The plane was waiting. It took a while to load baggage and TV filming equipment, so everyone waited in the terminal. They drank coffee and soft drinks.

It was eleven o'clock by the time they began boarding. Janet had surrendered all hope of Christopher's showing up for final goodbyes. Craig walked her to the gate, Janet lost in the pain of frustrated love. Craig was occupied with thoughts of his own. "Too bad this couldn't have worked out better for all of us," he said finally.

"Yes, isn't it?" Janet agreed. He kissed her cheek, and that was that. Janet joined the line of people filing across the runway.

"I expected you two to come up with a better show than that," Jill chided, catching up to Janet.

"What?" Janet responded absently. Her mind was elsewhere. She hoped to forget Christopher one day, but it was still too early. She couldn't blot his image out of her mind, couldn't forget how devastatingly sexy he looked with his shirt off and his belt unfastened.

"My brother gives me more affectionate good-bye kisses," Jill criticized her playfully.

"Yes? Well, Craig is less than my brother, isn't he?"

"So where's Christopher?" Jill asked hopefully "I'll bet he could do better."

"He's still out looking for gold," Janet said, attempting flippancy.

Jill's disbelieving shake of her head showed what she thought of that. Jill was a romantic, and romantics were freaks in an age of jaded realists, Janet reflected wryly. No one came to Africa and married the big white hunter, except in movies and story-books.

The plane was large and spacious. Jill sat with Tim. Roger didn't insist that Janet join him, and she chose a seat by herself. Her window faced away from the terminal. She buckled her seatbelt, closed her eyes and settled back. It had boiled down to this, and she had wanted so much more. Too bad Christopher couldn't deliver, but why should he? She had deserted him sixteen years before without a word. She had been naive to expect his open arms once her secret was out. She should have been content with second best. That was better than nothing.

The plane taxied along the tarmac to the end of the runway. It made a one-hundred-and-eighty-degree turn and stopped. The engines revved for takeoff, and Janet waited. The vibrations and the sounds died. "Did someone forget something?" Roger asked in the calm. Janet opened her eyes. Everyone turned toward her side of the plane, which now faced the terminal. A Land Rover and truck were headed for the aircraft. The truck carried boarding stairs piggyback. Despite Janet's hopes, the Land Rover was driven by Craig, not Christopher.

"Mrs. Westover?" The unfamiliar voice startled her. The pilot stood at the front of the aisle. He located her by the curious glances suddenly cast in her direction. "Will you please come forward for a minute?" he requested.

"You making off with the silverware again, Janet?" Roger asked. He got a howl of laughter from the passengers. Even Janet smiled.

The pilot waited for her by the door. Outside, someone jock-eyed the stairway into position. "What's this all about?" Janet asked.

The pilot shrugged. "Instructions from the flight tower," he said and opened the door.

Craig was on the other side. "Craig?" Janet queried. The

word asked a lot.

"Captain, will you excuse us for a minute?" Craig asked. The pilot returned to the cockpit, and Craig motioned Janet out onto the stairway for more privacy. "Christopher called from the hotel," he said. Chills danced along Janet's spine. The sound of Christopher's name released the usual flood of emotions inside her.

"What's that got to do with me?" she managed.

"He doesn't want you to leave," Craig said. He flashed an I-told-you-so smile, but Janet didn't believe him.

"Why didn't he tell me himself?" she asked. She had just faced up to her loss, and now this. It wasn't fair!

"He plans to tell you himself," Craig said. "He'll be here in fifteen minutes if he drives as fast as I expect. I won't hold the plane, but whether you leave on it or not is your decision. At least you're aware of your alternative."

It was hope where there was none. Only more pain and heartbreak loomed ahead, and Janet had suffered enough. If Christopher wanted her to stay, he would have said something before now.

"His Land Rover broke down early this morning," Craig said. "He was out driving at the time—without my knowing; his cell phone with no signal," he added. Janet knew the significance and danger of that. Already Christopher had forgotten the lesson learned by the wounding of Paul Spencer. "He had to walk back to the hotel. We were gone by the time he got back."

Janet shook her head. She wanted to believe, but she couldn't. Things didn't happen this way in real life.

"He sounded sincere," Craig judged. He checked his watch. "We should let these people get on their way."

"My suitcase?" Janet said. She was, stalling. Her bag was the least of her worries. There was the prospect of additional heartache to consider. Clean separations between people were the best—but that wasn't true, either. She'd left Lionspride sixteen years before with no goodbyes, and she'd regretted it ever since.

"Your bag can be flown back on the first commercial flight,"

Craig said, predictably.

"Let me tell Roger I'm staying," she said. It was the only decision she could make. Even the merest flicker of hope inside her had to be fanned.

"It's the right decision, Janet," Craig assured her.

Right or wrong, she'd made it.

"So," Roger asked when she reached him, "which one is it?" She pretended not to understand. "Captain Sylo or Van Hoon?" he asked with a laugh. Janet blushed.

"Christopher," she said. What else could she say? She didn't have the time for feeble excuses, and she couldn't leave without giving some reason.

"Good!" he said, pleased. "I wouldn't have said this before, but he's the better man—richer, too. Don't forget your poor camera crew when you make out the wedding invitations."

"It isn't close to any wedding!" Janet said. Her expectations no longer matched the silly fantasies shared by Roger, Tim and Jill.

"I don't believe that," Roger said. Janet wished she had his insight and confidence.

"Believe it," she told him, knowing she was running out of time. "I'll call."

"Should we wait for you in Salisbury?"

"No," she said. "Go to Seattle and oversee the editing, will you? I'll fix things with the boss myself. I have some holiday time coming to me anyway."

"And the angle for the piece?" Roger asked. He was enjoying himself. "It's one thing to do a hatchet job on Christopher Van Hoon," he explained, "but quite another to do one on the boss lady's love. Why don't we hold off on editing until you decide? We've enough shows in the can to start the new season. We can wait on this one."

"I'll call you," she repeated, giving him a quick kiss on the cheek.

"Van Hoon is the winner, everybody!" Roger announced loudly. Janet turned red. Everyone immediately applauded. He was impossible, but he was her friend.

Craig drove her to the terminal. "It's better if the two of you have time alone," he said, always the diplomat. He rejoined his soldiers. The line of vehicles headed toward Great Zimbabwe. Behind Janet, the aircraft lifted into clear African skies.

The terminal was deserted, between planes. Janet chose a chair that faced the doorway. Minutes ticked by with no Christopher. He wasn't coming; he'd changed his mind. Craig had mistaken what Christopher had said over the telephone. There were numerous excuses for his not showing, and Janet ran through them all.

She changed her seat. Watching water never made it boil faster, and the same principle applied here. If Christopher wasn't coming, he wasn't coming, and she wouldn't make him appear by watching the roadway. She stared at the empty tarmac. Craig had said Christopher would be there in fifteen minutes. Those minutes were up.

Suddenly he was there, and she realized with a jolt that she hadn't really been expecting him. She didn't believe he was standing in front of her. "I'm glad you waited," he said apologetically. "I didn't know if you would."

He wore faded jeans that molded his firm legs and hugged his slim waist. His khaki shirt was open almost to his waist, revealing his chest, which glistened with perspiration, as did his face and muscular arms. His blond hair clung to his damp forehead. He was the most handsome man she had ever seen. "Oh, Christopher," she moaned, "I thought it was over!"

His arms supported her when she could no longer stand. He drew her close and kissed her hair while she inhaled the heady fragrance of his masculine scent. "Janet," he whispered, "what a fool I've been!" She put her forefinger to his lips, excited by the touch and smell of him. She savored the moment in silence, afraid words would spoil it. However, they couldn't stand where they were forever, and they both knew it. "Come on," he said, taking her hand.

They drove through Fort Victoria and into the surrounding

farm country. They didn't speak, and Janet was comfortable in the silence. Things needed saying, but all in good time. She didn't know what to say anyway. She couldn't explain her wondrous feelings.

They passed two barricades manned by soldiers. At each, Janet's and Christopher's names were checked against a list of authorized personnel before they were allowed through. Until a few minutes earlier, Janet's name hadn't been on the list. Craig had added it once he knew she was returning with Christopher.

Christopher pulled the car off the main road, after they entered the wilderness of the reserve, parking among the towering acacias. He waited until the dust settled around them and then turned to her. "I think I knew who you were all along," he confessed. He touched her cheek gently with his fingertips. "Why did I react the way I did?" He shrugged. "Subconsciously knowing something and facing up to the reality are two different things. The fear comes when you're on the threshold of some-thing only dreamed of for sixteen years."

"Yes," she said. She knew. Oh, yes, she knew!

His fingers lingered lovingly against her cheek. "I wonder where we go from here," he said.

"We go to the hotel," Janet said, more in control than she had ever been. Now that it boiled down to boy loves total girl, woman loves total man, no matter what the past or what the future, the moment demanded more than probing discussion.

She kissed his fingers before he pulled them away. He started the Land Rover and drove them to the hotel.

* * * * * * *

HE LOCKED the door of his room behind them. A pair of his pants hung over the back of one chair. Beyond the open bath-room door, his toilet articles neatly lined the glass shelf above the sink. A pair of scuffed hiking shoes was on the floor at the foot of the bed, his blue jockey shorts from the day before casu-ally tented on top of them. The draperies were open, but gauzy curtains allowed filtered sunlight to fill the room.

"I need to shower," he said, taking her in his arms and kissing her forehead. "My unscheduled walk this morning has left me less than fresh."

"It's sexy," she said, kissing the sweaty hollow of his neck. She slipped her hands into the opening of his shirt and explored the scalloped contours of his chest and stomach. "Very, very sexy," she assured him, pulling back to look into his sunny eyes. "Did your Land Rover really break down this morning?" she asked. To think a faulty car had almost deprived them of this glorious moment!

"It ran out of gas," Christopher said, his fingers combing through the silky strands of her shiny black hair.

"You're supposed to have a woman along whenever you pull that old stunt," Janet teased, rubbing her cheek against the velvety-smooth hardness of his chest.

"I planned for the gas to run out," he confessed. One of his nipples hardened as she kissed it. She was excited that he was excited. "I convinced myself that I didn't want to get back to you in time," he said. "When I changed my mind, I was almost too late."

"I'm glad you made it to a phone," Janet said.

"I'm the one who's glad," he replied, putting his forefinger beneath her chin and lifting her face to his. He kissed her forehead, the bridge of her nose, her cheeks. He kissed her lips, the length of his body also kissing hers. His desire was sensually evident, so powerful that it was difficult to control. "About that shower?" he said; his voice low and gravelly with passion.

"I'll help you undress for it," she said, feeling deliciously bold. She wouldn't have suggested it to Bob. He would have been shocked by his wife wanting to undress him. Lovemaking with him had been less than adventurous. He got all the adventure he needed from his job without carrying it over into the bedroom. He had married Janet to give a sense of normalcy to his life. To Bob, home had been a quiet retreat, a place to escape to when the excitement of the outside world became too much to bear.

Janet flattened her hands against the ripples of Christopher's stomach and slid her fingers up over his chest to nudge his shirt off his broad shoulders. He pulled his arms from the short sleeves. The shirt hung from his waist, held there by two fastened buttons and the tuck of the shirttail in his trousers. Janet dislodged the material from beneath the waistband of his jeans. Without bothering with the buttons, she let the shirt drop around his feet.

She remembered how he had loosened his belt buckle the night before, and she mirrored the procedure. She slipped her fingers beneath the front of the waistband to begin unzipping his jeans, and Christopher groaned in helpless response. An accompanying tremor went through his body. Her power over him made her more excited. Love was meant to be this two-way exchange, this give and take of pleasure, this mutual sharing of ecstasy.

He groaned again when she slid the zipper down still farther. The backs of her fingers slid along his sensitized skin. His hand squeezed and released her shoulders in cadence with the waves of pleasure washing through him.

Trembling, she finally had his jeans completely undone. She helped him wriggle out of them, revealing white shorts and the muscled columns of his legs.

He leaned forward, nuzzling his mouth against the soft arch of her neck and kissing upward to her ear. "One small problem," he whispered; his low-timbered voice sexy. Her heart stopped. "My pants won't come off over my boots," he said.

"Oh," she said, relieved enough to giggle. The problem was funny, not tragic. She hadn't undressed a man before, and she hadn't thought it out beforehand. She had known what she wanted to see, and she had gone for it. She hadn't thought of starting from the bottom and working up. So much for spontaneity! His golden eyes sparked with amusement as well as passion. "Why didn't you tell me, you beast?" she said, her wide smile adding beauty to an attractively flushed face.

"I was counting on this moment of levity to keep me from prematurely losing control," he said, his smile deeply dimpling both cheeks.

"How's that?"

"A guy can't really get too carried away with his pants thoroughly binding his ankles, can he?" Christopher pointed out with a chuckle.

"So where do we go from here?" Janet asked. Rather than diminishing her excitement, their light banter increased it. She had always suspected sex was more than the serious business Bob had insisted on making it, and a few brief moments with Christopher had already confirmed as much.

"I can do my flamingo routine, standing on one leg at a time to take my boots off," he suggested. "That's good for a laugh. Or I can play duck and waddle to the nearest chair. Either of those strike your fancy?"

"Is this happening?" Janet asked. Everything was too right, too perfect, too charmingly enjoyable.

"Oh, yes," he guaranteed, "and it's going to get better. I promise."

"So which is quicker?" Janet asked, shaking her head. "Flamingo or duck?" Where had she been all of her life that she had missed the pure pleasure of such moments?

"The duck routine is quicker," he said. "Want to walk along to give me balance?"

"I got you into this, didn't I?" Janet reminded him. "The least I can do is give you a helping hand."

He put his arm around her neck and executed an exaggerated shuffle to the nearest chair. Janet couldn't help laughing aloud. It was funny and exciting at the same time.

She helped him off with both boots and freed his legs from the tangled pants and shirt, laughing all the while. She extended her hands to his, thrilling to the touch and squeeze of his fingers as he came to his feet. "I love you," she said, her forefinger tracing a line from the hollow at the base of his throat to the indentation of his navel. Golden hair curled on his lower stomach, disappearing beneath his shorts.

"I assure you, the feeling is mutual," he said, and kissed the sensitive spot where her neck smoothly curved to meet her shoulder.

He wasn't shy about his body. Bob had been, and Bob's uneasiness had made her feel guilty and embarrassed for enjoying the sight of her husband's muscled nakedness. It was different with Christopher. He made something undeniably right about taking lovemaking out of the darkness.

"I prefer my lovemaking with the lights on," he had told her when they were poised at the entrance of a dark basement room at Lionspride, Janet afraid to enter for fear of what advantage he would take there.

"My shower," he reminded her, although he seemed less and less determined to take it.

"In a minute," she assured him. Hooking the elastic top of his shorts in her fingers, she pulled them down, revealing an un-tanned part of his body that she had never seen before. The sheer powerful beauty of him numbed her. "About that shower," she muttered. She was going to tell him to forget it, but she didn't. "I think *we* should take it," she said instead.

"We?" He held her at arm's length, her suggestion obviously meeting with his approval.

"We," she affirmed, taking his hand. She led the way to the bathroom, where Christopher hurriedly adjusted the temperature of the water while Janet took off her shoes and clothes.

"Need a little help undressing?" he asked. She shook her head. It was quicker this way, and there would be time later for more leisurely explorations. The sooner she was naked in his arms, the sooner they could treat themselves to the pleasures they both craved.

Christopher stepped into the shower, leaving the curtain partially open and glancing at Janet. She faced him, blushing because of his obvious approval. He adjusted the water to make it more comfortable for her, but he needn't have bothered. She would have joined him no matter what the temperature. She had a heat burning inside of her that would have survived the worst Arctic storm.

The tub of the bath-and-shower combination was over six feet long. There were several strips of special no-skid adhesive along the bottom to keep them from slipping.

"Oh, Janet, Janet," Christopher murmured, taking her in his arms when she stepped into join him. He kissed her eager lips, and then turned her beneath the soothing jets of warm water. His hard chest flattened her yielding breasts.

The combination of hot skin and warm water was undeniably sensuous as his hungry mouth traced the smooth curve of her neck to her shoulder. His butterfly kisses sexily backtracked along the arch of her throat, pausing where the frantic race of her pulse heralded her increasing excitement.

She caressed the length of his strong back and the twin mounds sculptured at the base of his spine. Resting her hands there, she pulled him nearer. They were as close as two people could get without achieving the ultimate closeness.

He outlined her lips and teeth with his tongue, adding fuel to their mutual fire. He turned his back to block Janet from the jets of water, reaching for the soap in the nearby niche and hastily ripping off its wrapper. Within seconds his fingers were lathered and beginning slow and smoothly caressing movements down her back and farther. He slid his hands around her sensitive derrière, igniting sparks of pleasure wherever he touched.

He turned her soapy back toward the hardness of his stomach and chest. Leaning back, she rested her head against his neck, her wet black hair clinging to his chest. He drew slippery whorls up her stomach to her breasts. Her nipples hardened. His nipples, too, were as hard as thumbtacks against the foamy slickness of her back. He massaged her breasts tenderly, lovingly. "Christopher, oh, Christopher," she moaned, nothing but her utterances of his name adequate to express her feelings at that sublime moment. He moaned a guttural undecipherable reply into her ear.

On weak legs, she shifted her position and took the soap from him, lathering his corded neck and broad shoulders while his hands held her waist and offered support. She soaped his chest and his stomach, his body still a barrier protecting her from all but an occasional splatter of spray. She touched him as she hadn't touched any man. Her fingers explored, and Christopher made no move to interrupt the freedom of their movement.

She watched what she did, and her pleasure was increased by her seeing.

She stretched to put the soap back in its niche, then flattened her hands on the ripples of his stomach and gazed deeply into the black-flecked sunny quality of his eyes. "Love me," she said, stirring the lather caught within the curls of golden hair beneath his navel. "Love me," she repeated, pulling her hands away. He groaned loudly when next she touched him, reflexively thrusting his hips closer.

"I do love you," he said, his voice husky with pleasure. She gasped in accompanying wonder, her mouth exploring his shoulder. She wrapped her arms around his neck and held on tightly. He looked down, his stare wide and glassy. Quickly, though, he focused and smiled. "And this," he said, "is heaven."

"Yes," she agreed. "Yes, oh, yes, oh, yes!" She tilted her head so her lips were easily his. At the same time, his hips revolved slowly, conjuring up a flaming heat that quickly melted her insides to golden dew. Her fingernails dug into his strong neck. They were both gasping for breath. She was caught in a super-nova of exploding emotion. She eagerly entered the special world of love's golden spell, and Christopher joined her in the flames.

It was all Janet imagined it would be and more. Much, much more.

* * * * * * *

HE SLEPT on his stomach, his cheek resting against her heart. His arm was thrown covetously across her waist. The sheets were in disarray, kicked that way during the heat of the night. Her head was propped on the pillow, and she had an excellent view of the tapering of his body from his broad shoulders to his narrow waist.

Lazily she combed the silky softness of his hair with her fingers. He groaned contentedly in his sleep, like a cat purring after a feast on heavy cream. The blond strands caught the light from the lamp left on all night. Outside the sky paled as morning approached.

She took pleasure in the moment and wished it would last. But he stirred, on the verge of waking. He turned his face to her breast, nuzzling her nipple. She was excited by the sensuousness he exhibited even in sleep. Her nipple hardened in response, and she slid her hand along the gentle curve of his spine.

Begun in sleep, his desire increased when he awakened fully to find her beside him. There was no denying the force that merged them in love.

The magic of their union had not diminished. The feel of him, the taste of his lips, the sound of his breathless sighs were pure unadulterated enchantment.

There had been ecstasy in their adventurous lovemaking in the shower and in the eager embraces that followed, but their present pleasure was more intense because of its slowness. There was a delicious tension in carefully layering one degree of enjoyment upon another.

His hand flattened on the bed, his arms straightening to push himself up. "I want to see you clearly while we make love," he said huskily.

"And I want to see you," she murmured, gripping his forearms and looking deeply into his eyes. He was virile and handsome, his striated muscles working sensuously beneath his tanned skin. His arms strained with the effort to keep his torso curved away from hers.

She splayed her fingers across his chest, delighting in his nearness, in the mere fact of having him this close, this touchable, after so many hopeless years. "Oh, Christopher!" she whispered.

He released the tension of his strong arms, lowering himself. "Janet," he whispered; his voice soft yet rough.

She moaned in reply, her hands sliding out from under his chest to clamp his shoulders. Through blurred eyes, she saw his neck arch back. She heard his response. She shut her eyes and tossed her head helplessly from side to side in fevered passion, her black tresses whipping the whiteness of the pillow.

Her long and sensuous slide into oblivion wasn't disappointing, because it was a true sharing. He didn't stop his kisses and caresses too soon. As he sighed "I love you," his hands stroked gently at her breasts, and then lovingly cupped her undulating hips. He snuggled closer and kissed her eyes, her nose, her cheeks, her chin, and the curve of her neck.

"I love you, too," she said finally on a long sigh of her own, gently biting his shoulder, even now hungry for the taste of him.

They cuddled in the warmth of passion's afterglow. When they finally parted, he stretched, turned toward her and smiled. "And what do you say to two people very much in love witnessing the beginning of this new day in a very special way?" he suggested, drawing his finger delicately along her jaw line. He obviously didn't mean from the comfort of their bed, either. "Come on," he said, getting up. The sheer beauty of his naked and athletic body still took her breath away. "We can make it to the top of the Acropolis before sunrise."

"The Acropolis?" she echoed disbelievingly.

"When Christopher Van Hoon plans to propose marriage to the woman he loves, he deserves the entire glorious backdrop Mother Nature can provide. Right?" She'd heard what he'd said, but it didn't sink in. Love and marriage did go together, but somehow marriage to Christopher had remained an unattainable dream, despite what had happened between them. "Well?" he insisted. His pants were on, belted and buttoned. She was too dumbfounded to move. "Get up, Janet! Do get up!" he insisted playfully.

She remained in a daze while she dressed. He was standing at the window, checking the skyline and his watch when she finished. "We'll have to hurry," he said, taking her hand.

Her feet seemed to have wings as he pulled her across the parking lot to his Land Rover. The moon had set, and it wouldn't be long before the rising sun bleached all remaining starlight from the sky. For the moment the valley was still in shadow, the horizon not yet tinged with morning gold. The Acropolis was a dark silhouette that loomed on their left as the Land Rover sped along the deserted roadway.

There were three routes to the top of the Acropolis, all of which required walking. The Northwest Stairway and the Southeast Stairway had been major approaches during the heyday of Great Zimbabwe. The former was presently over-grown and hardly used. The latter was a steep climb. The third approach was a more gradual ascent constructed for tourists who preferred sight-seeing with the least possible exertion. But even it was no piece of cake. Janet was panting within minutes of leaving the Land Rover and starting the climb. "I've got to rest," she insisted, leaning against a massive boulder that was incorporated into the wall of the stairway.

"Maybe I should have been less spontaneous," he suggested with an apologetic grin. He wasn't even breathing hard. "It seemed a good idea at the time."

"If I survive, it *will* be a good idea," she grudgingly admitted. There was something romantic about getting up before sunrise and hiking up a mountainside to witness the dawn of a new day and the dawn of her new life with the man she loved. He was proposing marriage to her once they got to the top of this moun-tain—if they ever got there. "Let's move," she said, pushing away from the boulder and heading up more steps. There was still no evidence of sunlight frosting the distant outcroppings, but it wouldn't be long.

"Funny, but I don't remember the climb being this strenuous," he said magnanimously. Janet blushed. He was being gallant.

When they reached the ruins at the top, there was a warren of pathways from which to choose. Christopher knew the way. He'd been there before, but not under such special circumstances, he told her.

The Royal Enclosure was on the western tip of the escarpment on a natural ledge in the Turret Wall. The wall had been named after the succession of small round towers along its top. By entering the Royal Enclosure and climbing the Turret Wall directly to the left of the Cliff Entrance, and by facing east, Janet and Christopher had an uninterrupted view of the horizon.

Janet was initially too tired to enjoy her successful race with the sun, but when she got her breath, she took in her surroundings and could understand why the locale had been picked for a fortress. It commanded a spectacular panorama of the surrounding countryside, so there would have been plenty of forewarning of attack from any direction. The narrow pathways to the summit assured an easy defense of the top.

But the breathtaking landscape and the defense capabilities of the citadel weren't what held Janet's interest at the moment. Christopher had that. When he enclosed her in a tender embrace, she was concentrating totally on her undeniable love for him.

"Janet Kelley Westover, will you marry me?" he asked as the sun spilled golden light over the horizon. It was a wondrous moment, one to tell their children and grandchildren about. She was glad he had brought her to this special place at this special moment.

For a brief instant she remembered that he might yet find gold at Great Zimbabwe, which would interfere with the survival of the animals left in the area. On the other hand, his chances of discovering gold were remote, by his own admission. There was no point in cluttering her life with maybes.

"Yes, I'll marry you, Christopher Van Hoon," she said, because for her it was a dream come true.

The Great Zimbabwe Valley emerged fully from the darkness, revealing the work of others who had stood and dreamed on that very spot. As blissfully optimistic as Janet, nothing but heaps of deteriorating rubble came of their expectations.

CHAPTER TWELVE

FOR JANET, the next few days were happy ones, despite the overhanging threat of a major gold find by Christopher's team. The team left each morning, sometimes not reappearing with ore samples until nightfall. The samples were shipped to Salisbury every night on a special plane out of Fort Victoria. In Salisbury, the ore was analyzed for gold content and the results telephoned back to Great Zimbabwe before the team left the next morning.

Janet wanted to spend more time with Christopher, but each of his trips into the bush assured a quicker completion of the V.H.A.M. project. The sooner he was sure none of the old sites were reusable, the sooner Janet and he could get on with their lives. More and more assay reports came back negative, and Janet continued to hope for her fairytale ending.

The time she managed to have alone with Christopher was marvelous. To her delight, there was much of the boy still left in the man. Vincent Van Hoon had been less successful in distorting his son's character than Janet had first thought. Christopher was loving and caring, and it was true that he hunted animals only with his camera since promising Janet all those years ago that he would never kill another gazelle.

Their hours together were spent rediscovering joys of each other's company. There was a lot catching up to do. Neither one's life had stood still during the past sixteen years.

With Christopher so often out in the field, Janet's days settled into a fairly predictable routine. Immediately after his early-morning departures, she had coffee with Craig, during which she either confirmed or amended the daily itineraries the V.H.A.M. team had officially filed the night before. For the most part, Christopher's people were pretty good at keeping Craig accurately informed of their whereabouts—which pleased Craig and made Janet more confident of Christopher's safety.

Perhaps her confidence was misplaced. After all, Dr. Nhari's radio transmitters, which gave Craig knowledge of the elephants' whereabouts, didn't keep those animals out of harm's way. Since the research team had been ordered out of the reserve there had been thirty more elephants found slaughtered. No one knew how many other dead ones were unfound and uncounted. The two hundred elephants that Dr. Nhari's team had estimated were in the reserve for transfer were being cut down to zero in no time.

Janet didn't visit each new spot of unfeeling slaughter, but she did keep up on the killings. She knew that whoever was supplying the poachers with information on troop movement was continuing do so. Elephants were continually attacked in sections of the reserve not assigned a patrol for that day.

Janet often drove out with Christopher or Craig to check on Melissa and Suzy. The safety of the mother and daughter rhinos was important to her. It proved another endangered species could breed naturally and survive in the reserve.

"Well, one more day of miracles!" Craig exclaimed, pointing out Melissa and Suzy grazing contentedly among some nearby trees. Craig looked haggard, an aftereffect of his latest bout with his superiors in Salisbury a couple of days before. Rumor had it that he would be replaced as commander if he didn't start getting results—and fast.

"Do you want to find some shade and catch a catnap?" she suggested, concerned by his evident fatigue.

"The lack of sleep is beginning to tell, is it?" he asked, giving her a small smile of gratitude.

"Maybe you were always ragged around the edges," Janet ventured with a good-natured shrug.

"No," he admitted, putting the Land Rover in gear and heading back toward the hotel. "Actually, I'd love that catnap," he said. "However, I can't spare the time. I shouldn't be out here now, but I needed a few minutes away from the rat race."

"They came down on you pretty hard in Salisbury this last time, did they?" she ventured. He obviously wanted to talk about it.

"Can't blame them, can I?" he said with a shake of his head. "I'm not getting results, am I? Dr. Nhari is screaming bloody murder that whatever chances the elephants had were shot out from under them when I kicked out his transfer team. Who knows? Maybe he's right."

"You were thinking of his and his men's safety," Janet reminded him.

"Try telling that to Dr. Nhari," Craig replied bitterly.

"What are you going to do?"

"Don't tell anyone, but I haven't the foggiest," he admitted. "All my efforts to get the poachers have me chasing phantoms. All my clever plans to trap their informant have been even less successful."

"I wish I could help," Janet said sincerely, It was hard to see someone like Craig depressed because of poachers who cared nothing about Africa or the preservation of the continent's wild-life.

"You've been a great help in monitoring the team's itiner-aries," Craig complimented her. "We haven't had any mishap like Spencer's since you started." Paul Spencer, the member of the team who had been wounded by the poachers, had died shortly after Craig's unsuccessful attempt to evacuate the rest of the V.H.A.M. team from the area. "Just keep that up, and I'll do my best to keep your fiancé alive and well for his wedding."

Janet felt a chill overcome her at the thought that the life of the man she loved might be threatened, too.

They lapsed into a silence that remained unbroken until they were flagged down at the hotel by a soldier. Craig was handed a clipboard, and he scanned the attached information sheet before turning an accusing eye on Janet. "So where in the hell is your lover boy today?" he asked. His belligerent tone caught her off guard. "The south ten section, wasn't it?" he asked.

"Yes," she affirmed.

"Then why did he take the road to Fort Victoria this morning?" Craig asked, returning the clipboard to the soldier and dismissing him with a curt nod. "Van Hoon passed through the two checkpoints on the Fort Victoria road, and he hasn't checked back through." Janet didn't have the slightest idea why. As far as she knew, Christopher was scheduled to examine three old mine sites in the south ten. "I have my men patrolling a section of reserve to protect a man who isn't even there!" Craig shouted.

"Don't forget Carl and Jacob," Janet reminded him. Carl Mason and Jacob Phillips were the two remaining members of the V.H.A.M. team. Both were supposed to be in the south ten at the moment. That didn't mean they were—any more than it had meant that Christopher was.

"It's vital that I know where everyone is at every moment of every day," Craig insisted. "You tell Mr. Van Hoon that for me when he turns up, if he turns up. And remind him about what happened to Spencer." He left Janet in the parking lot, the tires of his Land Rover squealing as he pulled away.

The soldier returned with his clipboard. "Is Captain Sylo returning to headquarters?" he asked. He was in his twenties; blond-haired and blue-eyed. Janet sometimes saw him working on the hotel switchboard.

"He didn't say," Janet said, "but he was headed in that direction."

"Right," the young soldier said and made a smart about-face.

"Anything the matter?" she called after. The soldier wouldn't tell her even if there was. She was a civilian with no need to know.

"No trouble," the young man answered over his shoulder. "We got a call that Mr. Van Hoon just checked back through Checkpoint Alpha."

"Oh," Janet said noncommittally. She sat on one of the chairs on the hotel veranda, waiting for Christopher. Craig wasn't the only one who was curious about the mix-up in Christopher's filed itinerary.

Checkpoint Alpha was the first military blockade of two on the highway from Fort Victoria. It was followed, a few miles later, by Checkpoint Bravo. It took a car half an hour to reach the hotel from Alpha. Janet had time to think.

She had taken it for granted that Christopher would be in the south ten that day. He knew that Janet reported any changes to Craig. By doing so, she saved Christopher and his men a lot of last-minute paperwork. Since he hadn't mentioned the change to Fort Victoria, his reason for going there must have come up after he'd left her that morning...or he hadn't wanted her to know he was going in the first place.

If he had come across an ore sample that looked too promising to wait for the evening plane, he would have shipped it off immediately on a morning flight. That was one explanation Janet didn't want to be true. A promising sample could be disastrous to hers and Christopher's relationship. She wouldn't love him any the less, but a gold discovery would make this situation too similar to what had happened at Lackland. She wasn't up to seeing more wildlife bite the dust because of profits sought by Van Hoon Afrikaner Minerals. A gold rush to Great Zimbabwe would endanger what little there was left of the reserve.

Christopher's Land Rover pulled into the hotel parking lot and stopped. Janet went to meet him. "Hi," he said, and gave her a big kiss. He didn't sound or act as though he had set the ball rolling that would shatter all their chances for a happy future.

"Your little side trip to Fort Victoria has Craig in a snit," Janet informed him. There was no point in beating around the bush.

"His men at the checkpoints got back to him, did they?" Christopher said, taking her arm and walking with her to the veranda. They sat opposite each other at a small table. "I figured they would," he said. "This is why I didn't check in with him this morning."

"I could have told him about the change," Janet said, sounding hurt, "but you didn't mention it to me, either."

"That's because I made my decision after I left you," Christopher explained. "Anyway, I don't know why the captain is upset. He wasn't expecting me to get into trouble in Fort Victoria, was he?"

"He put some men in the south ten to look after you, and you weren't there to be looked after."

"Carl and Jacob were there to use those services," Christopher pointed out. "I'm not the only one who deserves protection."

"Which I mentioned to him," Janet said. "I hope you have better luck pacifying him than I did. Meanwhile, tell me what you expect from your latest find."

"What latest find?" he asked. He sounded innocent. Probably he wanted to avoid a confrontation until the assay reports confirmed he'd found pay dirt.

"You've found an ore sample that looks good, right?" she said. There was a lump building in her throat. She'd been expecting this. Somehow the scale had been tipped too far on the side of happiness. Something had to be done to put things back into balance.

"I'd be happy to hear how you came to that conclusion," Christopher said.

"You headed off this morning to get ore samples," Janet said obligingly. "Suddenly you're heading for Fort Victoria. Adding one and one tells me you found something that looked good and couldn't wait to ship it off on the evening plane."

"Well, you've figured all wrong, lady," he said. "Remind me to do the bookkeeping in our family, since you can't add two and two. Donald Geiger called, and I went to meet him. You remember Donald, don't you?" She remembered. "You met him at Lionspride," he added. Donald was the man with the diamond. He hadn't seen her at her best.

"Oh," she said. She didn't know where that left her.

"Actually, Donald did bring news about one ore sample we'd

already sent to Salisbury."

It did have something to do with gold. Janet's heart sank. She wanted to return to her Cinderella existence and forget that the clock struck midnight every time and ended the ball. "What about the ore sample?" she asked. She dreaded his answer.

"I can see the black picture you're painting," Christopher said, shaking his head. "It's not that way at all. There was a mix-up, and one ore batch got thrown out before it was tested. That's all. The problem merely requires a second sample. The mine site is just up the road a piece."

"Mr. Geiger came all this way from Johannesburg to tell you that?" Janet said disbelievingly.

"No," Christopher admitted. "That was just news he brought along to save the company the cost of another phone call."

"I see," Janet said. She was as much in the dark as ever.

"You haven't seen anything until you've seen this," he said. He reached into the pocket of his bush jacket and pulled out a small black box. He held it out to her. "Donald was hand-delivering this."

"What is it?" she asked. Her hand trembled. She knew what it looked like.

"I'll give you a hint," he said. His smile was wide attractive. "What does an engaged lady usually have that you don't?" She opened the box and gasped. "No, Janet, it's not a yellow topaz!" he said with a laugh. She had once wrongly identified the same stone when she had seen it rolled uncut onto black velvet at Lionspride. The diamond was cut now. It flashed rainbow sparks from a heart-shaped surface that was the color of warm summer sunshine.

"It's beautiful!" she exclaimed. That was the understatement of the year. Only the stronger attraction of Christopher's eyes could pull her gaze away from the gorgeous display of color reflecting from the faceted surface.

"Yes, it did turn out nicely," Christopher unabashedly boasted. "What's the point of my owning a diamond mine if I can't pick up a bauble now and again when the occasion warrants it? I thought this stone particularly appropriate; since it came into my life at the exact moment you came back to Lionspride." He reached for the box, and she surrendered it to him. Their fingers touched in the exchange, and she felt the familiar electricity that always sparked between them. "It's a ring, or haven't you noticed?" he chided, freeing it from its nesting of plush velvet. The stone caught more light and was transformed into a miniature sun. "It's your engagement ring."

"I'd be afraid to wear it," she said. "It must be worth a fortune."

"It is, but it's insured," he said casually. Putting the box down, he reached for her hand and slipped the ring on her finger. "It was meant from its beginning to be worn by you," he said gallantly. "It was fired to crystal in the forges of the earth for just this very moment."

"Oh, Christopher," she said, "I'm so very happy." He used the tip of his forefinger to catch the first of her tears, then lift the drop to his lips and kiss away its moisture. She cupped his hands in hers, resting her wet cheek against his fingers. "Will we pay for such moments of exquisite joy?" she asked. She had once had a whole summer of happiness, and look what price she'd paid for that. "Must there be more heartache and sorrow to balance the scales?"

"Of course not!" he said. His head was bowed so that he spoke softly into her hair. "Besides, haven't we suffered enough? Sixteen years apart should be credit enough on anyone's balance sheet."

"I do so love you," she said, looking up. His face was close to hers, and she couldn't believe any man could be so handsome.

"Let's get married very soon," he said, gently wiping her cheeks free of tears with the back of his hand. "I'm too selfish in my old age to wait much longer. "Luckily," he added, "we're almost finished here. If there's no gold in the south ten that wraps it up—unless, of course, some mix-up should occur that makes it necessary to go back for more seconds."

Surely the fates wouldn't be so cruel as to turn up a major

gold find at this late date! She and Christopher had come so far. They didn't deserve that final obstacle. "Speaking of second samples," he said, "why don't I take care of the one Salisbury wants now? The site isn't far."

"Now?" she echoed. She didn't want him to leave. She wanted him with her forever. She feared the gold that he might find would turn the area into an industrial wasteland like the one she'd seen at the Van Hoon Deep Levels Mine. The expansion of farm and ranchland had destroyed most of the original Great Zimbabwe Reserve. Not even the smaller animals would survive once Van Hoon Afrikaner Minerals arrived in force.

But leaving things unfinished wouldn't solve anything, either. This was an issue they would have to come to terms with in their life together—starting now. If the land was exploitable, someone would exploit it; that was the way of things. It was ridiculous to turn the advantage over to an even less caring competitor. "We'll have to tell Craig where you're going," she said. She felt safer when he knew where they all were.

"Yes, we'll tell Craig," he assured her.

Craig wasn't in his tent, though. "There was a report of unauthorized personnel on the reserve about here," Lieutenant Walkford said, pointing to the map on Craig's desk. The lieutenant had seen a lot of African sun in his twenty-five years. His face was a deep chestnut shade, the lightness of his pale blue eyes somehow out of place in all that tan. "Captain Sylo took a few of the troop out to take a look."

"I have to take another ore sample from a dig located here," Christopher said, pointing to the locale for the lieutenant. "It's close to camp, and I foresee no problems, but Captain Sylo insists I keep him posted on my movements. I don't need to wait until he gets back, do I?"

"I don't see why," Lieutenant Walkford agreed. "There's been no poaching activity in that area for quite some time, and it's too close to our camp for even those brazen bastards to try anything."

"Thanks," Christopher said. Taking Janet's hand, he led her

into the sunlight. He asked her if she wanted to go with him, and she said no. She'd gone on a couple of his ore-gathering trips, and she'd been in his way each time. He scrambled over rocks and through underbrush and never complained about giving her a hand, but she felt she was a chain dragging along behind him.

He returned her to the hotel and kissed her goodbye. She went to the veranda. The hotel staff was out of sight, doing assigned chores. The V.H.A.M. team was in the south ten and wouldn't be back until nightfall. The activities of the military focused around their tent community near the Great Enclosure. Christopher was looking for gold.

She was alone and suddenly uneasy. She intuitively sensed something was wrong and nervously glanced down at her engagement ring. It was worth a fortune. Poachers who killed helpless animals for profit wouldn't think twice about killing a woman and snatching up a king's ransom that could be carried away in a pants pocket. She twisted her ring on her finger, palming the crystal. So much fire inside a stone should burn, but it was cool to the touch.

The danger had something to do with what Lieutenant Walkford had done or said—or hadn't done or said. But what? He had pointed to one spot on the map, showing where Craig had gone. Christopher had pointed to another spot, indicating the ancient mine site. The two spots were miles apart, and it was those miles of separation that bothered her. Whenever the poachers struck, they did so well away from existing patrols.

She was being silly. There were no reports of elephants where Christopher was going. If a herd was there, any poachers' gunfire would send Lieutenant Walkford and his men on the run. It took time to remove tusks from an elephant, which were, after all, well-anchored teeth.

Yet seven elephants had been mowed down at a waterhole not much farther from camp than Christopher's destination. Poachers had removed fourteen tusks and made away with them, no one the wiser until a swirl of vultures betrayed the deed. How far did the sound of machine-gun fire travel, muted by shrubbery, hills and distance, before it faded to nothing or arrived distorted beyond recognition?

She walked to the Land Rover in the parking lot. Christopher left it for her whenever he was in the field. Everything she needed was within walking distance, but riding was convenient and comfortable once the summer sun began its daily baking of the landscape, and she was used to taking a car out now and then. She got in and sat behind the wheel. Lieutenant Walkford would laugh at her intuition. He wouldn't follow Christopher on the basis of her gut feeling.

She started the Land Rover and eased it out of the parking lot. Janet to the rescue. How ludicrous! One woman against how many guns? She didn't even own a gun. She hated them. But she couldn't sit and do nothing. Something inside her demanded action. The man she loved was in possible danger. She knew that, whether Lieutenant Walkford could be convinced or not.

She knew the route. She had traveled it often in her searches for Melissa and Suzy. The mine site was on an outcrop she and Craig had seen while watching the rhinos graze that morning.

Turning off the dirt road, she headed across country. The African sky was dark blue and cloudless. Shrubs and tall acacias seemed to brush up against it, and wavy lines of heat seemed to distort the distant horizons. There was no sound except the rattle of the Land Rover across rough terrain, stirring up a feeble breeze as it cut through the stagnant air. Plants, green when she had arrived at Great Zimbabwe, were fading fast to browns, rusts and pale golds during these increasingly hot days. There was no wildlife to be seen. There was no Christopher to be seen. His dust trail had settled without a trace.

Her panic gradually faded, giving way to reason. Her initial impulse seemed foolish now. She had rushed off half-cocked.

Janet braked to a stop, and dust settled like gold flour on the windshield and dashboard. She was surprised at how far she had driven. One edge of the mined outcrop was visible through the trees. She had to decide whether to go forward or back.

The decision was made for her by the loud gunshot blasts she heard, followed by the flutter of frightened birds airborne from nearby trees. *"Christopher!"*

It seemed as if her aching heart screamed her verbal protest.

* * * * * * *

AFTER THE GUNSHOTS came absolute silence. It was easy to imagine no shots had been fired at all, but Janet knew differently. Christopher was lying dead somewhere, a meal for the vultures. Or he was badly wounded. Either way, she had to find him. She had no medical supplies. If he'd fallen outside his Land Rover, she didn't have the strength to lug his dead weight any great distance. However, those difficulties made no difference. She had to do something, and going for Lieutenant Walkford would waste time. Anyway, the lieutenant would have heard the gunfire. He'd be on his way.

She turned the Land Rover in the direction of the shots—at least she thought it was the direction. It was hard to tell. Distance distorted. Rocky outcrops bounced sounds, even amplified them. The shots seemed to have originated from close by, but they could have come from the next valley or the next ridge.

It could have been a poacher downing an elephant. Two shots were more than enough. Vincent Van Hoon had considered his marksmanship off whenever it took him more than one shot to down any animal. One elephant could be stripped of its ivory before Lieutenant Walkford arrived to investigate—except that Great Zimbabwe poachers seldom bothered with just one elephant. They worked on the assembly-line principle, shooting them five or more at a time. It might be an independent operator, a native out to supplement his low income. There were always a few of them. Whoever it might have been, however, Janet's thoughts were back on Christopher and what one of those bullets might have done to him.

She steered the Land Rover around bushes and trees, expecting horror beyond each turn. She feared what she might find, but Christopher's life might depend on her reaching him in time. She became more and more frantic but strove to stay calm and cool. She was no good to anyone if she didn't keep her wits about her.

She almost didn't hear it. It wasn't loud like the gunshots. It was a muted thumping, a sound like a muffled dissonant pounding on a tom-tom. She tested the air like an animal sensing prey without seeing it. The sound was very near. It stopped and began again. She made a quick turn to avoid an impenetrable stretch of thorn bushes and low-growing scrub. She almost hit Christopher's parked Land Rover. She braked, and her engine stalled.

More low thumping. She unfastened her seatbelt and got out. Her subconscious was putting meaning to the sounds, even though she had never heard them before. She shuddered, fighting off the awareness of what they could be.

The ground dipped into a depression. She walked toward the edge. The heat of the sun burned the back of her neck. She was perspiring. Her heart was racing. Her lips and throat were dry.

There would have been nothing worse than seeing her lover dead, but what she did see came in a close second. He was very much alive, stripped to the waist and bent over. His back muscles rippled beneath the African sun, turning glossy with the sweat of his exertion. His shirt was wrapped around the large stone he was using to knock the second of two large horns from the dead rhinoceros. The first horn was lying in the dust beside Melissa's deformed snout. More pathetic than the ongoing mutilation was the sight of Suzy dead within a few feet of her mother. All hope that these two animals had represented for the survival of their species had been erased by two bullets from a rifle. Christopher's rifle lay on the ground within easy reach.

Janet watched, and a blow of the stone loosened the second horn. The three-foot projection tilted precariously without coming loose. Another blow knocked it off.

The full impact of what she was seeing, and what it did to their relationship, dropped on her like a ton of bricks. "Oh, Christopher!" she groaned.

He heard her and looked up the incline to where she stood. "Janet?" he said in surprise. He believed she was back at camp. He knew Craig was miles away with a patrol. Had Craig been sent out on a wild-goose chase while Christopher moved in for the real prize?

She turned and ran, but the picture of Christopher's half-naked body laboring over Melissa's horn, Suzy's lifeless carcass close by, was forever branded on her memory. It was the perverted mingling of the man's living beauty with the ugliness of the dead animals that she found so abhorrent and obscene.

Christopher's brutality and wanton slaughter spoiled everything for her. There was no forgiving him. He knew what those rhinos symbolized, but he had snuffed it all out with two bullets, snuffing his and Janet's love out in the process.

If only it were that simple! It wasn't, though. Because she still loved him. Not even this act erased sixteen years of caring and dreaming. But it did make her determined to fight those feelings. Whether she loved him or not, she couldn't find happiness with a man who killed helpless animals for profit. No matter how much gold those horns brought on the black markets of the Orient, it was a drop in the bucket compared to what the Van Hoon empire poured into Christopher's pockets every minute of every day. Why had he done it? For a few bucks he had put a species one step closer to extinction. Once a species was gone, there was no resurrecting it. Millions of years of evolution were lost forever with the death of the last rhinoceros, or elephant, or zebra, or wildebeest. Had Christopher thought of that?

She was in the Land Rover, driving. She didn't know where she was going. She didn't care. She wanted to be as far away from Christopher as possible. She couldn't face him after what she'd seen.

She had thought he was in danger, but he was alive and well. She resented the way she'd been drawn toward his naked torso even as that horn came loose. She resented loving Christopher too much to put him in jail where he belonged. She resented his becoming more important than her ideals. Considering that she had come to Africa for sweet vengeance, she was missing the perfect opportunity to keep the promise she had made to her dead father, which showed that her values had become doubly warped—not only for harboring a deep resentment all these years but for nurturing an unnatural love for Christopher Van Hoon in the present.

She gave the Land Rover more gas, speeding over rugged terrain meant to be taken at lower speeds. Her spine was jarred repeatedly as she bumped along. Her teeth chattered. Her hands, wet with sweat, kept slipping off the wheel. She welcomed the discomfort. It kept her mind off crushed dreams of love and happy endings.

Suddenly the land disappeared in front of her. The Land Rover tilted precariously forward. Braking didn't help. The wheels locked in soil that was already collapsing beneath the weight of the vehicle. The Land Rover slid to a jarring stop amid a spray of water. Janet's knuckles were white, her fingers frantically clutching the wheel. She was lucky she wasn't hurt. In her hurry to escape Christopher, she hadn't bothered to fasten her seatbelt.

She had driven over a steep embankment and into a small stream. From the size of the splash, she thought she'd landed in a river at the very least. The Land Rover had stalled on impact, but it started promptly when she tried it. The far bank of the stream was at water level, and the Land Rover left the water with little trouble.

She parked beneath a graceful fever tree; an acacia that got its name from its association with areas free from fever. Its bark was yellow. Christopher's tanned skin, bright eyes and hair were yellow gold. "Oh, Christopher!" she said, her words a lament. So many wonderful things that might have been were now shattered beyond repair.

Where did she go from here? She was disoriented, and not just geographically. She couldn't put Christopher out of her life after accepting him so totally—not without causing herself considerable emotional pain. Nevertheless, there could never be anything between them after what had happened.

The bubbling of stream water over loose stones suddenly sounded inviting, considering her hot and flustered condition. She opened the door and got out. It was pleasant beneath the shading branches, the greenness of the leaves offsetting the tawny sameness of plant life beyond the reach of the water. A ray of sunlight ignited the beauty of her ring. Offended by the gaudy display, she tugged the ring off her finger and put it in her pocket, where it couldn't trigger thoughts of the man who had given it to her.

Kneeling beside the water, she dropped her cupped hands into the coolness. She splashed her face, drawing wet fingertips down to her cleavage.

She caught a somehow familiar glitter in the water-covered gravel recently disturbed by the Land Rover. For a horror-struck moment, she thought the engagement ring had dropped from her pocket. She reached for the glitter, but the water distorted her aim, and she came up with a plain brown stone. The sparkle disappeared in the swirl of disturbance made by her hand.

Frantic, she got to her feet, automatically searching her pockets. Christopher would never forgive her for losing the ring. She would never forgive herself. She had every intention of giving it back to him, for it was something whose value and beauty could give a lot of joy to many people. For her, it would always bring back too many painful memories.

Surprisingly, the ring was in her pocket where she'd put it. She could have sworn she'd seen it sparkling in the water. Wrapping it in her handkerchief, she tucked it securely away, then squatted by the stream and methodically scanned the gravel. Sunlight reflected on the surface of the water, and she blamed it for the illusion—until she saw the unmistakable glitter again. She reached for it, more careful this time. She sank her fingers slowly into the loose gravel and pulled out a stone almost buried beneath some smaller ones.

She brought it to the light. She had seen it before. Donald Geiger had tumbled it out on the black velvet at Lionspride. But that was impossible! That uncut stone was now the cut diamond in her pocket. Here, then, was an octahedron similar to that original rough stone, as yellow in color but actually bigger. But no amateur stooped by a stream and nonchalantly came up with a diamond—not since the twenty-one-point-seventy-five-carat *Eureka*, the diamond that had started it all in South Africa, had been picked up from the banks of the Orange River by Erasmus Jacobs, fifteen year old son of a poor laborer, and taken home as a plaything. Not since a local native had retrieved a similar bauble from the Vaal River and traded it for a pittance to crafty Petre Van Hoon, who used the handsome profits from the sale to spearhead the present Van Hoon fortune.

Christopher would know if the stone was worth pennies or a fortune, but she wasn't talking to him. She didn't ever want to see him again.

If by some wild stretch of the imagination it was a diamond, she would have in her hands the one sure bomb to sink all hopes for the survival of the Great Zimbabwe Reserve. There would be no end to the hordes of get-rich-quickers who would come with visions of diamonds growing on each and every tree. Under those circumstances, any ecological balance wouldn't have the chance of a snowball in hell. No; it wasn't a diamond, but a pretty stone, a memento to take home, since she wasn't keeping the engagement ring. Every time she felt sorry for herself in the days to come, she would look at this keepsake, remembering the day Christopher's golden body had labored to knock the horns off a dead rhinoceros.

She took the rock to the Land Rover and put it in the glove compartment. Such wild fantasies—thinking it was a diamond!

She noted the position of the sun and got a rough idea of which direction would take her back to the hotel. If she was lucky, she would make it back soon. If she was lucky, she would be out of Great Zimbabwe tomorrow and out of Africa as fast as her legs could carry her.

She heard him before she saw him. His foot dislodged a stone on the top of the embankment and caused a small slide. He was standing there, his shirt still off. He was an Adonis bathed in sunlight. He was evil in the guise of ethereal perfection.

She fled to her Land Rover, hurrying to turn the key in the ignition and put the car in gear. He came down the embankment after her, running and leaping like a young lion intent on downing his fleeing prey. The Land Rover moved forward. Christopher's running feet splashed through the water of the stream. Escape would have been easy had there been a straightaway through the trees, but there wasn't one. She steered with difficulty around obstacles that Christopher's athletic body took with far greater speed and dexterity.

Desperate, she tried for an opening in the bush. It was too small. A sapling bent at the collision, the splintering wood sounding almost like a gunshot. The Land Rover came to a grating stop.

She opened the door and stumbled out. He was panting loudly as he narrowed the distance between them.

She ran from him, and he grabbed her from behind. When they fell, he twisted them so he hit the ground first and she came down on top of him. He had intended to cushion her fall, but his muscular body was as hard as well-packed rock.

"Let me go!" she screamed, fighting him and his power to excite her. She refused to surrender. She refused to forgive. She had sacrificed too many ideals to love this money-hungry animal. He was worse than an animal. He didn't kill for food but for profit. He kept killing, although he had more money than he could spend in ten lifetimes.

He held her while she struggled, letting her expend her energy while he got his breath back. It was a foregone conclusion that he would win, because he was stronger. He was a brute!

He rolled her onto her back, pinning her arms above her head. The weight of his body kept her under control. She wiggled fiercely, hoping to get free. "Keep struggling," he said. "It feels sexy." This made her so furious that she almost mustered the strength she needed to dislodge him. "Now what in the hell is this all about?" he asked when he again had her under control.

What unmitigated gall! Was she blind? Was she stupid? There was no talking himself out of this one. She turned her head and shut her eyes. She wasn't seduced by his good looks, either. Not this time. The man was rotten to the core! "Why don't I tell you, then?" he suggested. "You heard two shots. You arrived to find me knocking the horns off Melissa. You jumped to your usual biased conclusions."

"My usual what?" she asked, her eyes popping open and locking with his. "My usual biased conclusions?" she echoed. "There isn't anyone alive who wouldn't have come to the very same conclusions!" she insisted. She put her hands against the hardness of his chest and pushed. He wouldn't budge.

"What are you afraid of, Janet?" he asked. "What's this hang-up you have that makes you look in every corner for some rationalization to dump me?" She heard what he said, but she wasn't taking it in. "You and I have a good thing here," he said. "If anyone blows it, it's going to be you. I've tried my damnedest, but one of these days I'm going to expect you to listen to my side of a story without my having to run you to ground to tell it."

"You haven't the time or the imagination to come up with a good enough story to get you out of this one," she said sarcastically. If only he could!

"The truth always works," he said. "I see no reason why this time should be an exception."

"And you'll let me up whether I swallow your hogwash or not?" she asked. What was he planning to do with her? He wouldn't believe she wasn't going to tell Craig what she had seen.

"The rhinos were poisoned," he said, bringing her back from her frantic imaginings. "I found them dead. I also found the two men who were there to collect the horns. They spotted me, and those two shots were their little gifts to me in parting."

"Poisoned?" Janet asked weakly.

"I couldn't leave the horns," Christopher explained. "The poachers would come back for them."

"Poisoned," Janet repeated. It was an explanation that cleared him. It was an explanation she had doubted could be found.

"Poisoned grass to be specific," Christopher said. "There's enough of the stuff scattered around that area to kill a hundred rhinos. We can pick up samples on the way back for a lab test, if you like."

"That won't be necessary," she said. He wasn't guilty, and she was a fool! "I believe you, but can you forgive me?"

"Forgive you for what?" he asked, flashing a wide smile. "Anybody alive would have jumped to the same conclusion."

"But I, of all people, shouldn't have," Janet conceded. "I should have known there was an explanation, shouldn't I?"

"Just because two people love one another doesn't mean they know each other inside and out," Christopher said. "It doesn't mean they should stop questioning each other, either. Humans are complex animals. They're not read like a book. Their relationships are complex, too, built and strengthened by trial and error. There's no perfect man, no perfect woman, no perfect love, no perfect marriage. That's what makes a relationship exciting. What makes a relationship work is knowing the truth when you hear it."

"I love you," she said. "Do you know that's the truth when you hear it?"

"Sure do," he said, kissing her forehead. "You don't think I'd go through all of this bother for a woman who didn't love me, do you?"

"Maybe you get excited by the idea of making up after a fight?" she suggested. She wiggled beneath him, but she had no desire to get free now. "I know I do."

"That was quite a fight, wasn't it?" he said, his dimples sinking deeper.

She wound her arms around his back and pulled him closer. She kissed the tanned skin of his powerful shoulder. Her desire blossomed like a flower opening its silky petals to the caress of the sun. "Let me love you, Christopher," she begged, luxuriating in their reprieve, enjoying one more moment before some other obstacle arose to challenge their happiness.

"Yes," he said, as eager as she was.

A blaring sound interrupted them. It was the horn of Christopher's Land Rover parked up the distant embankment. "Christopher? Janet? Where are you?" It was Lieutenant Walkford.

"Damn!" Christopher said. "Damn!"

"Don't worry, darling," Janet murmured. "There's always later...."

CHAPTER THIRTEEN

JANET WAS AWAKE most of the night, anticipating the phone call. Christopher slept calmly beside her, content that whatever the news, they would work things out. Janet wasn't so sure. This was too much a replay of what had happened sixteen years before. Oh, she saw the dissimilarities. There was nothing clandestine about V.H.A.M.'s looking for gold around Great Zimbabwe. There was no fake attempt to carve an animal preserve out of new territory. The Great Zimbabwe Reserve, or what was left of it after land reform, was already there—which made the threat against it an even sadder state of affairs. A major gold discovery meant that animals supposedly protected would suffer, no thought given to them in the mad rush to fill corporate and government pocketbooks. There was no Jack Kelley to die a second time when betrayed by a man who had hired him as an unwitting cover for gold prospecting. But his daughter was alive to witness another victory of greed over wildlife preservation. Janet respected those things that her father had stood for, and she stood for those very same things. A duplicate victory here by Van Hoon Afrikaner Minerals might yet taint her relationship with the head of that company.

The phone rang promptly at five o'clock, as it did every morning.

Janet shook Christopher awake. He groaned and let the phone ring three more times before he reached for it. He listened to the caller as he always listened. "You're sure about that?" he said, which he didn't always say. He hung up the phone and scooted down in the bed, pulling the covers over his head.

"Well?" Janet asked.

"Let's sleep another hour," he suggested. His voice was muffled by the sheet and blanket across his face.

"Let's not!" she insisted, uncovering him from his head to the tight golden curls on his lower stomach. As always, she marveled at the sensuous perfection of his body.

"You have something better in mind?" he asked playfully and slyly winked.

"What did the assay reports say?" she asked. He was teasing her. Either that or one of the last reports was positive, and he was sparing her the news. Bad news for Janet. Good news for Van Hoon Afrikaner Minerals.

"You have this virile hunk in bed with you, and all you can think about is assay reports?" Christopher asked in mock disbelief. "I must be losing my sex appeal in my old age."

"One of the assay reports is positive!" she said. She truly believed it; it was just her luck. The final samples to be taken at Great Zimbabwe had been shipped to Salisbury the night before, and substantial gold might well have been discovered in one of those last possible sources. "Please, tell me the truth."

"Oh, there's gold all right," he said. The teasing had gone far enough. "We've always known there's gold. The question is whether or not we can get it out at a profit."

"And?" Janet prodded.

"We can't," he said with a wide smile.

"You can't?" Janet asked, needing to hear it again. Even then, she wouldn't believe it. "C-A-N-N-O-T?"

"That's R-I-G-H-T!" he answered. "The price of gold would have to skyrocket substantially before we could make any profit on what's left around here." She knelt on the bed beside him, and his eyes caught the new happiness in her own. "Why does that news please me?" he asked. "Because it pleases you— although a feasible gold extraction here could have been oh so good for company profits." Taking her arm, he pulled her gently down to him. "What do you say to the two of us heading back to Lionspride and making those long overdue wedding plans to console me and help you celebrate?"

"Soon, but not this very minute," she said, uncovering the rest of him.

She should have been the happiest woman alive. She had been close to that when she'd found out Christopher had had no part in killing Melissa and Suzy. He had turned their horns over to Lieutenant Walkford, who turned them over to Craig. Yesterday Craig told her and Christopher that the horns had been shipped off to whatever bureaucratic office in Salisbury took care of such contraband. Now, with no major deposits of gold in the Great Zimbabwe Reserve, its animals—at least those without valuable horns and tusks—should have a chance to live out their lives in peace.

Except that there was another problem: the sizable yellow stone she had transferred from the glove compartment of the Land Rover to the bottom drawer of her hotel dresser. There it rested, beneath a couple of folded blouses. Whatever threat to her happiness had ridden on the gold or lack of gold at Great Zimbabwe, it dimmed in comparison to this new threat of her own making.

She could hand the stone over to Christopher and know within seconds its estimated value. There would be blissful happiness if it was a pretty stone and nothing more. There would be wretched despair if it was a diamond, because Christopher would convert from lover to ruthless businessman as quickly as Dr. Jekyll ever changed into Mr. Hyde. He would persuade her to tell him where she'd found it, because she was helpless to resist her love for him. There would be more weeks spent on the spot while a V.H.A.M. team decided if there were more diamonds worth exploiting. Any news that leaked out would bring thousands of prospectors on the run to the Great Zimbabwe Reserve—none of them particularly interested in ecology.

"That doesn't seem to be an expression of unmitigated joy on your beautiful face," Christopher observed, nestling closer to her on the bed. "Are you disappointed that our relationship wasn't put through the acid test to see if it would survive?"

"I'm glad there's no gold," she said, committing herself to no more than that.

"Gold or no gold, our relationship would have held fast," he guaranteed. "I believe that, and you do, too. There should have been gold if for no other reason than to prove we have something that can survive against all odds and emerge stronger because of the struggle."

She wanted to believe it, because the yellow stone in the dresser was an acid eating away at their love for as long as she kept the rock hidden from him. She should have left it in the stream or spontaneously thrown it back when she'd had the chance. There was no throwing it back now. Doing so would be her admission that their love couldn't survive the test.

She had promised herself no more second-class love. Marrying Bob had been the mistake to prove for sure that settling for less was never better. She had told Christopher she was Janet Kelley, because she had wanted to be sure their love was strong enough to surmount old obstacles. And it was. However, she had risked all that before she had found out that the ecstasy of loving Christopher was something she could never bear to lose again. Now she was beyond the point of willingly sacrificing what she had on any further all-or-nothing gambles.

The importance of her newfound happiness was brought forcefully home to her by the thrilling rush that warmed and excited her whenever she was near him. He didn't even have to touch her. She simply couldn't bear the thought of spending her life without him or waking up to his empty pillow day after day. No man could give her more. She didn't need more. She didn't have to spoil it. The yellow stone was her secret.

That it was a secret, though, was a danger in itself. Beginning her marriage with something like that bottled up inside her was no way to strengthen and build a relationship. If only she could be sure she had a worthless rock on her hands!

It wasn't as if she could take her find to a reputable jeweler in Johannesburg, not as long as there was the faintest chance it was a diamond. The South African government had stringent rules and regulations about the possession, sale and transfer of all diamonds. Not even the fiancée of Christopher Van Hoon walked in off the street and asked about the potential value of an uncut stone without setting off a chain reaction. There would be questions from Christopher and from government authorities, who would be curious as to how she had obtained a diamond nowhere recorded in their minutely detailed mine inventories.

She was damned if she did. She was damned if she didn't. If she hadn't found the blasted thing, everything would be so perfect! She shouldn't have bolted when she'd seen Christopher knocking off Melissa's horns. Common sense should have told her there was a logical explanation—which there was. But she had run off impetuously, had fished herself a pretty rock and a whole bag of trouble out of a stream.

She kissed the spot where Christopher's strong neck met his muscular shoulder. His hand gently cupped her head, to bring her lips nearer to his, but the motion was interrupted as a sudden unexpected vibration shook the room. "Earthquake?" she immediately asked in a frightened voice. She had been in an earthquake in California. Any massive shifting of land wasn't something she cared to have repeated.

"No," he said, and put a finger to her lips for silence. He got up and went to the window. Sound accompanied the vibration beneath his feet. He parted the curtains far enough to see outside. "Get dressed!" he whispered.

Suddenly Janet remembered how the ground had vibrated during the stampede. "Elephants?" she asked nervously. There was a movie called *Elephant Walk*, in which a whole herd came rampaging through a plantation house.

"Not elephants, either. In fact, it's probably nothing," he assured her. "But whatever it is, we'll be best able to handle it if we're dressed."

She scrambled for her clothes, which she'd hastily discarded the night before. Christopher pulled on his pants, his shirt and walked quickly across the room to the dresser. He took a pistol from the top drawer, checking to make sure it was loaded.

"What's going on out there, Christopher?" Janet persisted. If a gun was presently necessary, that at least insinuated something out of the ordinary. She would have looked out the window herself, but getting dressed seemed more important at the moment.

"It's a troop convoy," Christopher said, "and a big one—headed for the military encampment by the looks of it. Three trucks, though, have pulled into the hotel parking lot. Armed soldiers are holding some of Captain Sylo's men, ushered from the hotel office, at gunpoint."

"Maybe the soldiers are merely reinforcements," Janet suggested feebly. "Craig certainly could use them."

"Maybe they are," Christopher said but didn't seem convinced. "But neither reinforcements nor replacements would be acting like siege troops," he added. Janet joined him at the window, and they watched for a moment, unable to comprehend the scene any better. "Here comes someone who might have the answers," Christopher commented as a car pulled next to the trucks. The doors opened, and four men got out. Only three of them wore uniforms.

"Dr. Nhari!" Janet said, identifying the fourth as the chief of the elephant tagging team that Craig had evacuated to Salisbury.

"So it is," Christopher agreed. "Think he got tired of waiting for Captain Sylo to call him back?" Craig had never mentioned anything about the doctor's return. Janet didn't know what to think. "Take this," Christopher said, offering her the pistol.

"I won't use it!" she protested.

"Never say never." His words scared her, but she knew she had to face facts. A military coup of any kind in volatile Zimbabwe could mean real trouble for civilians caught in the crossfire.

"Why? Where are you going?" she asked. She didn't want him to go anywhere. Those soldiers had guns. Craig's parents had been killed not that far away and not that long ago. She didn't want Christopher to die—not after all they'd gone through to get this far.

"It'll be easier to get answers while there's a familiar face in the crowd," he said.

"Then I'm coming with you!" she insisted. There was no way he was leaving her. If he died, she would rather die with him than go on alone.

"Maybe I can persuade him to come to us," Christopher suggested. "I have to admit I'm not all that keen on either of us getting shot. It's worth a try." He walked to the phone and dialed the front desk.

The blond corporal who usually operated the hotel switchboard had been one of those escorted out on the lawn. He and the rest of his duty group from the hotel office were being watched over by several newcomers with machine guns.

"Someone is going inside for the phone," Janet informed.

"The corporal?" Christopher asked.

Janet shook her head. "He started to go, but Nhari said something, and one of the military men from the car went instead."

Christopher responded to a voice on the other end of the phone. "This is Christopher Van Hoon. Could you put Dr. Nhari on the line, please." He covered the mouthpiece. "What's happening?" he asked Janet.

"The military man is at the office door," Janet answered. "Dr. Nhari is following him inside."

"Doctor," Christopher said on the phone a few seconds later, "Christopher Van Hoon here. Yes. Mrs. Westover and I were wondering if you could explain all the troop activity this morning." He listened. "You remember my room?" he asked. "And doctor, come alone, won't you? I do have a gun." He replaced the receiver and came back to the window. He put a protective arm around Janet. She gained comfort and strength from his presence, not sure how she would have reacted on her own. "He's coming over for a little chat," Christopher said. "He says there's nothing to worry about."

Dr. Nhari reappeared at the office doorway. He circumvented the milling soldiers outside and was soon greeting Janet and

Christopher inside the latter's room. He didn't have to ask what Janet was doing there at that hour of the morning. He smiled when Christopher frisked him. "Sorry to drop in on you without forewarning," he said. "Under the circumstances, it was decided a surprise visit was best."

"What circumstances?" Janet asked. Surely Dr. Nhari couldn't be involved in anything illegal. "Best for whom?"

"The authorities in Salisbury got a hot tip from a reliable source regarding the location of a large cache of ivory collected by the poachers who have been operating on the Great Zimbabwe Reserve," Dr. Nhari explained. "A break like this doesn't come along every day, and Salisbury is determined to make the best of it. Since it's obvious someone in Captain Sylo's camp is leaking vital information to the poachers, the plan is to launch an independent operation under Major Jenkins, making damned sure all of Sylo's men are present and accounted for right up until zero hour. I had enough pull in Salisbury to get assigned as an advisor to the major's team. I'm well acquainted with the reserve, whereas. Major Jenkins isn't."

"Craig will be glad to hear there's been a breakthrough," Janet said. She was more at ease. The doctor's statement made sense.

"I hope that's the case," Dr. Nhari said, although he sounded doubtful. "The captain keeps insisting he has everything under control, but it's obvious he hasn't. He shouldn't have been allowed a free rein as long as he has, but that's finally been rectified. Major Jenkins has brought along Captain Sylo's replacement. As of this moment, Captain Sylo no longer has any say around here."

Christopher didn't say anything. Janet knew what he thought of Craig. Here were two men, one of whom she loved, and both of whom she respected—neither impressed by Craig Sylo. Her own favorable impression of the man was colored by her emotional state at the time she had met him. Out to find someone or something as a diversion from Christopher, she had thought Craig perfect for the part. "He's certainly tried his best to get the poachers," Janet insisted. She wasn't a fair-weather friend, and she wasn't deserting anybody until more evidence was in, especially since Craig had been responsible for getting her and Christopher back together by suggesting they talk at Victoria Falls. And he had tried again when he was unsuccessful in evacuating the V.H.A.M. team, that time asking Janet to stay on.

"If a good many dead elephants could rise up and talk, they would tell you his best wasn't enough," Dr. Nhari said. "'For the sake of the few elephants left alive on the reserve, I hope Captain Sylo welcomes this breakthrough with the enthusiasm it warrants."

"He will!" Janet assured the doctor defensively. Dr. Nhari might doubt it, but Craig wouldn't begrudge a solution to the problem just because he hadn't come up with it himself. If he did, he wasn't the man Janet thought he was.

But she had to admit she wasn't always a perfect judge of character. She'd made mistakes—such as the one she'd made with that writer friend of Bob. She thought he had asked her to supper as a courtesy after Bob's death, but he had had other things in mind. She had been genuinely surprised by his pass. She hadn't pegged Christopher right, either—not in the beginning. She had seen him as someone intent upon punishing a woman who was trying to besmirch the Van Hoon name.

"When is the raid on the cache taking place?" Christopher asked.

"We'll head out within the hour," Dr. Nhari said. He chose one of the available chairs and sat in it. "Jenkins would prefer being assured he's snared all of Sylo's troops, but a roll call to be sure would take too long. Even if word gets through to the poachers, though, there won't be time for anyone to clear out all the incriminating evidence—too much of it. Still, the sooner we move the better. We would like to nab at least a couple of the culprits."

"I want to come with you," Christopher said.

"No!" Janet protested. She didn't believe her ears.

"I want to go along, Janet," he insisted, turning toward her.

"But why needlessly expose yourself to danger?" she asked. The poachers weren't giving up the fruits of their labors without a fight. Getting involved was an unfeeling risk on his part, considering how worried she would be about him.

"Yes, why?" Dr. Nhari asked, curious himself. "Major Jenkins will appreciate your offer, but why get involved?"

"The bastards killed one of my men, that's why," Christopher reminded. "They made his wife a widow and his children fatherless. I owe it to Paul Spencer to be there when his killers are brought to justice. I owe it to his wife and kids, and to myself."

"Admirable sentiments," Dr. Nhari admitted, "but I suspect that Major Jenkins will prefer that you stay here. It would be too embarrassing if *the* Christopher Van Hoon ended up dead in a Zimbabwe shoot-out." He turned to Janet. "Nor would it do to have a famous American television personality wounded or killed."

He had anticipated her asking to go along. The blow-by-blow description of flushing out poachers was perfect for a dramatic television report. But joining the attack group was the last thing on Janet's mind. She had too much of what she wanted out of life to risk it on some harebrained adventure without even a camera crew to record her efforts. She resented Christopher's volunteering, but she understood. He was a friend of the dead man and his family. But neither Janet nor Christopher would have a family if Christopher got killed.

"I might remind you to remind Major Jenkins that I have friends in high places," Christopher said.

"We could bring Captain Sylo in to verify that, couldn't we?" Dr. Nhari observed with wry humor. "The captain's efforts to remove you and your team from Great Zimbabwe were certainly nipped in the bud by a few of your phone calls, but Major Jenkins might be less willing to give you access to an outside line."

"Then there'll be phone calls afterward," Christopher guaranteed. "Just because Van Hoon Afrikaner Minerals hasn't come up with any gold at Great Zimbabwe doesn't mean that it doesn't have its tentacles in enough other pies to assure me the continued goodwill of your government and its supporting military hierarchy. The latter are always on the lookout for those among their ranks who show potential for upward mobility."

"Like Major Jenkins?" Dr. Nhari suggested.

"There are higher ranks to which an ambitious man can aspire than major," Christopher said. "Promotions are undeniably made on the basis of qualification and merit, but a good word dropped here and there never hurt anyone. Wouldn't you agree? A bad word, on the other hand...."

"I'm not in the military," Dr. Nhari said, "and I don't know how Major Jenkins would respond to that theory. However, you did have a friend who was murdered, and Major Jenkins does appreciate sentiments like loyalty and friendship."

Janet read through the double-talk. Christopher wanted to go, and he was going. He got everything he wanted, including her. Janet had wants of her own. She wanted a lover and a husband in one piece.

"I'll see what Major Jenkins says," Dr. Nhari promised, coming to his feet. "You'll hear his decision shortly." He bowed smartly in Janet's direction and left.

"You're angry," Christopher said, and it wasn't a question. Her feelings were clearly visible on her face.

"Don't you dare tell me you don't know why!"

"These poachers have to be stopped," Christopher insisted. "I've seen what they've done, remember? I saw seven bloated elephants dead at the waterhole. I lost a friend because he was in the wrong place at the wrong time. I saw Melissa poisoned, her calf dead within a few feet of her. I can't forget all of that; I can't forget that I almost lost you beneath a stampeding herd of elephants. And you don't understand why I want to make sure this is handled effectively?"

"I understand it," Janet said, "but there are men out there who've killed animals and people, and they may kill you. That's what upsets me."

"I promise to keep out of the way of their bullets," he said, making light of something in which Janet could see no humor. He was going. She would, too, if she were in his shoes. Christopher felt a sense of responsibility; he was not the sort of person to leave things entirely up to others. Knowing that, though, didn't erase the fact that her man was going into a danger zone and might not come back. The poacher who killed the last elephant would wipe out millions of years of evolution, and the man who killed Christopher would wipe out Janet's future. "I'm coming back," he said. "I promise."

How could he promise? No man knew his future. Anyway, it wasn't his worthless promise that would make her let him go. His need to participate was a vital part of the man she loved, and she wouldn't have him any other way. "You'd better come back to me," she said, wrapping her arms around his waist, laying her cheek against the hard smoothness of chest. His shirt was unbuttoned, and his skin was warm. One bullet could turn his flesh cold and lifeless. "I won't forgive you if you don't. Never!"

He kissed her. It was ended too briefly, interrupted by Dr. Nhari's return. "Major Jenkins wants to welcome you aboard," Dr. Nhari said.

"I'm delighted to be aboard," Christopher said.

"We're leaving immediately," Dr. Nhari informed him. "Time is of the essence in these matters of surprise."

Christopher left Janet with another brief kiss and a mental scrapbook of wonderful memories. It wasn't enough, even if some people never got that much.

Major Jenkins was waiting outside with a wide smile and a friendly handshake. He looked like a military man, ramrod straight and ruggedly thin, somewhere in his late fifties. Craig was there, too, not looking pleased. Janet couldn't blame him. It would have been a feather in his cap had he solved the problem before losing his command. On the other hand, Dr. Nhari was right: Craig had wasted too much time. Too many elephants had died, too many kept dying while Craig struggled helplessly for solutions. They all hoped the present plan would end the slaughter; Craig should chalk Major Jenkins's success up against his own bruised ego. This was a one-time operation that had to work. Soldiers couldn't be spared every day from more pressing duties, as Craig himself had explained to Janet some time ago.

Janet waved after them, and Dr. Nhari and Christopher waved back. Major Jenkins talked strategy with his aide-de-camp. Craig stared straight ahead. The driver steered the car toward the troop convoy regrouped at the military encampment. The three trucks in the parking lot remained where they were. The soldiers who had arrived in them stayed to make sure no one else left the surrounding area.

Janet didn't know where Christopher was going or how long he would be gone. The Great Zimbabwe Reserve, even shrunk from its original nineteen-thousand square kilometers, had plenty of rugged terrain that made travel time-consuming. He could be gone all day and all night. He could be gone longer.

She had early-morning coffee in the restaurant. She saw no one she knew, and after coffee she went to her room. The yellow stone was still hidden away in her drawer, and after a moment's thought, she went to the dresser and removed the gem. Whatever threat it offered would be nonexistent if Christopher didn't come back. She'd rather have the problem. "Oh, Christopher, please don't die!" she said. She put the stone back in the drawer. If he came back alive and well, they would work out their problems, including the one presented by the diamond—if that was what it proved to be.

She wanted to marry him. She wanted to bear his children. She wanted to love him into old age. Maybe a marriage contract was nothing more than a piece of paper, but she wanted that seal of approval. Her need to do the right thing was deep, and she didn't consider herself or Christopher a sinner because of the wonderful nights they had already spent together. But she did want to make their commitment formal and legal. If he came back, she would have love, marriage and children. If he didn't, she would have wonderful memories. She wanted more than just the memories.

She left the room and began walking from the hotel to the military encampment. The road was deserted except for two trucks parked in the roadway in an apparent attempt to prevent anyone from taking off in the airplane. She saw sentries on duty among the trees. None paid any attention to her. They wouldn't unless she tried to break through their ranks. No one or no message was to get through until Major Jenkins sent word back that his mission was completed.

She crossed the field to the Acropolis. The craggy prominence of granite had been special to her since she'd climbed to the top to hear Christopher's proposal of marriage. She had once preferred the geometric beauty of the Great Enclosure, laid out in the valley among green grass and shady trees—but no longer. The view from the top of the Acropolis was stupendous, and she hoped to see the military convoy and Christopher from there.

She walked through the ruins of the Outspan Gate and began the ascent of the Southeast Stairway, welcoming the physical strain of the climb. She welcomed anything that took her mind off what might happen to Christopher.

The pathway narrowed between huge granite boulders and man-made walls. She paused, looking out over the valley below. There was no sign of the convoy, no sign of Christopher.

She was alone with her thoughts. The sky was cloudless, the sun growing warmer. There wasn't even the breath of a breeze. Everything was waiting. For what?

The stairway ended in the Covered Entrance. Janet stooped through the low passageway that penetrated the Turret Wall as far as the Royal Enclosure. She remembered things she had read about this place, using memory as a mental exercise to keep her thoughts off Christopher's fate.

Household rubbish had been thrown over the sides of the cliff in the old days, and high piles of garbage had been formed. When partially excavated, one turned up cattle bones, broken pottery, copper bangles and the remains of five dogs. There were few wild animal bones. The inhabitants apparently relied more on domestic animals and plants for their food.

Several hut floors were stratified in the sides of the large pit in the Royal Enclosure. Fragments of a soapstone bowl, gold, glass beads, copper spearheads and the head of a soapstone bird had been found there. Several complete soapstone birds were found farther along the rim in the Ritual Enclosure. Janet headed there.

Much of Great Zimbabwe—its Conical Tower, its carved birds and its monoliths incised with geometrical designs—remained a mystery.

In the Ritual Enclosure, she turned from the man-made wall and climbed up through the natural rock. The ledge was called the Balcony. It faced out over the Ritual Enclosure and gave one of the best views from the Acropolis. She surveyed the exquisite interplay of rugged hills and tree-lined valleys stretched to the horizon. On the landscape below, the Great Enclosure was wondrous to behold. The adjoining military encampment, a toy-like miniature among milkwood trees, was insignificant in comparison. The dirt road, blocked by the parked trucks, was a dusty scar among faded greens, rusts, browns and golds.

The gunfire started, and it was closer than she suspected it would be. For a moment it sounded as it was coming from the camp below, but it was farther afield. The elevation of her vantage point gave a clarity to faraway sounds that was missing lower on the Acropolis.

She sat on the Balcony, her chin on her knees, her arms around her legs. With each burst of automatic weapon fire, she tried to place the source. Each time she failed. Except for a few startled birds, no wildlife moved to the accompaniment of that deadly background music.

It was warm on the Balcony, and it got hotter as the sun climbed higher in the sky. But Janet was chilly; her mind insisting that Christopher's vital living body was in the path of each and every shot cracking in the distance.

Surely a day would come when she could look ahead to the next day, or next week, or next month—even next year—and see nothing standing in the way of her and Christopher's happiness. There had been so many obstacles, one after another. Her need for vengeance had dissolved when her love for him took precedence over an oath to her dead father. Her doubts that Christopher loved her were erased completely by what had since happened between them. Their past wouldn't interfere with their future, because she had admitted their childhood relationship. Then there was the poisoning of Melissa and Suzy, but he wasn't responsible for that. There was the gold that could have been found at Great Zimbabwe but wasn't. There was this battle over illegal ivory that had popped up out of nowhere.

But if he returned alive and well from it, that didn't necessarily mean any happy-ever-after ending. There was the rock in the dresser drawer, waiting to plunge their relationship into new chaos if all else failed. There should be an end to it! Even Christopher admitted that the sixteen years they had spent apart should count for something—not to mention obstacles already surmounted.

The gunfire stopped. Had the soldiers and poachers all been killed? Civilians? Had Dr. Nhari and Christopher been shot in a fight over the ivory of animals already dead?

The beauty of the vista disturbed her, and not for the first time. It hid too much. Africa was crumbling into ruin, but no one would know that by looking at the landscape spread out before her. How deceptive those greens, rusts, browns, ochers and golds, the radiant blueness of the cloudless sky. Beneath it all, there was decay running rampant: animals dead and dying; men dead and dying; a way of life dead and dying. Behold the new Africa of farms, ranches, highways, power stations— hamburger and fried chicken stands just waiting to take over.

Janet left the Balcony, climbing down a pathway that ancient sentinels had taken to and from their posts. She walked through the Ritual Enclosure, where soapstone birds hinting of pagan rites had been found. She walked beside fortress walls so impressive that they were acclaimed as the work of Sabaeans, Phoenicians and Egyptians. This was the fabled Ophir of King

Solomon: a city born of gold and left to die when gold deserted it. Death and ruin were natural parts of Africa.

She bent over and scuttled through the low tunnel from the Royal Enclosure to the Southeast Stairway, descending steps too narrow for her feet. She could fall and break her neck. Christopher could return from battle to find her dead on the mountainside! Because he was alive. He was coming back. Together they would solve whatever heaven or hell put in their path. Love had to conquer all. It was as simple as that, after all.

She listened for the returning convoy. With each step she tested the ground for vibrations. The last time she hadn't recognized the sounds. She would now. She would welcome them. They would mean her lover was back.

Her climb and descent of the Acropolis had made her hot and sticky, so she showered when she got back to her room. She put on a blouse of light orange. The color set off her dark hair and radiant tan. She wanted to be beautiful for her man, and she was.

There was a knock at the door, and she hurried to answer it. Her heart beat faster. Her skin flushed attractively. She floated across the floor.

It wasn't Christopher but a black soldier with a machine gun. His weapon wasn't menacing, merely strapped over one shoulder. His presence drained away happy expectations, replacing them with sinister foreboding. "Mrs. Westover?" the soldier asked. He was young but looked older because of the strain evident in his face. "Captain Frazier would like to see you."

She didn't know Captain Frazier. "Yes, of course," she said. The soldier had a Land Rover in the parking lot. "Who's Captain Frazier?" she asked finally. The soldier frowned, not understanding her question. "I don't remember him," she said.

"He came with Major Jenkins," the soldier explained.

"Of course," she said, leaving it at that. Only the captain would say what he wanted with her, obviously.

They stopped at Craig's tent. Captain Frazier, then, was Craig's replacement. The familiarity of their meeting place didn't put her any more at ease. The soldier motioned for her to wait. He left.

She didn't expect the person who emerged from the tent. "Craig!" she exclaimed, her response automatic. If Craig was there, Christopher was back, too. They had left in the same car with Major Jenkins and Dr. Nhari. Where was Major Jenkins? Where was Dr. Nhari? "Where is Christopher?" she asked.

"Come inside, Janet," he urged, taking her hand and leading her into a shade no less hot than the sunshine.

"Mrs. Westover," Captain Frazier said in greeting. He was younger than Craig but not as good looking. His hair was red and thinning, and his complexion hadn't stood up well beneath the tropical sun. His morning at the Great Zimbabwe encampment had left him painfully sunburned. The burn ointment he had slicked on his face gave his plain features a plastic gloss and did nothing for his discomfort. The pleasant-smelling goo attracted flies which he irritably flicked away with quick spastic movements of his left hand. "Do sit down," he said moving a chair toward her.

"What's this about?" Janet asked. She didn't want to sit, but she did. She kept looking for Christopher, knowing he wasn't there.

"I'll let Captain Sylo explain," Captain Frazier said.

"Christopher is wounded, Janet," Craig obliged, wasting no more time.

"Wounded?" Janet responded. She had convinced herself Christopher was all right. Foolish! "Badly?" she asked, the word catching in her throat.

"I'm afraid so," Craig said. The bottom dropped out of Janet's world "He's asking for you," he added.

CHAPTER FOURTEEN

"I MUST go to him!"

"Yes, of course," Craig agreed, coming to his feet. "That's why I'm here. I'm going to fly you. The landing will be a little difficult, but I'll manage."

She didn't care how difficult the landing would be. The sooner she got to Christopher the better. Christopher was her life. Anxious to get out of the tent, she collided with a soldier who was on his way in. He was embarrassed, mumbling apologies.

"Yes, Private Choma?" Captain Frazier asked irritably.

The only thing on Janet's mind was getting to the man she loved. But, Craig paused.

"Word from Major Jenkins," the private said. He handed the communiqué to Captain Frazier. As the captain unfolded the paper, Janet's heart skipped a beat. She thought it was word about Christopher's condition, and fear made her drop her eyes. She didn't want to read bad news in Frazier's face. It was only later that she recalled having noticed the curious fact that Craig had kept his hand on the gun in his holster from the moment Choma had appeared.

"Mission a success," Captain Frazier read aloud. "Notify Salisbury." Craig reached for the paper, and Captain Frazier reluctantly surrendered it. Craig scanned the communiqué and confirmed what Frazier had read. Instead of the look of relief that Janet had expected, she saw with astonishment that Craig's features hardened. In an almost imperceptible motion, his hand drew out his gun.

"What's the meaning of this, Sylo?" Frazier sputtered.

But Craig didn't answer, his eyes riveted on Choma. "I wouldn't do anything foolish if I were you, soldier," he warned the young man.

"Where's Christopher?" Janet demanded. She was beginning to panic. What was happening here made no sense at all. "You've got to get me to him. He may be dying...."

"Christopher is fine," Craig said coolly.

Janet was stunned. "But you said—"

"He's fine!" he interrupted. "I lied when I said he was wounded."

"You said Christopher was badly hurt!" she said in an accusing tone. She was confused. What did he mean, it was a lie?

"I need a plane," Craig explained. "With Captain Frazier now in charge in the absence of Major Jenkins, I foresaw difficulty in getting it."

What was he saying? Why was he acting so strangely?

"Is Christopher wounded or isn't he?" Janet persisted. Christopher's condition was the most important thing to her. Concern for him overrode her powers of reasoning.

"It was a ploy, Mrs. Westover," Captain Frazier enlightened her, and suddenly a lot of jigsaw pieces began to fit into place. "He arrives on a mission of mercy, here to fly you off to the wounded man you love. I wave goodbye with my blessing."

"You'll still wave goodbye," Craig promised, "although you'll now be less content to see me go."

"Craig, what's this all about?" Janet asked. She wouldn't easily forgive the torment of his cruel lie about Christopher—if it was a lie. Her heart was still thumping madly from the scare.

"Here's the man who kept the poachers informed of the best times and places for their strikes," Captain Frazier conjectured further. "As soon as I saw that communiqué, I realized that some of his cohorts must have been taken, which was also part of the plan. Captured men sometimes have the nasty little habit of spilling the beans. They would quite likely, for instance, reveal who their ringleader was."

"I don't believe it!" Janet protested.

"Ask him," Captain Frazier challenged. "No wonder he was banging his head against the wall when it came to coming up with the guilty party. He couldn't haul himself off to jail, could he?"

"Craig?" Janet asked, more than one question implied by her simple speaking of his name.

"It's true," Craig admitted. "There's no point in my playing innocent any longer."

"Why?" Janet asked, aghast. "Your grandfather and father devoted their lives to wildlife preservation, and you've been instrumental in destroying all they worked to achieve."

"My grandfather died as poor as a country church mouse. My father was shot down with hardly enough in his savings account to pay for his and my mother's funerals. Here's one Sylo who's getting out of Africa what Africa owes him—and don't tell me it doesn't owe me!" he said. "I've as much right to some of the gravy as your boyfriend does. Hell, I've *more* right. My grandfather and my old man worked their lives away to keep Africa unsullied, while the Van Hoons raped the countryside for everything it was worth. In the end, all my grandfather and father did wasn't worth a damned thing. It's men like the Van Hoons who always win in this world. So why shouldn't I be out for number one?"

"You used me!" Janet shouted. He had worked so hard to get her and Christopher together, because he had wanted her daily reports on where the V.H.A.M. team was headed. He couldn't count on their filed itineraries. Team members were always wandering off, as Paul Spencer had done. Unmonitored, they could stumble onto things they weren't supposed to see.

Paul Spencer was dead. If Craig hadn't pulled the trigger, he might as well have. In the stampede designed to scare away the research team, a soldier had been trampled to death, Janet had almost been killed and Christopher had had to shoot an elephant to save her. Melissa and Suzy were dead—all because of Craig!

"You're despicable and crude!" she exclaimed. To think she had once actually held him up as some kind of model.

"Yes, go ahead and damn me for my ill-gotten gains, while you guiltlessly plan to marry into a fortune built from more exploitation of Africa than my killing of a few elephants and rhinos!" Craig declared. "Then you tell me, while you're busy spending your husband's money, which of us is more honest— which of us is more the hypocrite."

As much as she longed to deny any truth to Craig's words, Janet felt a niggling uneasiness. She and Christopher still had so much to resolve....

"You're not getting away with this, Sylo!" Captain Frazier warned.

"And who's going to stop me? You, Captain Frazier?" he asked before answering his own question. "I think not. You're going to let me go, because that'll be better than dying in any attempt to play hero and stop me. But we're wasting valuable time with this idle chitchat, aren't we? Is that what you're counting on? Do you expect Major Jenkins to realize I've slipped through his fingers in the confusion?"

"Major Jenkins has the ivory," Janet reminded Craig triumphantly.

"Only some of it," Craig replied. "We've a lot already funneled through the pipeline; believe me—far more than I ever dreamed possible. When I first got involved, I was thinking of only four or five elephants. That was big money compared to my yearly income. I was even upset when my partners started getting greedy and endangering my cover by continually going for more. However, I'm going to be the one to enjoy the fruits of their greed while they sit out their time in some jail cell. There is justice in the world, after all, yes? Now about that plane...."

"You won't get far!" Captain Frazier vowed, stalling for time. But Craig had obviously already gauged his position. Even if the prisoners had revealed their informant's identity to Major Jenkins by now, no doubt hoping to gain lighter sentences in return for their information, by the time they all returned it would be too late. Craig would be long gone.

"I'll get far enough with Janet along," Craig assured the captain. "It's not as if I haven't made some plans for this day, you know. My cover could have been blown a long time ago. In fact, I was expecting it to be. It was sheer luck it wasn't. It was even luckier that my optimistic superiors in Salisbury held out until now, figuring a guy, like me, with my father and my grandfather, would surely come through for them. So don't worry about me. I've greased enough palms with ivory to get me out of Africa and to a certain sizable bank account awaiting me elsewhere."

It was his tent, and he knew where things were. He picked up a jacket and draped it over his arm, hiding the gun. No one would look that closely, anyway. It wouldn't occur to anyone to suspect the ex-commandant of holding a gun on the man brought in to replace him. Craig didn't rush. He proceeded calmly and coolly but efficiently.

"Captain Frazier and Private Choma, step outside first," Craig instructed, waving the gun. "Janet and I will follow. The private will drive the captain's Jeep; Captain Frazier in front with him. Janet and I will sit in back. And don't any of you try anything, will you? I'll shoot one or all of you if I have to."

"You should give yourself up, Craig," Janet said. Craig laughed in genuine good humor. "I'm serious," she insisted.

"I know you are," he replied. "You see salvation awaiting this poor sinner if he repents his wicked ways. However, I have no such illusions. I would be put away for far longer than I have any mind to be. So save your breath, Janet. Surrender is out of the question. Let's get on with the better alternative."

They left the tent and got into the Jeep. Janet hoped Christopher wouldn't show up and attempt any dangerous heroics. She didn't want him dead, and Craig would shoot if pressed—she was convinced of that now.

Before leaving the encampment that morning, Major Jenkins had ordered two trucks left in the middle of the dirt road that doubled as a runway. There was no way the airplane could take off around or over them. This had offered Craig his main obstacle in making any escape without first enlisting the aid of Captain Frazier, whose men manned those vehicles. It took only one command from Frazier to have the trucks pulled back. No one was the wiser, since the word was out that Christopher Van Hoon had been shot and Craig had come to fetch the wounded man's fiancée.

"Excellent," Craig said when the Jeep pulled to a stop not far from where the plane stood beneath the shade of several milkwood trees. "Now if the private will disengage the mooring cables and slide the blocks free of the wheels, we'll wait." Private Choma proceeded to do as he was told.

"How long are you planning to have me along as your hostage?" Janet asked. She wasn't afraid; she merely wanted this out of the way so she could get back to her life with Christopher.

"Counting the minutes, are you?" Craig asked. His smile was an unattractive smirk. "Relax and take things as they come, Janet. After all, you now know Van Hoon has nothing I can't offer, including money. Oh, I can't match him bank account for bank account, but I'm no longer a pauper—that's for certain. I might even have him beat in a few other departments. You can tell me for sure later."

Janet snapped to attention. He was planning more for her than a little side trip. "If I were you, I wouldn't make comparisons between you and Christopher," she warned. "As far as I'm concerned, you'll always come out on the short end."

"We'll see what you have to say about further comparisons after our little trip gets underway," Craig said. His suggestive wink gave Janet no comfort.

"You're disgusting, Sylo!" Captain Frazier spat. He, too, was catching Craig's none-too-subtle innuendos. "You be damned careful what you attempt with Mrs. Westover."

"I'll keep that in mind," Craig retorted, sneering.

Janet was appalled—more disgusted than fearful. Her mind flashed back to the times she had innocently spent alone with

Craig. There hadn't been that many—once after Christopher had unexpectedly shown up at Great Zimbabwe and insisted they talk; again at Victoria Falls. She had been looking for someone to offset the disturbing effect Christopher had on her, and Craig had been a likely choice. However, there hadn't been any magic between them, or any danger. Clearly there was danger now.

"You look nervous, Janet," Craig said mockingly. She didn't like the way he said it. She didn't like anything about this situation. She should have seen the man as he was long before this too-late moment. There had been hints—something he had said about money not being the best thing in life, but everything else coming in a distant second. There had been that comment on how he would like, just once, to be in Christopher's shoes long enough to know the feeling of having all that money and all those women. She had thought he was joking, because she had been confident at the time that she had him and Christopher correctly labeled and filed into categories. Craig was honest, trustworthy, loyal, friendly, courteous, kind—a veritable boy scout, interested not in material things but in endeavors like saving the animals of Africa. Christopher had been born with a gold spoon in his mouth and expected everything and everyone he wanted—money, power, beautiful women—to fall into his lap: a money-mad businessman who ran over anyone or anything at the hint of possible profit. Since then, she had at least partially adjusted her opinion of Christopher, but she hadn't stopped to rethink Craig. It was an oversight for which she was to pay dearly, if Craig was to have his way.

"So? Which one is it, Captain Sylo or Van Hoon?" Roger had asked on the plane just before the camera crew was evacuated to Salisbury on Craig's orders. She had told him it was Christopher. "Good," he had answered. "I couldn't say this before, but he's the better man." And Dr. Nhari didn't like Craig. And Christopher didn't like him. Still, Janet had seen what she'd wanted to see. She had wanted an ideal man who labored for good causes and battled evil and avarice in a world gone mad. She had wanted a friendship with a man who had all the good qualities she had once thought missing in Christopher. Yet she had never seriously considered Craig as anything more than a friend. It had quickly become obvious that he was no match for Christopher, with all his faults. Her preference for Christopher must have been one more blow to an ego already bruised and battered by jealousy and envy.

"You'll never get anything from me, Craig," she said.

"Never is a very long time," he said cryptically, sending chills up and down her spine—and it wasn't a pleasurable sensation.

She turned desperately to Captain Frazier then, but despite the commanding appearance of his uniform, he was as helpless as she. The ointment smeared on his sunburned face drew more flies, and sweat glistened on his brow. Craig was calm, cool and collected. He was in control: He was the enemy, and he was about to win.

Private Choma returned to the Jeep, his mission accomplished. "We'll be saying goodbye to you gentlemen now," Craig said, his gun ready for any necessity. "I'll expect Captain Frazier to remain in view of his men until we're airborne. I want everyone to see his full stamp of approval set on this mercy mission. Slide over this way, Janet. That's right. Now step on out."

"If you harm Mrs. Westover, there's going to be hell to pay!" Captain Frazier said.

Craig wasn't impressed. "Harm Janet?" he asked incredulously. He reached for her with his free arm and drew her close. She wanted to pull away, but a scene was out of the question as long as Craig had a gun. "Janet and I are dear friends, aren't we, Janet?"

"I once thought we were friends, but I was mistaken," she said.

"Yes, we're dear, dear friends," Craig said, ignoring her denial. "But as much as it would pain me to hurt a dear, dear friend, I will if either of you gentlemen makes what even looks like one false move."

"You bastard!" Captain Frazier barked. Private Choma, as

helpless as the captain, could only nod his agreement. "You're a disgrace to your uniform!" Frazier added.

Craig merely laughed at that comment. He kept his arm firmly around Janet's waist and walked her to the plane. "You first, Janet," he said. She moved slowly, hoping for a miracle. Christopher would save her, but she didn't want him exposed to the dangerous risks any rescue would require. Besides, he was with Major Jenkins and out of temptation's way. Janet would carry on as best she could, hoping this predicament promised none of the horrors she was reading into it. "A little faster, please, Janet!" Craig insisted, his impatient tone belying the politeness of his words.

She entered the plane and turned into the aisle between the seats, heading toward the cockpit. The other times she had been in the plane, the seats, recently replaced, had been removed to make additional cargo space.

Suddenly there was a loud noise behind her. "What the hell?" Craig exclaimed. Something deflected off Janet's foot, and she looked down instantly to see Craig's pistol skid beneath the seats. She turned to confront the continuing noise.

"Christopher!" she gasped. There was no mistaking his powerful body locked in battle with Craig for control of Christopher's gun. She marveled at how he could be there. Since Craig had shut the door of the plane, Christopher must have been waiting in the tail section all along. But how had he known enough to be there?

The two men grappled for the gun still in Christopher's possession, moving slowly down the aisle toward her. Janet automatically stepped back. With the seats bolted in place, there wasn't much space for two large men to move. Clearly well matched, they tumbled over seat backs that collapsed beneath the combined weight. The gun dropped from Christopher's hand and clattered in between the seats.

Janet dropped to her knees, looking for either gun. She spotted Craig's, but not the other. Because of where the two men were fighting, she couldn't reach it. Frustrated, she got up and hurried into the cockpit. Through the window she saw Captain Frazier and Private Choma sitting dutifully in the Jeep. She waved to them frantically, but neither was looking in her direction. She pounded on the sealed window. She put her mouth close to the glass and screamed, "Help, damn it, help!" She was behaving like the heroine in a B-movie, but she didn't care. She had to get the attention of Frazier and the private.

Craig and Christopher were fighting harder now, but the cramped quarters kept them from doing as much damage as they might have. Their momentum carried them back toward the tail section. Outside, Captain Frazier and Private Choma had finally caught sight of Janet, had run to the plane and were trying unsuccessfully to open its locked door. The captain, having shouted for assistance, had brought soldiers running from the sidelines.

Janet went down on all fours in another attempt to get Craig's gun, and this time she succeeded. The other gun was still nowhere to be seen, probably wedged between two seats. Janet hated guns. The feel of the one in her hand was especially disturbing. "Stop, or I'll shoot!" she commanded. It was another hackneyed line from some late-night movie; it didn't get any results. The two men kept slugging it out as if they hadn't heard her. Anyway, she hadn't aimed the gun for fear of shooting Christopher.

The wrench had been left on the floor by one of the crew who had bolted down the seats, and Craig was the first to find it. Janet saw him with it before Christopher did. "He has a wrench!" she screamed in warning, watching Craig raise the piece of heavy metal. The blow grazed Christopher's already bruised cheek-bone and whacked his shoulder. Encouraged, Craig raised the wrench again.

Janet fired a shot into the air. Disoriented by the sound, Craig turned toward her for a fraction of a second. And it was long enough for Christopher to bend down and retrieve the gun that had lain out of sight not far from his feet.

"This is it, Sylo," he said quietly, training the weapon on the other man, whose face was a mask of despair and disgust.

* * * * * * *

SHE SAT with her back against the trunk of a milkwood tree. Christopher lay with his head in her lap. His eyes were closed, and she gently traced the edge of the bruise growing more defined along his cheekbone. His hair was glowingly blond against the orange of her blouse. "You're going to end up with a black eye, too," she prophesied.

"Will you love me anyway?" he asked.

"Of course," she said. His question and her answer were superfluous. It was accepted that she loved him and would do so forever.

"Did I thank you for saving my life?" he asked, opening eyes as golden and as attractively hypnotic as ever.

"Yes, I believe you did," she said with a smile, "shortly after I thanked you for once again coming to my rescue."

Captain Frazier broke away from the group of soldiers gathered around the airplane. "We're ready to fly Sylo out," he said. "He won't thank you for what you did; he has a lot of time in the stockade stretching ahead of him." He dropped to his haunches to put himself on eye level with the two of them.

Christopher anticipated the captain's next question and asked it for him. "How did I happen to show up at the right place at the right time?"

"I guess the prisoners taken during the raid talked their heads off, huh?" Captain Frazier speculated. He brushed away the fly that was trying so persistently to sample the ointment on the bridge of his nose. "Sylo was convinced no one would spill the beans about him until the legal people were brought in for plea bargaining."

"For all I know, he was right," Christopher said. "It wasn't anyone's confession that had me looking to see where Captain Sylo had got himself off to."

"Then what?" Captain Frazier asked. Janet was as curious,

too. She might be willing even to believe in incidents of E.S.P. and mental telepathy, especially between two people as closely in tune as she and Christopher, but she didn't think any of her mental calls for help had brought Christopher running this time.

"I was one of the first into the storage room," Christopher said. "Actually, it was a cave. They had all of their booty laid out for transport." Captain Frazier didn't see how that had tipped Sylo's hand. "Mainly tusks," Christopher continued. "About sixty of them. But there were several rhino horns, too, including a couple of distinctively long and large ones."

"Melissa's!" Janet said, immediately making the connection. "They were Melissa's weren't they?"

"Who's Melissa?" Captain Frazier asked, puzzled.

"Melissa was a rhino that grazed around here until a few days ago," Christopher explained. "She had a pair of horns that were unique in this day and age. She and her calf were poisoned by poachers."

The captain still needed more information, and Janet obliged. "Christopher scared off the poachers before they got her horns." That was the same day she had found the yellow stone in the stream, but she had no desire to think about that now. "Christopher took the horns to Craig for safekeeping."

"Sylo told us he shipped them off to Salisbury," Christopher said.

It all clicked for Captain Frazier then. "And they weren't in Salisbury," he verified. "They were in the cave with the contraband."

"So they either got there before Sylo shipped them to Salisbury or afterward," Christopher said. "I was most interested in hearing Captain Sylo's opinion on that. Suspiciously, he was nowhere to be found."

"You figured he'd come back here instead of head across country?" Captain Frazier asked.

"There was a plane here," Christopher reminded him. "When you want to get far fast, you don't drive the distance if you have access to an airplane. If he was guilty and making a break for it, this was where he'd come. I didn't waste time trying to explain all of that to Major Jenkins, either. I headed back here like a shot. Rather than comb the whole camp and tip my hand, or miss him, I staked myself out in the plane."

"Lucky for us you did," Captain Frazier congratulated him. Janet readily agreed.

"I was a little taken aback when he ushered Janet aboard," Christopher confessed. "Especially when I suspected he had a gun under that rather conspicuously draped jacket. I didn't want bullets to go flying indiscriminately. We had quite a little tussle," he said, gingerly fingering his bruised face. "But Janet ended up saving the day," Christopher added, looking at her with loving pride.

"You both handled things well, very well indeed," Captain Frazier assured them magnanimously. Christopher and Janet's fast action meant the captain's military record would look a lot different than it would have if Craig had kidnapped Janet and flown into the wild blue yonder.

"And I see a medal of commendation in your immediate future, Captain Frazier," Christopher commented shrewdly, but with a smile.

The captain nodded complacently as a soldier yelled something from the plane and double-timed it to his superior. Frazier came to his feet. "I have to be on my way," he said.

"Before you go, could you arrange for someone to give Janet and me a lift back to the hotel?" Christopher asked, getting up. "I could use a shower. How about you, Janet?"

She knew to what he was referring, and she blushed bright red. Fortunately it all went completely over the captain's head. "I'll have Private Choma drive you," Captain Frazier said obligingly. He walked toward the plane in order to single the private out of the group of curious onlookers.

"What you need is a good long soak in a tub full of hot water," Janet said when the captain was out of earshot. "Not a strenuous workout in the shower."

"You're right," Christopher agreed. "Besides, the tub is

plenty big enough for two, isn't it?"

"You're incorrigible!" she said, shaking her head. She took his proffered hands, and he pulled her to her feet, groaning with the pressure of her weight on his injured shoulder as she came up against him. "Doesn't sound to me as if you're up to much of anything," Janet said with a wide smile.

"We'll see," Christopher said. Their peals of merry laughter reached the soldiers gathered in a solemn group several hundred yards away.

And Janet thought how perfect things would be if it weren't for a yellow stone still in her hotel dresser.

CHAPTER FIFTEEN

"IT'S A DIAMOND, isn't it?" she said.

Christopher looked up from the stone she had placed before him on his desk at Lionspride. Surprisingly, he didn't touch it but left it where it was: a miniature sun, collecting light from the desk lamp and holding it. Her engagement ring was more actively on fire, flashing sparks from its faceted surface.

"What do you think?" Christopher parried noncommittally, leaning back in his chair and folding his arms across his chest. His hair and eyes, like the stones, trapped the light.

"It *is* a diamond," she said. It had been obvious from the moment she'd seen it reflecting sunlight through the water of the stream.

He leaned forward and touched the stone for the first time. He moved it this way and that with his forefinger and finally lifted it for a closer examination. "Yes," he verified, "a diamond. A yellow fancy, approximately one-hundred-and-fifty carats. Its two readily noticeable flaws will still leave a seventy-carat cut gemstone, and there's a good chance the right cutter can salvage even more."

"You don't seem surprised I have it," Janet said. She was sure he hadn't known.

"I'm always surprised to see a diamond of this color and size," he said. "It's just that it does explain the air of impending disaster you've been carrying around with you since our return to Lionspride. You found this on the Great Zimbabwe reserve, didn't you?"

"If I did, what then?" she asked, so afraid that he wouldn't have the right answers yet again.

"If so, there must be compromises," Christopher said, putting the stone back on the blotter. "We talked about compromises once, didn't we?"

"We could forget I found it," Janet said.

"Flush it down the toilet, you mean?" Christopher suggested wryly. "Send it out to sea with the fish? I don't think so. You don't, either. Nothing is washed away by pretending the problem doesn't exist. We'll face this squarely, as we would have faced a large gold discovery at Great Zimbabwe. Besides, it's a rare find you have here, Janet. Compare what Donald Geiger dropped on the desk to the final product on your finger. Now imagine a faceted stone at least twice that size. The two yellow fancies will make quite a pair—big and little, mother and daughter."

Melissa and Suzy were mother and daughter—big and little, both dead. Killed by poison. This stone could kill all Janet wanted out of life—such a deceptively beautiful death weapon.

"Do whatever you must," Janet said. "I'm glad it's out in the open."

"Yes," Christopher agreed. "There shouldn't be secrets between two people as much in love as we are. Whatever the problem, it should be worked out together. You see that." It wasn't a question.

"Behold the acid test the gold wouldn't give us!" Janet said sadly. She couldn't keep the fear out of her voice. She had come so close to keeping the secret, but she had spent too much of the past sixteen years living in fantasies to do so any longer. She had to start dealing with realities.

"This won't make any difference to the way I feel about you, or to the way you feel about me," he assured her. "Except that I love you more, because I know the effort it took for you to bring this forward." He thought he understood, but he didn't. Wildlife preservation remained a vital part of her life. Love didn't cancel out that importance. Maybe true love was supposed to, and that's what pained her, because she couldn't stand by docilely and accept the dissolution of the Great Zimbabwe Reserve just because of her feelings for Christopher.

"Anyway, the Great Zimbabwe Reserve doesn't stand much chance of surviving with or without interference from my company," he said, reading her thoughts. He was preparing the way for her surrender, she knew, giving her the rationalizations that would make it all right. Janet had to be careful, because she so badly wanted to be won over. "Look at its history," he continued. "It was once nineteen-thousand square kilometers but was carved up by land reform and converted, piece by piece, to farms and ranches. It's no longer large enough to support the big cats. It's no longer large enough to support the elephants. The cats are long gone, and Dr. Nhari's team is transferring the last of the elephants to Wankie. So we're not talking about a major animal sanctuary, are we? The irrigation potential of Lake Kyle has a lot of covetous eyes looking at what's left of the reserve, and who do you think will win the final struggle between animals and agriculture? Past victories point to the likely winner, don't you agree?"

His arguments were valid, but were they valid enough for her to accept them without compromising her ideals? "There are more and more people like Dr. Cunningham and Dr. Nhari who are beginning to speak out for wildlife preservation," Janet reminded him.

"One diamond doesn't make a diamond field, right?" he said. "Maybe we should find out more before imagining a problem where one might not exist. We nearly had a serious problem over the question of gold, didn't we? And there was no gold."

But Janet couldn't shake off her pessimism. "And if there are more diamonds?" she asked. She expected the worst, because there had been no major gold discovery to complicate her life. She wouldn't luck out twice.

"We'll confront that problem and deal with it," Christopher answered confidently.

"Yes, of course, you're right," she agreed; hoping the problem could be solved. She left him with the diamond and went back to her room. She lay on her bed. He wouldn't come to her. He wouldn't use his body to seduce her into his way of thinking, and that was admirable. But she wondered what he *would* do. He needed to use every persuasive weapon in his arsenal or he would lose her, and she didn't want to be lost. She wanted him to take her in his arms, pull her against the comforting hardness of his chest and promise her everything would be all right. She wanted reassurance that she was his and he was hers for time and all eternity—that there was nothing powerful enough to break the bond between them. She wanted to believe, really believe that somehow there was merit in sacrificing the Great Zimbabwe Reserve, where there had been none whatsoever in dissolving the dream her father had once had for Lackland.

During the next few weeks, Christopher became more and more preoccupied with telephone conversations and meetings behind closed doors. A good deal of his activity concerned the ongoing efforts to pinpoint the mother source of Janet's diamond find on the Great Zimbabwe Reserve. She didn't press for progress reports, and Christopher didn't volunteer them. For Janet, no news was good news, because she foresaw no suitable solution to their dilemma.

He continued to avoid her bedroom. She missed him beside her, but she needed a clear head to analyze things objectively, and Christopher's lovemaking would cloud the real issue. Blessed irrationality might be welcome for a time, but Janet knew she would regret it later. There was wisdom in keeping each other at arm's length for the moment, even with her fading hopes for a return to their previous closeness.

There were ways to get the information he didn't give her. She could have scanned the financial pages of the newspaper for hints of things in the works, on which newspapermen were always quick to speculate. But she didn't bother with the newspapers. She didn't watch television or listen to the radio She didn't go into Johannesburg. Lionspride was its own isolated and self-contained world, a connoisseur's paradise. There was fine food, fine wine, elegant domestic employees to serve both.

There was a sauna, steam room and Jacuzzi that did wonders for the aches and pains obtained during long hours of horseback riding. Most importantly, there was Christopher.

By mutual consent, all planning for their wedding was put on hold. Ann Tiompkin, a social secretary originally brought in from Johannesburg to help Janet coordinate the arrangements, was told her services would not be needed so soon, after all. Christopher explained that business matters had momentarily made definite plans impossible. Ann was sufficiently compensated for her inconvenience to accept the delay in the best of humor.

Janet's well-being fluctuated. Her leisurely weeks at Lionspride recalled the idyllic days she had spent there in her childhood, especially whenever Christopher realized he was neglecting her and showed up at the pool to join her in the water and in the sun. Sometimes he would be at the stables, his horse saddled and ready to join hers on one of her frequent rides. Often enough, it seemed so perfect. But it was as flawed as the largest diamond could be flawed, and thus could be valueless.

It might have been better for Janet to face the impossibility of the situation and call it quits. It wasn't as if she didn't have anything to go back to, because she had her life in the States. She had her job. She detected a good deal of curiosity on the other end of the transatlantic telephone line whenever she called to give her latest excuses for staying on in South Africa, but she was never threatened with dismissal by her supervisors. There were enough of her television shows shot and in the can for the start of the new season. She had plenty of time before her job would be in jeopardy. Jokingly, Roger continued to ask how she wanted the Great Zimbabwe tapes edited— "As the original hatchet job, or with more consideration for your husband?" She and Christopher weren't married yet, she would painfully remind him. "When is he going to make an honest woman of you?" he would respond predictably. She promised he would be the first to know.

She contemplated a return to her old life, but she knew what kept her at Lionspride. It was a faint, die-hard glimmer of hope that there was a solution somewhere. Christopher talked of compromises, and maybe there was one...maybe.

The visitors to Lionspride became more numerous, more frequent and more varied. Donald Geiger was often there. Janet usually saw him coming to or from the library, where Christopher stayed closeted for long hours at a time. Janet got no news out of Donald, although he was her most logical information source after Christopher. She knew none of the other men who came in and out of the house. Some wore expensive business suits; some wore soiled blue jeans. A few wore the military uniforms of South Africa and Zimbabwe. Some had manicured fingernails; some had nails encrusted with dirt and grime. Some nodded to her and offered polite greetings with the aplomb of men comfortable with women; some were embarrassed and unable to manage anything but tongue-tied grunts in passing.

At first, Janet looked over each man closely. One of them might provide the solution to hers and Christopher's problem. Later, she realized all of them were probably there to discuss potential profits for Van Hoon Afrikaner Minerals, and she began to pay less attention. She returned to her swimming and her riding. She spent long hours reading: *Moby Dick*, *War and Peace*. She re-read *Gone with the Wind*. She grew despondent with *Anna Karenina*, whose problems were only solvable by suicide beneath a speeding train. She exulted in the victory of Jenny Mowry over all her trials and tribulations in *From This Beloved Hour*.

There were more horseback rides—more returns to find cars filling the driveway. More of Christopher's conferences from which she was excluded.

But one afternoon Ashanti announced the moment she came through the door, "Mr. Van Hoon would like to see you in the library."

She didn't know how to handle this news. Christopher never included her in his business meetings. She stalled for time. "He might prefer that I change out of my riding clothes," she said.

"You're to go right in," Ashanti contradicted her.

"He is in a meeting, isn't he?" she asked. This could mean something she didn't want to hear—some decision reached about diamonds on the Great Zimbabwe Reserve, a decision that affected her last chance for happiness with Christopher.

"You are to join him nevertheless," Ashanti confirmed, "*immediately* upon your return. Mr. Van Hoon was quite specific."

Janet surrendered to the inevitable. At the library door, she knocked. Sliding the doors to one side, she stepped inside.

"Janet... good!" Christopher greeted her, apparently delighted to see her. He was obviously confident, but she doubted he had good news.

"You wanted to see me *immediately*?" she asked. It was her way of excusing her riding clothes.

"Yes, indeed!" Christopher affirmed, introducing the various people in the room. Janet had difficulty catching all the names and titles, but there was a cross section from both the South African and Zimbabwe governments. "Come on over here and sit down," Christopher invited, motioning to a wing chair close to where he stood. Self-conscious, Janet crossed the expensive Persian carpet and took the seat. "Janet has been most anxious," Christopher said to the others in the room. The men nodded their understanding. But they didn't understand, she thought. Christopher stepped up to the presentation easel set up in front of his desk. Displayed was a large map of the Great Zimbabwe Reserve. A blue outline designated the reserve boundaries as they had existed a few days before. A substantially smaller area, clinging precariously to a section of one sideline, was outlined in red. Janet braced herself for whatever was to follow.

"First, the diamond field looks like an extensive one," Christopher continued. The Zimbabwe representatives murmured appreciative agreement of Janet's worst fears. "Thanks to you, Janet," Christopher said, "we were able to stake out the claim before word got out confusing matters."

There were more nods and grunts of approval. Bully for Van Hoon Afrikaner Minerals! Janet's attention remained riveted on the map on the easel. "We've optioned all this area in blue," Christopher informed her, his finger designating the area, "with the full approval and cooperation of the Zimbabwe government."

"Most positively so!" one of the men said from his chair. Janet couldn't remember his name or his impressive title. Of course the Zimbabwe government wasn't protesting! It had contracted the survey for gold and would have been disappointed when the project fell through. It was delighted that diamonds had come to light as a replacement. Diamonds meant big profits for a poor country like Zimbabwe, profits that certainly weren't to be passed over at the prospect of losing one wildlife sanctuary that was fading fast anyway.

"However, these gentlemen have agreed to block off eight-thousand hectares of the original reserve for wildlife."

Eight-thousand hectares weren't much. They were piddling compared to the nineteen-thousand square kilometers that the Great Zimbabwe Reserve had encompassed at its conception. It was even a shockingly small area compared to the existing, much-diminished reserve. "I take it there was no sign of diamonds along that section of one sideline?" Janet said sarcastically.

"None!" Christopher admitted, ignoring or not recognizing her sarcasm. "While the potential remains for agricultural development, the Zimbabwe government has made it clear it desires this smaller game park to be set aside as a permanent sanctuary for area wildlife."

It was something; Janet admitted that. If the government wanted the game park left there, it would get its wish. But eight-thousand hectares were something less than a compromise—a token and nothing more. But there wasn't much she could do about it. She'd put Christopher in control the moment she turned the diamond over to him. But that small parcel of land wasn't enough to salve her guilty conscience about the animals.

Janet didn't know whether to reveal her feelings to Christopher now or when they were alone. It was easier now. If they were alone, he could revert to other means of persuasion. He could take her in his arms, kiss her and beg her to see this as the solution to keep them together. He had what he wanted—diamond-bearing rock to be mined and exploited for profit. She had what she wanted—a nice little animal reserve, set up by the government, for a few giraffes, buffalos, zebras and rhinos... except she wanted more. Her love and need for Christopher didn't blind her to the tragedy happening here. The animals on the land taken over by the Zimbabwe government couldn't all survive in the eight-thousand hectares they had left. There wasn't enough room. More animals would be dead and dying for want of grazing land and sanctuary.

"Here is the real *pièce de resistance!*" Christopher assured them all before she had a chance to protest, flipping the map over to reveal another one beneath it. The new map had a large area outlined in gold. Janet couldn't place the land mass, but it didn't include the Great Zimbabwe Reserve, and that was her interest at the moment. "A jointly operated and sizable wildlife reserve!" Christopher proclaimed dramatically. Everyone in the room broke out in warm applause, but Janet was confused by the revelation. "Ten-thousand square kilometers straddling the Limpopo River on both the South African and Zimbabwe sides," Christopher continued, "and joined by a land corridor to Kruger National Park in the east. Van Hoon Afrikaner Minerals has had extensive mining interests in this area for years—" his finger jabbed spots near the proposed animal sanctuary but not included in it "—copper mines in Messina, copper and phosphates in Phalaborwa. However, nearby is an extensive mass that is unsuitable for mineral development but still suited for wildlife. Since ownership of that land has been in dispute for a long while, it has, therefore, been decided that both the South African and Zimbabwe governments will stock such land with the displaced animals from the Great Zimbahwe Reserve—including those that won't be able to graze on the smaller game park. A share of both reserves' future maintenance costs will be offset from profits realized from the Westover-Van Hoon Diamond Mine, which the Zimbabwe government has agreed to allow me to set up under the corporate umbrella of Van Hoon Afrikaner Minerals, as long as a generous portion of the profits are donated to the country of origin."

"What?" Janet responded automatically. Her head was swimming. Her heart was filled with joy. If only she could believe what she was hearing.

Christopher smiled, very pleased with himself. Janet had noticeably rejected the compromise offered by the salvaged portion of the Great Zimbabwe Reserve alone, but this was another ball game. "Diamonds aren't found everywhere, Janet, and I have to take advantage of them where and when they're found. But there's no reason why non-mineral producing land donated by the two governments—since they will be sharing in V.H.A.M. profits, after all—couldn't be converted into an animal reserve. And since you picked the diamond up from the stream, it seems only fitting and fair that some of the profits from the mine be devoted to your concern for wildlife. We named the mine after its founder and the man you're going to marry," Christopher concluded. "You are still planning to marry me, aren't you, Janet?"

He had taken the Great Zimbabwe Reserve and shrunk it to a pitiful eight-thousand hectares with the diamond discovery, but he had compensated with a suitable replacement. The man was a true magician! "Yes, I'm marrying you!" she said. How could she not marry the man she loved and who helped to work such miracles? All the walls were finally down!

The men in the room again broke into hearty applause, with resounding cheers of, "Here! Here!" Janet was embarrassed. In her swelling happiness, she'd forgotten she and Christopher weren't alone.

"If you gentlemen will excuse us," Christopher announced in dismissal, "my fiancée and I have to take care of some long overdue plans for our wedding." There was much shuffling of chairs and cheerful best wishes. When the last man was gone, Christopher smiled in well-deserved self-congratulations. "Well, what you think of compromises now?" he asked her.

"Oh, Christopher!" she said, running to him and falling into his hearty embrace that was eagerly awaiting her. "Do you know how happy I am at this moment?"

"I think so," he admitted, laughing affectionately. "Yes, I do believe I do—but I've one last surprise for you," he added, stepping away from her. She wanted to be back in his arms, but he moved behind his desk.

"I'm not sure I can take any more," she replied with a tremulous smile.

"But I thought diamonds were a girl's best friend?" he teased. "Diamond one on your finger, and—" Christopher paused, pulling a long jewelry case out of the top desk drawer "—diamond two, here." He flipped open the lid, revealing the large golden heart-cut diamond set in a necklace of white gold.

"Oh, Christopher!" Janet exclaimed. "It's beautiful!"

"It doesn't hold a candle to your beauty," he said, lifting the necklace from its black velvet and fastening it around her neck. "But it does look spectacular, doesn't it? Going for the heart-cut to match your engagement ring gave us the maximum seventy-two carats salvageable from the original stone you picked up from the stream." He turned her toward a mirror on the wall. It wasn't the golden diamond hanging around her neck or the one on her finger that held Janet's attention, but the reflection of the man she loved standing behind her. He slipped his arms around her waist and kissed the top of her head. "I promise I'll try to be more sensitive to the wildlife issue from now on," he said on a suddenly serious note.

"And God knows, you've conceded enough to me that I can be generous, too. I suppose I should have realized long ago that a certain amount of mining—gold and diamonds—has its place in the South African and Zimbabwe economies. I love you, Christopher Van Hoon," she added, turning within his embrace and slipping her arms securely around his neck. "Errant ways and all."

"I love you, Janet Kelley Westover Van Hoon, stubbornness and all," he replied, pulling her closer, his lips lowering to her inviting mouth with a caressing firmness. After a long breathless moment, he raised his head to murmur, "You never have asked me about the ivory collection at Lionspride, although I've known about your suspicions all along."

"Well, I now know, without your telling me, that you're not still stockpiling," Janet replied with confidence.

"Thank God," Christopher said with a sigh, "but I can go even one better than that. I'm donating that particular Van Hoon treasure to the South African government, a kind of national monument. I can't do anything about the past, but you've managed to bring my dormant guilty conscience to life."

"Thank you, darling," Janet replied simply.

Two diamonds flashed golden fire, but that fire was nothing compared to the gold of Christopher's hair and the gold of his eyes. The legendary hardness of the diamonds was nothing compared to the hardness of his muscled body.

"I want you, Christopher." Her voice was a whisper against his sweet lips.

"You have me," he told her, lifting her into his strong arms. "You've had me for the past sixteen years, and you'll have me for a lifetime!" He carried her exultantly out of the library and up the curving staircase.

ABOUT THE AUTHOR

WILLIAM MALTESE, an international best-selling author of non-fiction and fiction articles, short stories, and novels, including his popular Wildside Mystery Double, *Incident at Aberlene* and *Incident at Brimzinsky* (Spies & Lies #1-#2), has published (under various pseudonyms) over 200 books in genres ranging from straight mainstream, to straight and gay erotica, as well as mystery, romance, western, adventure, espionage, cooking, wine, young adults and children, plus twenty-four science fiction/fantasy/horror novels, beginning with *Five Roads to Tlen* in 1969 (as "William J. Lambert III") through *Bond-Shattering* (2007). He's anything but a newcomer by way of writing fictionalized autobiographies and biographies, including his *Diary of a Hustler* (with "Joey"), *Slovakian Boy* (with "Pavel"), and his shocking Lambda-Award-nominated *ARDENNIAN BOY* (written with eminent gay scholar Professor Drewey Wayne Gunn) that raised more than a few eyebrows, while gleaning rave reviews, in its graphic portrayal of the scandalous literary and sexual relationship between the French poets Paul Verlaine and Arthur Rimbaud. For a comprehensive list of his literary output, see *Draqualian Silk: A Collector's and Bibliographical Guide to the Books of William Maltese, 1969-2010* (Borgo Press, 2010). Maltese enlisted in the U.S. Army, where he achieved and was honorably discharged with the rank of Sergeant (E-5).

You can email him at: williammaltese@yahoo.com

You can locate him on the internet at:

http://www.williammaltese.com
http://www.facebook.com/williammaltese
http://www.theglutenfreewaymyway.com/
http://www.facebook.com/backoftheboatgourmetcooking
http://www.facebook.com/winetastersdiary
https://www.facebook.com/DinnerWithCecileAndWilliamACo
okbook?fref=ts
http://www.facebook.com/evengourmandshavetodiet
http://www.facebook.com/flickerwarriors
http://www.facebook.com/draqual
http://www.myspace.com/williammaltese
http://www.myspace.com/draqual
http://www.myspace.com/flickerwarriors

William's Xocai® chocolate site:

http://www.mxi.myvoffice.com/williammaltese/